LIBERATOR

Also by Richard Harland
Worldshaker

LIBERATOR

Richard Harland

SIMON & SCHUSTER BFYR

New York London Toronto Sydney New Delhi

SIMON & SCHUSTER BFYR

An imprint of Simon & Schuster Children's Publishing Division
1230 Avenue of the Americas, New York, New York 10020

SIMON & SCHUSTER BFYR is a trademark of Simon & Schuster, Inc.
For information about special discounts for bulk purchases, please contact Simon &
Schuster Special Sales at 1-866-506-1949 or business@simonandschuster.com.
The Simon & Schuster Speakers Bureau can bring authors to your live event. For more
information or to book an event, contact the Simon & Schuster Speakers Bureau at 1-866-248-3049
or visit our website at www.simonspeakers.com.
Also available in a SIMON & SCHUSTER BFYR hardcover edition
Book design by Tom Daly, based on a line look by Laurent Linn
The text for this book is set in Augustal.
Manufactured in the United States of America
First SIMON & SCHUSTER BFYR paperback edition April 2013
2 4 6 8 10 9 7 5 3 1
The Library of Congress has cataloged the hardcover edition as follows:
Harland, Richard, 1947–
Liberator / Richard Harland. — 1st U.S. ed.
p. cm.
Summary: After the Filthies seize control of the massive juggernaut Worldshaker,
now called Liberator, members of the former elite, Swanks, remain to teach them, but class
differences continue to cause strife and even Col and Riff may be unable to bring unity.
ISBN 978-1-4424-2333-6 (hardcover)
[1. Fantasy. 2. Social classes—Fiction.] I. Title.
PZ7.H22652Lib 2012
[Fic]—dc22
2010050911
ISBN 978-1-4424-2334-3 (pbk)
ISBN 978-1-4424-2335-0 (eBook)

To Aileen, for your unswerving support, inspiration, and partnership

Acknowledgments

My deepest gratitude—

To Konstantin Sheiko for translating the speech
of the svolochi into authentic Russian.

To Henri Jeanjean for researching Napoleon's
plan for an under-the-Channel tunnel.
(The plan really existed, but the tunnel didn't!)

To Deirdre Beaumont for volunteer proofreading
in desperate last-minute circumstances.

To Aileen for the same, and for everything else as well.

To Rowena Cory Daniells, Maxine MacArthur,
Dirk Flinthart, Carol Ryles, Dawn Hort, and
Laura Goodin for much-valued feedback.

To Selwa Anthony as the very best of agents ever, anywhere.

And last but definitely not least to David Gale, Navah Wolfe,
Adam Leposa, and the whole team at Simon & Schuster, who babysat
Antrobus, watched over the relationship of Col and Riff, kept Lye
on her implacable course, and absolutely demanded to know what
happened to the Menials. Oh, and did I mention the nurturing care
over every single word and sentence in the whole novel? Thanks, guys!
You made it happen!

1

Something bad had happened on First Deck. The news traveled the length and breadth of the iron juggernaut: from the storage decks to the old Imperial Staterooms, from the coal bunkers on Bottom Deck to the bridge on Fifty-fourth Deck. The saboteur had struck again, and the Revolutionary Council had called a general meeting of Filthies in the Grand Assembly Hall.

In the Norfolk Library, Col Porpentine and his family looked at one another with dismay.

"They never called a general meeting before," said Orris Porpentine.

Col nodded. "Must be worse than ordinary sabotage."

"I'm going to the meeting," said Gillabeth. "I'll find out." She thrust out her jaw in characteristic Porpentine fashion—unstoppable as the mighty steam-powered juggernaut itself.

Col's mother fluttered in ineffectual protest. "But it's so . . . so dangerous, dear. Wouldn't you rather stay safe in here?"

"They need me," said Gillabeth.

Col's sister took her role as adviser to the Revolutionary Council very seriously. In the three months since the Liberation, she more than anyone had taught the Filthies how to drive the juggernaut over land and sea. But she overestimated her own importance, Col thought. The Filthies were fast learners and could do almost everything for themselves by now.

"I'll go too," he muttered, and followed her out of the library.

There was a great stir of Filthies in the corridors—countless hurrying footsteps, a murmur like an ocean, and grim, set faces in the yellowish light. They were all heading one way, toward the Grand Assembly Hall.

Gillabeth inserted herself into the flow, and Col trailed in her wake. The Filthies ignored them and made no eye contact. A few times Col heard the scornful word "Swanks" directed at their backs. It was the Filthies' name for those Upper Decks people who had chosen to stay on after the Liberation. Col bristled at the word, though it was hardly worse than "Filthies" as a name for those who had once been trapped Below.

Everything had gone downhill over the past three months. Col and Riff had dreamed of a golden age of harmony and cooperation between Filthies and Upper Decks people. The change to the juggernaut's name said it all: from *Worldshaker* to *Liberator*, from tyranny to freedom. But it hadn't happened. Instead of harmony there was distrust; instead of freedom the Swanks lived in restricted ghettos. And all because of this saboteur . . .

It had to be somebody who'd stayed on out of a desire for revenge. But who? And why should all Swanks be blamed?

The Grand Assembly Hall was on Forty-fourth Deck,

the same level as the Norfolk Library. When Col and his sister entered, it was already packed full. Gillabeth plowed her way forward through the crowd.

The hall was a vast oval with white marble columns and a high domed ceiling. In the days before the Liberation it had served mostly for balls and receptions, bedecked with flowers, urns, sculptures, and streamers. Col remembered his own wedding reception here, after his arranged marriage to Sephaltina Turbot. Now, though, it was a more utilitarian space that served for public and political meetings. Only the chandelier remained as a witness to past splendor: a shimmering pyramid of light and glass.

The press of Filthies grew thicker as they advanced. Halfway to the front Col decided it was time to stop.

"Far enough," he said, and halted beside a column.

Whether Gillabeth heard or not, she pushed on regardless. Hostile glares followed her as she elbowed her way to a position ten paces from the front, where four members of the Council stood facing the crowd. Riff, Dunga, Padder, and Gansy were there, but not Shiv or Zeb. Gansy was the new member voted in to replace Fossie, who had been killed at the time of the Liberation.

Col tuned his attention to the voices talking in low tones all around. He caught a mention of Zeb and a mention of Shiv, but he couldn't hear what was being said about them. Why weren't they present in the hall?

He recognized a face he knew in a group nearby. It was one of the young Filthies who'd fought beside him when he and Riff had stopped Sir Mormus Porpentine from blowing up the juggernaut. He hoped the boy would remember.

"What's the sabotage this time?" he asked.

The boy turned and recognized him—Col saw the look of recognition in his eyes. Instead of answering, however, he glowered at Col in silent condemnation. Col's past deeds on behalf of the revolution counted for nothing. The boy curled his lip and turned away again.

It was like a sudden drop in temperature. The mood among the Filthies was ugly in a way that Col had never seen before. Something had changed; some boundary had been crossed. What could have happened that was so bad?

He rose on his toes and scanned the crowd. At sixteen he was already tall—taller than most adult male Swanks. Compared to the Swanks the Filthies tended to be short and lean, a result of their previous living conditions Below. They no longer wore rags, but simple tops or undershirts and baggy pants. They had never taken to the more formal fashions of the Upper Decks.

There were only two other Swanks in the hall: Col's old teacher, Mr. Bartrim Gibber, and his old headmaster, Dr. Blessamy. They were standing off to the side, and Col wondered why they had turned up at all. Mr. Gibber had always taken a very low view of Filthies in his lessons.

"Be patient, everyone. Shiv will be here soon. Please clear a way."

Riff was addressing the meeting on behalf of the Revolutionary Council. Col spun to face the front, and his heart leaped at the sight of her. Huge, dark eyes, mobile mouth, hair that was black in some places and blond in others—she was as amazing as that very first time when she'd begged to hide in his bedroom.

Right now, though, there was a curious catch in her throat. And when he looked, weren't those patches of wet on her cheeks? Why? Tears over an act of sabotage?

He learned the reason a minute later. There was a disturbance at the back of the hall as a new group entered. The crowd opened up a path for them to come forward to the front.

It was a procession of half a dozen Filthies, with Shiv at their head. They supported a makeshift stretcher of netting and poles. A heavy, lumpish shape sagged down between the poles, under a bloodstained cloth.

The crowd broke out in a hubbub of cries and moans and groans. Gripped by a dreadful foreboding, Col wished he could look away—but he couldn't. The bloodstained cloth wasn't large enough to cover the body properly, and the man's feet stuck out at one end, his head at the other.

The eyes were glassy and staring, the mouth wide and slack; the back of the skull had been smashed to a pulp. The face belonged to Zeb of the Revolutionary Council.

2

"Zeb was coming down to see me about our stocks of coal. It was Darram who found the body."

Shiv spoke, and the crowd listened in absolute silence. Darram was one of the bearers of the stretcher, which had now been lowered to the ground. When introduced, he stood forward to present his account. He was bare from the waist up, suggesting that he worked under Shiv's supervision in the engine room Below.

"I come up from Door Fourteen at the end of me shift, see," Darram began. "I was goin' to take a steam elevator on First Deck. Then I see the blood. Zeb was lyin' in the bottom of the elevator, sort of curled up. I rolled him over, and his skull was all bashed in."

He snuffled and wiped his nose with the back of his hand. He appeared no more than fourteen years old.

"Go on," Shiv prompted. "You called for help."

"Right, called for help. An' I was the one that found the murder weapon. On top of a barrel of flour it was. Just left lyin' for anyone to see."

Shiv turned to a girl who had come in with the procession. "Hold it up, Lye."

The girl held up a massive wrench as long as her forearm.

"Blood on the end," Shiv announced, pointing. "The saboteur must've hit Zeb at least twice with it."

"Why the saboteur?" asked Riff. "How do you know?"

"Oh, yes, it was the saboteur." Shiv turned again to the girl. "Show them, Lye."

Col had never seen the girl before, and he would have remembered if he had. She was very striking, with a pale complexion and jet-black hair pulled back under a band. She was neither short nor tall, but held herself upright in a way unusual for Filthies.

The distance was too great for Col to recognize the small metal objects she held up, but Shiv's next words to the crowd explained.

"Every steam elevator has a guide cable that runs round a wheel at the bottom. These are nuts from the bolts that hold the wheel. The saboteur must have been trying to wreck the elevator, because he'd already undone two of the four."

The crowd stirred and seethed as a ripple of comprehension traveled around the hall.

"Here's what we think," Shiv continued. "The saboteur was using his wrench on the bolts when he saw Zeb coming down in the elevator. So he used the wrench to strike Zeb instead."

Padder of the Revolutionary Council spoke through gritted teeth. "He could have walked away. He didn't have to kill."

"If he's done it once, he'll do it again," said Gansy.

Dunga nodded agreement. "He has to be stopped."

"I propose an investigation team." Shiv spoke half to the crowd and half to his fellow Council members. "We need someone to gather a full-time security force. Hunt him down till he's caught."

"I'll do it," said a loud, firm voice.

Col's jaw dropped when he saw whose hand was raised. It was his sister Gillabeth.

"*You?*" Riff voiced the general disbelief.

"I can do it."

"You're a *Swank*," hissed Shiv.

"Exactly. Swanks want to catch this person as much as Filthies. More. Put me in charge and I'll prove it."

The crowd recovered from their surprise. There were jeers and contemptuous whistles.

Gillabeth wore her most obstinate expression. "Be fair. You can't blame us all because of one lunatic."

Shiv's pale eyes narrowed. "Unless some of you are sheltering the lunatic. Unless all of you secretly support him."

A redness crept up over Gillabeth's neck, but she wouldn't yield. "You know how much I've helped the revolution. I can organize better than anyone. Let me lead the team, and I'll get results."

Col groaned inwardly. Her claims were right, but her timing was terrible. Couldn't she see she didn't have a hope?

The Council members hardly needed to discuss their decision.

"I don't think any of our people would follow your leadership," said Riff.

Her mild tone had more effect than Shiv's hostility. Gillabeth fell silent.

Then the girl Lye made a suggestion. "What about Shiv?"

She seemed immediately embarrassed to have spoken, and dropped her gaze to the floor. But the crowd took up the idea with enthusiasm.

"Yeah, why not?"

"Shiv to lead the team."

"He'll uncover the saboteur."

"And the supporters."

Dunga raised a hand. "Hold it!" She was the tattooed member of the Council, with blunt features and short-cropped hair. Her manner was equally blunt. "Shiv has a job to do. He's in charge of Below."

"Hmm." Shiv scratched his chin. "There is a way. Lye could take over my job."

Lye continued to look down at the floor. A tiny shake of her head showed modest reluctance.

Dunga frowned. "We don't know anything about her. Nothing personal, mind."

"I vouch for her," said Shiv. "She's been helping me supervise for two months now. She's very competent."

Still Dunga frowned. "Never met her before."

"Because you never come down Below." Shiv's tone sharpened. "I *vouch* for her."

Col wondered if there was more to it than competence. Shiv seemed the last person in the world to get carried away by impulse or infatuation, but still . . . Lye was extremely attractive. It was obvious that many male Filthies thought so too. There was a general murmur of approval.

"Are you willing to take on Shiv's job?" Riff asked Lye.

"If that's what the Council wants," Lye answered quietly.

The Council members exchanged glances, but the mass of Filthies had clearly made up their minds. Three young males near Col burst into cheers and whoops.

"So be it," said Riff. "Lye supervises Below, while Shiv gathers a team and leads the investigation."

"Not only investigation," Shiv put in. "We'll need a security force to patrol the corridors and watch for suspicious activity. An armed security force."

"Why armed?" Riff bristled. "They don't need to be armed."

For a moment Shiv seemed about to challenge her. Then he thought better of it. Although all Council members were equal, Riff's preeminent role in the Liberation gave her special status and popularity.

"Okay, not armed," he agreed.

"Good." Riff was back in control. "Now we need to make funeral arrangements for Zeb."

"There's something else first," said Shiv.

"What?"

"We have to vote in a new Council member."

Riff shook her head angrily. "What's the rush?" She gestured toward Zeb's body on the floor. "Show some respect."

Shiv stood firm. "Not lack of respect. This saboteur is

threatening us, so we have to show we won't be threatened. The Council will go on with its work no matter what he does. We have to make a statement."

It was a good point, Col had to admit. Riff had to admit it too, and her anger subsided.

"It'll need a democratic vote," said Dunga.

"We have the numbers here now," Shiv pointed out.

"If we have the nominations," said Padder.

"I nominate Lye." Shiv turned to face the crowd. "The person in charge of Below *ought* to be a member of the Council."

A dark scowl flitted across Riff's face. Col knew exactly what she was thinking. She'd had no time to prepare any other candidate for nomination. Lye would support whatever Shiv said on the Council, tilting the balance of power in his favor.

Col longed to help, but it was impossible. If he spoke up for Riff, the Filthies would react the other way. He hated Shiv for himself, and hated him twice as much on Riff's behalf. She had been completely outmaneuvered.

Shiv smiled, scenting victory. He turned mockingly toward Gillabeth. "Anyone else? Would you like to be nominated, perhaps?"

Boos and hisses from all sides. Gillabeth stood impassive as a rock while the abuse washed over her.

"No other nominations." Shiv turned to Riff. "So it's a simple yes or no. Would you like to conduct the voting?"

Riff showed no outward signs, but Col felt her inner rage. She addressed the crowd. "All those in favor. If you choose Lye as your new Council member, raise your hand."

A forest of hands shot up.

"All those against."

There were no negative votes. Lye inclined her head in acknowledgment. Her face had an almost unnatural calm. Perfectly modeled nose, high cheekbones, arched eyebrows, clear-cut mouth—yet her only expression was a kind of tightly drawn seriousness.

Riff turned to her. "You are our new Council member." She extended a hand. "Welcome."

Lye shook Riff's hand. "I'd give my life for our revolution," she said.

"As Zeb gave his life for our revolution." Shiv pointed to the body on the stretcher. "Remember Zeb's blood!"

If Lye was calm, Shiv put on all the intensity he could muster. He looked out over the crowd, swung his arms, and raised his voice. "Remember who struck him down! Defend the Liberation! Fight against tyranny!"

Heads nodded in the crowd, but Riff cut him short before he could arouse them further.

"Enough," she said. "You have your new Council member. We still have to grieve for Zeb."

"We must never forget," he muttered, and dropped his arms.

"I'd like to inspect the scene of this murder," said Gansy.

Dunga nodded. "Me too."

"First the Council has to make arrangements for Zeb's funeral," said Riff. "Can we close the meeting?"

The Filthies shuffled their feet. No one had any more to say.

Riff took it upon herself to declare the meeting closed. However, there was no immediate move to disperse. The Filthies stood around talking among themselves, while the Council, now including Lye, discussed funeral arrangements.

Col also stayed where he was, deep in reflection. Riff had just suffered a political defeat on top of the emotional blow of Zeb's death. She surely needed a sympathetic ear and a shoulder to lean on. Although she no longer liked to be seen talking with him in public, they could set up one of their secret meetings. Sharing her problems was the only help he could offer nowadays.

First, though, he had to talk to her long enough to set up the meeting. How? Impossible here. And impossible while the Council arranged the lying in state of Zeb's body—probably in his cabin, surrounded by mourners.

It would have to be later, then. No doubt Riff would go with the other Council members to view the place where Zeb had been killed. If he could lie in wait for her somewhere along the way . . . He calculated their likeliest route. They couldn't descend by the elevator that had now become a crime scene, so they would have to use the one nearest, then walk back along First Deck. That was his best chance to draw her aside, among the aisles and passages between the stored provisions on First Deck.

Keeping his face lowered, he threaded through the crowd and headed for the exit.

3

Col avoided the elevators and went down by the stairs. He had forty-three levels to descend.

The Upper Decks had changed since the time of the old regime. Rooms taken over by the Filthies had spread out into the corridors, which had become communal living spaces furnished with chairs and small tables. Some of the decks had been repainted, with bright yellows and blues replacing dull green and chocolate. However, the two thousand Filthies who had moved up into the Upper Decks were fewer than the Upper Decks people who had departed, and many of the rooms stood empty.

Down past the Westmoreland Gallery he went, down past the workshops on the manufacturing decks. Here and there were memorials to the Liberation, marking the sites of particular triumphs or heroic deaths. The usual form of memorial was a tripod of three rifles fastened together, barrels pointing skyward.

He passed one of the Swank ghettos, too, a cluster of interconnecting rooms that had once been nurseries. The corridors outside the ghetto were bare and the doors all closed and locked.

He dropped his eyes whenever he met individual Filthies on the stairs or in the corridors. Even so, he sensed hostility and suspicion, a sudden stiffening of body language. Clearly, everyone knew about the murder, whether or not they'd been in the Grand Assembly Hall.

By the time Col arrived on First Deck, his calves were aching and his legs were wobbly. He made his way forward more slowly between stacks of crates, bags, boxes, and barrels. The air was thick with mingled food smells, especially smoked fish and dried fruit. Some of the stacks reached up to the ceiling, but most were only shoulder-high.

When he reached the aisle where he expected Riff to pass, he turned off into a small passage at the side. How long would he have to wait?

Five days had gone by since their last secret meeting. Their precious, stolen hours together seemed harder and harder to manage all the time. He understood that Riff had a position to maintain, and he wouldn't want to jeopardize that. Still, he longed to see more of her.

It had been different immediately after the Liberation. Then their relationship had been more out in the open, though never quite as public as he would have liked. He'd expected that he and Riff would grow closer and closer until they could declare themselves partnered, but instead they'd grown further and further apart. All because of this saboteur, all because of the increasing distrust between Filthies and Swanks.

Everything had turned upside down since the Liberation. In the time of the old regime *he'd* been the one who couldn't be seen in public with *her*. She'd had to disguise herself as a Menial and come secretly to his room. He remembered how she'd taught him fighting skills, using pillows and a tie. In return he'd taught her to read, sitting on his bed with a book spread across their knees. . . .

He was so absorbed in his memories that the voices were almost upon him before he realized. The Council members came walking along the main aisle, exactly as he'd calculated. He dropped down on one knee and pretended to be tying a shoelace.

They went past while he watched from his side passage. First Shiv and Lye, then Padder and Gansy, then Dunga and Riff. He tried to signal to Riff, but she didn't notice.

He counted to ten, then walked out into the main aisle behind them. He gave a cough just loud enough for Riff to hear. But when she looked back over her shoulder, Dunga looked too.

Dunga was more on his side than any other member of the Council, but that didn't stop her from scowling at him. "What are you doing here?"

He had to take a chance. "I wanted a couple of words with Riff."

Riff's eyes flashed. "Now? Don't you know what's been happening?"

"It's okay," said Dunga. "I don't want to hear your conversation."

She lengthened her stride and moved up to walk with Padder and Gansy. Col and Riff dawdled at the tail of the party.

"This is crazy," Riff muttered.

"Dunga's okay," said Col. "She always acts gruff."

"Not Dunga. Everyone's against you."

"I know, I was in the hall. I thought you'd want to talk."

"Not now."

"Later. We could—"

She shook her head before he could finish. "I can't think about it now."

They continued on in silence. She was angry and snappy, but not with him . . . at least he hoped it was not with him. She had a lot to be upset about. He wished he could comfort her with a hug. Who else did she have with whom she could let her guard down? Her closeness had an overpowering effect on him.

They were passing another side passage between crates and barrels. He touched her on the elbow, suggesting a private moment out of view.

She flung off his hand with contempt.

Col was stunned—until he realized where she was looking. Lye, the new Council member, was no longer walking with Shiv, but had dropped back through the rest of the party. How much had she seen?

She fell in on the other side of Riff. "What's his problem?" she asked.

"Oh, nothing important." Riff temporized. "Wants to talk about the running of the juggernaut. As usual." She turned to Col, her face expressionless. "You can explain at tomorrow's Council meeting."

Lye accepted Riff's explanation without challenge. But

she challenged something else. "Why should *he* come to our Council meeting?"

Col noted the word "our." So recently elected, and already she was making assumptions!

Riff shrugged. "Didn't you know? Colbert or his sister are often asked to attend Council meetings."

"Porpentines!" Lye was indignant. "The old ruling family! The oppressors!"

"We have to be practical," said Riff. "They can tell us things we need to know. Of course we exclude them from all debate and decision making."

Col gritted his teeth. He resented the way Riff talked like other Filthies when she was in their company. She was so popular and admired; he was sure she could afford to stand up a little more for the Swanks.

She turned to him again. "Will your sister come to the meeting?"

Col made no reply. He didn't know how Gillabeth would react to her humiliation in the Grand Assembly Hall.

"Well, you be there," said Riff. "Ten o'clock tomorrow on the bridge."

The topic was closed, and Col found himself excluded from further conversation. He stopped and stood in the middle of the aisle while Riff and Lye walked on. Riff had set no time or place for a secret meeting.

He raised his eyes at the very instant Lye turned her head to look back at him. Two impressions struck him like a thunderbolt.

The first was that she wasn't just striking or attractive, but beautiful. An extraordinary, gaunt kind of beauty: high cheekbones accentuated by hollow cheeks, mouth drawn down at the sides, the planes of her face as sharp as cut glass. She was beautiful like a burning arrow.

The second impression was that she *hated* him. He almost staggered under the violence of it. Loathing poured out of her eyes like a jet of poison. He had thought her calm and impassive, but not in this moment, not now. Her hatred lashed him like a blow to the face.

It lasted barely a second before she looked away again. He might have thought he'd imagined it—but he hadn't. It wasn't just hatred for Swanks in general, or even hatred for all Porpentines. It was somehow more personal than that. He had acquired an enemy, and he couldn't guess why.

4

Gillabeth must have told everyone the latest developments long before Col returned to the Norfolk Library. They were all abuzz with the news: Orris and Quinnea at one end of the central table, Septimus and Professor Twillip at the other. Only Gillabeth took no part. She had thrown herself into one of her mad bursts of cleaning, sorting, and tidying up.

The library was no longer merely a library, but living quarters for seven people. They had moved into it temporarily after the Liberation while the Filthies selected cabins on the Upper Decks, and somehow the move had become permanent. Everyone had a sleeping berth between the bookshelves, with a mattress on the floor and a chair for hanging clothes. There were a few other pieces of furniture, such as chests, cabinets, and bedside tables that they had salvaged from their old rooms. A small kerosene stove and stocks of preserved food made them virtually self-sufficient.

The Filthies accused them of choosing to segregate themselves, but it had happened simply because they all felt safer gathered together in the same place. Whether it was the still, hushed atmosphere or the lofty rows of bookshelves or the smell of leather-bound books, the Norfolk Library seemed like a haven of peace and security.

Col took a seat in the middle of the table. On top of the table, directly in front of him, sat his baby brother, Antrobus. Though only three years old, Antrobus had his own personal pen and bottle of ink, supplied by Professor Twillip. He never touched the bottle or picked up the pen, but he liked to sit beside them, contemplating them with satisfaction and apparent affection.

Professor Twillip drew Col into the discussion he was having with Septimus. "What do you think? Is there any way this can turn out well for us?"

Col turned to their end of the table. The professor smiled and blinked behind his glasses. Col's old tutor was an eternal optimist, but even his smile was a little wan.

"The Filthies will hate Swanks even more because of the murder," Col answered gloomily. "And Shiv will have even more power on the Council."

Septimus frowned. "Whoever this saboteur is, he doesn't care what happens to the rest of us."

Septimus had been Professor Twillip's research assistant for the past three months. His voice had recently broken, and his new deep bass seemed to surprise its owner as much as anyone else. He had matured in other ways too, his long limbs becoming less gangly and his features filling out until he was quite good-looking.

"Perhaps the new investigation team will help," said Professor Twillip. "If they can actually discover the saboteur . . ."

"I don't believe it." Col shook his head. "Shiv will use

them to harass us and interrogate us, but he's got no clues to go on. I bet there's not much real investigation."

"I wish we could discover the saboteur ourselves," said Septimus. "He must be an amazing actor."

"I've checked around," Col agreed. "Nobody has any idea who to suspect. I'm sure he has no secret helpers in the ghettos."

"A complete loner." Professor Twillip pursed his lips and put his fingertips together. "So strange. Such ruthlessness. I just don't know anyone like that."

Col had a less rosy view of human nature than the professor, but he didn't know anyone like that either. Many Upper Decks people had committed monstrous deeds under the old regime, but never as individuals acting on their own. It had always been more of a social cruelty.

A small gasp made Col switch his attention to the other end of the table. Quinnea was working herself up into a state.

"Nothing like this ever used to happen in the old days! It's too much for me! All of these Filthies getting themselves murdered!"

Col's mother was an ethereally thin woman, perpetually atremble, with wisps of hair the color of dead autumn leaves. Orris was trying to calm her down, without effect. He turned to Col in silent appeal for help.

"It's only one Filthy, Mother," Col said. "And *he* didn't choose to get himself murdered."

Quinnea shook her head. "I should never have listened. Dreadful, dreadful. It's bad for me to hear that kind of news."

"Yes, but you mustn't blame the Liberation." Orris tried to pat her hand, which caused her to jump like a startled rabbit. "One small unpleasant thing compared to many, many improvements. We're all much happier now."

Col had no doubt that his father *was* happier since the guilt of the past had been lifted from his shoulders. But he hardly looked happy, with his bulging eyes and sagging jowls. The habit of a lifetime couldn't be so quickly shuffled off. Even when he talked of being happier, his voice still sounded lugubrious.

Quinnea sniffled. "I can't help it. Perhaps I'm a— what do you say?—a reactionary. I can't cope. Too many changes. Too fast. And all of my friends have left."

"We stayed to play our part in the new order," said Orris.

"Nobody else did. The Turbots. The Trumpingtons. The Squellinghams. All gone."

Col could have pointed out that the Squellinghams had been anything but friends to the Porpentines. But instead he said, "Victoria and Albert stayed."

"Not the same." Quinnea wouldn't be consoled. "Not Queen Victoria the Second and her consort, Prince Albert. Why can't we say that anymore?"

"Because we don't live under a monarchy anymore," said Orris. "It's a republic now. We have to move with the times."

"I don't like the times. I liked it the way it was."

"We can learn new ways," Orris insisted. "I'm learning to be more like a Filthy. Not so slow and stuffy. More spontaneous. Look what I learned this morning."

He raised his right hand and snapped his fingers—except they didn't snap. Just a dull, muffled noise. He stared at them in disappointment.

"It worked this morning," he said. "I practiced until I could do it three times out of four."

Quinnea looked away. "I don't care about doing things with my fingers."

"No, that's only an example," said Orris earnestly. "We can learn a new attitude to life. More lighthearted. We're free to be happy now. I'm sure I've started breaking into unexpected smiles."

Col said nothing. Light-hearted or heavy-hearted, his father was not an easy man to show love to. But Col felt a deep fondness for him. He was a good man, a very good man.

"I was happy before," said Quinnea. "Do you know what was the happiest day of my life? The wedding day of my eldest son." She turned big, brimming eyes to Col. "Do you remember? So many well-wishers as we walked to the chapel. Hundreds of guests at the reception. Flowers and banners. Music and dancing. And the desserts. I ate three darling little cupcakes."

Col nodded without enthusiasm. He had only a vague recollection of the ceremony in the chapel, when he had exchanged rings and vows with Sephaltina Turbot.

The reception was memorable mainly because Riff had let her disguise slip. Then Grandmother Ebnolia had marched her off to the Changing Room . . . and he'd rescued her . . . and together they'd launched the revolution. . . .

"I remember the day," said Professor Twillip. He must have been listening from the other end of the table. "It was indeed a very happy occasion."

"Oh." Quinnea looked at him. "Were you a well-wisher, or were you invited to the reception?"

It was an innocent question. Grandmother Ebnolia had decided the guest list for the reception. Professor Twillip wouldn't normally have mingled in the same social circles; Septimus hadn't been invited at all.

"At the reception," said the professor with a small bow.

"Do you remember the ceremony in the chapel?" Quinnea turned to Col and continued her reminiscences. "You in your tailcoat, very smart and handsome. And your bride so pretty in her tiara and wedding dress. All beaded with pearls. And your baby brother, too, with his own pink boutonniere. Like a proper little gentleman. Weren't you, Antrobus?"

Nobody expected an answer, and Antrobus didn't give one. His only response was a solemn, owl-like stare. Though he appeared to be always preparing for speech, the three-year-old had still not managed to utter his first words. He had already passed through the phase of baby babble without indulging in a single word.

Then a whirlwind arrived out of nowhere. "This place is a *pigsty*!"

It was Gillabeth striding forward with a broom in her hand. She pointed at the books and papers stacked up around the table legs. Professor Twillip and Septimus always accumulated vast quantities of research material for whatever project engaged them.

"Look at it all! Mess, mess, mess!"

Septimus sprang to defend their books and papers as Gillabeth made threatening motions with the broom.

"No!" He stood blocking her way. "You can't! You mustn't!"

"Tidy it up, then."

"Where?"

"On the table. That's the proper place for books."

Septimus and the professor set to work lifting stacks of books and papers onto the table. Gillabeth stood watching with folded arms.

"Set them out neatly," she warned.

Even on the table the stacks had to be arranged symmetrically side by side. Gillabeth made her own contribution to symmetry by picking up Antrobus and arranging him more tidily on the tabletop. With his wide, unblinking eyes he *did* look a little like a table ornament.

Then she went off with the snort of someone who still disapproved but couldn't find anything more to criticize. She began bustling and busying around the bookshelves, straightening mattresses, pummeling pillows, and generally reorganizing everyone's personal possessions.

Col went after her. He had seen this mood in his sister before, though never quite so manic.

She was muttering to herself as he came up behind her. "Things get done properly when I'm in charge. . . . No one can say they don't. . . . Just let them try and say it, that's all. . . ."

"Er, Gillabeth."

She swung around savagely with a pillow in her hands. "What?"

"There's a Council meeting tomorrow at ten."

"So?"

"Will you go?"

"Phh! They chose to do without my help. Now they can look after themselves."

"But it's in our interest to—"

"You go, then. You can drool over black-haired beauty too."

"You mean Lye?"

"Looks, looks, looks! That's all it is for a girl. That's all anyone cares about. Padder's half in love already. Shiv's the whole way there."

"Do you think Shiv and Lye . . . ?"

Gillabeth curled her lip. "He's a fool. What does she know about running the engines? I bet she can't organize herself out of bed in the mornings."

"She'll take his side on the Council."

"Take his side? More than that. She'll be his puppet.

She doesn't have the brains to make her own decisions."
Gillabeth gripped the pillow in both hands as if wringing
its neck. "If you think things are bad now, just wait and
see what happens next."

"Worse?"

Gillabeth spoke with a perverse kind of satisfaction.
"Much, much worse."

5

The Council meeting took place over Gansy's map desk at the back of the bridge. It was very informal compared to the meetings of the Executive under the old regime. The rest of the bridge continued to function as normal. Four Filthies moved among the control units; two Filthies looked out through the curved strip of windows at the front. Occasionally the two at the front called back to the four among the control units; then levers were pulled, wheels turned, and orders spoken quietly into voice pipes. The bridge was all gleaming brass and polished woodwork, humming with smooth efficiency.

There was a seat around the desk for each of the six Council members—folding chairs of the type that had been used for picnics before the Liberation. Lye took a seat beside Shiv, while Dunga sat next to Riff. Compared to Shiv, Dunga and Riff were the moderate faction. Gansy swung between moderate and radical, while Padder voted sometimes out of loyalty to Riff, his sister, and sometimes out of an instinctive dislike of Swanks.

Col stood unobtrusively a couple of paces farther back.

The meeting began with discussion of the murder. Inspection of the area around the crime scene had uncovered no new clues. As leader of the investigation Shiv reported on his activities so far, mainly the recruitment of several dozen Filthies onto his team.

"They'll need a mark of office," he said. "I suggest a red armband."

Riff raised an eyebrow. "Why?"

"To give them the right to ask questions. So everyone knows they're security force."

Shiv preferred the term "security force" to "investigation team." There was some debate over the red armbands but no real opposition, and the proposal was passed.

Then Shiv brought up another topic. "We're running out of coal," he announced.

"How come?" Padder demanded. "We've been traveling so slowly."

Gansy nodded. "Only eighteen hundred miles. And all by sea. Surely that takes less coal than using our rollers on land?"

Shiv turned to Lye. "Would you like to explain? It's your responsibility now."

Lye had been sitting very quietly, keeping her views to herself. She continued to defer to Shiv. "I think you should explain. You're the real expert."

Shiv shrugged, though he appeared pleased. *She's playing up to him*, thought Col.

"We don't burn coal only when we're traveling," Shiv began. "We have to keep the boilers always heated. And even when we're stopped, the turbines are still driving the dynamos to generate electricity. It's been three months since the Liberation, and our bunkers were only a quarter full then."

"That's why Zeb was coming down to meet us," Lye put in. "To see the problem for himself."

"How much in the bunkers now?" Padder began by addressing Lye, then gravitated to Shiv.

Shiv pursed his thin lips. "Enough for a month if we continue like this. Or a few hundred miles of traveling."

"So." Riff swung and focused everyone's attention on Col. "What did *Worldshaker* do about coal?"

Shiv repeated the question with a barb. "Yes, what would your grandfather have done?"

Col ignored the barb. "Coaling stations. The juggernauts go to coaling stations to load up with coal."

"Where?"

Col tried to remember what Sir Mormus had told him. "Singapore is one. And Hong Kong."

"Singapore!" Dunga cried. "Didn't we pass there three months ago?"

"Yes." Gansy nodded. "Let me think."

Although her frizzy, unkempt hair and scatterbrained manner suggested otherwise, Gansy had a very sharp mind. After a moment's thought she dived into a box under the desk and emerged with a long scroll of paper.

"Help me hold this flat," she said.

It was a map of the world, which she unfurled on the desk. Col craned for a view over the shoulders of the Council members.

"See, Singapore and Hong Kong!" Gansy pointed. "Marked with red dots. I bet a red dot means a coaling station."

"Where are we?" asked Dunga.

Gansy's finger stabbed out again. "Here. And here's the nearest red dot."

"What does it say?"

Riff read it out. "Botany Bay."

"Three hundred miles south," said Gansy. "We've been traveling down the east coast of Australia. All we need do is keep heading in the same direction."

"But faster," said Riff. "No more stops. No more fishing."

"Right." Gansy clapped her hands, releasing her end of the map, which sprang back and refurled.

Col foresaw a problem, but he couldn't speak unless he was asked. He made desperate hand signals to catch Riff's attention.

At last she noticed. "Does that seem a good plan to our adviser?"

"They may not want to trade coal with you," he said.

Shiv scowled. "Why not?"

Riff caught on first. "He means because of the Liberation. They may not want to trade coal with Filthies."

There were mutters among the Council as the implications sank in.

"You haven't communicated about the Liberation," Col pointed out. "You've been picking up messages by wireless telegraph from other juggernauts, but you haven't sent any messages of your own."

"Why should that make a difference?" Padder demanded.

"It *shouldn't*," growled Dunga.

But everyone could see that it might. There was a long, thoughtful silence.

"Do they have to know?" asked Gansy.

Riff snapped her fingers. "Just what I was thinking. We could behave as if the Liberation never happened." She turned to Col. "You could be our representative."

"Me?"

"You could go on shore and negotiate with the imperialists. Pretend you're in command."

"A bit young, aren't I?"

"You and the old royalty. Victoria and Albert can go with you."

A look of distrust sharpened Shiv's already sharp features. "We can't let them go on their own."

"Ah, but we'll be there too," said Riff. "Pretending to be their servants. Disguised as Menials."

Col remembered Riff's old disguise as a Menial. She could play the part perfectly.

"We shouldn't have to do this." Lye spoke up suddenly. "It's humiliating."

Riff silenced her. "We'll be proud as you like when our bunkers are full."

"How do I negotiate?" asked Col. "What do I trade for coal?"

"Hmm. What would *Worldshaker* have traded?"

"I don't know. Stuff scooped up from the ground, I suppose. We don't do that anymore."

"No, we barter and exchange. We don't steal from native people."

An idea popped into Col's head. "We could trade Old Country antiques. There's plenty on board, and you don't care about keeping them."

"No use to us."

"But they'd be worth a lot to the imperialists. Old furniture, vases, paintings—anything from the Old Country."

"Okay, problem solved." Again Riff snapped her fingers. "Everyone agreed?"

The others nodded agreement. Riff's energy had a way of sweeping people along.

"Who'll look after it?" she asked.

"I will," said Padder.

"Excellent. No further business, then?"

There was no further business. In spite of Gillabeth's dire predictions, the Council hadn't made any decision that immediately threatened the Swanks.

"Let's get moving," said Riff, rising to her feet. Her next words were directed to Col alone. "Find out all you can about coaling stations, and report back."

She gave him a wink.

Col's heart leaped. He didn't know what it meant, but that wink was for him, a personal aside.

Padder, Dunga, and Lye moved out among the control units. Padder and Dunga issued instructions to the Filthies on the bridge; Lye spoke orders into a voice pipe. Shiv disappeared on other business. Gansy remained at her desk and set to work with ruler and pencil, plotting their route to Botany Bay.

"I'm going to observe from above," Riff announced to no one in particular.

Now Col understood that wink. She was offering him the chance to talk to her alone. He tracked her out of the corner of his eye as she mounted the metal stairs to the platform above the bridge.

He waited another minute before wandering in the same direction. Then quietly, casually, he made his way up the steps. He prayed nobody would notice or challenge him, and nobody did.

6

When Col emerged from the turret, his senses swam in the overpowering brightness. Out on the platform the air was crisp and thin, and the sun seemed enormous. Riff was a silhouette against the steel barrier at the front. He hurried forward.

"I should've known you'd find a way," he said as she turned.

She grinned. "Glad you got the idea."

"I thought you were brushing me off yesterday."

"Yesterday was a bad time. You need to trust me a little more, don't you?"

They stood facing each other. Open space was all around, yet they were entirely private and alone.

"I hate having to meet in secret," he said.

"Yes, well." The grin vanished from her face. "Nothing I can do about it."

He had been about to hug her—the hug left over from yesterday—but her sharp tone made him pause. Why did it keep happening like this? So many of their meetings lately started out on the wrong foot. He didn't want to argue.

It seemed Riff didn't want to argue either. "Anyway, we're here now," she said, and the grin reappeared.

He loved that grin. It reminded him of the Riff of old,

the daredevil risk taker. He drank in the smell of her hair, the warmth of her skin. . . .

The turret door clanged behind them.

They moved apart, trying not to look guilty. It was Lye. What did she want? Col could have shrieked at the unfairness and frustration of it. Lye, of all people!

She showed him no look of hatred as she advanced; instead she ignored him completely. Her black hair was radiant in the sunlight, her complexion so pale it looked white by comparison. She moved with poise and deliberation, almost a glide.

"I thought I'd watch from up here," she said.

Riff nodded, and Col sensed that she was studying Lye with admiration and just a hint of envy. The idea infuriated him. Riff ought to know she was infinitely more attractive. Not more beautiful, perhaps—but Lye's beauty was a cold, inhuman thing. Riff's features were less perfectly proportioned, but they were infinitely more alive. Her face flickered with the same energy that made her body so lithe and quick.

Lye came up on Riff's other side.

"You're not needed Below?" Riff asked.

"No, I've given the orders," Lye replied. "Shiv will be going down to keep a check."

"Fair enough." Riff turned and gazed out over the barrier. "You've come to the best place for a view."

Col remembered Riff's scowl when Shiv had maneuvered his own supporter onto the Council. Lye had been the enemy then, so why speak pleasantly to her now?

Was it all an act? If the friendliness in Riff's voice wasn't genuine, Col couldn't tell the difference.

"Look, they're bringing up the scoops," Riff said, and pointed.

Col leaned over the barrier and focused on the scene that spread out below the bridge. The superstructure dropped vertically for five hundred feet, then widened level by level in tiers of gray metal. Over the tiers hung a webbing of rope ladders and cradles, newly added by the Filthies for climbing around on the outside of the juggernaut. There were hundreds of them on the webbing right now, enjoying the air and sunshine, watching the preparations for departure.

The lowest tier was Garden Deck. Once parkland, it was now used for food production, and Menials tiny as dots went about their work on a multicolored patchwork of vegetable plots. Below Garden Deck came the sheer drop of hull, another five hundred feet.

All around, the sea was a beautiful turquoise blue, absolutely smooth and still. The scoops that had been lowered for trading with the natives were now being raised, and the natives in their canoes and rafts were paddling away. Other scoops that were used for fishing came up trailing lines and nets. It was a scene of swarming activity, yet curiously tranquil at a distance.

"Won't be long now," Riff commented.

"I was looking at the Menials," said Lye.

Riff sighed. "It was the best we could do for them after the Liberation. The Council relocated them from their old dormitories to Garden Deck. At least they have fresh air and simple tasks to keep them active."

"But they can't be liberated in themselves, can they?"

"No."

"Because of what the Upper Decks surgeons did?"

"The surgeons implanted things in Filthies' brains to produce obedient servants who could never answer back." Riff spoke flatly, as if reciting a lesson. Col recalled that she herself had narrowly escaped having limiters implanted. "And no, we can't change them back."

A sudden vibration ran through the metal under their feet. Col looked back and saw a voluminous puff of smoke issue from one of the juggernaut's funnels. A second puff blossomed from a second funnel; then all six funnels vented together. The boilers and turbines were building up steam.

Meanwhile the native craft had put on speed and were scurrying away like water beetles. Turning forward again, Col saw that the scoops were halfway up the side of the hull, dangling on cables from the juggernaut's great cranes. A medley of faraway sounds mingled with the blowing of the breeze.

Although Lye had supposedly come to watch the departure, she hardly paid attention to what was happening below. Now she was talking to Riff again.

"This is the place where you defeated the tyrant, isn't it? The supreme commander jumped to his death from this platform?"

Riff nodded. "You heard the story?"

"Of course. I know every detail. He was trying to blow *Liberator* up."

"Yes, except it was called *Worldshaker* then. He couldn't stand the idea of Filthies in charge."

"And you stopped him. You had to go hand over hand round the outside of this barrier." Lye breathed a sigh of awe as she studied the five-hundred-foot drop. "Certain death if you lost your grip."

Riff laughed. "In the middle of a thunderstorm. I must've been mad."

"No, brave. You did what had to be done."

Col clenched his fists. He'd been there; he knew how brave Riff had been. But couldn't she see how Lye was flattering her? Exactly the same as she did with Shiv, he was sure.

"You've done so much," Lye went on, "and still only the same age as me."

"Fifteen."

"Same as me." She leaned in a little closer to Riff. "You're such an inspiration. We owe our Liberation to you."

"I was one of many."

"Yes, but you led the way. You spied out the Upper Decks for us, then you let down the rope so we could break out from Below. We'd still be trapped down there if not for you."

What about me? Col thought. *I discovered the way to let the Filthies up. I made the decision.*

He expected Riff to speak out on his behalf, but she

didn't. He had been written out of the story, his role forgotten.

"I wish I'd been with you when you overthrew the
tyrant." Lye's voice had taken on a deep, fervent quality,
and her eyes shone with enthusiasm.

Col couldn't stand it anymore. "Where were you,
then?" he burst out.

Lye simply continued talking as if he weren't there—
until Riff repeated the question. "Where were you, Lye?"

"I did what I could." Lye addressed her answer to Riff
alone. "It wasn't easy for me. I killed one of their officers."

Riff raised an eyebrow. "Why not easy?"

Two white spots burned on Lye's cheekbones. "Let me
tell you another time," she said.

Col felt he'd won a small victory. She wouldn't explain
in front of him—so at least she'd had to acknowledge his
presence.

A murmurous sound rose up from below—from the
Filthies on the webbing and in the scoops. It was the
sound of hundreds of voices cheering. The juggernaut
was underway. Tiny white waves fanned out all along the
hull.

BRAHH-AHH-AHH!

An almighty blast of noise made all three of them
jump. They clapped their hands over their ears and
whirled around. The juggernaut was sounding its horn:
a trumpet-shaped Klaxon mounted on the front funnel.

BRAHH-AHH-AHH! On and on and on it went.

Riff fell into helpless laughter, dancing around with her hands over her ears. Amazingly, Lye started laughing too. Col would never have guessed she even had a sense of humor. Her perfect face changed and lit up. She seemed to be almost trying to outdo Riff in whoops and giggles.

Col didn't have the heart to laugh himself. He felt somehow excluded from the joke.

The juggernaut curved several degrees to port, then took a course straight ahead. Although they hardly appeared to be moving, the breeze became a wind that blew on their cheeks and ruffled their hair. Soon the native canoes and rafts were left behind. One by one the cranes swung their scoops into the trays on Thirty-first Deck at the side of the superstructure.

At last the horn fell silent. Col tried to think of something to say, but nothing would come. He was desperate to work his way back into the mood of the moment.

"On to Botany Bay!" he cried, and raised his arm in a kind of salutation.

The phrase sounded lame even as it left his lips. So stiff and pompous, so oddly old-fashioned. It sounded like the phrase of a Swank.

Lye turned to Riff and whispered something behind her hand. Col could only imagine that it was something mocking and malicious. Riff laughed out loud, and Lye echoed her laughter.

If Col had felt excluded before, he felt a hundred times

more excluded now. He stood there in mute defeat, facing the two of them as they had fun at his expense.

Finally Riff took pity and spoke to him directly. "It's okay. Don't worry. It was nothing so bad."

But she still didn't say what it was. Lye's laughter dried up when Riff ceased to be amused.

"Time we were going?" she suggested in Riff's ear.

Riff nodded, and turned to Col before leaving. "You should go and tell your Victoria and Albert about the coaling station. Make sure they know what to do."

Col watched as they walked off side by side. Lye's upright glide was like a stalking motion.

Oh, I hate you, he thought. *I hate you every bit as much as you can ever hate me.* A lead weight settled in the pit of his stomach.

Lye entered the turret with Riff following. The door clanged behind them.

Riff's earlier words floated back into Col's mind: *You need to trust me a little more.* But even if he trusted *her,* how could he trust the situation? He certainly couldn't trust Lye. She would have countless opportunities to talk to her fellow Council member, and he had no doubt she would make the most of them.

His enemy was socially acceptable in a way that he wasn't.

7

Col didn't visit ex-queen Victoria that day or the next. Back in the Norfolk Library he asked Professor Twillip and Septimus to find out all the facts on coaling stations. The professor threw himself into the task with his usual scholarly ardor, clambering over mattresses and upsetting furniture in his quest for books. Septimus pored through volume after volume, making copious notes. Antrobus helped by sitting on books to hold the pages open. Even as an infant paperweight, he maintained his deeply serious expression, suggesting he was somehow absorbing the information on which he sat.

Col paid his call the following day. With their old staterooms taken over by Filthies, Victoria and Albert now inhabited the Imperial Chapel on Forty-fifth Deck. Col was saddened to see that since the time of his last visit someone had defaced the carved entrance arch and chipped away the imperial coat of arms.

The ex-queen's majordomo answered his knock on the door, and the lady-in-waiting came hurrying up behind. Both wore the high-buttoned collars of the previous regime, and their unnatural waistlines indicated corsets under their clothes. Col knew they had stayed on board only out of loyalty to the imperial household.

"Master Colbert Porpentine." The majordomo's

expression was as grave as an oil painting. "You would be wishing to meet with Her Majesty and His Highness?"

"Yes, thanks, Beddle."

The majordomo and lady-in-waiting escorted him as though he didn't know perfectly well where to find the ex–royal couple. They progressed between stone pillars in the red and purple light filtering through stained glass. The place had changed since Col's wedding, having been subdivided into separate rooms. Fabric hangings served as screens between the pillars, and there were solid partitions made out of stacked wooden pews.

They halted in front of one particular closed-off area. The lady-in-waiting coughed twice and spoke through a curtain. "Master Colbert Porpentine craves audience with Her Majesty and—"

"Colbert? Come on in."

Col pushed aside the curtain and entered. With a loud sniff the lady-in-waiting followed him through. "And His Highness," she concluded.

Victoria and Albert were sitting on the side of their bed, which had been raised to a dignified height by dint of piling four mattresses one on top of the other. All around were furnishings salvaged from the Imperial Staterooms: a writing desk, a cabinet, two wing chairs, and a great many velvet cushions embroidered in gold thread with the v & a monogram.

"Oh, Morkins." Victoria smiled and shook her head. "We're just plain Mr. Albert and Mrs. Victoria now."

Col had never seen her so glowing and radiant. She had lost the creases in her brow produced by the heavy imperial crown and appeared even younger than her thirty-two years. However, she was no beauty by anyone's standards. Her face had a long, horsey look, and her large, square teeth might have been designed for cropping grass. Her eyes were her most attractive feature, brown and soft and melting.

"Sit down, sit down, Colbert." Albert gestured toward the wing chairs. "No need for formality. We're all equal now."

It was in recognition of the new equality that he had shaved off his mustache. Every now and then he couldn't help fingering the place where it had once flourished. Yet he too looked remarkably pleased with himself. What was their secret? Col wondered.

He sat in the wing chair and explained the role that the Council wanted them to play at the coaling station.

"But we left all of that behind." The creases came back to Victoria's brow. "We were *glad* to leave it all behind. We enjoy being Mr. Albert and Mrs. Victoria."

"We don't want to pretend," added Albert.

"Just an ordinary married couple," said Victoria. "Like anyone else. Doing the same things as any other married couple."

The gentle appeal in her eyes was hard to resist. Col steeled himself. "It's important. You heard about this murder?"

"Dreadful business." Albert blew out his cheeks.

"Beddle told us. The blackguard. I mean the saboteur, not Beddle."

"The Filthies have turned against us more than ever. We have to *prove* our cooperation. This is our chance."

"I suppose I could do it," Victoria conceded. "If it's so important."

Albert wrapped an arm protectively over her shoulder. "Only if you're strong enough, my dear. You mustn't overtax yourself."

"I won't. I'll do it."

"Thank you." Col looked from Victoria to Albert, then back again to Victoria. "You're not unwell, are you?"

"No, no." Victoria broke into a sudden smile and snuggled a little against Albert's arm. "Shall we tell him?"

"I think so. Yes."

Victoria's teeth shone like the sun uncovered by clouds. "We're pregnant."

"Pregnant?"

"With child."

The lady-in-waiting, who still hovered in the background, couldn't contain herself. "An heir to the imperial line," she proclaimed.

"No, Morkins. Just an ordinary child. The most ordinary child. And we shall be the most ordinary parents."

"Ordinary, *loving* parents," Albert amended.

"Of course. But we mustn't spoil him."

"Of course not. Or her."

"If it's a him, I'm sure he'll look just like you. Handsome and manly."

"Or like you if it's a her. Gracious and womanly."

Col cleared his throat. "Congratulations," he said. "I'm really happy for you."

Victoria inclined her head. "Thank you, Colbert."

She sat smiling and snuggling against Albert's arm. Then, giving herself a tiny shake, she turned again to Col.

"Such a pity *your* wife isn't here, Colbert. You made a lovely couple when I married you."

She nodded at the wedding ring on Col's finger. In fact it was only there because Col hadn't been able to pull it off.

"You might have started a family of your own by now," said Albert.

Col didn't try to explain his true feelings. Of course he'd already fallen for Riff before he'd ever spoken to Sephaltina Turbot, but even if he hadn't, he would have thought Sephaltina a very strange person. For some reason she had wanted to marry him, yet they had nothing in common at all. Her sweet and girlish mannerisms set his teeth on edge. It had been an arranged marriage from the start, simply an alliance between Turbots and Porpentines.

"I can't believe she put her parents ahead of her husband," Victoria went on. "I can't believe she went off with them."

"Seems so," said Col.

"I would have stayed with my husband on the juggernaut." Victoria exchanged fond glances with Albert. "Whatever the dangers."

Albert put out a hand, and Victoria took it. In a moment

they were lost in their own private world. Col realized it was time to leave.

He made his farewells, and Morkins hurried up to escort him out of the chapel. All the way back he tugged at the ring on his finger, and, as always, it slid up as far as the knuckle, then stuck.

If only everyone would just forget that he'd been married. If only they'd stop reminding him about Sephaltina Turbot . . .

8

Day by day *Liberator* continued south toward Botany Bay. Septimus and the professor completed their research on coaling stations and passed the information to Col. Col had been hoping that Riff might call for him to hear his report, but he received no summons. He wondered if she was avoiding him.

It was the middle of the night when he awoke to the sound of an argument in the Norfolk Library, an argument conducted in lowered voices. All the library lights had been turned off except for the one above the central table. He could see shadows moving across the ceiling and over the bookcases.

He recognized one voice as belonging to Septimus. Three other voices belonged to Filthies. What were they doing in the Norfolk Library? He came fully awake when he realized that one of the Filthies was Padder.

He got up from his mattress, pulled on a jacket, and made his way to the end of the bookcases.

Padder and two male Filthies stood halfway between the central table and the door. Septimus confronted them with flapping arms. No one else in the library was awake; the air resonated with short, sharp snores from Gillabeth and drawn-out snores from Orris.

Sensing Col's approach, Septimus turned for support. "They want to take our books."

Padder barely spared Col a glance. "Things from the Old Country to trade for coal. He knows all about it."

"But . . . but . . . ," Septimus spluttered, unable to find the words.

Although Padder bore a family resemblance to Riff, the perpetual stubble on his chin gave him a harder, older look. His red, flushed cheeks often seemed to be smoldering with inner anger, ready to fire up at any provocation.

He swung round suddenly and snapped at Col. "You were there at the meeting."

"Right." Col stood face to face with him. "The Council decided to collect things from the Old Country. They also asked for information on coaling stations."

"So?"

"That's what books are for. That's where we get you the information."

Padder's lips twisted in an uncertain sneer. Many of the Filthies had learned to read, following Riff's example, but Padder wasn't one of them. He obviously feared he was being duped.

"All of these on coaling stations?" His gesture took in every shelf of books in the library. "I don't believe you."

"Not on coaling stations, no. All sorts of useful information. We don't know which books we'll need until you ask for particular information."

"That's right," Septimus put in.

"Ask your sister," said Col. "She understands. Ask anyone who can read."

Padder's cheeks flamed at the insult. But he struck back with a different form of attack. "You leave my sister out of it!"

"What?"

"You and my sister. I don't like you hanging round her. She's not your friend. Get it? She belongs with us. She's a Filthy, not a Swank. I don't want my sister associating with your lot."

"You can't tell her what to do."

"No one needs you. No one wants you. We all think it, and I'm saying it. My sister is our inspiration, see? Our figurehead. We don't want you dragging her down. So stay away from her, *Swank*!"

His eyes were popping with anger. He spun on his heel and strode to the door.

"What about collecting books?" asked one of his helpers.

"Leave them be."

The two male Filthies followed Padder out of the library. For the first time Col noticed they were both wearing red armbands.

The snorers continued to snore; the library returned to its previous state of hush. Col stood there shaking. Did Padder really speak for most Filthies? Why had he described Riff as "our inspiration"? It was the very same phrase Lye had used.

"You were wonderful," said a voice at his shoulder. "I could never have done that."

It was Septimus. He was bouncing up and down on his toes with enthusiasm.

"He hates the idea of me and Riff," said Col.

"So what do you care? You love her, don't you?"

"Love" wasn't a word Col thought about much, but he nodded.

"Then you'll get her. You're a winner."

Col shrugged. Septimus believed in him more than he believed in himself. "It's hard for her, when all her friends are against me."

"But if she loves you, too . . ."

"Hmm." Col considered. "I have to fight for her, right?"

"You're good at fighting. I wish I could be like you."

"You're good with books."

"Yes, and hopeless in real life. I can always think what I should have done, but never at the time."

Col didn't know what to say, so he said nothing. Septimus's admiration could be embarrassing.

"It's like I'm living on the outside of real life. I'm never totally *there*. Or I'm there five minutes after, when it's too late. Whereas you . . ."

Septimus kept talking, but Col was no longer listening. He was busy with his own thoughts. He did love Riff, and he had to trust that she loved him. It was as simple as that. He *would* fight for her.

9

"Disengage propellers." Gansy called out the order from the raised level of the bridge.

Down among the control units Shiv repeated the orders into a voice pipe, while Padder and three other Filthies pulled levers and checked dials. Col, Victoria, and Albert stood on the raised level with Gansy, gazing out through the curved strip of windows at the front.

"Engage rollers."

There was more repeating of orders, more pulling of levers. A shudder ran though the juggernaut like a change of gears. Three months ago they had changed from rollers to propellers on leaving the Malay Peninsula; now they changed back. The Filthies had already mastered the procedure.

Further orders followed in swift succession. "Forward drive. Quarter power. Three knots."

There was another kind of vibration as the rollers rode up over the seaboard shallows. They had been closing in on the coast ever since dawn broke on an overcast day, half an hour ago. Directly before them were the wooded green headlands enclosing the harbor of Botany Bay. Other man-made shapes showed behind, spiky and metallic and incomprehensible.

Col was still trying to make sense of the shapes

when three new figures entered the bridge on the lower level. Riff, Lye, and Dunga were dressed for their role as Menials accompanying the imperial party.

Col would have been amazed at the transformation, except that he'd seen Riff in Menial disguise before. They wore loose, sacklike uniforms; their skin had been rendered pale with powder and ash, and their grayed hair was tied back in buns. Even Lye's jet-black hair had been made to look drab and dull.

Victoria groaned. "Oh, no! Not those things again."

She was staring at the crowns carried by Riff and Dunga: the massive steel-and-gold one for Her Majesty and the smaller one for His Highness. Obviously Victoria and Albert were expected to dress up in full regalia.

Riff shambled her way forward to the front of the bridge. Her movements were no less convincing than her physical appearance. She must have been teaching the others, because Dunga moved in a similar way. Only Lye seemed halfhearted about her performance.

"Okay." Riff halted before the raised level and snapped out of her act. She addressed herself to Col. "Give us the facts about coaling stations."

"Now?" Col frowned. "We're nearly there."

"So talk fast."

Col launched into a compressed version of all that Professor Twillip and Septimus had told him. He found he could remember whole slabs of information word for word.

"Coaling stations are what's left of the old colonies.

Before the French Revolution, the nations of Europe started up colonies on every continent—British, Dutch, French, Spanish, Portuguese. Britain had the most. After the revolution, when the wars between France and the rest of Europe dragged on and on, the fighting took up all of their manpower and resources. Especially with the race to industrialization. They didn't have time to worry about colonies anymore.

"Britain held on longest, until Napoleon invaded and encouraged the English working classes to revolution. Then everything was concentrated on crushing the uprising. Britain's colonies went the way of the rest. They had to look after themselves, not very successfully. Native tribes drove them back until they held only the ports they'd started out with.

"They'd have vanished completely except for the Age of Imperialism. With Europe in ruins at the end of the Fifty Years' War, the juggernauts became the new mobile colonies traveling round the globe. They needed to refuel and restock without ever returning to their home countries. That's where the remnants of the old colonies came in. They turned into coaling stations and storage depots and repair yards."

"What about *this* coaling station?" Riff demanded. "What about Botany Bay?"

"It used to be called New South Wales until it shrank back to just a port," said Col. "It was the last British colony founded before the French Revolution, mainly as a place to transport convicts. Britain was still sending convicts right up to the time when Napoleon dug his tunnel under the English Channel. Soldiers and colonists turned the convicts into a slave labor force."

"Like us, then," put in Dunga. "Like the Filthies."

"Anything else we should know?" asked Riff.

Col searched his memory. "They've been self-governing for over a century and a half, but they still think of themselves as loyal subjects of the British Empire. And they mine their own coal nearby, unlike most coaling stations."

"I can see coal," said Gansy, pointing ahead.

Col swung around to look. *Liberator* was passing through the headlands and riding higher, now almost wholly out of the water.

The bay was a mazy patchwork of mud and pools and channels; the land seemed to have been mashed and remashed into a kind of porridge. All around stood great conical pyramids of coal, a hundred times bigger than the mounds on Bottom Deck. The blackness of the coal spread into water, mud, land, and every part of the landscape. It was an infinitely dreary sight.

"Slow. Straight ahead. One knot," Gansy called back to the operators among the control units.

The spiky shapes seen previously turned out to be metal structures along the shoreline, almost as tall as *Liberator* itself. They looked like a nest of spiders on towering, spindly legs.

"Any other juggernauts?" Riff called out. She couldn't see through the forward windows from the lower level of the bridge.

"None," answered Gansy.

Little by little, two broad tracks of brick and gravel surfaced out of the bay. *Liberator's* prow was approaching a slipway.

Riff clapped her hands. "Time for the imperial party to get moving. Let's go."

She strode off with Dunga and Lye. Victoria, Albert, and Col descended from the raised level and followed.

"Carefully, my dear," said Albert, taking Victoria by the arm.

They were heading for one of the scoops, which would lower them to the ground. They went down twenty levels by steam elevator, then walked through the manufacturing decks.

Col registered a change when the vibration of rollers suddenly fell away. The juggernaut had come to a halt.

"Hurry up," said Riff. She stopped before the entrance to one of the sorting trays. "Here's where you start acting," she told Victoria and Albert.

Reluctantly, the ex-royal couple accepted the massive crowns on their heads.

"Now you walk in front," said Riff.

So Victoria and Albert walked out onto the sorting tray, followed by Col, with the three Council members shuffling along behind like mute Menial servants.

The air outside was fresh, with just a hint of rain. The scoop lay in the middle of the tray, ready to be lifted and lowered by a crane overhead. But before they could climb in, there was a mighty grinding, rumbling noise.

"Something approaching," said Col.

"See what it is," ordered Riff.

Col walked around the scoop to the lip of the tray at the front. There was no barrier, just a sheer, sudden drop. He stopped a couple of paces back and looked out.

The source of the noise was a skeletal steel frame coming toward them. It moved on wheels in the strangest way, expanding and telescoping outward and upward.

"I know," said Victoria. The others had followed Col to the front of the tray. "It's coming to meet us." She turned to Albert. "Do you remember the Cape?"

"Um, Africa? We visited the governor there, didn't we?"

"Yes, and a thing like that came to meet us. With a little trolley . . ."

"There it is!" said Albert, pointing.

An open-sided vehicle was trundling along the top of the frame, even as the frame continued to telescope outward and upward. Five officers rode in it under a tentlike canopy. At the back a brass and copper engine puffed out clouds of steam.

"We travel in that?" muttered Riff from behind.

"Yes," said Col. "No need to go down in the scoop."

All at once the officers began waving their arms with great excitement.

"I think they've seen us," Victoria observed.

"I think they've seen your crowns," added Col.

Riff spoke to the other Council members. "Do as I do. Not another word."

The frame creaked and veered, angling toward the lip of their particular tray. Soon the trolley was within hailing distance.

"Welcome, Your Imperial Majesty!" cried the officers. "Welcome, Your Imperial Highness! Welcome to Botany Bay!"

10

The officers attached a metal plate like a gangplank between the frame and the juggernaut, and helped Victoria, Albert, and Col across to the trolley. Muddy smears and coal grime somewhat marred the effect of their smart black jackets and red epaulettes. The sham Menial servants were left to make their own way across.

Only two officers made the return journey; the rest remained on guard by the gangplank. One of the two controlled the trolley from the front, while the other operated the engine at the back. Victoria, Albert, and Col sat in the middle with their servants bundled in behind.

The officer at the front addressed Victoria with exaggerated deference and a faint peevishness. "You should have given us warning of your arrival, Your Majesty."

"Standard procedure, Your Majesty," added the officer at the back.

"Then we could have prepared a proper imperial welcome."

"Ah, um," said Victoria, and turned to Col for assistance.

Col thought fast. "Our wireless telegraph equipment has been malfunctioning," he explained. "We're still fixing it."

"I see." The officer frowned. "And you are?"

"Colbert Porpentine. The grandson of Sir Mormus Porpentine. I'm acting as his deputy and representative."

Obviously the name Porpentine rang a bell. The officer saluted from a sitting position. "An honor to meet you, sir."

The trolley's engine huffed and chuffed; the wheels clack-clacked over the iron track. On either side was a dizzying drop. The frame itself seemed less than secure, swaying and shivering in the breeze. The hint of rain became a light drizzle that blew in over their legs.

The officer at the front turned again. "Do you see our coal loaders?"

He was pointing to the spidery structures on towering, spindly legs.

"Where's the coal?" asked Albert.

"In the pipe at the top. Carried in buckets on a chain inside the pipe. One loader can load up to three hundred tons a day." The officer spoke with as much satisfaction as if he were performing the feat himself.

They traveled on in silence for a while. Then the trolley tilted sharply downward, and they descended inside the frame on a rack-and-pinion system. The cogs and gears made a tremendous din that rattled the teeth in their heads.

Down and down they went, bracing themselves until they were almost standing in their seats. Crisscross girders went past in front of their faces, left and right. The girders had been painted a green-gray color but were everywhere streaked orange and red with rust.

At last the descent came to an end. The officer at the front worked levers and handles, the rack-and-pinion system disengaged, and the trolley trundled forward on a level once more. In the next moment they had left the frame behind and were chugging forward along an embankment high above muddy ground.

Two hundred yards ahead was a curious building, rounded at either end like a boat. It rose from a base of marble steps, four stories high with verandas on every side. Its yellow, pink, and lilac paintwork looked completely out of place against the coal-blackened landscape.

"The Governor's Residence," announced the officer at the front, with evident pride.

"Where Sir Peggerton Poltney resides," added the officer at the back.

"And Lady Poltney."

"And the Peggerton Poltney household."

As they continued along the embankment, the officer at the front drew attention to the buildings on either side. "On your left, the convict quarters. On your right, the soldiers' and officers' barracks."

The barracks consisted of a dozen long, humped buildings made of corrugated iron. The convict quarters consisted of wooden huts and lean-tos, enclosed by wire fencing. Several convicts stood gripping the fence as the trolley went past. They wore loose brown uniforms that appeared to be made of burlap, each with a number stenciled on the back.

"Not as submissive as your servants, I'm afraid," said

the officer at the front. "We don't have the surgical techniques to create proper Menials. We have to use constant beatings instead."

Col sensed the silent anger of Riff, Lye, and Dunga like a heat in the air. He prayed they wouldn't give themselves away—and they didn't.

Beyond the convict quarters the ground on the left became a network of sad, dark puddles and ponds of standing water. On the right the barracks buildings were succeeded by a storage area, where wheels, pipes, and assorted industrial objects had been piled in rusty stacks.

Directly ahead the marble steps of the Governor's Residence rose from the muddy ground like a white beach out of a black sea. Three female convicts struggled to unroll a red carpet under the orders of a red-jacketed soldier with a whip.

The trolley came up to the steps and bumped to a halt at the end of the track. Clouds of steam billowed all around. The soldier held the whip behind his back and saluted with his other hand.

The officers guided Victoria, Albert, and Col onto the red carpet. Their three sham servants had to mount the uncarpeted steps at the side. The front door of the residence swung open as if by magic.

Everyone trooped through a lobby and into a large reception hall. It was a light, airy space with painted wall panels depicting pastoral scenes from the Old Country. There were items of furniture from the Old Country too, artfully arranged like museum pieces. Col noted an elaborate carved hat stand, three footstools, a glass-fronted cabinet, and an ottoman covered in floral silk brocade. His plan to trade antiques for coal looked like a good one.

Escorted by the officers, they advanced across the hall to the foot of a grand staircase. While the imperial party waited, one of the officers hurried upstairs.

Whispers floated down to them from a higher floor: impatient, irritated whispers. They heard a sound like a stamping foot and an exclamation like an angry quack.

Then Sir Peggerton Poltney and Lady Poltney appeared. They looked as though they had put on their best clothes in a rush. Sir Peggerton's high white collar was all askew; his wife was still patting down her hair.

"Welcome to our humble outpost of Empire, Your Majesty, Your Highness," Sir Peggerton drawled as they descended the stairs. "The Peggerton Poltneys are at your service."

"We shall shower you with hospitality," added Lady Poltney eagerly.

Her voice was deeper than her husband's. Although she wore a floating, gauzy gown over a dress of pale green flounces and bows, her shoulders were brawny, and she was built like a blacksmith.

"As befitting your gracious presence," Sir Peggerton confirmed.

"We shall positively drench you with hospitality," Lady Poltney gushed. Then she checked and looked to her husband. "Perhaps I shouldn't have said 'drench'?"

Sir Peggerton pursed his lips and waggled his neck

to show that indeed she shouldn't have said "drench."
His neck was his most impressive feature, long and slen-
der. Lower down he was less impressive, with a rotund
little body and short splayed legs. But his neck was very
refined, and his chin sloped down into it with barely a
hint of projection.

Col stepped into the momentary silence. "Actually,
we'd like to do business as soon as possible. We want to
trade for a full load of coal."

Lady Poltney blanched. "Oh, such dirty stuff, coal. So
uncouth. Let's not mention it yet."

Sir Peggerton agreed. "Yes, formalities first. Due ceremony and etiquette." He frowned. "You should have
given us notice of your arrival. We do have wireless telegraph in the residence, you know."

Col was about to repeat the excuse of malfunctioning
equipment, but Sir Peggerton addressed himself exclusively to Victoria.

"I suggest an early luncheon, Your Majesty," he went
on. "Let us forget about matters of trade while we make
polite conversation and partake of a light repast."

"Oh yes, with wine and all our best cutlery." Lady
Poltney took up the idea with enthusiasm. "We can serve
it alfresco out in the open."

"Your Majesty?"

Victoria looked uncomfortable under Sir Peggerton's
pressure. "Very well. Then a discussion of other matters
afterward."

Sir Peggerton craned his neck in triumph. "So that's settled."

Col's spirits sank, but there was nothing to do about it. How long could Riff, Lye, and Dunga maintain their role as Menials? How long before Victoria and Albert let something slip? Every minute of conversation increased the danger of discovery.

11

The luncheon was not a social success. Col, Victoria, and Albert sat with the governor and his wife under a gaily striped awning on the flat-topped roof of the residence. The tablecloth was a huge Union Jack; the napkins were smaller versions of the same. Muddy marks spoiled the whiteness of the fine china plates, cups, and saucers.

"Oh, la!" Lady Poltney had acquired gloves and a fan on the way up to lunch. She flourished the fan like a fly-swatter. "Such a problem, mud, don't you find?"

The drizzle had turned to a patter of steady rain on the canvas overhead. Bunting hung sodden and forlorn from the ironwork railing that encircled the roof. Looking out on the side of the convict quarters, they watched as needling raindrops made circles on the surfaces of black water.

Convict servants carried up pot plants and created a ring of greenery around the table. Riff, Lye, and Dunga waited outside the ring like dumb, patient animals. Other convicts carried up musical instruments and began to prepare for a performance.

Lady Poltney tried to be the perfect hostess. At first Col was taken aback by the way she kept fluttering her eyelashes—a flutter so slow and heavy that she appeared to be falling asleep. Equally disconcerting was her voice, which ranged between bass and treble.

"Oh, here come the hors d'oeuvres!" she trilled.

"Do try the squid," she rumbled.

"Would anyone care to taste our"—rumble transposed suddenly into trill—"delicious mulberry wine?"

She ate little herself, perhaps because the tightness of her gloves made it too hard to pick anything up. Sitting across from her, Col couldn't help noticing the musty, mothball smell of her clothes.

Sir Peggerton hardly bothered to be the perfect host. He kept wriggling his neck in his collar, which obviously aggravated him by its misalignment. An absence of accessories aggravated him too: He called for his fob watch to be brought, then his silver snuffbox, then a favorite lavender handkerchief.

"He's very particular, you know," Lady Poltney confided admiringly to her guests.

The serving of the meal proceeded in fits and starts. The convict servants, who had been dressed in Union Jack waistcoats, dropped dishes, spilled food, and slopped drinks. Coal grit had found its way into the soup, and a rusty bolt lay buried in the middle of the mashed potatoes.

At every new mishap Sir Peggerton arched his neck and let out a sound somewhere between a hiss and a snarl: *"Skwa!"* Clearly, he felt very ill used.

Flying beetles were another problem. They skimmed in over the ironwork railing and flung themselves bodily into the food on the table. Lady Poltney gave one such a whack with her fan that the blow not only flattened the beetle but rocked the table, cracked the dish, and spattered meat loaf in all directions.

"*Skwa-skwa!*"

Lady Poltney shrank back as her husband darted his head out at her. "I shouldn't have done that, should I?" she said humbly.

Sir Peggerton fingered his fob watch, toyed with his snuffbox, and recovered his equilibrium. With redoubled breeding and courtesy he addressed himself to Victoria.

"Such a shame, Your Majesty. We would have put on a magnificent banquet if you'd given advance notice of your arrival."

Victoria said nothing, her forehead furrowing under the weight of her crown. Col knew that her severe look was the sign of a headache.

"We put on two days and three nights of festivities for your predecessor, King George the Ninth. Sixty roasted peacocks. Lobsters, crabs, and crayfish. The finest local produce and the finest conversation. At least three days and four nights."

Lady Poltney lowered her fan, from which she had been quietly licking morsels of meat loaf. "When was that, dear?"

"Before your time, dear." Sir Peggerton's tone was like cut glass.

Lady Poltney turned to her guests. "I remember the tsar of Russia. Such a charming and elegant man. Alexander the Sixth and his tsarina. They were most graciously pleased with our fireworks display. And the Austrian

Emperor, when the *Grosse Wien* put in last year. The whole family came onshore to meet us."

"Naturally." Sir Peggerton's neck seemed to lengthen an extra inch. "Naturally they came to meet us."

"They were here for a month," Lady Poltney went on. "We cleaned and serviced their turbines."

Sir Peggerton drew down the corners of his mouth at the word "cleaned"—or perhaps it was the word "serviced." "We lent them our ablutionary assistance," he drawled.

The meal continued. Rainwater percolated through the awning and dripped here and there on the table-cloth. When a drip fell on Lady Poltney's shoulder, she gave it a mighty smack with her hand.

At last dessert was served: glass bowls of fruit and cream. At the same time, the convict band struck up a tune. After three bars of "Land of Hope and Glory," the trombone player dropped his instrument, which hit the ground with a brassy clatter.

"Skwa-a!"

Sir Peggerton's hiss was so vitriolic that the drummer jumped up, knocked over a drum, and put his foot through it.

Sir Peggerton turned to the nearest officer, unnaturally calm. "Take that one below and flog him. To within an inch of his life. The other one too."

That was the end of the musical performance. As they ate their dessert, a different kind of performance started up on the floor below: the swishing of a whip and howls of pain.

Col continued to spoon fruit and cream into his mouth without tasting a thing. When he risked a glance toward Riff, Lye, and Dunga, their eyes were alight with fury. Had anyone else observed them, it would have been obvious they weren't genuine Menials. Lye wasn't even hunched or slouched; she was on her toes and ready to lash out.

Finally, thankfully, the meal came to an end. When Lady Poltney proposed a cup of local coffee, even Sir Peggerton pulled a face and waved the idea away.

"We'd like to do business now, if that's all right," Col spoke up. "We need a full load of coal, and we have fine Old Country antiques to offer in exchange."

"Old Country antiques?" A note of eagerness came into Sir Peggerton's drawl. "Such as?"

"Vases, rugs, urns, mirrors, furniture."

"Ah." Sir Peggerton craned forward. Col had his full attention now.

"And statues, portraits of the royal family, imperial heirloom jewelry."

Sir Peggerton was almost salivating at the prospect. Still, he swung toward Victoria with a puzzled expression. "You really want to trade away your heirloom jewelry?"

Victoria found her voice. "Yes."

"But how can you bear to part with such treasures?"

"Not treasures. Ugly old things."

"Ugly?"

"I never liked them even when I was queen."

Sir Peggerton sat up very straight. "'Even when I was

queen'?" he repeated. "'*Was*'? Why do you say 'was'?"

Victoria realized her mistake. "I mean . . . that is . . ." She floundered to a stop.

Albert tried to come to her rescue. "What she means is . . . well . . . um . . ." He also floundered to a stop.

Col was still trying to come up with an innocent explanation when Lye exploded.

"What she means is she's not in charge anymore!" she yelled at the Poltneys from five yards away. "*We've* taken over the juggernaut!"

12

The frozen moment seemed to last forever. The governor and his wife swiveled to gawk at the three sham Menials on the other side of the pot plants.

"I thought they couldn't speak," said Lady Poltney.

"We're not Menials, we're *Filthies!*" Lye beat at her hair and pulled out the bun, shedding gray clouds of ash. "The ones you crush and oppress! But not us! Not any more! Not on *Liberator!*"

Sir Peggerton gulped for air. "*Liberator?* What's *Liberator?*"

Riff spoke up more calmly than Lye. "*Liberator* is our new name for *Worldshaker*. We had a revolution three months ago."

"We live under a new system of government," added Dunga.

Lady Poltney's eyes skittered from face to face. "They *all* speak!"

"It's only babble and nonsense," said Sir Peggerton. "Meaningless sounds."

"I thought it didn't make sense."

"Cover your ears, my dear."

Col rose from his chair. "It's a fairer system. Many of us from the old Upper Decks chose to stay and help."

Sir Peggerton stared at him in disbelief. "*Help?*"

"We showed the Filthies how to run the juggernaut. Everyone cooperates now. Mutual respect."

"*Respect?*" Sir Peggerton's voice had faded to a whisper.

"No more exploitation. We trade honestly with the native people, too. And we're offering you an honest trade. Our antiques for your coal."

Lady Poltney had her hands over her ears. The nearby officers and soldiers stood aghast.

Sir Peggerton struggled to rise, but he was unsteady on his feet. He grabbed hold of one of the poles that supported the awning. Immediately a deluge of rainwater came through the canvas and showered down over heads and shoulders.

"*Skwa!*" Sir Peggerton squawked and shook himself.

"A full load of coal and we'll be on our way," said Col.

Sir Peggerton shot his neck out of his collar and turned on Col. "You make me sick! Sick! Sick! Sick!"

As if matching deed to word, Lady Poltney leaned forward, heaved, and vomited over the tablecloth.

"You see?" Sir Peggerton gestured. "No decent human being can stand to hear you. *Cooperating!* With *Filthies!* How can you stand there and utter such obscenity? How can you live with yourselves?"

"*You're* obscene!" shouted Lye. "*You're* the obscenity!"

"You're as bad as Filthies yourselves." Sir Peggerton continued his tirade against Col. "No, worse, because they were born as animals. Whereas you—you debase yourselves. You're a disgrace to the human species." He swung toward Victoria and Albert. "And you participate in this perversion, this blasphemy, this abomination! You ought to be ashamed! I'm ashamed *for* you!"

"Filthies are born as human as us," Col disagreed. "We're all the same species. There was no difference before the Fifty Years' War."

Sir Peggerton wasn't listening. "I want you out! Out of my residence! Out of Botany Bay! Get out, get out, get out!" He flapped his arms. *"Skwaa-aa!"*

"We're going," said Riff.

The three Council members strode across to the stairs. Victoria and Albert followed, and Col brought up the rear.

Sir Peggerton turned to his officers. "Armed guard. Back to their juggernaut. Make sure they go."

Officers and soldiers accompanied them down from floor to floor. They kept at a distance as though wary of contaminating influence.

Sir Peggerton's voice could be heard still screeching on the roof. Now he was taking out his rage on the crockery.

"They ate off our plates!" *Smash!*

"Defiled our glasses!" *Smash! Tinkle!*

"Touched our knives and forks and spoons!" *Rattle! Clatter! Crash!*

Victoria paused when they came to the front door, and turned to Albert. "Help me with this, dear."

Together they lifted the crown from her head and deposited it on the floor.

"That's better. Beastly thing." The creases were already melting from her brow.

Albert followed suit, leaving his own smaller crown next to hers.

The seating arrangements in the trolley were different on the way back. Riff, Lye, and Dunga now sat in the middle, while Victoria, Albert, and Col squeezed in behind. The officer at the front kept his back turned; the officer in charge of the engine averted his face.

A second trolley followed, containing half a dozen armed soldiers. They kept their rifles trained constantly upon the passengers in the first trolley.

Victoria hung her head. "I let us down, didn't I?"

"Don't worry about it, my dear," said Albert.

"But I did."

"Don't worry about it," said Col.

The return journey was a dismal, silent affair. Col stayed sunk in his own thoughts until they were traveling along the top of the frame, approaching the sorting tray. *Liberator* blotted out the sky and the landscape with its vast, gray bulk.

The tray was deserted, but the three officers who had remained by the gangplank were still at their post in spite of the rain. Naturally, they were bewildered by the soldiers with rifles in the second trolley.

The two officers brought the first trolley to a halt and jumped out to explain. They were in a great hurry to escape from the presence of Filthies—and class traitors.

Victoria, Albert, and Col crossed the gangplank to the tray, followed by the three Council members. The discussion among the officers came to their ears—not only

words like "abnormal" and "monsters," but tones of contempt and disgust.

Lye had no sooner stepped off the gangplank than
she swung around. Her face blazed with the same violence of hatred she had once directed at Col.

"This isn't the end! You'll see! You'll pay!"

It seemed that her voice possessed another register
quite unlike her usual quiet manner: ringing and powerful, a deep-throated scream. The officers looked at her
and backed a step farther away.

"You won't get rid of us so easily!" she roared. "We'll
crush you! We'll destroy you!"

The rifles of the soldiers in the second trolley came
up, ready to fire.

"Enough," said Dunga, and grabbed Lye by the shoulder. "Stop now."

"Don't tell me what to do!" Lye broke away, advanced
to the extreme edge of the tray, and brandished her fists.
"Cowards! Imperialist dogs! We don't need to trade with
you! We'll take what we want by force!"

"Shut her up," muttered Riff.

Dunga got Lye in a bear hug and wrestled her back
from the edge. Lye twisted and wrapped her hands
around Dunga's neck. Riff sprang forward and quelled
the aggression.

"Don't give them the idea," she hissed at Lye. "Keep
it to ourselves."

Lye dropped her hands, though she continued to
glare at Dunga.

Riff led them both farther back, into the shadow of the scoop. "I'm calling a meeting of the Council," she announced. "Right now, on the bridge."

Col caught her eye with a silent question. She didn't meet his gaze, but gave a warning shake of the head.

"No advisers or observers," she said. "Council members only."

13

When Col returned to the Norfolk Library, Septimus, Orris, Quinnea, Professor Twillip, and even Gillabeth gathered round to hear the news. Col tried not to make it sound too depressing.

He was depressed in himself, though. He had told Victoria and Albert that the negotiations with Botany Bay were the Swanks' best chance to prove their cooperation; now that they'd failed, the Swanks would be more unpopular than ever.

He could imagine how Lye would describe events to the Council. If it hadn't been for Lye's outburst, Col still believed he could have found a plausible explanation and saved the situation. But Lye wouldn't be accepting any of the blame, and he doubted Riff or Dunga would expect her to. The blame would fall entirely on Victoria. They might even accuse her of intending to make the negotiations fail.

He was equally gloomy about the Council's future plans. When Lye had threatened to take what they wanted by force, Riff had said, *Don't give them the idea.* It wasn't the idea she objected to, but letting it out in advance.

Perhaps there was no other option. But did the Filthies understand the dangers involved? The Botany Bay imperialists would have the support of all other imperialists everywhere.

Shiv and Lye wouldn't care. They'd probably welcome an all-out confrontation, the bigger the better. Would the moderates argue against them? Could Riff and Dunga plot a way to seize coal with a minimum of damage?

It was infuriating that he'd been excluded from Council meetings just when they needed his advice—and the research of Septimus and Professor Twillip—more than ever. Perhaps Riff had had no option about that either. But he hated not knowing what the Council had decided.

Life in the Norfolk Library settled back into its normal pattern. Gillabeth continued her self-imposed task of organizing everything to the ultimate degree. Her current obsession was with building up their stocks of food, and she sent Col, Orris, and Septimus on gathering expeditions to the storage decks and other places where she knew food was kept. There was very little that Gillabeth didn't know about the juggernaut.

When Septimus wasn't out on food-gathering expeditions, he joined Professor Twillip in their latest research project. They were seeking information on all the other juggernauts: dimensions, engines, performance, armaments, and crew numbers.

Orris went back to practicing ways of being more spontaneous. He had discovered he could snap his fingers better when he did it without thinking, so he kept trying to surprise himself by doing it at unexpected moments. Quinnea jumped and shook whenever he

actually managed to produce a snap. His sudden bray-
ing laughs and garish grins were even more unnerving.

It was late in the afternoon when Septimus came up to
Col and asked, "Do you want to see something funny?"

"Funny ha-ha or funny peculiar?"

"Funny peculiar."

He led Col in among the bookshelves, to the spot
between two rows where Antrobus had his sleeping place.

"I was searching for books when I found them." He
lowered his voice and pointed.

There was Col's baby brother, sitting cross-legged
and motionless on one end of his mattress. On the other
end sat a mangy-looking animal that Col recognized at
once.

"Mr. Gibber's pet!"

"Yes. Murgatrude."

Murgatrude had rusty-colored fur with bald patches,
a nose like a pug, and long, yellowish whiskers. At
school, when he dwelled in Mr. Gibber's wastepaper
basket, the students had never been able to tell what
sort of animal he was. Even now, in full view, he could
have been either a doggish breed of cat or a cattish
breed of dog.

"They get on well together, don't they?" Septimus
nodded at the two small creatures facing each other on
the mattress. They were equally enigmatic in their different ways.

Col clicked his tongue. "We ought to return Murgatrude to Mr. Gibber."

"You want to get a good scratching? You're braver than me if you pick him up."

Col addressed his baby brother. "Antrobus, we have to return your new friend to his owner now."

Antrobus looked at Col: a long, silent stare. Then his owl-like eyes swiveled back to Murgatrude. Impossible to tell what spark of intelligence passed across—but Murgatrude began to purr.

"He *is* a cat!" cried Septimus.

Col still wasn't so sure. He knelt down and encircled Murgatrude in one arm. No reaction.

He lifted the animal in both arms and rose to his feet. Amazingly, Murgatrude continued to purr.

Septimus laughed. "So you're braver than me. As if I didn't know that."

Col's grin was a grin of sheer relief. "Fancy a visit to Mr. Gibber?"

"No, but I'll come anyway."

14

They made their way down to Dr. Blessamy's Academy on Thirty-seventh Deck. Their school had become a Swank ghetto inhabited mainly by grindboys and grindgirls, the most humble level of student in the old school hierarchy. Mr. Gibber and Dr. Blessamy were the only two teachers who had stayed on.

The entrance to the academy had been closed off with a barricade of overlapping blackboards. Someone had drawn cartoonlike figures on the blackboards—some Filthy, presumably, mocking the Swanks inside. None of the Filthies had yet learned to write, but they were very good at drawing pictures.

Half a dozen heads popped up above the barricade as they approached. Col recognized Snellshott and Clatterick from class 4A. They were still wearing their old school uniforms, green jackets with red piping. There were whistles of amazement at the sight of Murgatrude curled up in Col's arms.

They made a gap in the barricade, and Col and Septimus passed through. Murgatrude continued to purr with frequent rasps and creaks and wheezes. The students escorted the visitors across the schoolyard to Dr. Blessamy's rooms, where Mr. Gibber now also resided.

Septimus knocked on the door.

"Come!" answered Mr. Gibber's voice, after a count of thirty.

They entered the study. Mr. Gibber was leaning back in the headmaster's chair, feet propped on the head-master's desk, in an attitude of posed nonchalance. The desk itself was overspread with sheets and a quilt, and appeared to double as a bed. Dr. Blessamy sat sleeping in an armchair on the other side of the room. A blanket covered him up to the shoulders, a pillow supported his head, and his mouth hung open.

"Ah, students to see me." Mr. Gibber cracked his knuckles, smirked, then wiped the smirk from his face. "Porpentine, isn't it? How can I help you, Porpentine?"

Col simply held out his arms. "Murgatrude."

Mr. Gibber almost overbalanced in his chair. He jumped up and waggled a finger.

"Oh, you *bad* Murgatrude. Where have you been?"

Murgatrude switched from a purr to a low spitting sound like a firework getting ready to explode. Mr. Gibber withdrew his finger.

"I've been so worried," he told Col. "I've been beside myself with worry." He turned to Dr. Blessamy. "Haven't I? Beside myself?"

Dr. Blessamy remained fast asleep. Mr. Gibber pro-duced an eraser and lobbed it in the direction of the old headmaster's open mouth. He missed, and the eraser bounced off Dr. Blessamy's chin.

"Wha—wha—what time is it?"

"I said, *beside myself.*" Mr. Gibber raised his voice. "Haven't I?"

"You have? Who has?"

"Pacing the floor, crying uncontrollably, tearing my hair out." Mr. Gibber reached up to demonstrate, yanked at a few gingery strands, then desisted. "Well, perhaps not quite tearing my hair out." He turned to Col and Septimus. "That would be going too far. A bit excessive, wouldn't you say?" For the first time he focused on Septimus. "You were in my class too."

"Septimus Trant."

"Yes, I remember a Trant." Mr. Gibber swung round to Dr. Blessamy. "Do you remember a Trant?"

Dr. Blessamy scratched at his eyebrows. "What's today? Is it the end of term yet?"

Mr. Gibber twirled a finger to indicate a screw loose. "One of our students has come back to say hello. Two of our students. Are you pleased?"

"Oh, yes." Dr. Blessamy sat up straighter. "Very pleased and . . . more than pleased. Hello to their dear old headmaster. Very . . . er . . . very . . . er . . ."

"Pleased."

"Indeed. My young charges. Every Dr. Blessamy has a duty to educate the young. Fine young boys and girls." Dr. Blessamy seemed to have difficulty focusing. "Are they fine young boys and girls, Mr. Gibber?"

Mr. Gibber stuck out his tongue at his old employer and turned back to Col and Septimus. "He stayed here out of devotion to his young charges. Calls it his sacred duty. Sad, sad, sad."

Dr. Blessamy rocked his head from side to side. "What's sad, Mr. Gibber?"

"You are. Going downhill fast."

"I'm not going downhill."

Mr. Gibber addressed himself to Col and Septimus. "One foot in the grave. On his last legs. He needs me to tuck him in and adjust his pillow and give him his daily glass of milk. Me!" Mr. Gibber appeared highly delighted. "A hired teacher! How demeaning for him!"

"I don't *think* I'm going downhill," mumbled Dr. Blessamy.

Again Mr. Gibber indicated a screw loose. "Which one are you today?" he shot out.

"Which one? I don't know." Dr. Blessamy picked at his bald scalp, releasing a small shower of scurfy flakes. "The first?"

"Think carefully. The second? Or the fourth? Or the twenty-first?"

"The twenty-first?" Dr. Blessamy brightened for a moment, before Mr. Gibber's expression deflated him. "Not the twenty-first."

"Rack your brains."

"The seventh?"

"Keep racking."

"Oh, dear. Can I have a clue?"

"No, you have to work it out for yourself. Which one are you?"

Col could hold back no longer. "Which what?"

"Which Dr. Blessamy. There have been nine since the first Dr. Blessamy founded the Academy in 1851. He knows he's one of them, but he can't remember which."

"You suggested the twenty-first," Septimus accused. "There never was a twenty-first."

"Just a little test for him." Mr. Gibber sniggered. "I try to keep his mind active. It's for his own good."

It seemed more like cruelty than kindness to Col. He'd had enough of Mr. Gibber's conversation.

"Here's Murgatrude," he said, and leaned forward.

Mr. Gibber didn't take the animal directly from Col's arms, but dived under the desk and emerged bearing a wastepaper basket. He held it out, and Col deposited Murgatrude into the bottom of the basket.

"Home again, home again," Mr. Gibber crooned softly. "You *bad* Murgatrude."

"We'll be off, then," said Col.

Mr. Gibber looked up before they could leave. "And how are the two of you? Doing well?" Mr. Gibber directed a smile toward Septimus. "You're doing *very* well for a grindboy, I hear. Keeping company with the Porpentines in the Norfolk Library."

"We're all equal now," Septimus retorted.

"Of course we are." Mr. Gibber's smile widened until it was more of a grimace. "You are, I am, he is. All Swanks together, all equally inferior to our new masters. High or low, Porpentines or Trants—they despise every one of us exactly the same."

Col never knew how to react to Mr. Gibber. "What are you saying?"

"Nothing, nothing. Why would *I* say anything? I've been wrong so many times before. All my lessons gone into the garbage bin. Nobody would want to hear my views." He clapped his hands. "Would they, Dr. Blessamy? Do you want to hear my views?"

"Wha—? Did I fall asleep again?"

"You see? He couldn't care less about my views."

"The Liberation hasn't worked out as well as we hoped," said Col slowly. "But it's still better than the tyranny of the old system."

"If that's what you think. Of course, of course. Optimism! You'll need all your optimism after what happened with Victoria and the governor."

"You heard?"

"Only rumors." Mr. Gibber licked his rubbery lips. "What will the Filthies do next?"

"I don't know. Have you heard any rumors about that?"

"Oh, what would *I* hear? I'm only your humble Mr. Gibber."

Col wondered whether Mr. Gibber *had* heard rumors; he was smirking so much. But getting the truth out of him would be more trouble than it was worth.

With a nod to Septimus, Col turned on his heel and headed for the door.

15

For the next twenty-four hours *Liberator* remained exactly where it was. No vibration of turbines, no movement of rollers. Col visited other ghettos, but no one knew what was happening.

On the evening of the second day he decided to make contact with Riff. It would have to be a conversation in public, but perhaps that would lead to a meeting in private. His best chance of finding her was on the bridge.

He went by way of rarely used staircases, hoping to avoid awkward questions and confrontations. The few Filthies that he couldn't avoid appeared preoccupied.

He remained unchallenged until the final set of steps up to the bridge. At the bottom stood two Filthies wearing the red armbands of Shiv's new security force. Since when had Shiv been guarding access to the bridge?

It was too late to turn back, however. He summoned up an air of confidence. "I have to talk with Riff."

They looked him up and down. "Yeah?"

"Is she on the bridge?"

"Nah."

"Only Gansy and Dunga."

Dunga was more on his side than most, Col remembered. "I'll talk to Dunga, then."

"Nah."

Col didn't register that he'd been denied access until a raised arm barred his way.

"*You* can't talk to anyone."

"I need to speak to her."

"Yeah, but does she need to speak to you?"

The two red armbands shared a guffaw as though they'd just made a joke.

"Go back to your own kind, Swank."

Col held his temper and retreated. He could have told them he was an adviser to the Council, but he could see it would make no difference.

How would he ever manage to talk to Riff again? Hanging around in corridors lying in wait would only draw the attention of the security force. There was only one sure way to catch her alone—and he was desperate enough to take it.

He directed his steps toward Riff's cabin on Forty-second Deck.

She wouldn't like it, he knew. Some weeks after the Liberation she had told him it was too risky to meet in her bedroom. Yet hadn't she always gotten away with it herself, when she used to pay secret visits to his room before the Liberation?

Forty-second Deck was the same deck on which the Porpentines had once lived. But Riff, like many of the Filthies, had chosen an outer room right next to the juggernaut's exterior walls. The portholes in those rooms had stayed sealed for more than a century—until the Filthies uncovered them.

Col was in luck. There were no Filthies in the corridor outside Riff's room. He strode up to the door and made a show of knocking. Then he turned the handle, walked in, and shut the door behind him.

His eyes took a while to adjust. The light filtering down from the porthole was thin and pale, a bluish shade of moonlight.

Riff's room seemed both strange and familiar to him. It was familiar because he'd often visited her in the weeks after she'd moved in, up until the time of the first act of sabotage. It was strange because everything looked different, waiting here alone in the moonlight. How long would he have to wait?

The porthole was high up on the wall, with a chair placed underneath. To his left was the bed, to his right the wardrobe, washstand, and chest of drawers. A three-shelf bookcase filled in the angle between the chest of drawers and the back wall.

He remembered helping Riff install that bookcase. It was her pride and joy, scavenged from a drawing room two corridors away. Together they'd chosen the volumes to fill it: not only the collection from Col's old room, but the most interesting-looking volumes from far and wide. It had been like a treasure hunt, competing and comparing their finds.

A wave of sadness washed over him. He sat on the side of the bed and felt like crying. Those first few weeks had been such a magical, golden time. They'd sat here on the bed and talked everything over, from plans for the route of the juggernaut to plans for the redecoration of Riff's bedroom. The future had seemed so bright and beckoning, and he'd been so much a part of it.

Looking around, he saw that Riff had done almost no further redecorating on her own. Was that a good sign? They'd talked of hanging pictures, putting up new lampshades, finding better rugs. But Riff hadn't gotten around to any of it.

One particular memory almost broke his heart. It was a memory from the very beginning after Riff had selected this room, when he'd helped her pry the metal cover off the porthole and the sunlight had come streaming in. They'd sat side by side just touching hands and letting it pour over them. Simple, glorious sunlight . . .

And he'd expected it to last forever. He shook his head, rose to his feet, and crossed to the porthole.

The chair was where they'd put it on that very first day. Many times they'd stood on it to look out together—gripping each other round the waist, laughing and barely balancing. He mounted now, and applied his eye to the thick convex glass.

The scene outside was dark and ugly. The moon was no more than a sliver, low in the sky, and the buildings of the coaling station were drowned in shadow. The frame that had telescoped out to meet them had now telescoped back in again, until it was barely distinguishable from the other great spidery structures that carried the coal-loading pipes. No human activity anywhere. It was as though Botany Bay and the juggernaut were ignoring each other.

His memories took a darker turn too. He remembered how Riff had started to discourage his visits, and he'd been so blind he hadn't even realized what was happening. He'd kept on saying the same things, the wrong things—like the time he'd tried to persuade her they should become partnered. Too late, too late! As the acts of sabotage continued, the periods of distance between them had grown longer and longer, the periods of closeness shorter and shorter.

A sudden sound made him spin round. Someone had laughed in the corridor outside.

He knew that laugh. Riff had returned to her room—and she wasn't alone!

He stepped down from the chair in a hurry. What if the other person came in? This was something he hadn't expected.

He looked around frantically. Where to hide?

The handle turned, and the door opened a few inches. He saw Riff silhouetted in the strip of light.

"Come in," she said. "We've got a while yet."

His gaze fell on the bookcase in the corner. It was waist-high, with a triangular space behind. He crossed to it in three noiseless strides, squeezed in, and ducked down out of sight.

Two people entered the room. Col crouched even lower as the ceiling light snapped on.

"So this is your room," the other person said.

Col could have groaned. It was Lye.

16

He heard the sound of a chair sliding across the carpet. Edging forward on hands and knees, he peeked out around the end of the bookcase. Riff had shifted the chair from under the porthole to sit facing Lye, who perched on the side of Riff's bed.

The blood beat in his ears, and he felt a surge of rage. Lye had taken his place. Why had Riff invited her in? Why was Riff so friendly with the girl who was his worst enemy?

Strangely, they were both dressed all in black. Lye sat up very straight on the bed, with that cool, posed manner of hers. Why couldn't Riff see through her?

For a while the rage in his mind distracted him from what they were saying. When he did concentrate, it was as he'd expected: Lye was trying to ingratiate herself with Riff. She was claiming some connection between the two of them, something to do with a long-dead relative by the name of Arrod.

Riff seemed impressed. "You mean the Arrod who . . ."

"Who was hooked up to be changed into a Menial. Just like you. But he burst his straps and escaped from the Changing Room before they could operate. He hid on the Upper Decks for more than a week. Then they caught him. They broke every bone in his body and flung him back down Below."

"As a warning," said Riff. "I know the story."

"Everyone does. He was already dying, but he wouldn't die. He hung on for three hours. He wouldn't die until he'd passed on every scrap of precious information. He was a hero. A martyr."

"*And* your great-grandfather."

"Yes. My mam used to tell me his story over and over. It was the bedtime story I always wanted to hear. He brought back precious information, just like you."

"Except I didn't have to die for it."

"But you would have. If you'd had to."

"Would I?"

Col saw Riff's shrug. *You didn't have to die, because I let you down the food chute,* he thought. *I was the difference.*

"No one could believe it when you came back to us alive," Lye went on. "I was there near the food chute. I saw you first of anyone."

"I don't remember."

"You wouldn't have noticed me then."

"No?" Riff sounded incredulous. "You're a bit of a mystery figure. No one knows where you sprang from."

"Do you want to me to tell you?"

"Now?"

"I never tell anyone. Not even Shiv. I used to be a cripple."

Col had to hold back a gasp of surprise.

"You know the drive shafts next to the gears?" Lye went on. "The gears that switch power between rollers and propellers."

"Below the main turbine." Riff nodded.

"When I was six years old, I fell thirty feet onto the drive shafts next to those gears. Landed on my back and did something to my spine. I couldn't move. My mam jumped down to save me."

"But it's all grease down there."

"Yes."

"So how could she climb out?"

"She couldn't. She knew what would happen. She stood in the channel beside the shafts and grabbed hold of me. My da had come down too, to the bottom of the nearest ladder. Mam threw me up, and Da caught me. Working like a team, same as they always did. He slung me around his neck and started to climb. Then the jets of steam shot out."

There was a long silence. Riff knew about the jets of steam Below, and so did Col. The officers of the old regime had used them to quell and control the Filthies.

"They shot out and blasted his chest and belly and legs," Lye went on. "He held me out of the way, but he couldn't avoid them himself. He was screaming with the pain. He climbed three quarters of the way up the ladder till he couldn't climb any further. He hung on with one arm, lifted me with the other, and threw me up onto the platform. Then he fell backward."

"Killed?"

"Of course. It happened all in a second. I saw him die, but I never saw my mam die. They told me she kept on sliding down and down in the channel until she slid into the gears. Chewed up. Her life for mine."

Lye's voice trembled, but there were no tears. Her expression was set and fixed, her features more gaunt than ever.

"I lost my mam and da too," said Riff. "Both hooked up to be made into Menials."

Col digested this new piece of information. In all the conversations he had had with Riff, she had never once mentioned her parents.

Lye went on with·her story. "It was a poor trade they made. My life was hardly worth living. Whatever had happened to my spine, it was agony to stand up straight. I got used to going around bent over." Her voice no longer trembled, but sounded flat and hard and matter-of-fact. "I should never have survived."

"It's a miracle you did."

"Oh, I concentrated on it. I learned other ways to do things. Or other things instead of what I couldn't do. I ran errands and carried messages, any job that didn't need a straight back. I never expected anyone to take care of me."

Remembering the time he'd fallen down Below, Col understood why her survival was a miracle. Before the Liberation, conditions among the boilers and turbines had been so dangerous that almost nobody lived past the age of thirty. It had been a world where no one made allowances, where compassion was an unaffordable luxury.

"So how come you're not a cripple now?" asked Riff.

"Let me tell it in order. All that time my life was like a tunnel, narrowed down. I had nothing to live for, but I was determined not to die. My only pleasure was before I went to sleep, telling over the stories my mam used to tell me."

"About Arrod."

"Yes, Arrod most of all. He'd been broken like me, only a hundred times worse, and still he refused to die. But he had a purpose. I had no purpose until you came back to us. Everyone knew you'd been hooked up and lost forever—and suddenly there you were. I saw you first and called for everyone to come."

"I *should've* remembered you," said Riff.

Lye shook her head. "I was a nobody. I didn't *want* to be noticed. It wasn't just my back. I *made* myself dirty and grimy."

"We were all dirty and grimy."

"Yes, but I did it deliberately."

"Even your beautiful hair?"

"I never thought of it as beautiful. I still don't. But *you* were beautiful. When you talked to us, when you told us what you'd learned, your precious information. You were . . . I can't describe it."

Riff pulled an ironic face. "I hadn't changed."

"But you had. You had become our symbol of hope. You told us the Swanks were useless and ineffectual. You told us the time was ripe for revolution. You made us believe we could do it. That we *would* do it."

"We'd been talking and planning revolution for a long time before then."

"Talking and planning, yes. But never anything more. It was like a dream of justice that would never come true. But when you talked about it . . . you'd been there and come back. I followed you around and listened to every speech you made."

Col had to think twice to work out the time frame. Riff must have been making her revolutionary speeches in the period after she'd dropped down the food chute—therefore the period when he'd started to attend Dr. Blessamy's Academy. His own life had been filled with Mr. Gibber and the Squellingham twins and a hundred other new school experiences; he'd never even considered what Riff had been doing in those weeks.

It was a strange realization, and he didn't much like it. The food chute was something he'd shared with Riff, but what she'd done after was a complete blank to him. In fact her whole life down Below was a blank to him. Lye and Riff shared a world in the past from which he was forever excluded.

And now Lye was playing up to Riff even more blatantly. "You gave me faith in myself. You made me understand my life in a different way. I'd been surviving so long, it was just a habit to keep going. Suddenly I understood that my life was a very little thing, quite unimportant. I didn't need it. I didn't enjoy it. It only mattered for what I could do with it. I dedicated it to our revolutionary cause. To justice."

"So you were there in the fighting?" asked Riff.

"Of course. I followed you up to the armory. You

didn't pick me in your team to attack from behind, so I stayed with Shiv and fought with him."

"Ah, right. When you killed an officer. Was that when Shiv noticed you?"

Lye let out a harsh sound that might have been a laugh. "I could've killed a dozen officers and he wouldn't have noticed. I only made an impression later, when I could stand up straight."

"So what *did* happen to your spine?"

"Nothing happened. Only this."

Lye lifted the loose black blouse that covered her from the waist up. She was staring at Riff, and Riff was staring at her. Col took a risk and stuck his head out farther for a better look.

"What's *that*?" Riff gasped.

"An Upper Decks corset. I found it in some Swank lady's cupboard."

Col had never seen a corset before, but he knew about them. His grandmother had worn one to pinch her waist in. Lye's was a fearsome-looking garment like a case of vertical bones tied with crisscross laces.

"It holds me so tight that my back can't bend," Lye explained.

"You wear it all the time?"

"Every minute of every day."

"And it takes away the pain?"

"No. Why would it?"

"But . . ."

"I don't *care* about the pain. If I wanted to avoid pain,

I'd stay bent over." Lye let her blouse fall back into place. "This way I can *do* something with my life. I don't want to live bowed down like a grub. This way I can make a difference." Her voice was fierce, implacable. "And don't pity me either."

There was a long moment's silence. Riff pursed her lips.

"Hmm. So Shiv noticed you when you wore the corset?"

"And when I washed my hair and cleaned myself up. Men started noticing me. Admiring me. I realized there was a sort of power in the way I looked." Lye's expression conveyed distaste. "It's not even *me*, it's this thing I wear. I never asked to be beautiful. It means nothing to me. I have to pay for it every day of my life. But it's power I can use."

"You used it on Shiv."

"He'll do what I say. Men don't think with their brains, do they? He claims he's in love with me. Lust, more like."

"I'd never have thought Shiv was the type. Lust or love."

"I don't know about types. I don't understand men. I think he's surprised at himself."

"You don't care for him, then? Not at all?"

Lye hardly appeared to take in the question. "He wants what I want, but not in the same way. For him our revolution is about keeping what we have. He can't dream big dreams. His mind is riddled with little doubts and fears. He's too worried, too suspicious—too *small*. He sees enemies everywhere."

"Like the saboteur."

"He's obsessed. He thinks these acts of sabotage could be the start of a counterrevolution."

"You don't?"

"Of course not. The Swanks are finished. It's not about what happens inside our juggernaut. It's about universal revolution. It's about justice for every Filthy in every juggernaut in the world."

"That's your dream?"

"Isn't it yours, as well? I know we're alike. The revolution can't just stop with *Liberator*. You gave us that name. We're *Liberator*, and we have to *liberate*."

Riff leaned forward intently on the chair but said nothing. What was she thinking?

"We see clearly, you and me." Lye was unstoppable. "We judge by something bigger than ourselves. No wavering. We see what has to be done."

This was more than just playing up to Riff, Col realized. Lye made no gestures, sat on the bed in exactly the same position, barely raised her voice. Yet she spoke with an absolute conviction that allowed no room for doubt or complication. There was an almost spiritual passion in her, cold and pure as a blade of ice.

Shivers ran up and down his back. He resisted her intensity, even as he felt its appeal. He wished Riff would resist too.

Perhaps she did. "Well, one step at a time," she said.

Lye didn't disagree. "True. There's tonight's work to do first. Time to get ready."

She rose from the bed and stood upright. Her strange

way of moving was no longer so inexplicable. Even the down-turned look of her mouth might be an effect of chronic pain.

Riff nodded. "Gather your team and take them down to the armory. Then assemble for final preparations on Thirty-first Deck."

Lye headed for the door. "It's wonderful to be fighting for the revolution." She paused. "And fighting with you."

Col counted to twenty after she had left the room. Then he stood up behind the bookcase.

17

"What's happening?" he demanded. "Final preparations for what?"

Riff whirled. Her mouth opened in amazement; her eyebrows came down in an angry black line.

"Why are you hiding in my room?" she snapped.

"You're attacking the coaling station, aren't you?"

Riff jumped up and confronted him face-to-face over the top of the bookcase. *"Why are you hiding in my room?"*

"I came to talk to you."

"Are you a complete idiot?"

Col flushed, and squeezed out from behind the bookcase. Still Riff confronted him.

"Eavesdropping on a private conversation. You ought to be ashamed."

"I'd have been a complete idiot to come out and say hi."

Riff snapped her fingers and swung away. Col hated the reference to a "private conversation." Was she now more of a friend to Lye than to him?

"Since when have you and Lye been so close?"

"You wouldn't understand."

"Sharing secrets."

"We're not close, except we grew up in the same way."

"You didn't even remember her."

"Same background. Same way of life. Same history."

"What way of life?"

"Our own customs. Our rites of birth and death. Our ceremony for getting partnered. Whistle tunes. Coal carvings."

Col remembered the tiny figurines carved from lumps of coal that he'd discovered in the Filthies' sleeping niches. "I know about coal carvings," he said.

"What? From when you fell down Below and stayed a couple of hours? You don't know what coal carvings *mean*. You don't know what any of it means."

It was true. Col felt excluded all over again.

"What about history?" he asked. "Do Filthies have their own history?"

"Of course we do. Better than yours. We remember back to Bony-Part and the Duke in Wellingtons."

Col reflected a moment and made the connection.

"You mean Napoleon Bonaparte. The Duke of Wellington."

Riff frowned. "You can say it your way. But you never knew it till you read it in books. We handed it down one generation to the next. We remembered how Bony-Part invaded England and our people made the Uprising in London Town. Then the Duke in Wellingtons turned his armies on us, drove out the Frenchies, and imprisoned us in the Black Camps. They separated us off and pretended we were animals."

She was right that Col had known nothing of history until he'd read it in books. Or more accurately, until

Professor Twillip and Septimus had read it in books. She hadn't seemed particularly surprised when he'd told her about their discoveries. Now he knew why: She already had her own version of history.

"Then there was the Great Deception, when they trapped us into the juggernaut. The Dark Days. The Fifty Martyrs. The Long Hunger. What do you know about the Long Hunger?"

Col shrugged. "I don't."

"It was a dozen generations ago, when the Upper Decks started hooking us up for Menials. Probably when they found out how to change us. We formed the first Revolutionary Council and refused to work the engines. The juggernaut never moved for eight weeks. They tried to use steam on us, and turned the whole of Below into one scalding steam chamber. But we never gave in—not until they starved us out. People were skeletons, chewing on rags and coal. Half of all Filthies at that time starved to death. *Half!* A thousand of us!"

The mention of Menials jogged Col's memory of something he'd heard before.

"You said your own parents were hooked up for Menials."

"Yes."

"You told Lye, but you never told me."

"So now you know." Her tone was aggressive, but she lowered her gaze to the floor.

"How old were you when it happened?"

"My da when I was eight. My mam when I was ten."

"Oh. So they're probably living with the other Menials on Garden Deck."

"They're not living." Riff spoke in a tight, small voice. "Don't call *that* living."

"Have you tried to find—"

"Shut up about them!"

"I just thought—"

"*Shut up!*" Riff swung her arms violently, as if lashing out. "I don't think about them! They don't exist as people anymore, because of what your lot did. Changed them into vegetables! Don't you *dare* speak about them!"

It was an explosion out of nowhere. Obviously, she had never looked for her parents on Garden Deck and never intended to. The idea of them as Menials must be absolutely unbearable for her.

"Okay, okay," he said. "Forget it."

There was a drawn-out silence. Riff was breathing in slow, deep breaths. When she finally spoke, she was almost unnaturally calm.

"You've finished talking to me, then? Done what you came to do?"

Col went back to the question he'd started with. "Are you attacking the coaling station?"

"Yes. At dawn."

"You and Lye will lead the attack teams?"

"Every Council member will lead a team. Except Gansy. She'll stay with *Liberator*."

"Can I come with your team?"

Even as he said it, he knew it was a bad time to be asking.

"Why?"

"To help in the fighting."

"You're no great fighter."

"I can do my bit."

"Not as good as a Filthy."

"This isn't fair. You won't let us help, and then you blame us for not helping."

"What's fairness? We had two hundred years of unfairness before the Liberation."

Her jaw was set, and her eyes were stony. It was a similar expression to the one Lye had worn when describing the deaths of her parents. Col could see there was no use arguing with her.

He left the room with a formal farewell. He hadn't given up on the idea of joining the attack, however. A Swank *could* help the Filthies, and he was determined to prove it. There had to be a way!

18

Wandering down from deck to deck, Col met members of the attack teams on their way back up from the armory. They carried rifles and talked in low, excited voices. Presumably, they were heading to their assembly points on Thirty-first Deck, and the scoops on Thirty-first Deck would lower them to the ground.

They were dressed all in black like Riff and Lye. They had blackened their faces, too, making them strange and unrecognizable. Col kept out of their way and watched them go by.

An idea was starting to form in his head. If the Filthies were unrecognizable with blackened faces, then he could be too. It was the perfect disguise for merging in among the attack teams.

He hurried back to the Norfolk Library. Orris, Quinnea, and Gillabeth had retired early to bed, while Professor Twillip and Septimus sat at the central table with their noses buried in books. All was hushed and still.

Col pulled on a black sweater over his shirt. He put on a pair of dark breeches, not quite the same cut as the Filthies' loose pants but hopefully not too noticeable. For blackening his face he had to request assistance from Septimus and the professor.

Professor Twillip didn't approve of wasting good

black ink on such an unscholarly enterprise, but his benevolence was stronger than his disapproval. He and Septimus used blotting paper to dab the ink all over Col's face until there wasn't a patch of white skin left. If Col didn't look quite like a Filthy, at least he no longer looked like a Swank.

He made his way back down to Thirty-first Deck. He had to tell himself to walk like a Filthy and resist the urge to lower his head.

There was no one around in the corridors on Thirty-first Deck, and at first Col thought the attack teams must have already gone down in the scoops. Then he realized they'd assembled in separate rooms. He hung around the doorway of one room where Dunga stood in front of her team, demonstrating the way to work a rifle. Her face was also blackened, but he recognized her voice and her close-cropped hair.

Col remembered how he, Riff, and Fossie had discovered the way to work a rifle at the time of the Liberation. Dunga showed how to load a clip of bullets, how to flick the safety catch on and off, how to press the butt into one's shoulder, aim, and fire.

There were about thirty members in her team. After a while the Filthies began to practice with their own rifles. Not having a rifle, Col stayed and watched from outside. Merging in was going to be more of a problem than he'd anticipated.

When the practice was over, Dunga produced a sheet of paper and began calling out names. It was a roll call for the members of her team. One Filthy after another answered, "Here!" Col was thankful he hadn't tried to sneak into the room.

Then the roll call stalled. "Megra . . . Megra? . . . *Megra?*"

Wherever Megra was, she wasn't responding. A hubbub of discussion rose among the Filthies in the room. "Did anyone tell her?" "I thought you had." "Haven't seen her to tell."

Someone called out to Dunga. "Shall we go look for her?"

"No time." Dunga shook her head. "We'll be one short, that's all."

She obviously wasn't happy about it. As she continued the roll call, a glimmer of hope lifted Col's spirits. Dunga needed one more person to make up the numbers. Would she accept him as a volunteer?

He liked Dunga, while she . . . well, at least she didn't hate him. She was more sympathetic to Swanks than any other member of the Council. It was worth a try.

He moved a little farther down the corridor and lay in wait. Five minutes, ten minutes . . . at last the preparations were over, and Dunga's team streamed out from the doorway.

He watched for Dunga out of the corner of his eye. As the Filthies brushed past, he let himself get swept up by the crowd and fell in alongside her.

"Hi," he said.

She looked at him, then looked again. "Porpentine?"

She lowered her voice. "Why are you here?"

"Your team's one short. Let me take Megra's place."

"You're a Swank."

"I'm on your side."

"You don't have a gun."

"Do you want me to have a gun?"

Dunga thought about it. "No."

A no for the gun, but a yes for taking Megra's place? Col couldn't tell.

Dunga remained tight-lipped as they marched on. She still hadn't answered by the time they arrived at the entrance to one of the sorting trays.

Col took the plunge. "So? Am I in?"

"Okay. Just don't make a show of yourself."

19

A single scoop lowered the Filthies to the ground, twenty at a time. Dunga's team was the last to go down, and had to march fast to catch up with the others. Some of the team carried gunnysacks as well as rifles, bags that made clinking metallic sounds as they marched.

Dunga led them round by the stern of the juggernaut. By now the sliver of moon had sunk out of the sky, and twinkling stars were the sole source of light. The vast cylindrical shapes of the juggernaut's rollers loomed high over their heads in the dark.

Beyond the slipway the ground turned into a glutinous paste of mud and coal dust, which sucked at their feet and made every step a struggle. Col marched close behind Dunga and ahead of the rest of the team. Only Dunga knew he was a Swank, and he aimed to keep it that way.

The Botany Bay buildings and pyramids of coal were a jumble of indistinct shadows. They passed engines of some kind on their right, all lumps and domes, like quietly sleeping beasts. After a while the ground became more irregular, until they were walking up and over a series of parallel ridges. Between the ridges they splashed in and out of puddles. There were many stumbles and muttered curses.

"Stop!" Riff's voice called out from the front. "We wait here."

The first team had reached a line of steel tanks, half buried in the earth. One by one the other teams came up and ducked down. Some Filthies found dry spots for sitting; the rest squatted on their heels and leaned back against the tanks. There were patches of black oil on the ground and a thick, oily smell in the air.

"What are we waiting for?" Col asked Dunga.

"Dawn." Dunga never used two words where one would do.

She gathered her team and divided them into smaller groups of five or six. Col noticed there was one gunnysack in every squad. He stood with the members of his group, silent and uncomfortable, while they chatted among themselves.

It wasn't long before the first hint of dawn crept up into the sky. A dim light outlined a chain of hills behind the pyramids of coal. Riff called the attack force to readiness.

"You know the plan," she told them. "We fix the barracks, move on the residence, and take hostages. Especially the governor and his wife—we want them captured and alive. You've got guns, but try not to use them. Minimal bloodshed."

They filed forward again, passing between the tanks. Ahead lay the rounded, corrugated-iron buildings of the barracks. They fell into the same order as before, with Riff's team at the front and Dunga's at the rear. Col wondered what Riff meant when she said "fix the barracks."

All was quiet and deserted, with no sign of any guards. The soldiers and officers must all be asleep in their beds. The teams moved with increasing caution as they approached the buildings. They kept to the bare, soft earth and avoided the gravel paths.

Then the teams split up into squads. Dunga pointed and whispered. "Take the window end there." "You take the door end." "Window end." "Door end."

Squad after squad glided away in the darkness. Dunga directed her last two squads toward a third building. "Window end." "Door end."

Every building was constructed to exactly the same pattern. Continuous curved sheets of corrugated iron formed the sides and roof, but the ends were filled in with brick. A window pierced the brick at one end, and a door gave access at the other.

Col was happy to see that Dunga had included herself in the final squad, which was also his squad. There were five other Filthies in the squad, including one with a broken pug nose who carried a gunnysack.

Dunga stepped up and pressed an ear to the door. A long moment later she nodded with satisfaction; obviously there was no one moving or stirring within.

She gestured to the pug-nosed man, who lowered his bag to the ground, undid the drawstring, and brought out a metal clamp, an adjustable wrench, and a length of chain. Dunga signaled to Col to come forward and assist.

The pug-nosed man loosened the screw of the clamp,

then pointed to the projecting frame that ran around the door. Col got the idea. He took the clamp and held it over the frame in the place indicated. The man used the wrench to tighten the screw, twisting and turning until the clamp gripped fast.

Dunga looked after the next part of the operation, fastening the chain tight around the clamp and the door handle. No one from within would be able to turn the handle, Col realized. They were locking the soldiers and officers in their own barracks!

The chain was only the beginning of it. There were more items of equipment in the bag. The pug-nosed man and Col fixed another eight clamps onto the frame. Then Dunga took up a spool of wire and wound it back and forth from clamp to clamp, taut as a spider's web over the doorway. A final clamp pinned it to the frame.

The only miscalculation was when the pug-nosed man snipped off the end of the wire with a pair of pliers. The springy metal flew back and whipped against the door with a sharp *swack!*

The other Filthies trained their rifles on the door. Had the sound been heard within? Dunga bent forward against the web and listened.

When she straightened, she was giving a thumbs-up. "Deaf as posts," she whispered with a grin.

The whole operation had taken just five minutes. Already the other squads were reassembling around Riff in the center of the barracks area.

"Like rats in a trap," said the pug-nosed man, walking

beside Col. "They won't get out of that in a hurry."

Col only grunted agreement. He was afraid his Swank accent would give him away if he spoke more.

Every door and every window had been webbed over with wire. Elated with success, the Filthies no longer bothered to keep their voices down. Riff called for hush.

"What's the need?" someone objected. "They can't stop us now."

"Quiet!" ordered Dunga and the other team leaders.

In the silence that followed, a faint sound could be heard. Music? It seemed to come from the direction of the residence.

"They're havin' a party," someone suggested.

"Not much longer they ain't."

There were a few laughs, while others shook their heads and looked puzzled.

Riff raised and swung her arm. "Makes no difference. Come on."

Emerging from the barracks area, they saw that there was indeed a party going on. Lights blazed in the upper-story windows of the residence; silvery notes of music floated on the air. Was it the tail end of a party that had been going all night? But why hadn't they heard it earlier?

Between the barracks and the residence the ground was low-lying and boggy. They kept close to the embankment, where a line of wooden duckboards served as a causeway. Their weight on the duckboards made the mud squish and squelch as they walked.

The light in the sky was spreading, but the sun hadn't

yet appeared. On their right was the storage area with its stacks of miscellaneous rusty objects. Everything remained indistinct in the gloom.

As they advanced, the music grew louder and more martial. The party certainly wasn't dying down yet. On the contrary, it seemed to be spilling upward onto the flat-topped roof. Figures moved around, lighting tiny colored lamps that hung in strings from the awning. All very festive . . .

The Filthies sped up to a jog. No need for any word of command; everyone understood the risk of being spotted from the roof.

And the party guests *were* coming out on top. Not servants, but officers, ladies, and gentlemen, laughing and talking in loud voices. Some carried drinks; others carried lanterns.

They must be drunk not to have noticed the Filthies already. *Faster, faster,* Col urged the attack force on in his head.

The marble steps were just a short dash away when Riff raised and swung her arm to signal the start of the assault.

"Now! Fire at will!"

For one second Col couldn't adjust to the fact that the voice was male. The command hadn't come from Riff at all.

In the next second the lanterns on the roof of the residence lined up and redirected their beams upon the Filthies.

A second later and there was a clatter of falling metal from the storage stacks. Ten, twenty, a hundred soldiers flung aside their cover and raised rifles to their shoulders.

On the other side even more heads and rifles stuck out over the top of the embankment.

Then they were firing—flash after flash after flash, so many cracks of gunfire that it was like rolling thunder. Bullets sang through the air and smashed into flesh and bone. Filthies screamed and staggered and slumped to the ground.

They had become the rats in a trap!

20

Only Riff's quick thinking saved them from total massacre. "Get down!" she yelled. "Use the duckboards!"

They threw themselves down on all fours and grabbed at the duckboards. They levered them up from the sucking mud and held them raised like a fence.

"Double up! Double up!" Col heard Dunga's voice bellowing in his ear.

They slid the duckboards forward or back to form fences on both sides. Now they were better protected, but isolated in a score of separate refuges. The initial storm of gunfire died away.

They knew we were coming, thought Col. *We locked up the barracks with nobody inside.*

He supported one duckboard with his arms and the other on his shoulder. Crouching or kneeling in the same refuge were Dunga, the pug-nosed man, and two other Filthies. The duckboards gave them cover to a height of only three feet.

The soldiers held their fire, momentarily baffled. There were cries of disappointment from the roof of the residence.

"Don't stop!"

"Give them what for!"

Col applied his eye to the nearest slot between the

planks of the duckboard. The officers, ladies, and gentlemen hung out over the ironwork railing and watched the fighting with obvious relish. The officers held and directed the lanterns; the ladies and gentlemen sipped from their glasses and nibbled party snacks.

Unfortunately, the slots between the planks were not only a means of looking out—as the officers soon realized.

"Aim for the gaps, lads! Pick them off! Show your marksmanship!"

The shooting began again, more measured this time. Bullets splintered the wood of the duckboards—and, inevitably, some penetrated the slots. There was a howl of pain from one of the other refuges, then another.

The ladies and gentlemen applauded and clinked glasses.

"Oh, well done!"

"Good shot, that man!"

The shooting continued. Every now and then there was a yelp, a shriek, a moan.

Col turned to Dunga. "They'll get us all in the end. We have to do something."

But Dunga was listening to something else. "What's that noise?"

Col refocused his attention. She meant a noise away to their left, a noise on the other side of the embankment. Dull and muffled, clamorous like an ocean . . .

"Must be the convicts," he said.

Dunga had already reached the same conclusion. "The fighting's stirred 'em up."

"Sounds like they're going crazy," Col agreed.

The noise rose until it drowned out the applause from the roof of the residence—though not the *crack-crack* of rifle fire. The convicts must be hollering at the tops of their voices. Col had a sudden desperate idea.

He spoke to the pug-nosed man on his other side. "Have you still got your tools with you?"

There was no reply. But Col felt around and found the shape of the gunnysack beside the man's knee.

"Okay if I take your tools?"

Still no reply. Col looked again. The man was kneeling, leaning forward with his head against the duckboard. Was he propping it up, or was it propping him?

Col pushed at his shoulder, and his head lolled sideways. At first Col could hardly see in the half-light, but then he did. There was a hole in the center of the man's forehead, round and red-edged. Blood trickled down the sides of his nose, over his mouth and chin. He had been shot and had died without uttering a sound.

Col shuddered. They'd all be dead if he didn't act fast. He picked up the bag and turned to Dunga.

"The convicts," he said. "We have to get over there and set them free."

Dunga grunted. "A distraction?"

"A new front in the fighting."

"We'll be shot before we can go ten yards."

"Right. But if we *can* go ten yards—look."

He directed Dunga's gaze back over the route they'd taken. Dunga's team had been at the rear of the attack force when the ambush began, and now they were farthest away from the beams of the lanterns. It was only a short distance before the light petered out altogether.

Dunga nodded. "Go back around? Across the embankment?"

"What have we got to lose?"

"You and me, then." She looked along the passage between the duckboards. "Clear a way." She raised her voice. "We're coming through."

She didn't move, however, except for a sudden small jerk. She let out a grunt of surprise.

Col didn't need to see the blood to know she'd been hit. She was holding her leg above the knee, gripping hard. An artery?

"You're on your own," she said between clenched teeth. "Go."

"But—"

"Go."

Col went. He clambered over her legs, and over the legs of the other two Filthies.

At the end of the duckboards he paused and looked out over the low-lying ground. The empty barracks buildings were straight ahead; the embankment was to his right. But first he had to get out of the light.

Every nerve in his body screamed at him not to do it. In his heart he was sure he was going to die. But his head held to its merciless logic: *Stay where you are and you'll die anyway.*

He launched forward and ran. One pace, three paces, five paces. Then the shooting swung his way. Bullets sang through the air around him, smacked and spattered in the mud.

He tried to jink from side to side, but the soft, wet earth dragged at his soles and made him leaden-footed.

Eight paces, ten paces, twelve paces . . .

He was almost out of the light when something struck him on the hip. Except it didn't strike flesh, only the gunnysack at his side. There was a metallic reverberation and a blow like a hammer that knocked him off his feet. He fell flat and helpless in the mud.

He waited for them to finish him off. But the coup de grâce never came.

Did they think he was already dead? Was he too hard to see, lying prone and almost out of the light? He flinched at every crack of rifle fire, but no shots came his way. They had turned their attention back to the duckboard refuges.

He crawled forward, dragging the bag. Still nothing happened. He kept on crawling until he was completely out of the light.

Then he rose cautiously to his feet and moved on in a crouch. The line of duckboards leading back to the barracks was just a short way to his left. He veered onto it and began running again.

The flashes of gunfire were behind him now, both on the embankment side and the storage-stacks side. But crossing over the embankment was another matter. As soon as he climbed up to the trolley rails, he would be fully exposed.

He had made up his mind to a wide detour when he noticed something circular at the foot of the embankment. A pipe? A drainage pipe?

He swung across and ran up to it. It was made of iron, flaky with rust and green with slime. The bottom part was filled with silt, but it was wide enough for his shoulders to fit. Peering inside, his eyes met absolute darkness. However, he could hear the convicts' clamor with an echoing sound, so it probably went all the way through.

He got down on elbows and knees, held the bag in front of him, and wriggled forward. Darkness closed over him—along with a stench of stagnation and decay. He fought down the urge to gag and kept crawling.

The pipe sloped fractionally downward, and the silt filled up more and more of it. He pressed himself flat as his back scraped against the iron at the top. Pushing the bag in front of him, he had no idea what lay ahead. Fresher air, an upward turn? Or less and less space and an impassable blockage?

I can breathe, I'm okay, he told himself. The air was foul and clogged his throat, but he could still take it into his lungs a little at a time.

The space continued to shrink; the silt continued to rise. Soon he had to twist his head to the side. When he could no longer use his elbows, he stretched his arms out in front and propelled himself forward with just the leverage of his toes.

The roof of the pipe tightened over him until he was half submerged in the silt. If he couldn't force a way through, he doubted he would be able to move in reverse.

Desperation kept him going, and in the end desperation paid off. The air stayed foul, the pipe maintained its downward slope, but gradually the tightness eased and there was more space above the silt. He was past the narrowest part.

He wriggled along faster and faster. Soon he was pushing the bag out of the pipe, emerging headfirst into the open, gulping beautiful, clean air.

He would have liked to rub his aching muscles and take a minute to recover. But the convict quarters were straight ahead, and he had a task to finish first.

He moved out from the shadow of the embankment. The sky was lighter than before—not long to sunrise now. Looking over his right shoulder, he could see a line of silhouetted soldiers along the top of the embankment, stretching all the way to the residence. They were kneeling, rifles to shoulders, firing down at the besieged Filthies. There must have been a hundred of them.

Col could only hope they stayed focused on the Filthies. He set off running across the open ground. Before him the convicts were massed along the wire fence that caged them in. They shook the wire, shook their fists, cursed and roared and screeched. It was an ugly, brutal sound, full of threat.

Some noticed Col as he ran up. They began shouting

at *him*, creating even more of a din. To Col it sounded
much the same as their fury against their oppressors.

He stopped ten feet away and rummaged in his bag.
Pliers . . . wrench . . . spare clamps. He brought out the
pliers and eyed the fence. It was fifteen feet high, with
barbed strands along the top. He wondered if the pliers
could snip through wire as thick as that.

The convicts had all seen him now. Their faces were
full of wild passion, frenzy, hysteria. They pushed forward against the fence until it bulged . . . which gave
him a new and better idea.

The posts supporting the fence were braced on the
outside by struts that angled back to iron plates in the
ground. With the weight of so many bodies pushing
together, only the struts kept the posts from collapsing.
And the struts were fixed to the plates by great bolts with
protruding bolt heads. . . .

He dropped the pliers and took up the wrench. He
ran to the nearest plate, knelt, and adjusted the wrench
to the size of the bolt heads. He turned his back on the
convicts to shut out their distracting racket.

There were three bolts, and Col unscrewed them one
by one. He sensed the strut bowing and bending under
pressure from the fence behind. When he applied the
final twist to the final bolt head, the bolt sprang out of
its socket, and the wrench flew out of his hand.

He jumped to his feet and spun around, just as a
whole section of fence gave way. He leaped back as the
barbed strands came down nearly on top of him.

In the next moment the convicts streamed forth, trampling the fence under their feet. Men and women, old and young, all in brown burlap uniforms with numbers on their backs. Cheering, whooping, cursing, they surged forward on a tidal wave of sound.

21

The mass of bodies knocked Col flat to the ground. He curled up in a ball, shielded his head with his arms, and waited for the trampling feet to pass. He didn't see the imperialist soldiers turn to face the new threat, didn't see them start shooting. He heard only a chaos of gunfire, yelling, and screaming.

By the time he was able to rise to his feet, a multitude of dark figures were struggling hand to hand all along the top of the embankment. Obviously the soldiers had failed to halt the horde with rifle fire. Col hadn't just opened a new front in the fighting; he had unleashed a convulsion of rage and violence.

He stood watching, no more than an observer now. The figures were outlined against a brightening glow in the sky, pink and pearly. Sunrise had come at last.

After a while a fresh movement started up. The soldiers on the embankment had been slaughtered or driven back, and the convicts were rushing toward the residence.

He hoped the Filthies would grasp the situation and seize their chance to attack while the imperialists were in disarray. Dunga, for one, would understand what was happening. That is, if Dunga was still alive . . .

He made his way toward the embankment. Everything was happening so quickly. The convict quarters were deserted; the fighting on the embankment was over; already the convicts were storming the residence.

At least he didn't have to crawl through the pipe again. As he climbed the slope, a faint but distinctive smell came to his nostrils. Smoke?

He had a better view when he reached the top. The convicts milled around the marble steps that surrounded the residence, while officers fired shots from the roof and upper verandas. Tendrils of smoke crept out from the lower windows and main door. Some of the attackers must have penetrated the ground floor and set fire to the building.

On the other side, the barracks side, it was a scene of death and devastation. Col crossed the trolley rails and looked out over the boggy ground.

The Filthies *had* seized their chance to attack. They had thrown aside the duckboards and turned on the soldiers shooting from behind the storage stacks. Many of the soldiers had retreated to the cover of stacks farther back; others had abandoned the fight and were fleeing the field.

But that wasn't what made Col's heart contract. The boggy ground was dotted with sad, huddled bodies, like sea creatures abandoned by a receding tide. The near-horizontal rays of the sun picked out their shapes and cast a long, thin shadow of each individual death toward the embankment. Col couldn't bear to count, but it looked as though a third of the attack force had been slaughtered.

Minimal bloodshed, he thought bitterly. The imperialists had shot them down for sport.

He scanned the area for Dunga. The duckboards of their refuge now lay flat on the ground, and there between them lay two motionless bodies. Even at a distance he could recognize Dunga's close-cropped hair. Had she died in the time he'd been gone?

He scrambled down from the embankment and squelched his way toward her.

She lay curled on her side in the middle of a patch of blood-reddened mud. But he didn't think she was dead. As he came up, he sensed a flicker of movement, eyelids and mouth.

He had a lump in his throat as he bent over her. "Are you okay?"

Her response was a babble. "Who did it? Who did it? Who did it?"

"Did what?"

She didn't recognize Col and probably didn't understand the question. But her next words gave him his answer anyway.

"Someone's to blame . . . betrayed us . . . revealed our attack . . ." Her voice faded, and she lapsed into delirium.

Col examined the wound. She was half covered in mud, and the blood was still seeping out through the mud that caked her leg. No point trying to clean away the mess, which at least helped staunch the flow.

He stripped off his sweater and shirt, then ripped one shirtsleeve away at the armpit. He tied the sleeve around

Dunga's thigh and made a tourniquet above the wound. But he still needed something to tighten it.

He found the solution almost at once. Dunga herself was carrying one of the sharpened metal spikes that the Filthies used as weapons. He slid the spike in under the knot and twisted it around and around. Then he sat on the mud beside her and held the spike in place.

"I let out the convicts," he said. "Just as we planned."

But Dunga was beyond listening. Col looked away, and became aware that the light had changed. Smoke blanketed the sky, and the sun that came through was an eerie orange.

He swiveled toward the residence. Now the whole building was in flames. Even as he watched, a veranda came crashing down, and a corner of the roof caved in. Then officers appeared, bursting out through the main doors, coughing and staggering.

Although the convicts had backed away from the steps, they stood waiting on the muddy ground. When they saw the officers, they let out a bloodcurdling roar and converged. The fleeing men didn't stand a chance.

So many lives lost, thought Col. *So senseless.* All because the imperialists couldn't bear to trade with Filthies. A melancholy mood washed over him. There should have been another way. He didn't know what it was, but there should have been one.

For a long while he was hardly aware of time passing. At regular intervals he loosened the tourniquet for a minute or two, then tightened it again. Dunga seemed to have sunk into a more natural kind of sleep. He felt sleepy himself. He hunched forward and half closed his eyes.

"Hey! Who's this?"

He blinked and looked up at two female Filthies standing over him. He didn't know whether they were talking about him or Dunga.

"Dunga," he said.

"How badly hurt?"

"Bad. But she'll survive."

They were staring at him curiously, he realized. Though his face was blackened with ink and still unrecognizable, he was bare from the waist up—and his build was not the thin, wiry build of a typical Filthy.

He let go of the spike, which immediately swung round in a half circle.

"Look after her," he said.

He sprang to his feet, collected his sweater and what remained of his shirt, and left them to it. Twenty paces away he checked over his shoulder and saw that they were attending to Dunga.

He pulled on his sweater and discarded his shirt. Then he turned to survey the residence.

The scene had changed; the convicts had gone. The fire had burned itself out, with only a few wisps of smoke still drifting up into the air. The building was no more than a skeleton of bare, blackened ribs. Several Filthies strode around on the marble steps, inspecting the ruins.

One of them looked like Riff, except that there were

no streaks of blond in her hair. But if Riff had blackened her hair for the attack . . . had she? He'd only seen her in the dark; he couldn't remember.

It had never previously crossed his mind that Riff might have been shot and killed. But it crossed his mind now. In sudden panic he hurried toward the ruins of the residence.

22

It *was* Riff. She was leaning forward, probing about in the ashes with the tip of her rifle. No doubt the ashes were as hot as the bits of charcoal that littered the marble steps. Col burned his foot on one as he ran up the steps toward her.

"You're okay," he cried.

Riff was preoccupied with something in the ashes, but she turned at the sound of his voice. She stared into his face for a moment.

"It's you! What are you doing here?"

Col couldn't find the words to reply. He was just relieved to find her still alive.

"Ha! I might've known you'd find a way to come along." She swung back to the ashes. "Look at this."

She pointed with her rifle. The blackened, blobby mess no longer bore any resemblance to a human being, but the stench of burned flesh was unmistakable.

"See?"

"What?"

She prodded at something round and shiny under the ash. Metal and glass . . . a fob watch!

"Sir Peggerton Poltney!"

"Yeah, that's his watch. And that's him. His wife's just over there."

Col shook his head. "It should never have been like this."

Riff turned on him, eyes blazing. "You think they didn't deserve to die?"

"I didn't mean that."

"They'd have shot every last one of us. We'd all be dead if the convicts hadn't broken out."

"They didn't break out by themselves," said Col. "I let them out."

Riff's fierceness faded. "You did?" She pursed her lips and considered.

"Where are they now?" asked Col.

Riff turned from the ruins and swung her rifle in a wide gesture. "All over."

Looking out across the marshy areas on the convict-quarters side of the embankment, Col saw a hundred scattered groups, near and far. The convicts sat or sprawled in the mud, and appeared to be singing.

"They looted the residence before it burned down," Riff explained. "Made off with the governor's store of wine and spirits." She shrugged—then suddenly stiffened. "What's that?"

Col had heard it too. Somewhere close by, the sound of a drawn-out groan.

Bodies lay at the foot of the steps, where they had rolled down after the fighting. Some in the brown uniforms of convicts, some in the red jackets of soldiers, some in the black jackets of officers. One of the bodies seemed to move.

"Alive," muttered Riff. "Let's see if he knows."

"Knows what?"

Riff didn't bother to reply. Col followed her down the steps to where one of the officers lay sprawling. The man's midriff was soaked in blood, and his right leg was bent out at an impossible angle.

Col recognized him at once. "It's that officer who sat at the front of the trolley! Remember? When they escorted us to the residence."

"I remember." Riff gave the officer a push with her foot. "How did you know about our attack?" she demanded. "Who betrayed us?"

"I won't tell," said the officer faintly.

"I think you will." Riff gave him a harder push with her foot.

Col was about to protest when a male Filthy burst upon the scene.

"Scum!" he yelled, and aimed his rifle at the officer's chest.

Riff swung her rifle before he could pull the trigger. Barrel smashed against barrel, and both weapons clattered to the ground.

The male Filthy snarled and whirled. Most of the blacking on his face had already rubbed off, and Col recognized the pale eyes and sharp features of Council member Shiv.

"Imperialist scum!" He reached inside his undershirt and pulled out a long-bladed knife with a pearl handle. "Kill 'em all!"

Riff's reactions were instantaneous. She sprang forward and grabbed hold of Shiv's arm before he could cut the officer's throat. The officer struggled to draw away as the knife quivered six inches in front of his face.

For a moment it was a frozen tableau of straining arms and legs. Then Shiv seemed to relax.

Riff addressed the officer. "I want answers. Or I let him kill you."

The officer was going cross-eyed from staring at the blade.

"You even knew the exact time," Riff continued. "Who told you?"

She made a move as if to release Shiv's arm. The officer flinched and gave in.

"Nobody," he muttered. "It was a note."

"Go on."

"Pinned to a barracks door. We found it yesterday morning."

"Saying what?"

"It said, 'You die tomorrow. Attack at dawn.'"

Shiv lowered his arm and let out a savage, humorless laugh. "What did you expect? A Swank betrayed us."

Riff nodded agreement, but Col didn't understand at first.

"Why does it have to be a Swank?" he asked.

Shiv's narrowed eyes focused on Col. "Only Swanks can write."

It was undeniably true. Many Filthies had learned to read since the Liberation, but none of them had yet learned to write.

"The saboteur, then," Riff mused. "Must've been."

Shiv was still looking at Col, suspiciously, probingly. Col wished he could fade into the background. Then Shiv turned back to Riff and the officer.

"So we're done with him now?" He gestured toward the officer's throat with point of his knife.

"No."

"He's told us all he knows."

"And I said I'd let you kill him if he *didn't*." Riff was obviously ready to spring into action again. "Besides, he hasn't finished yet. He can tell us how the coal loading works."

She spoke to the officer, while keeping one eye on Shiv. "You show us what to do, and we'll let you live."

Shiv wasn't happy about that, and an argument started up. Shiv claimed that Riff had no right to make promises until the Council made a decision; Riff countered that he had no right to execute anyone without approval from the Council.

Col stood back a pace and let them fight it out. He watched the expressions on Shiv's face: the instinctive defensiveness, the pinched and wary look. For Shiv the officer was an enemy to be eliminated, and, just at that moment, perhaps Riff was too. Lye had described him as *small* and *riddled with little fears,* and, much as Col hated Lye, the description fit. Shiv *was* small, but a dangerous sort of small, like a rat.

Col urged Riff on in his mind, and she appeared to be winning. Then a movement on the embankment diverted his attention.

"Someone's coming," he announced.

A Filthy was running toward them, a young girl. Riff and Shiv broke off their argument.

"Looks like urgent news," muttered Shiv.

"News from *Liberator,*" said Riff.

The girl was panting for breath as she ran up. "All the other juggernauts!" she brought out. "Wireless telegraph! Messages intercepted! All the other juggernauts coming against us!"

23

The girl, whose name was Ellet, told the full story as soon as she got her breath back. The operators in *Liberator*'s wireless telegraph offices had intercepted messages from the imperialist juggernauts communicating among themselves, after an SOS message from Botany Bay.

"They must've sent off their SOS before the residence burned down," said Riff, and flicked her eyes toward the charred ruins.

"Every juggernaut in two thousand miles is heading top speed to Botany Bay." Ellet waved her arms, wide-eyed. "The Russians and French and Austrians and more."

"They know about us now," Shiv commented.

Other Filthies came hurrying up to hear the news, and Col retreated to observe from a distance. There was a great deal of excited discussion, followed by much issuing of orders.

Twenty minutes later, organized teams set to work burying the dead and tending to the injured. Col would have liked to help, but he didn't want to be recognized. He wandered off as far as the storage area and found himself a secluded spot beside a stack of rusty metal drums.

The injured were carried back along the embankment on makeshift stretchers. Col thought he spotted

Dunga on one stretcher. The juggernaut's cranes and scoops began lifting up the injured and lowering more Filthies to swell the work parties.

For two hours Col stayed watching the activity, which proceeded with perfect efficiency. The Filthies had learned the art of cooperation through long practice in the terrifying conditions of Below. Col was no longer surprised by anything they could do.

When all of the injured had been transported and most of the dead had been buried, a new operation started up on the other side of the embankment. One of the huge spidery steel structures, one of the coal loaders, was moving. Col stared in fascination as the girders telescoped out and out.

Obviously the Filthies still intended to refuel *Liberator*. Perhaps the imperialist juggernauts were many days' travel away; perhaps their intercepted messages would reveal when they were getting near.

As the loader extended and expanded toward *Liberator*, so *Liberator* changed too. A flap opened up in the smooth surface of its hull, exposing a wide rectangular hole. Col guessed that the hole was on a level with Bottom Deck, where the coal bunkers were.

He decided to take a closer look. Avoiding the teams of Filthies, he cut across the embankment and over the coal-blackened ground on the other side. Now he had a better view of the loader and its spindly legs—except that white clouds of steam obscured the very bottom of the structure.

The grinding, grating sound he could hear was obviously the sound of telescoping girders. But there was a second sound as well, like the chuff and chug of engines. The second sound appeared to come from out of the middle of the steam.

Again he moved forward. He was thirty yards away when he saw a vague, dark shape through the blanketing whiteness. He walked on into the steam, and the shape resolved into an outline of lumps and domes.

So this was probably one of the engines they'd seen on their way to attack the residence. It labored along with glacial slowness, puffing out vast quantities of steam. Col stood to watch as it went past. It was attached by cable to the girders of the loader, and he realized that it was actually hauling the whole structure forward.

There were two Filthies operating the engine at the back, but they were so wrapped up in noise and steam he hardly thought they'd notice him. He was wrong, however. One of the two jumped down and stepped up to him.

"Why are you dawdling around? Don't you have work to do?"

She had lost most of the blacking from her face, and he staggered with the shock. It was Lye!

He could only hope that his own ink-blackened face was a better disguise. He spun on his heel to hurry away. But he had gone only three paces when she snapped out a direct command.

"Wait!"

Reluctantly, he stopped and turned. She stood very upright, in that odd stance of hers. The remnants of the blacking made her features more gauntly beautiful than ever. She was studying his breeches, which were not quite the same as the Filthies' loose pants. No one else had noticed—but Lye had.

"Who are you?" she demanded. "Wash your face."

"It's ink. It doesn't come off."

"*Ink?*" She pointed to a puddle nearby. "Wash. There."

Col had no choice. He went across, squatted, and scooped up water. He hoped the ink would refuse to move, but in fact it washed off easily enough.

Meanwhile the haulage engine had trundled on and vanished from sight. However, by the time Col stood up again, a second haulage engine was chugging forward, looming out of the steam. Apparently, it took more than one of them to pull the loader.

Lye's lip curled when she recognized Col. She muttered something under her breath, then swung round at the sound of the approaching engine. One Filthy rode on the engine while another walked alongside.

"Look what I found," she called to the one walking alongside. She spoke as if Col were something she'd discovered on her shoe.

His heart sank further when he realized she was addressing Padder.

"Porpentine?" Padder halted. "What's he doing here?"

"Dunga let me join her team," Col retorted. "You can ask her."

"No one will be asking her anything for a very long time," said Lye. "Not until she recovers."

Padder snorted. "Why would Dunga want you on her team?"

"I *saved* you," said Col. "It was me that let the convicts out."

"Don't believe you." Padder shook his head.

"He's a liar," said Lye. "The convicts broke free by themselves. He's a liar, same as all Swanks are liars."

"It's the truth. I—"

"And he has no right to be out here." Lye cut Col off short. "Someone should march him back on board."

"Right." Padder agreed willingly, though he didn't seem so eager to act.

Lye turned suddenly on Col. "Stop that!" she snapped.

"What?"

"Stop looking at me!"

Col goggled at her.

"I can't bear him leering at me," she confided to Padder. "Nasty, greasy little Swank eyes crawling all over my skin. It makes me sick."

Padder swung toward Col with his fist raised. Col shrugged and looked away.

"He's always doing it," Lye went on. "It's the same with your sister. I've seen him pawing her over in his mind. She's sick of it too. I know she is."

Col had so many different denials jostling on the tip of his tongue that he couldn't manage to utter any of them.

An angry red color suffused Padder's face. "I'll deal with him."

"You'll march him back on board?"

"Right this minute."

"Good, then," said Lye.

She turned her back and walked on after the haulage engines. Padder continued to watch her retreating figure. *He was the one leering at her if anyone was,* thought Col. But, of course, Padder wasn't a Swank.

When he spoke to Col, it was as though he was returning to an unpleasant reality. "You come with me," he growled.

24

When Col got back to the Norfolk Library, everyone already knew about the imperialist juggernauts converging on *Liberator*. Septimus drew Col aside.

"We've been researching the other juggernauts, you know," he said. "Me and the professor found out all the facts. You ought to tell the Council."

"They won't listen."

"Riff will."

Col shrugged. "What did you find out?"

"The other juggernauts were built later than *Worldshaker*, not quite as big but faster and more powerful. They carry all kinds of special weapons. Mortars, toxic gas, pedal-bombs, loblights, pufferbugs . . ."

"We don't?"

"*Worldshaker* was built right after the Fifty Years' War, in a period of peace. Nobody wanted to think about armaments. We only have rifles and Maxim guns."

"Maxim guns?"

"They fire nonstop with a belt of bullets."

Col thought back to the Liberation. "I remember one of them three months ago. Where are they stored?"

"No idea. Books don't tell you things like that."

At that moment Gillabeth came bustling up with a pile of books in her arms. Her Porpentine chin jutted toward Septimus. "You left these lying on the floor," she said accusingly.

Septimus blinked. "Only a minute ago."

"You *left* them. Tidy them away."

She thrust the books into his arms and marched off with an air of civic duty performed.

Septimus chewed at his lower lip, then went across and deposited the books on the central table. Col followed and sat down beside him.

Septimus looked at Col, looked away, then looked back at him again.

"What's on your mind?" Col asked at last.

"I . . . um . . . doesn't matter."

"What?"

"You and Riff." Septimus checked that no one was listening, leaned forward, and lowered his voice. "How does it feel to be in love with someone?"

Col was half amused and half embarrassed. "What do you mean?"

"I mean, do you want to be close to Riff all the time? Is it the most wonderful feeling in the world?"

Lye's recent words echoed in Col's head: *She's sick of it too.* He didn't believe Lye, not for a moment, yet . . .

"I don't know about wonderful," he said. "Just as often miserable. Lots of little things hurt you."

"But it must be *intense*, even when it hurts. I could put up with the hurt if my whole life was heightened. Is it? Is it like being on top of the world?"

Col wanted to say, *It's more like being turned into a*

pathetic, helpless moron who never knows what's going on. But Septimus was so earnest; Col didn't have the heart to deflate him. So he said nothing.

"Do you think about Riff every second of every day? Does the thought of her make you go all hot and cold? I know I shouldn't be asking—you don't have to answer—but . . ."

Col shook his head. "You shouldn't be asking *me* about love. I'm not very good at it."

"Don't say that." Septimus's eyes shone with innocent envy and admiration. "I bet you—"

Professor Twillip burst upon the conversation out of nowhere. The woolly white fleece of his hair stuck out like a halo. "Look at this!"

He set down a massive leather-bound tome on the table. It was open at a page of diagrams colored red, black, and blue.

"It's a medical text," he announced. "That's a human head."

"So . . . ?"

"It shows where limiters were implanted in the brain. There. And there. And there." The professor jabbed a chubby pink finger at points in the diagram. "See, deep inside the skull. It shows how Filthies were changed into Menials."

Col shuddered to recall the time when he'd helped Riff escape from that horrific operation in the Changing Room. He couldn't make much sense of the diagram, but

Septimus studied it, then turned a few pages forward, a few pages backward.

"It's more diagrams than explanations," he said.

"Yes," Professor Twillip agreed, "but if there's one medical text, there are sure to be others. We have to search for them."

He could hardly wait to begin, rocking back and forth on his toes. Though well past middle age, he was like a ten-year-old when a new enthusiasm seized hold of him.

"We've finished with juggernauts, then?" asked Septimus.

"Yes! Come on!"

As the professor bounded away, Septimus turned to Col with a grin. "Care to join us?"

"No, thanks." Col knew there was no system for locating books in the library. A search like this could go on for days, even weeks.

Septimus followed the professor in among the bookshelves. Col heard thuds and thumps as they clambered over mattresses, then a crash as one of them knocked over a chair.

He wished they could have kept on researching juggernauts. If only there was a way to find out where the Maxim guns were stored, that *would* be something to tell the Council. It wasn't as if anyone had the surgical skills to help Menials. . . .

25

The next day Professor Twillip's new interest took an unexpected turn. He made his announcement over lunch, when the library's residents were gathered for a meal of cold rusks, cheese, dried fruit, and hot tea boiled on their kerosene stove.

"I want to look at the Menials on Garden Deck," he declared. "I need to examine their skulls."

"Garden Deck?" Col frowned. "Might not be a good idea."

"Why not? We can go anywhere on the juggernaut, can't we?"

Orris nodded. "The Filthies trust us. We're all on the same side now."

There was no denting the professor's blithe enthusiasm or Orris's high opinion of Filthies. Col shrugged.

"Okay," he said. "I'll come with you."

"Perhaps you'll see Missy Jip there," mused Quinnea. "I do so wish she was still with me."

As often was the case, Quinnea seemed adrift in her memories. Orris cleared his throat to speak, but she forestalled him.

"I know, I know, I shouldn't be saying things like that. You don't need to tell me it was wrong to have Menial servants. But Missy Jip was always so nice and helpful."

She turned to Col. "Look out for her on Garden Deck. I'd like to hear that she's still all right."

Septimus and Orris added themselves to the expedition, which set out for Garden Deck after lunch. Col led the way along corridors and down staircases little used by the Filthies. Professor Twillip carried a sketch pad and tape measure, while Septimus carried the three medical texts they'd discovered so far.

It was a while since Col had seen Garden Deck. The transformation was amazing. Before the revolution the area had been a large park divided into varying botanical zones and re-creations of rural scenes from the Old Country. Now it was turned over to farming, so that *Liberator* could produce its own fresh vegetables. The trees in their buried pots remained, but the lawns had been dug up and converted to a thousand small patches of onions, carrots, tomatoes, potatoes, and cucumbers.

It was peaceful and pretty in the afternoon sunlight: the light green of shoots and leaves, the brown soil, the darker green of foliage overhead. The Menials moved among the vegetable patches with trowels or buckets or watering cans. They still wore their gray, pajama-like uniforms and still shuffled along with hunched shoulders. They appeared contented enough, though it was hardly a very human form of contentment.

Col turned to Professor Twillip. "How many skulls do you need to inspect?"

"Dozens." The professor pointed. "Let's start there."

On the other side of a patch of squashes, two Menials

rested on a wooden bench. One was bald; the other was fast asleep and snoring.

Professor Twillip led the expedition around the squash patch. He studied the two Menials over the top of his glasses.

"I suppose there's no point asking for their consent," he said.

"They couldn't answer," said Col. "They can only obey orders."

Professor Twillip stood before the sleeper and started to sketch his head. Septimus opened up all three books on the grass.

Col left them to it. Since Garden Deck was fifty acres in area and there were probably three or four hundred Menials altogether, his chances of finding Missy Jip were slim. Still, he could try. He wandered at random among the vegetable patches, enjoying the sun on his face.

In fact he never did find Missy Jip. But he found another Menial he recognized: Wicky Popo. Compared to the waiflike individual almost starved to death by Ebnolia Porpentine, the liberated Wicky Popo was solid and well built.

"Hi, Wicky Popo!" Col grinned. "This is better than the old days, isn't it?"

Wicky Popo stopped weeding and rose up with his trowel in his hand. Col couldn't interpret the expression in his sad, soulful eyes, though he doubted there was any spark of recognition. He felt suddenly uncomfortable, and wished he hadn't intruded.

As he stood there, he became aware of a clamor of voices in the distance. He looked round and saw that the other three members of the expedition had gotten into an argument.

He raced back at top speed. Septimus, Orris, and the professor were waving their hands defensively, protesting innocence, while two men shouted at them. The two men wore the red armbands of Shiv's security force and carried wooden clubs.

Col was shocked to realize that only one of the two was a Filthy. The other was a convict from Botany Bay, dressed in the distinctive brown burlap uniform with a number on the back.

They swung toward Col and raised their clubs as he ran up.

"Here's another of 'em!" said the convict.

Professor Twillip turned unhappily to Col. "They don't want us examining the Menials."

The Filthy growled. "We don't want you on Garden Deck at all." He indicated the Menials on the bench, who were now wide awake but otherwise perfectly passive. "These were once people like us. Somebody's family, somebody's parents. Until your lot changed 'em."

The convict spat with contempt. "No Swanks allowed on Garden Deck."

"Is that an order from the Council?" Col asked.

"Council?" The convict tapped his red armband. "It's an order from Shiv."

"We prevent trouble," added the Filthy.

"We're not making any trouble," said Septimus.

"No? You've made plenty already." The Filthy waved his fist in Septimus's face. "Sixty-four killed, thanks to you and your lot."

It took Col a moment to realize that he meant those killed in the attack on Botany Bay. The Filthies blamed the Swanks for the handwritten note pinned to the door in the barracks. One Swank, all Swanks . . .

"Was it you?" the Filthy demanded, and jabbed his club into Septimus's chest.

"Me what?"

"Wrote that note."

"Of course not."

"I reckon you're lying." The Filthy turned to the convict. "Don't you reckon he's lying?"

They were working themselves up into a senseless rage. Col stooped and collected the three medical texts.

"Let's go," he said to the others.

They made their escape without another word. The two security-force men followed them all the way to the exit.

"Next time it's a beating!" The convict shouted a final threat.

Orris shook his head as they walked off. "I don't understand what's happening," he muttered. "I thought we were all on the same side."

"It's the red armbands," Septimus told him. "They're different."

Col said nothing, but he was thinking about the con-

vict. Shiv must have extended his recruiting for the secu-
rity force beyond their own juggernaut. And the Botany
Bay convicts hadn't even been present at the time of the
Liberation. It was an ominous development.

Just how ominous, Col was to discover over the next
few days.

26

The loading of coal proceeded at a slow pace. In quiet times or in the middle of the night the rattle of buckets could be heard, very faint and far away.

Col didn't get to go outside *Liberator* again. But he did leave the library to visit the other Swank ghettos—and everywhere, he heard the same story of heightened aggression from the Filthies. On top of the betrayal of the Botany Bay attack, they were now edgy and tense over the approaching imperialist juggernauts. The Swanks had grown used to being avoided and rejected, but this was something more: verbal abuse and small acts of bullying and persecution. Only the bolder spirits still dared roam beyond the safety of their own ghettos.

Moreover, the red armbands seemed to be multiplying in numbers, and an increasing proportion of them were convicts. Col couldn't understand why convicts had been allowed on board at all. It was even worse when Filthies with red armbands began carrying rifles. What did it mean? The Revolutionary Council had backed Riff's stand against arming the security force long ago. Had she been outvoted? Or had the new crisis situation made her change her mind?

Three days after the attack, the first refugees came seeking shelter in the Norfolk Library. They were a group of eight officers who had been living in a suite of administration offices on Forty-ninth Deck. One of them was bleeding from cuts to his cheeks and forehead. Col knew him by name as Warrant Officer Trockett.

"It's not safe on Forty-ninth Deck any more," said Trockett.

"We're getting blamed for the latest act of sabotage," said a chief petty officer called Chibling. "We're hoping you can take us in."

"I'm sure we can," said Col.

"*Hrrrumph!*" said Gillabeth.

Col turned to his sister. "We have space, don't we?"

"Of course we do." Gillabeth's "hrrrumph" wasn't the same as a no. "I'll just have to rearrange my organization."

The officers entered the library carrying cans, bags, and cartons of food—and not much else. They looked as though they had left their ghetto in a desperate hurry. The last one in made a point of closing and locking the door behind him.

"Tell us what happened," Col said.

They sat at the central table. Few officers had stayed on after the Liberation; as the most visible agents of oppression, they weren't exactly popular with the oppressed. This group had played a vital role in teaching the Filthies how to operate the juggernaut's equipment, but apparently their contribution was now forgotten.

"The first we knew was when they came to interrogate us," said Chibling. "Early this morning."

"Two of them were Council members," Trockett put in. "And two red armbands."

"Someone had discovered the wireless telegraph offices smashed up," added another warrant officer called Pollard. "And because we were close by on the same deck, we were the prime suspects."

"But they left without accusing anyone." Trockett took up the thread. "It was another gang that came along and attacked us later."

"Twenty or thirty of them," said Pollard. "More red armbands."

Col pictured the administration offices, with their large windows fronting onto the corridor. "You wouldn't have had much protection."

"They started by breaking the windows," said Trockett, and pointed to the cuts on his face. "I got these from fly-ing glass."

"We moved filing cabinets to make a defensive wall," Pollard went on. "We thought they were going to jump through the windows, or start shooting. But they just leaned in with clubs and rifles and wrecked everything within reach."

"We can't go back there." Chibling shook his head. "We really can't."

Gillabeth stood up with a snort. "I said I'd make space for you, didn't I? We'll need to find more mattresses, though." She clapped her hands. "A raid on some of the unoccupied bedrooms. Volunteers, please."

Col backed away as she singled out her volunteers.

Later he would help, but right now he wanted to see what had happened in the wireless telegraph offices.

"I'll be back soon," he said to no one in particular as he slipped out through the door.

Forty-ninth Deck was five levels above the Norfolk Library, and the wireless telegraph offices consisted of four interconnecting rooms with large windows, not unlike the administration offices. It took Col twenty minutes to reach the place, detouring to avoid Filthies on the stairs and in the corridors.

As soon as the coast was clear, he approached the nearest window and peered in through the glass.

The first thing he noticed was the absence of winking red and green lights on the cabinets inside. The wireless telegraph equipment was dead and out of action.

The second thing he noticed was that there were people in the first room—two shadowy figures deep in conversation. One had hair that was black in some parts and blond in others: Riff! But the other had jet-black hair, and he cursed his luck. He couldn't talk to Riff while Lye was there.

He was about to step backward when Riff glanced up and caught sight of him. Her eyes widened, and she said something inaudible through the glass.

In pantomime he pointed to his ears, shrugged, and made to move away again. She raised a peremptory hand and signaled for him to come inside.

He had no choice. Reluctantly, he nodded and went in through the doorway. Riff and Lye were standing by the desks where the operators normally sat with their headphones and telegraph keys.

"Go on, take a look." Riff swung an arm to indicate the damage. "Did a good job, didn't he?"

Col surveyed the room. Ripped-out wires dangled from the backs of cabinets; trampled glass and metal fragments littered the floor. Even the telegraph keys had been bent out of shape, and the headphones smashed and shattered. It was as if a hurricane had passed through.

"He must have been here half the night," said Lye.

"What about the other offices?" Col asked Riff.

"The same."

"Impossible to repair?"

It was a stupid question: Anyone could see that the equipment was impossible to repair. Riff glared at him.

"You know what this means?" she demanded.

"You can't intercept messages between the imperialist juggernauts."

"So we can't tell where they are. We can't tell when they're coming close."

"The saboteur must've known." Lye addressed herself exclusively to Riff. "He knew where to strike the most effective blow."

Riff knit her brow thoughtfully. "How?"

"Other Swanks would've told him. His secret supporters."

Col tried to deflect the discussion. "How long do you think before the other juggernauts arrive?" he asked Riff. "Gansy must have some idea."

Riff shrugged. "Five days. A week."

"We'll have loaded all the coal we need in a week," Lye insisted. She stood very close to Riff, claiming attention.

"It could be less than a week, though."

"Haven't we paid the price for that coal? Sixty-four dead! We've paid the price in blood!"

Lye seemed very eager to win Riff to her point of view, but Riff was not easily persuaded. Col stood on the sidelines, watching every expression on Riff's face. Signs of yielding, signs of resistance . . .

"We're not cowards, are we?" Lye's cheekbones burned with white spots of anger. "We can't let the tyrants chase us and frighten us!"

The talk went round and round in circles. Col prayed it would turn into an outright quarrel. Then Lye would leave, and he could talk to Riff on her own.

I can outlast you, he thought. *You won't drive me away.*

In the end he spoke up himself. "The imperialist juggernauts are more dangerous than anyone realizes. They're far better armed than us."

Riff turned to him, one eyebrow raised quizzically.

Lye lashed out with sudden violence. "What's he still doing here? We're discussing Council business! We don't want a Swank listening in!"

Riff sucked in her cheeks, and for a moment Col thought she was going to take his side.

"The other juggernauts have a whole lot of weapons we don't," he said.

"They're all puff and no blow!" cried Lye.

Riff looked from one to the other . . . and finally responded to Lye. "Why do you say that?"

"You remember the Liberation? How quickly the Swanks gave in? All we had to do was stand up to them, and they collapsed. It'll be the same with the other juggernauts."

Riff wasn't convinced. "Queen Victoria chose to surrender. That's what stopped the fighting."

"I *persuaded* her to surrender," said Col.

Lye focused all her intensity on Riff. "They had no guts for a real fight. Pampered parasites! You just have to look at them to see." She didn't actually look at Col, but it was obvious whom she meant. "The way they comb their hair, the way they dress, the superior way they talk. So full of their own self-importance. As if anyone cares. *Phuh!*"

She raised a hand and blew an imaginary speck of dust off her palm. She made sure that her hand was pointing in Col's direction.

Col felt his face turn red. He stared into Riff's eyes, but there was nothing for him there. She *had* to be aware of what Lye was doing, yet she didn't intend to come to his defense.

Enough! He spun on his heel and marched off.

"Oh, he's going already." Lye's mocking voice echoed in his ears on the way out. "Why do you even *bother* with him?"

27

There were more refugees the next day. The smaller groups in the smaller ghettos were starting to feel vulnerable. They came with tales of jeers and threats and banging in the night, of garbage left piled against their doors, of sinister stick-figure drawings on the walls outside.

"Someone's behind it all," said an elderly woman driven out from a workshop on the manufacturing decks.

"The red armbands," said her husband. "They stir up the trouble."

"But who's behind them?"

Gillabeth was in her element, telling everybody where to go and what to do. She let others look after the consoling and sympathizing; her task was to fit a growing number of people into a diminishing amount of space. Bookcases were pushed back, aisles created or closed up. Col had to transfer his mattress and belongings to another aisle altogether.

When four female supervisors from the Nursery Rooms came asking for refuge, Gillabeth decided that the central table had to be shifted to the side of the room. Septimus and the professor objected.

"You can't!"

"It's always been in the center!"

Gillabeth refused to listen to arguments. She grabbed one end of the table, but it was too heavy to shift on her own.

"Help me," she ordered.

Septimus helped—under protest.

"I don't see the point," he complained. "The table takes up the same amount of space wherever you put it."

Gillabeth let out a *whoof* of exasperation. "The point is that it gets in the way when it's in the center. And people can sleep under it more quietly at the side."

"Sleep under our table?"

"Just shut up and push."

Heaving and hauling, they slid the table across the library. Antrobus followed step for step, keeping an eye on his special pen and bottle of ink. Several sheets of paper wafted to the floor, but the pen and ink bottle remained in place. Septimus stooped to gather the fallen sheets of paper.

"You're a bully," he told her.

"And you're an intellectual egghead."

"I—"

"If you don't like it, I can let people sleep on top of the table too."

She dusted her hands triumphantly, and bustled away to the next job.

Col, who had observed the whole scene, came across. He lifted up his baby brother and set him down beside his pen and ink bottle.

"Don't worry about Gillabeth," he said to Septimus.
"She's always been like that."

"She's amazing."

"Uh?"

"So much drive and energy." Septimus was still gazing after her. "Do you know what I think? Not that I'm
an expert on people."

"What?"

"I think she doesn't have enough to do."

"She seems sort of busy now."

Col meant it as an understatement, but Septimus
shook his head. "Not really. Not for *her*. She needs ten
times more work than most people. A hundred times
more than me."

"You do plenty of work with your books."

Septimus brushed over the praise. "I've been watching her. She's been looking for things to do for weeks.
Trying to make tasks for herself."

"Well, she has a task now."

"Yes, but one library isn't big enough for her. She's
so competent and capable. She needs, I don't know . . ."
Septimus spread his arms. "A whole juggernaut to run."

Col grinned. "I don't think the Filthies would like
that."

Septimus spread his arms wider again. "A fleet of juggernauts."

"And the imperialists *definitely* wouldn't like that."

Septimus wasn't grinning. "You see, I do things in my

head because I'm an intellectual egghead. But she has to do things in the world. And when she can't . . ."

"It makes her angry and bossy." Col was beginning to get the idea.

"And frustrated. She ends up driving herself mad over things that aren't worthy of her. Too much energy turned in on little bits of arranging and tidying. I bet she'd be a different person if she had real scope for her powers. She's wasted as she is now, that's what I think."

Col followed Septimus's gaze across the room, to where his sister was taking out her frustration on a mattress. With one foot she kicked it into place while simultaneously taking down somebody's clothes from a washing line between the bookcases.

Real scope for her powers. Perhaps Septimus was more of an expert on people than he was. All the time he'd been growing up, Gillabeth had seemed relentlessly critical and disapproving. But she'd been trapped in the limited role of a female then . . . and she was trapped by other limits now. . . .

Gillabeth finished taking down the clothes and repositioning the mattress. Then she began folding the clothes in a neat pile while simultaneously unfastening the clothesline.

"Just look at her go," breathed Septimus.

28

Another refugee turned up the following morning: Mr. Bartrim Gibber. Gillabeth huffed and grumped but agreed to make room for him. Col was puzzled.

"Why have you come on your own?" he asked.

"I'm not on my own." Mr. Gibber joggled the wastepaper basket in his arms. "Here's Murgatrude with me."

The joggling prompted a deep, growly rumble from the bottom of the basket. Murgatrude didn't like to be disturbed.

"I meant Dr. Blessamy and the students."

"Dr. Blessamy has gone." The grimace on Mr. Gibber's face seemed to serve as an expression of grief.

"I'm sorry," said Col. "I hope it was peaceful."

"No, not that sort of gone." Mr. Gibber's grimace went through a number of rapid contortions. "Gone disappeared. Haven't you heard about the disappearances?"

"What disappearances?" Gillabeth demanded.

Mr. Gibber performed a small bow in her direction. "Upper Decks people gone without a trace. No one hears or sees anything, but suddenly they vanish and never come back. One boy from the ghetto on Thirty-eighth Deck. One mother from the engineers' group on Forty-fourth Deck. Maybe more."

"And Dr. Blessamy," said Col.

"Exactly the same, exactly the same. Last night he went to sleep in his favorite armchair. He thought he was the third Dr. Blessamy, and I told him if he was the third he'd have been dead for a hundred years. That put him to sleep straight away. Never fails. I tell him how long he's been dead, and he closes his eyes and drops off."

"And then?"

"Poof!" Mr. Gibber blew out his cheeks. "He was gone in the morning!"

"No sign of a struggle?"

"Nothing. Who could have done it?" Mr. Gibber waved his arms dramatically. "It's a complete mystery."

"The red armbands did it," said Gillabeth decisively. "Has to be."

"I'm afraid to stay in the academy." Mr. Gibber addressed Col's sister in a wheedling voice. "If they took Dr. Blessamy last night, it could be my turn tonight. I know I'll be safe with you. And Murgatrude." He rocked the wastepaper basket as though it held a human baby. "I couldn't bear to think of Murgy disappeared."

Col cut short the appeal. "We've already said yes."

"And it's so good of you. I don't ask for much, just a space to lay my head and—"

"You'll take what you're given," said Gillabeth.

"Of course, of course. And I shall be most grateful for it."

Gillabeth ignored his bowing and scraping. "Does the Council know about these disappearances?" she asked Col.

"I'm not welcome at Council meetings anymore."

"What about your friend on the Council? Riff?"

Col shook his head. He didn't know how to explain what had happened to his connection with Riff. He wasn't even sure himself.

Mr. Gibber seized the chance to re-enter the conversation. "Talking about Council meetings . . . I heard some news about the Council. And Riff."

"What?"

"Well." Mr. Gibber lowered his voice for the imparting of secrets. "That Riff doesn't have so much influence anymore. And the one called Dunga has stopped attending meetings."

"Only because she's still recovering from her injuries," Col put in.

"Whatever the reason. There's only one moderate, and the radicals have all the influence."

"You mean Shiv?" Gillabeth asked.

"Him and the other one. What's her name now? The one with the beautiful black hair."

"Lye," said Col.

"Ah, Lye. Yes, how could I forget?" Mr. Gibber licked his lips. "Shiv is madly in love with her. And Padder and Gansy are half in love with her. So I heard." He pulled a face. "Isn't that disgusting?"

Col said nothing. Mr. Gibber's account confirmed his suspicions—especially if Dunga wasn't attending meetings. Her injuries must be worse than he'd realized, because she certainly wasn't the type to play the invalid.

The loss of her vote made all the difference.

"Of course, those are only rumors," said Mr. Gibber suddenly. "Perhaps you shouldn't believe me."

"That's what you heard, though?"

"Oh, yes," Mr. Gibber sniffed, with just a hint of petulance. "At least I know more than most people."

By "most people" he seemed to mean Col and Gillabeth. Col had never understood the tangled workings of Mr. Gibber's mind, but the tone was beginning to sound familiar.

"We appreciate the information," he said firmly. "Thank you."

Mr. Gibber understood that the topic was closed, and looked down into the wastepaper basket. "I hope we can find a nice spot for you, Murgy. Somewhere quiet, with no drafts . . ."

"You'll take what you're given," Gillabeth said again. "Follow me."

She swung her arms and marched off. Mr. Gibber trailed along behind, still murmuring to his pet.

Col wished he could ask someone about Dunga, or visit her and check on her recovery himself. But he didn't know the location of her cabin. If only there were some way of getting hold of Riff . . .

Half an hour later, completely out of the blue, he received a summons to call on Riff in her room.

29

The two female Filthies who delivered the summons were unfamiliar to Col: one with a mop of frizzy hair, the other with a round face and yellowy teeth. They seemed very taciturn, and Col didn't bother to ask why Riff wanted to see him. They accompanied him all the way to her room on Forty-second Deck.

"You don't need to come any further," he told them, as they rounded the corner into the final corridor. "I can . . ."

He broke off, and his heart plummeted. A whole group of people stood waiting outside the door of Riff's room. There were two red armbands in the brown uniform of Botany Bay convicts, two Menials in their gray, pajama-like uniforms—and Shiv.

His heart sank even lower when the two Filthies who had accompanied him pulled red armbands out of their pockets and put them on.

"What's going on?" he demanded. "Riff wanted to see me."

"She *needs* to see you." Shiv smiled a thin-lipped smile. "But she doesn't know it yet."

Col whirled around—to discover that his two Filthy escorts had now become guards, and blocked his escape route.

"It was a trick," he said slowly, turning back. "*You* summoned me to her room."

Shiv stepped up to the door and knocked three times. A moment later Lye stuck out her head.

"You took your time," she snapped.

"I had to—" Shiv began, but she cut him off.

"Save it." She addressed the red armbands, first the convicts and then the Filthies. "You. Bring in the Menials. You. Bring *him* in."

"Yes, forward march," Shiv added weakly. It was obvious that the red armbands obeyed Lye's commands rather than his.

Col was swept forward into the room. He wondered how long Shiv had been subservient to Lye. Had it always been that way? Col had feared that Lye would act as Shiv's puppet on the Council; now he suspected it was actually the other way round. And the prospect of Lye's power was infinitely worse. . . .

"What is this?" Riff had been sitting on the chair under the porthole, but jumped up suddenly in amazement. "You said you wanted to chat!"

"This is more important," answered Lye. "A small deception for a larger truth."

Riff pointed at Col. "Why is he here?"

"You'll see." Lye signaled, and the two convicts propelled the two Menials forward.

"No." Riff shrank away and her voice quavered. "No."

Col followed the line of her gaze and saw what he'd

failed to notice before. One Menial was male, the other female—and the female Menial had hair that was black in some places, blond in others.

In spite of her hunched posture and dull eyes, Col understood immediately. This had to be Riff's mother. Riff's mother transformed into a Menial!

"I remembered what you told me about your mam and da," said Lye. "How they were hooked up to be made into Menials. I put Shiv onto the search. Tell her."

Shiv hardly seemed to mind being ordered around. "I didn't know what signs to look for at first. But the hair made it easy." He pointed to the female Menial's black and blond hair. "So I watched and noticed one particular male always hanging around near her."

Even now the two Menials were standing very close, almost touching. Shiv reached out, took hold of the male's chin and rotated it slightly this way and that. He was comparing the Menial's features to Riff's.

"Thought so," he said.

"Don't touch," said Riff in a whisper.

Shiv dropped his hand but continued his study. "Similar shape of the mouth," he said. "Similar large, dark eyes. I'm right, aren't I?"

"Be quiet," said Riff, still in a whisper.

She directed her gaze from one Menial to the other and back again. Her expression was uninterpretable. Horror? Hope? Yearning? Heartbreak? Col couldn't begin to guess at the feelings churning through her.

When she spoke, she addressed them both in an oddly tender voice. "Hello. I'm your daughter. Do you remember me?"

They couldn't speak, of course. Their only reaction was to move even closer, elbow to elbow. Could there be some spark remaining?

"Do you remember anything?" Riff's voice was barely audible, as though she were probing some infinitely fragile thing. The rest of the world had ceased to exist.

"Nod your heads if you remember," she said.

The two Menials nodded their heads.

Col held his breath. He had seen the operation in the Changing Room when the limiters were inserted: thin metal discs the size of buttons. He recalled what Grandmother Ebnolia had said about having *so many more thoughts than you really need* and about permanently blocking off *the nasty big ones*. But perhaps in exceptional cases . . .

"Nod your heads if you *don't* remember," said Riff.

Again the Menials nodded their heads.

"Put your hands on your heads," she said.

Slowly, clumsily, the Menials obeyed.

"Put your hands at your sides again."

They were like automatons, mindlessly following instructions. There was no spark. Riff's face had gone very white and sick-looking.

She continued to stare at them, chest heaving. Then the storm burst.

"Why?" She swung round to Lye and Shiv, and shrieked

at the top of her voice. "How could you do that?"

Shiv wilted before her rage. "We thought . . . we didn't know . . ."

But Lye was made of sterner stuff. "We did it for your own good."

Riff's lips drew back from her teeth, and for a moment she looked like a wild animal. "You must be mad! How *could* they remember me? What did you expect?"

"We expected nothing," said Lye. "We just wanted you to see. You have to face up to the truth."

"Don't tell me what to face up to!"

"The truth of what was done to your parents. You never backed away from anything in your life—except this. You must've known they could still be alive, but you kept away from Garden Deck. You didn't want to find out."

Riff seemed about to burst out in fury against Lye. Col hoped she would. Her mouth opened, but nothing came out.

"It's not worthy of you!" Lye stood very upright and implacable. "Taking the easy option. You're better than that. Don't back away. Expel the weakness. Accept the pain. Be pure and whole and strong."

Lye was certainly pure and whole and strong, as her voice rang out and filled the room. She was hard and inflexible like a blade—and it was Riff who crumpled. Suddenly there were tears streaming down her cheeks, and she was gulping for breath as though all the wind had been knocked out of her.

Lye pointed to the Menials. They hadn't stirred, hadn't moved their heads, had barely even blinked.

"Here is the truth," she told Riff. "Let it be burned into your brain. Remember it and live by it. The ultimate wrong that was done to your mam and da. The ultimate cruelty."

"Stop it," said Col.

He hardly knew he'd spoken. He was hurting for Riff, seeing her swamped with grief, her face all twisted up. He just wanted her pain to end.

Lye whirled on him at once. "Ah, the Swank would like me to stop. Wouldn't that be convenient? So that it can all be hushed up and forgotten. How very desirable!"

"What you're doing is cruel too," Col retorted.

"I'm not *doing* anything. I'm only showing what was done. What you did, when you turned people into vegetables."

"I didn't know about the Changing Room."

"Oh, of course, nobody knew about it!" Lye blazed with contempt. "Squirm away! Here's the living proof before us. And it'll never be forgotten. Not by me. Not in here." Lye pointed a finger at her forehead. "And not by *her*." She pointed to Riff.

Riff appeared shell-shocked, though no longer gasping for air.

Col appealed to her. "I didn't know about the Changing Room. You remember—"

"*Shut up!*" Riff spat the words in his face.

"You must remember." He couldn't adjust; he blundered on. "I *saved* you from the operation."

"You did it!" Riff was beside herself with rage. "All of you! All guilty!"

"No, listen to me."

"I don't want to listen! I'll never listen! You turned my mam and da into vegetables! You and your surgery! You and your limiters!"

Col shook his head and took a step backward. "You're just upset. You don't know what you're saying. I understand."

Riff came after him. "Then understand *this!*"

She swung her hand and dealt him a vicious blow across the face.

Col felt as though the ground had been pulled out from under his feet. It wasn't the pain; he hardly noticed that his cheeks were on fire and stinging. It was the way Riff looked straight at him without even seeing him. Col Porpentine had ceased to exist. He was no longer an individual, a friend, a person with whom she'd shared experiences. In her eyes he was a whole class, an example of the old regime and her Upper Decks oppressors.

"Get him out of my sight," she hissed. "Before I *really* hit him."

In the next moment all four of the red armbands had formed a guard around Col. He let them usher him away.

He saw Lye take Riff's hand in a show of sympathy. The two Menials remained hunched and unfocused, seemingly oblivious to all the drama. Shiv had a triumphant grin on his face.

Too late it all came clear. Lye and Shiv had brought him along to Riff's room for a reason. He wasn't there as an observer, but as the true object of their plan. The weakness that Lye wanted Riff to expel wasn't just a weakness over her parents, but a weakness over *him*. The scene had worked out exactly as they'd intended.

30

Col tried to tell himself that Riff's anger was just a reaction of the moment. He remembered what she had once said about needing to trust her a little more. And Septimus had told him he had to fight for her—if he loved her and she loved him. But did she love him?

Unpleasant images kept flashing up before his mind's eye. Lye taking Riff's hand . . . Riff's look of nonrecognition when she couldn't even see him as a person. He didn't deserve that. Lye had deliberately hurt Riff with the sight of her parents, but it wasn't Lye who had suffered the blame. As far as trust went, Riff seemed to trust him less than she trusted Lye.

That night he had the worst dream of his life, which went on and on for ages. It seemed that he was on Bottom Deck, the lowest level of the juggernaut above the engine room Below. Here, in the time of the old regime, he and Riff had hidden from officers behind the coal mounds. Now Lye and Riff were hiding from *him*.

At first when he spotted them, he called out and ran toward them. But they only shuddered and ran away. The look of disgust on Riff's face exactly matched the look on Lye's.

Another time he seemed to hear them laughing together. He hurried past pipes and iron piers and came out into a patch of blue-white light. There they were—and it was him they were laughing at. Vicious, mocking laughter, as though they'd known of his approach all along.

He tried to run after them, but they ducked round behind the nearest coal mound and disappeared.

So it went on. He went looking for them in one of the cagelike viewing bays that hung down from the ceiling of Below. Clouds of steam and smoke obscured everything.

"Where are you?" he shouted.

"Stop looking at us!" came the answer.

"Stop pawing us!" cried a second voice.

"Ugh! Nasty, greasy little Swank eyes!"

Then the steam and smoke cleared. Riff and Lye stood brushing each other down as though something unclean had crawled over them. When Col tried to justify himself, suddenly they were no longer there.

He made a rational decision in the dream, and stopped pursuing them. But, irrationally, he still couldn't avoid them. Wherever he was, they were always nearby, always together, always laughing and whispering. He was sure that Lye was poisoning Riff's mind against him.

At one point he was passing the piled-up food stores beside a food chute—the stores that had once been dropped down to Filthies, but that no longer existed in reality—when he heard a spitting sound. Two blobs of wetness landed on his cheek and the side of his neck.

He saw their faces then, sticking up above the bags and sacks.

"Stop it!" he yelled. "That's not fair!"

Lye's mouth moved, and he heard her cry, "We're sick of it! Sick of you!"

But the cry was in Riff's voice, not Lye's. Then Riff's mouth moved, echoing the same words. "Sick of it! Sick of you!"

Now it was Lye's voice coming from Riff. They shared everything, interchangeably!

"Sick, sick, sick, sick, *sick* of you!"

He woke up suddenly and gasped at the pain in his chest. It was sharp like a cut and dull like a bruise.

Only a dream, he told himself. *It'll pass, it'll pass.*

Yet it was a dream that had gone right through him and changed the color of his thoughts. He couldn't help thinking it had stripped away the illusions and revealed the true situation. Lye had triumphed, and Riff was lost.

A wave of bitterness washed over him. He lay on his mattress and stared up into the darkness—at the shadowy ceiling, at the dim bookshelves towering on either side. He just wished they would collapse and crush him.

He *hadn't* known about the Changing Room, and when he had found out, he'd turned against his own class and fought for the revolution. He could have been supreme commander of this juggernaut; he could have had everyone looking up to him and obeying his every command. Instead he'd given it all away for Riff. What had she given away for him?

She was more concerned about power and position than he'd ever been. They'd ended up meeting only in secret because she was afraid of what the Filthies would think of their relationship. And had she even cared very deeply about their secret meetings? Those few hours a week, so infinitely precious . . . No, if he was honest with himself, they'd never mattered as much to her as they mattered to him.

The thought twisted inside him like a worm. The feelings were all one way, from him to her.

He came to a resolution then: The relationship was over. He *declared* it dead. If she could forget everything they'd shared in the past, then he could too. No more wishing and hoping, no more humiliations, no more useless hankering, no more stupid ups and downs. Let Lye have her.

"It's over," he whispered aloud in the darkness. He felt numb, and somehow heavy and empty at the same time. "Over. Over. Over. Over."

31

"Colbert? There's something very interesting. Do you want to come and see?"

Col looked up at his father standing at the foot of his mattress. An unusual excitement animated Orris's lugubrious features.

Col could have happily stayed sleeping the whole day. But he roused and followed his father.

Orris led the way round into another aisle between bookcases. Everywhere they stumbled over bags and boxes, pillows and blankets, piles of clothing and assorted personal possessions.

The "something very interesting" turned out to be Murgatrude with Col's baby brother. Mr. Gibber's pet had hunkered down on Antrobus's mattress, while Antrobus sat facing him, cross-legged. They were absorbed in silent communion. Murgatrude seemed almost as good at silent communion as Antrobus.

Quinnea stood on the other side of the mattress, hands clasped to her chest as she looked on. "Aren't they amazing?" she murmured.

Col shrugged. "I saw them like that when Murgatrude came to the library a week ago."

Then he realized what his mother meant. It wasn't the same as a week ago, because Antrobus kept moving his lips as if forming silent syllables. Murgatrude might have been lip reading, the way his amber-colored eyes were fixed upon that tiny mouth.

"We think Antrobus is trying to talk," said Orris.

"Imagine!" gushed Quinnea. "His first words!"

"Keep trying, Antrobus."

"Go on, my little baby."

"You can do it, son."

"Just make the sounds."

Perhaps Antrobus *was* trying to make the sounds. His face certainly conveyed an impression of intense struggle. But no sounds emerged. Instead another voice cut in.

"Murgy! Murgy! Murgy! Murgy!"

It was Mr. Gibber, searching for his pet. He appeared at the other end of the aisle, carrying Murgatrude's wastepaper basket. Then he caught sight of Murgatrude over Quinnea's shoulder.

"*There* you are!" He came forward, grinning apologetically as he squeezed past Quinnea. "You bad pet! Leaving your wastepaper basket! Leaving your kind master! Murgy?"

Not a twitch of a whisker from Murgatrude. Mr. Gibber got down on his knees at the end of the mattress. He looked round at his audience and pulled his rubbery face into a huge smile.

"Here's what I do," he announced. "You have to understand how the animal mind works. This always does the trick."

He tilted the basket in Murgatrude's direction and

scratched in the bottom with his fingertips. Murgatrude continued to look at Antrobus.

"Murgy, Murgy." Mr. Gibber sighed. "Stop being such a show-off. You're making an exhibition of yourself in front of all these people." He spoke in an aside to his human audience. "This is where I use a little psychology. He can't resist this."

He placed the wastepaper basket on the floor in front of him, then folded his arms, leaned forward on all fours, and rested his elbows in the bottom of the basket.

"How comfy and cozy!" he exclaimed. "I think I'll just curl up and go to sleep in this nice basket."

Murgatrude remained completely indifferent. Mr. Gibber grimaced and rolled his eyes.

"He's being a real performer today," he said. "All for effect, you know. He'll do anything to get himself noticed." He switched back to his pet. "Very well, Murgatrude. You're the center of attention. We're all watching you. And now I'm going to steal your basket. Look!"

Mr. Gibber rose, then lowered himself into a squatting position and plumped his posterior down into the wastepaper basket, as far as it would go.

"Look, Murgy!"

He sat there with his knees up to his chin and waited for a reaction. He waved his arms and waddled the basket about on the floor. None of it made any difference to Murgatrude.

"Attention seeker!" he cried. "You're overdoing it, Murgatrude! No one's impressed anymore! We're all getting very bored with you! Enough of the stunts! Playing to the gallery, Murgatrude!"

Still sitting in the wastepaper basket, he reached forward and gave Murgatrude's tail a tweak. The tail flicked aside, and a deep-throated growl filled the air.

"Rrrrrr-ow-rrrr!"

Mr. Gibber drew back his hand in a hurry. "All right. You've embarrassed me now, Murgatrude. So be it. Stay with this . . . this babe in arms." For the first time, he deigned to recognize the presence of Antrobus. "This whippersnapper. I'm disappointed in you, Murgatrude. I thought you were more *mature.*"

He struggled to his feet, but the wastepaper basket had locked onto his posterior. He tugged and heaved and eventually hauled it off. Red in the face, he stood up straight and shouted at his pet.

"You disloyal creature! I abandon you! Do you hear? I *abandon* you!" When Murgatrude still didn't twitch a whisker, he turned to his human audience. "I abandon him," he explained.

He pushed past Quinnea and stomped off. They heard the sound of his footsteps heading toward the library door. A moment later there was a loud slam.

"I think he's gone out," said Orris, shaking his head.

"Don't worry," said Col. "He'll be back."

32

More refugees arrived the next day: a silversmith, a notary, and their wives and children. They came from a small ghetto on Thirty-seventh Deck, and one of their group had been mysteriously abducted in the middle of the night. They had decided to seek safety in numbers.

Their arrival jolted Col out of his dark mood over Riff and started him thinking about Victoria, Albert, and their attendants. They constituted an even smaller ghetto, just four of them on their own. Someone ought to encourage them to move to the relative safety of the Norfolk Library.

He set off at once for the Imperial Chapel. What if something bad had happened to them already?

He need not have troubled himself; they were all still there. A warm, loving atmosphere pervaded their make-shift residence, with Victoria's pregnancy the center of every attention.

When Col explained the increasing danger, the old majordomo puffed out his chest and stepped forward. "They'd better not try any of that here. I'll deal with them."

The ex-queen smiled. "No, Beddle, you can't fight them. You can barely tie your own shoelaces in the morning." From anyone else it might have sounded sharp, but not from Victoria. She turned to Albert. "What do you think, my dear?"

"Hmm . . ."

She nodded toward Col. "I'm sure he has our best interests at heart."

"No doubt, no doubt of it. And we have to think of little Henrietta."

"Or little Henry."

"Henrietta."

"Henry."

Albert took Victoria's hand. "We'll see."

"We will, we will." Victoria's smile lit up her whole face.

They were so tender to each other that Col thought of Riff and felt a sudden pang. The dark mood rushed back over him, and the world seemed to go into a blur. He looked down at his feet, trying to hide the wetness in his eyes.

Victoria noticed and empathized—or thought she did. "He's remembering his own Sephaltina," she whispered to Albert.

"Is he?" Whispering was outside of Albert's vocal range. "The wife who . . . ?"

"Abandoned him, yes."

"Bad show, bad show. She should have stayed."

"Shush."

Col pulled himself together and returned to the present. "So will you come to the Norfolk Library?" he asked.

"I think . . ." Albert twiddled a nonexistent mustache. "I believe . . . yes."

Victoria nodded and turned to her majordomo and lady-in-waiting. "You'll come with us, won't you?"

"We will, Your Majesty," said Morkins at once.

"Of course, Your Majesty." Beddle bristled, as though he would engage in fisticuffs with anyone who tried to stop them.

Col explained that they should bring only essential personal items, which troubled Victoria and Albert much less than it troubled Beddle and Morkins. For half an hour everyone bustled around except Victoria.

Col still couldn't wipe Riff from his mind. Somehow he'd been stronger and more determined yesterday. Declaring the relationship dead seemed to be growing harder rather than easier.

Back in the library Gillabeth shifted a bookcase to open up a new space for the ex–royal couple near the door. Col helped, although he found it difficult to concentrate. He moved around in a kind of cloud, which only Gillabeth's sharpest commands could penetrate.

All afternoon and evening the dark mood returned again and again. Any tiny thing could bring it on. *Be sensible,* he kept telling himself. *There's nothing to be done. Accept it.* He forced himself to recall the look of nonrecognition in Riff's eyes, but even that seemed less effective than before.

At night he lay curled up on his mattress, clenched in misery. He twisted and turned; he pressed with both hands to stop it from spreading. How could it be so physical?

He had never guessed it could hurt so much.

33

Mr. Gibber made his return the following morning. He had overcome his pique and decided to forgive and forget. He stood in the doorway and announced that he was ready to reconcile with Murgatrude.

"Where have you been?" asked Gillabeth.

"In depths of woe and realms of despair!" Mr. Gibber groaned, and flung out his arms. "Oh, Murgy!"

As it happened, Murgatrude had been on the prowl for scraps of unguarded food. When Mr. Gibber caught sight of him, he was licking a plate that one of the silversmith's children had left lying on the floor.

Mr. Gibber bounded across. "Murgy, my Murgy!"

Col, like everyone else, stopped what he was doing and turned to watch. Mr. Gibber didn't seem to mind. On the contrary, he redoubled his dramatics.

"How could we be apart? How could we let pride stand in the way? What's pride, compared to all we've been through?"

Murgatrude finished licking and directed an inscrutable amber gaze upon his master.

"Ah, you and I, old pet." Mr. Gibber sidled closer, half stooping at the knees. "You mangy old bag of bones. Arthritis in your joints and moths in your fur. A carcass on four legs is all you are. But still the best pet in the world to me."

He held out a hand, but Murgatrude merely looked at it. Mr. Gibber put on his most cajoling voice.

"So tatty and decrepit. You call that fur? You call that a tail? But Murgy, we were made for each other. You're what I deserve. I'm nothing, and you're nothing. Come here and be patted."

He moved his hand a little closer, and Murgatrude swatted it with his paw.

"Ow! Yow! Ow! You *scratched*!" Mr. Gibber held up the hand so that everyone could see a red line across the knuckles. "He scratched me!"

"Oh, be quiet, you silly man." Gillabeth snorted.

"Silly? Silly? She thinks I'm silly!" Mr. Gibber danced about, flapping his hand. "Perhaps I am. My loving heart makes me do silly things." He stopped and eyed Murgatrude severely. "My *rejected* loving heart."

"You make too much fuss," said Gillabeth. "It's only a . . . a . . ." Like everyone else, she wasn't sure whether Murgatrude was more of a cat or more of a dog. "A whatever-it-is animal."

"The bond between animal and human can be as strong as any bond," said Mr. Gibber sententiously, and laid a hand—the unscratched one—across his breast. "Never underestimate the power of that bond. Or the pain and jealousy when it's betrayed. When one is left for another."

"You mean Antrobus?" Gillabeth looked around, but Antrobus was nowhere to be seen. "So Murgatrude likes Antrobus better than you. So what? Antrobus likes Murgatrude better than me."

"It's not the same. I've done everything for Murgatrude. I've been his sole carer and provider." He glared at his pet. "After all I've done for *you*."

Gillabeth shrugged, and seemed about to dismiss the whole discussion. But instead she said, "You think I haven't done everything for Antrobus?"

"Well, you don't understand about love, then."

"I understand enough to know it's a waste of time."

"I love even the mangiest tip of his mangiest paw," Mr. Gibber declared. "I love each and every one of his whiskers. The ones he's got left."

"Stupid." Gillabeth stamped her foot with impatience. "You just do what you have to do. You shouldn't expect a return for it. You shouldn't make yourself unhappy over it."

It had become a private conversation between the two of them. Col wasn't sure whether his sister was talking more about Mr. Gibber and Murgatrude or about herself and Antrobus.

"Perhaps you're not very lovable." Mr. Gibber pulled one of his grimacing smiles.

"No, I'm not. I don't expect to be. And nor are you, by the look of it."

"I can hope."

"Yes, and I can do something useful with my life,

instead of deluding myself and carrying on like an idiot. At least I'll do what I do with dignity."

Murgatrude chose that particular moment to yawn, stretch, and stalk off. Mr. Gibber let out a cry and jumped across to stand in his way. Murgatrude merely detoured around his legs.

"Very well. I stand aside and let you go." Belatedly Mr. Gibber stepped aside. "I have my dignity too. Go, Murgatrude."

Murgatrude went—toward the aisle between the bookcases where Antrobus had his mattress.

"Go!" Mr. Gibber called out after him. "Go to your new carer and provider! Go to your whippersnapper! I won't stop you!"

Gillabeth clicked her tongue and walked away. She looked a little red in the face, as if embarrassed by the conversation she'd fallen into.

Col heard it all as a reflection on his own circumstances. *I can do something useful with my life.* He would make Gillabeth's phrase his own motto from now on. Better not to be deluded; better not to carry on like an idiot.

At the same time he couldn't help feeling a little sad and sorry for his sister.

34

While Murgatrude slept curled up on the end of Antrobus's mattress, Mr. Gibber remained in the library talking to anyone who would listen. In his time away he had heard more rumors about the Council. Apparently, Riff now kept to her room, so neither she nor Dunga was present at meetings. With no opposition the radical faction of Lye and Shiv refused to run from the approaching juggernauts and called anyone who thought otherwise a craven coward. *Liberator* would continue to load coal until every bunker was full, they said.

The juggernaut was becoming an increasingly dangerous place as tensions rose. Listening to the fearful tales told by refugees from other ghettos, Col and his family and friends counted themselves lucky.

But even the Norfolk Library was no longer a safe haven. That night everything changed.

It began with a knock on the door. Col was restless and brooding, and he remained awake long after everyone else had gone to sleep. He decided to act as doorman.

When he opened the door, a foot thrust forward immediately into the gap. Col planted his own foot to stop the door from opening further. He found himself looking into the eyes of a young Filthy: a girl with a red armband. An older female Filthy stood behind her, as

did a man in the brown uniform of a convict, also sport-
ing a red armband.

"We want to look," said the girl.

"Where?"

"Inside."

"It's too late now," said Col. "Everyone's asleep. Come
back in the morning."

For some reason the girl's attitude sent warning signals, while the pair behind were downright menacing.
They're here to cause trouble, said a voice at the back of his
mind.

"We're coming in now," growled the convict, and
pushed forward to take over from the girl.

But the moment the girl withdrew her foot, Col
slammed the door shut. He gripped the handle with
both hands to stop it from turning.

"What's going on?" "Who is it?" People in the library
were rousing and calling out.

The handle jiggled, and the whole door shook.

"Let us in!" a male voice cried.

"Or else!" added a female voice.

Col addressed the solid wood of the door. "In the
morning."

In the next moment Gillabeth had come up beside
him. She reached for the key and twisted it in the lock.

"There," she said. "No visitors tonight."

The visitors didn't leave for a long while. They
shouted threats; they kicked and rattled the door. Gillabeth turned to the library's residents, who were now all

awake and standing in a half circle, watching with wide eyes. She put her finger to her lips, and nobody answered the threats or made any sound at all.

Finally it grew quiet again. Col didn't feel like opening the door to check outside, in case they were still waiting, and Gillabeth made no move to check either. The library's residents sat down on bare floor or mattresses. A few talked among themselves, but their eyes kept returning to the locked door. It was obvious there would be no more sleep tonight.

"I could tell jokes," Orris offered. "I've been practicing some recently. I think they ought to cheer people up."

Under any other circumstances the idea of Col's gloomy father telling jokes would have been laughable—but nobody cracked a smile.

"I don't want to be cheered up," said Quinnea.

"Some of them are rather funny."

Quinnea shook her head. "No, thank you, dear."

An hour later the visitors returned with reinforcements. A score of yelling voices and stamping feet could be heard approaching along the corridor.

"Mattresses!" cried Gillabeth. "Quickly!"

Septimus helped her with the first mattress. They hauled it across, stood it on end, and set it up against the door, just as the attackers arrived. There were roars of abuse and a tremendous battering against the wood.

Inside the library others caught on to Gillabeth's plan and shifted more mattresses. They propped them against the door, two, three, four layers thick. Some officers from

Forty-ninth Deck stayed leaning against the final layer, arms outspread, keeping the mattresses in place and upright.

The violence against the door was ten times greater than before, yet muffled by the padding of the mattress. The sounds were surely too sharp and loud for fists.

Col frowned, and shouted across to Gillabeth, "Listen!"

"What?"

"Those are rifle butts!"

Gillabeth nodded. "They're armed, then."

"They might start shooting through the door."

"Through the door *and* the mattresses?"

"Possibly."

Col more than half expected Gillabeth to dismiss the possibility with a snort, but she didn't.

"Fall back!" she ordered. "We need more protection in case they start shooting."

She was in her element, like a general addressing troops. The officers from Forty-ninth Deck dropped back at once, and the mattresses stayed upright by themselves.

Then she set everyone to shifting bookcases. She created a barrier right across the library, leaving a small gap in the middle for the defenders to look out. She protected that gap with a shield of heavy books stacked up to shoulder height.

Professor Twillip blanched. "But those are *books*! Think what a bullet hole could do! Words lost! Whole sentences made meaningless! Septimus!"

But Septimus was already helping to build the shield

of books. In the end Professor Twillip gave in and involved himself in the selection of less precious volumes. Unfortunately, he was often sidetracked into reading what he was supposed to be selecting.

The battering on the door continued. The panels had probably cracked in many places, but the mattresses kept the door from disintegrating. There was still no shooting, just an ever-rising tide of jeers and catcalls. The residents waited, crowded in behind their barrier of books and bookcases.

"Why us? Why now?" Orris pondered aloud. "What have we done?"

Mr. Gibber tapped the side of his nose with one finger and directed his gaze toward the ex–royal couple nearby. "There's your answer."

"We're being attacked because of Victoria and Albert?"

"They're the symbol of the old regime, so they're a special target."

Mr. Gibber kept his voice down, but not so low that Victoria and Albert couldn't overhear.

"It's because of us?" Victoria whirled round with a look of distress. "What should we do?"

Mr. Gibber licked his lips. "Not for me to say."

"Should we leave?"

"No." Col intervened. "You're with us. You're my responsibility."

"We could go back to the Imperial Chapel."

"Absolutely not."

"I didn't say you should leave." Mr. Gibber smirked

and backed down at the same time. "Did I ever say—?"

"What's that?"

A new noise had started up directly over their heads. A pounding of feet, a thumping of heavy objects.

"They're on Forty-fifth Deck," said Septimus.

"What are they trying to do?" muttered the notary from Thirty-seventh Deck. "Attack from above?"

"Impossible," said Gillabeth with decision. "Every floor of this juggernaut is solid steel. They'll never break through."

Nonetheless they carried on as if they could.

Then the lights began to flicker: on-off, on-off, on-off. Col stared as white faces jumped in and out of existence all around him.

"Don't be afraid!" he cried in the firmest voice he could summon. "Lights and sounds won't hurt us! They're trying to make us panic!"

Clinging to one another for support, the library's residents fought down panic. For as long as they could remember, the nighttime lights and daytime lights had been a constant of their lives. To have that constant cut away was more than disturbing; it was traumatic.

Still they endured and held on—all except Quinnea. She didn't panic, exactly, but went into a state of trembling paralysis. It was as though all her reactions were happening so fast, so simultaneously, that they canceled each other out. Only her eyeballs continued to move, fluttering unfocused in every direction.

"Come on, my dear," Orris appealed. He began

patting her cheeks, more and more briskly. "It'll soon be over."

"Oh. Oh. Oh. Oh. Oh," said Quinnea, as the combs fell out of her hair. "Oh. Oh. Oh. Oh. Oh. Oh. Oh. Oh. *Oh!*"

The last "oh" must have marked some kind of watershed, because she drew away from her husband's patting and suddenly found her voice.

"I wish the other juggernauts would hurry up and come," she said.

Col and Orris exchanged glances. Orris tut-tutted. "You mustn't say that. We're not on the reactionary side."

"Whose side are we on, then?" Quinnea raised her eyes to the pounding and thumping overhead. "Theirs?"

Orris's shoulders slumped. "I don't know."

"At least the other juggernauts would make them behave," said Quinnea. "The way it used to be. More civilized."

Orris had no answer, and neither did Col. They believed in the Liberation, but not in *this*. On the other hand, Col remembered how the governor of Botany Bay had called them *a disgrace to the human species*. The imperialists regarded Swanks as traitors to the old cause, and the Filthies regarded them as traitors to the new. They were on nobody's side but their own.

"It's just a few hotheads," Orris said at last, completely without conviction.

Quinnea sniffled. "I wish we'd left the juggernaut when everyone else did."

There were murmurs of agreement from several

Swanks nearby. Being persecuted, they couldn't help but hate their persecutors.

That night, though, the persecution didn't pass beyond psychological warfare. The attackers weren't prepared to start shooting—yet. The on-off lights and jeering and thumping went on for hours, or what seemed like hours, but nothing worse happened. And in the end the thumping died down and the jeering faded away.

When the daytime lights came on and stayed on, they knew they'd survived.

Everyone breathed a sigh of relief. They waited a long while in blessed peace and silence. Finally Gillabeth commanded an opening to be made in their defensive barrier.

Septimus and the officers dismantled the shield of books. Then Gillabeth went through, followed by Col, followed by Septimus. Antrobus slipped out before anyone could stop him, and toddled along at their heels.

The library looked like a battlefield. Books, chairs, clothes, and personal possessions lay tumbled about everywhere. Col and Gillabeth went and pressed their ears against the wall near the door. Not a sound. They stayed listening a long time, then slid back the mattresses to partly uncover the door.

The wood was smashed, but the lock still held. Col opened up and peered out. The attackers had gone, and the corridor was empty.

"All clear." He drew back, relocking the door. "What now?"

"Sleep," said Gillabeth, decisive as ever. "Look at *him*." She meant Septimus, who was yawning and swaying on his feet. She turned to address all the residents as they emerged from behind the barrier. "Sleep for everyone. Till noon."

They needed no further encouragement. Dog-tired, they flopped down on the nearest mattress, regardless of whose it was. Many of them squeezed two or three together on a single mattress. Soon they were fast asleep.

When they awoke, five hours later, they discovered that Victoria and Albert had disappeared.

35

It was Professor Twillip who raised the alarm. "I'm sure that's where they were," he said, pointing to the empty mattress. "Next along from me."

Gillabeth organized a search: hunting for Victoria and Albert or clues to their disappearance. Nothing. They had vanished without a sound while everyone slept. Strangest of all, the door was still locked on the inside.

"It's like Dr. Blessamy all over again," said Mr. Gibber.

Col had only one faint hope. He remembered how Victoria had felt guilty about bringing trouble upon the Norfolk Library. Could she have followed through on her idea of returning to the Imperial Chapel? That didn't account for the locked door, of course. But then neither did the other explanation, of abduction by the red armbands.

"I'll search outside," he announced. "I'll check the Imperial Chapel."

He made his way up to the Imperial Chapel, one deck above the library. He crossed paths with a few Filthies, but only individuals, not a pack. They ignored him as he ignored them.

It was a different situation around the chapel, though. Gangs of red armbands lounged about, including convicts. Col bit his lip when he saw that even the convicts now carried rifles.

He walked on fast, head lowered, and passed a couple of groups before anyone thought to challenge him.

"Hey, where d'you think you're goin'?"

He walked on as though he hadn't heard. Then came a bark of command that he couldn't disregard.

"Stop right there!"

He stopped and raised his head. He had managed to get within twenty paces of the Imperial Chapel—and he could see at a glance there was no point going any farther. The entrance had been sealed off with a barricade of wooden posts and ropes. Two Filthies with red armbands stood at either end of the barricade.

"Oh!" He feigned surprise. "Victoria and Albert don't live here anymore?"

"Nah. Clear off."

They pointed their rifles at him. Col turned right around and marched back the way he'd come.

The situation had deteriorated a stage further. However, his immediate concern was with Victoria and Albert. If they'd tried to go back to the chapel, and red armbands had turned them away, where else might they have gone? Their old living quarters, perhaps? Some unoccupied corner of the imperial Staterooms?

He had to check out every possibility. He descended two levels to Forty-third Deck and headed toward the staterooms by side routes and lesser corridors.

He was one corridor away from the Imperial Dining Room when he heard a strange kind of laugh coming from behind a particular unmarked door. It was a female cackle, high in pitch, almost girlish. He couldn't believe that Victoria would ever laugh like that, but it wasn't the laugh of a female Filthy, either.

He rapped on the door. "Hello?"

No response.

Common sense told him to leave and forget it, but his curiosity was aroused. He turned the handle and opened the door just a fraction. In the same moment he peeped in, another door slammed shut at the other end of the room.

He stuck his head in a little farther. Whoever she was, she'd left in a hurry.

The room was a long pantry, with cupboards, shelves, and serving counters. Crockery was stacked on the shelves, along with wineglasses and decanters, place mats and folded napkins.

The bottles and flasks on the floor, however, were not normal supplies in any pantry. Col's nose caught the pungent smell of kerosene and other chemicals. He stepped forward to take a closer look.

There were about twenty bottles clustered together, along with a handkerchief and tinderbox. The bottles included cleaning fluid, cooking oil, and kerosene. The word FLAMMABLE was printed in big letters on many of the labels. The handkerchief had been twisted into a long roll and doused in kerosene.

He kicked the tinderbox away, although it could hardly start a fire without a human hand to strike the spark. No doubt the handkerchief would have served as a fuse, inserted into the top of one of the bottles. He picked it up by one corner. It was pink with a border of lace—clearly the handkerchief of an Upper Decks lady.

He had uncovered the next act of sabotage! In another minute the saboteur would have struck the spark, and the fire would have spread and engulfed many rooms. He had interrupted her just in time.

Her. No wonder the investigation had never made any progress. Everyone had automatically assumed that the saboteur was male. Whereas a female . . . what Upper Decks lady could have the will and capacity to commit such ruthless acts?

Obviously, the one who owned the handkerchief.

He didn't think of the danger; he didn't consider what had happened when Council member Zeb had stumbled across this saboteur once before. He took off in pursuit, racing to the door at the other end of the room.

36

On the other side of the door was a drawing room, deserted and unused, with velvet chairs and glass-topped tables. Col ran on to a farther door and came out suddenly into a main corridor.

Left or right? Pausing a moment, he thought he detected faint footfalls to the right. He sped on down the corridor and around the first corner. Yes, he *had* heard footfalls. There ahead of him were two familiar figures walking along. He recognized them instantly, even with their backs turned. His sister Gillabeth and baby brother Antrobus!

Gillabeth? The female saboteur? Could it be?

He was shocked—but then, he had been shocked three months ago, when Gillabeth had been exposed as his secret enemy, organizing the campaign of school bullies against him. It was impossible to understand her motives. Why she would conspire against the Filthies was no more or less mysterious than why she had previously conspired against her own family. She was capable of anything.

A million thoughts whirled through his head as he ran up. Gillabeth was holding Antrobus by the hand, and it was Antrobus who stopped and turned first. His big, solemn eyes were brimming with unuttered thoughts.

"What's this?" Col held out the kerosene-soaked handkerchief. "Is this yours?"

Gillabeth turned with a frown. "Phh! Kerosene!"

She pushed it away. It slipped from Col's fingers and fluttered to the floor.

"Yes, it's a fuse to start a fire. What do you know about it?"

Gillabeth's eyes narrowed. "Are you accusing me of something?"

"I found it in a room back there."

"So?"

"I think you came out of that room."

"You *think*."

"What are you doing here, then?"

"What are you accusing me of?"

Col pointed to the handkerchief on the floor. "That belongs to the saboteur."

"And you think it's mine? Don't be stupid."

"Prove it."

"You prove it. I don't have to justify myself to you."

"I *want* to believe you."

"Believe what you like. You'd only have my word for it, anyway. Come on, Antrobus."

Antrobus had dropped down on all fours and was making a close study of the handkerchief. Gillabeth flapped her hand, but he showed no inclination to take it. Observing his baby brother, Col came up with an idea.

"Antrobus could vouch for you," he said.

"*If* he could speak." Gillabeth snorted.

"He doesn't have to speak if he can nod."

"He still has to understand the question."

"Okay, let's see."

Col was more optimistic about his baby brother's powers of understanding. He dropped to one knee. "Antrobus, this is really important. You can clear your sister of a terribly serious accusation. Do you understand? Nod if you understand."

Antrobus raised his gaze from the handkerchief to Col. His expression was infinitely pensive, yet he gave not the slightest nod.

"You're wasting your time," Gillabeth sniffed.

Col persisted. "Antrobus, I'm sure you can understand. Have you ever seen this handkerchief before? Have you been in a room with a lot of bottles on the floor? Nod for yes, shake your head for no."

Still no movement of the head—but there was a movement of the lips. Antrobus was forming silent shapes with his mouth, as he'd done with Murgatrude. What was wrong with his voice?

Col tried to lip-read, but it was impossible with so many different shapes.

"Just a yes or a no, Antrobus. Did you see this handkerchief before? One-word answer."

If Antrobus understood, it made no difference. His mouth kept opening and closing; his lips kept wriggling and writhing.

"It's only imitation," said Gillabeth. "Not real talking."

Col was defeated. He straightened and stood upright.

"Ow . . . iss . . . em . . . ar . . . in," said Antrobus.

"What was that?" Col whirled. "Say it again, Antrobus."

"Our . . . iss . . . if . . . oo . . . ree . . . em . . . ar . . . ink."

"I still can't hear the words."

Antrobus struggled; he really struggled. His eyes bulged, and his cheeks puffed out with the effort. He appeared to be swelling up inside with something huge and indigestible.

Then it all came out in a single breath. "Our sister if you remember has never been partial to the color pink."

Col gaped, and Gillabeth goggled.

"Did I hear what I thought I heard?" Gillabeth asked.

"His first words," said Col in awe.

"A whole sentence. Where did he get that from?"

Antrobus had temporarily exhausted his tiny lungs. He was gasping for air like a stranded fish.

"It makes sense, too," said Col.

"It does?"

"Our sister—that's you. And you've always hated pink."

"True."

"So, don't you see? I wanted to know if you were guilty, and he's *proved* you're innocent. The handkerchief can't be yours, because it's pink."

"I wouldn't be seen dead with a pink handkerchief." Gillabeth turned to her baby brother. "That's amazing, Antrobus."

Antrobus was sucking in air again, swelling up with something else to say.

"Don't strain yourself," Col told him. "Say it in simple words."

"It appears," said Antrobus, "that the complexities of my mental processes require abstract words and complex grammatical structures, thus ruling out all simple forms of expression."

"He's done it again," said Gillabeth.

"And that makes sense too." Col nodded. "He could never speak before, because he couldn't speak in single words. Isn't that right, Antrobus?"

"Leave him be a moment," said Gillabeth. "Give him time to recover his breath. What's this about the saboteur?"

"I was looking for Victoria and Albert in the Imperial Staterooms when I heard a laugh behind a door. I walked in on the next act of sabotage."

"I was coming to check the staterooms too. I didn't know whether you'd think of them. What about the handkerchief?"

"It was the fuse to start a fire. She was all ready to light it, but she ran away as I walked in."

"A *female* saboteur?"

"Yes. But I didn't see who."

"Must be a Swank, with such a ladylike handkerchief. . . . What's he doing now?"

Antrobus had gone back to studying the handkerchief on the floor. At Gillabeth's words he turned, drew a deep breath, and produced another almost incomprehensible sentence.

"While the color of the handkerchief is in itself highly suggestive, the embroidered symbol is the most helpful aid to a rational deduction."

"Embroidered symbol!" Col worked out what he meant a fraction before Gillabeth. He swooped down on the handkerchief and held it up for examination. There in one corner was a tiny embroidered initial, white on pink.

"It's a *T*," said Gillabeth.

"Whose name starts with a *T*? Someone who might own a pink, lacy handkerchief?"

Col started running through possibilities in his mind—but he couldn't imagine any of them as the saboteur.

"Perhaps Antrobus knows," Gillabeth suggested.

Antrobus stared at them solemnly, then turned and toddled off along the corridor. They hurried after him and caught up.

"Do you know who she is, Antrobus? Are you taking us to her?"

But Antrobus didn't intend to waste breath on unnecessary answers. They were forced to accompany him in silence.

37

They must have looked like a family group on an outing. Col took Antrobus's hand on one side, Gillabeth on the other. The few Filthies they met let them pass without challenge or abuse.

They stayed on the same deck, but zigzagged by way of many corridors across to a different part of the juggernaut. Elite families had once lived here, but not anymore.

"Where on earth are we going?" Col asked.

"I'm beginning to guess," said Gillabeth.

Another two turns brought them to their destination. It wasn't any ghetto of Swanks that Col had ever visited, just an unexceptional door in an unexceptional corridor.

"Means nothing to me," said Col.

Gillabeth was nodding her head. "It nearly did. You nearly came here to live."

Col remained mystified. Gillabeth marched up to the door, turned the handle, and pushed—in vain.

"We'll have to batter a way in," she said.

Col understood that battering a way in was his task. He jumped forward and thumped on the door with the sole of his shoe. When that didn't work, he shoulder-charged it.

On the third attempt there was a sound of cracking

timber, and the door flew open. Off balance, Col hurtled forward and crashed to the floor.

His first impression was that the entire world had turned pink. He lay on a pink carpet and looked up at a pink bedspread, pink curtains, and pink wallpaper. The carpet was soft; the bedspread was frilly; the curtains were tasseled and flounced. The wallpaper was embossed with a P & T motif in a deeper shade of pink.

He sat up as the first glimmerings of comprehension dawned in his brain. Gillabeth hated the color pink, but there was someone else who loved it. At least there *had been* someone else. . . .

"*T* is for *Turbot!*" cried Gillabeth, standing in the doorway.

So that much made sense. This was to have been his bridal suite, decorated by Sephaltina Turbot. But . . .

"She's gone," he objected. "She left the juggernaut with her family."

"Doesn't look very gone to me." Gillabeth gestured toward one corner of the room. "Does she look gone to you?"

Col sprang to his feet. Crouching on the other side of the big double bed, between a lace-covered table and a pink-rimmed mirror, was his lawfully wedded wife, Sephaltina.

He hardly recognized her. Her eyes were sunken, her cheeks a hectic red; her flaxen hair draggled down in a mess of loose ends. She was no longer the fair, pretty girl of three months ago. Yet she still wore the tiara, pearl choker, and pearl-beaded dress in which she'd been married. The dress was now so stained and torn that it resembled pearl-beaded rags.

If he hardly recognized her, she had clearly forgotten him. She turned from Col to Gillabeth to Antrobus and made clawing motions in the air like a trapped wild animal. The snarl in her throat was as harsh as the cackling laugh that Col had heard earlier.

"I think she's lost her mind," said Gillabeth.

It wasn't just the snarl and the clawing motions. The corner where Sephaltina cowered was a litter of food remnants: rinds, crusts, and little bits of paper that looked like candy wrappers. There were even half-sucked candies stuck here and there on her wedding dress.

"It's okay." Col spoke soothingly. "We won't hurt you."

He advanced along by the side of the bed, one cautious step at a time.

"Watch out," Gillabeth warned. "Remember what she did to Zeb."

"Hate you, hate you, *hate* you!" Sephaltina hissed— and launched forward in a sudden dash for the door.

Col tried to grab hold of her, but she wriggled free of his outstretched arms. However, she hadn't reckoned on Antrobus standing in her way. She tripped over the tiny obstacle and rocketed headfirst into Gillabeth's midriff and thighs.

"Ooo-oof!"

While Gillabeth remained upright, solid as a tree

trunk, Sephaltina tumbled down on her knees.

Col came up behind her, knelt, and pinned her arms to her sides. Painfully thin and bony, she offered no resistance. She shot glances off in every direction but wouldn't look anyone in the eyes.

Gillabeth stood before her with arms akimbo. "So you've been living here all this time? We thought you'd left with the rest of your family."

Sephaltina raised her chin with a proud expression. "My bridal suite," she announced, swiveling her head to encompass the room. "I was a beautiful bride. The most beautiful bride. Everyone said so. It was my day of days. Then they took it all away. But I still have my bridal suite."

Gillabeth tried to keep the interrogation on track. "You decided to stay right here in this room?"

"Isn't it pretty? I chose the color and all the furnishings myself."

Col spoke to his sister over the top of Sephaltina's head. "Maybe she didn't even know when her family left. She fainted at the wedding reception, so she was probably taken off somewhere to recover. She must have come here straight afterward."

"I hate them." Sephaltina's voice switched in an instant from dreamy to vicious. "They didn't care. They spoiled my wedding. It was meant to be perfect for me, and they ruined everything."

Gillabeth frowned. "Who's 'they'? It wasn't your family that made the revolution."

"All of them. Everyone who changed things. They're all to blame."

"I don't think she knows who she means," Col told his sister.

Gillabeth shook her head. "I can't believe she never found herself a place in a ghetto."

"I'm a *bride*." Sephaltina pouted. "I'm special. No one else is a bride like me."

It was her most direct response so far. Col jumped in with the question he'd been waiting to ask.

"And you're the saboteur, aren't you?"

Sephaltina was momentarily distracted by a candy stuck to her dress. She picked it off and popped it in her mouth.

Col tried again. "You've been trying to sabotage the juggernaut, haven't you?"

Sephaltina sucked on her candy. "I like the red ones best," she said.

"Destroying things," Gillabeth accused. "Breaking and busting things."

Sephaltina let out a cackling laugh. Col and Gillabeth flinched at the craziness of it.

"Why?" Gillabeth demanded. "Is it revenge against the Filthies?"

"I like breaking things. I like hearing them go smash." After the harshness of the cackle, Sephaltina's voice changed and became soft and dreamy. "I never knew what I liked to do for myself. I was too young and innocent. Now there's nobody to tell me anymore. I dis-covered what *I* like to do."

"You realize you make trouble for us, too?"

Sephaltina didn't realize anything. "Everyone has to suffer. I'm not happy, so no one else should be either."

Col broke in again. "You were going to start a fire just now, weren't you? A fire in the pantry room?"

"Crackle, crackle! Spitter, sputter! Whoompf!" Sephaltina was off in a world of her own.

"How did you know how to start a fire? How did you know about making a fuse?"

Sephaltina's rosebud mouth took on a sly, shy look. "I'm *good* at destroying things. I can work out all sorts of ways. I'm very clever at it, you know."

"And the equipment smashed in the wireless telegraph offices. That was you too?"

"Bash, crash, mash!" Sephaltina reminisced cheerfully. "Lots and lots of little pieces."

Col addressed Gillabeth. "It must have been an accident, cutting off *Liberator*'s communications. She didn't know what she was doing."

"She was clever enough over starting a fire."

"That's a different sort of clever."

"What about betraying the attack on Botany Bay?"

"*If* the saboteur did it."

Gillabeth fixed Sephaltina with a stern look. "Did you write the note and pin it to a barracks door in Botany Bay?"

Sephaltina looked back with the blankest of blank expressions, as though the question were not even directed at her.

"She doesn't understand," said Col. "She just likes breaking things. She's a child."

"A deadly, dangerous child," said Gillabeth. "She killed Zeb when he interrupted one of her acts of sabotage. Don't forget that."

"She ran away when *I* interrupted, though. Perhaps she just panicked and lashed out with Zeb."

"Phh!" Gillabeth snorted her incredulity. "You just want to minimize her guilt."

"No. Why would I?"

"Because you're her husband, of course."

Col wished Gillabeth hadn't said that. He wished it even more when Sephaltina picked up on the word.

"Husband?"

She looked down at his left hand, where he was still gripping her by the shoulder. She raised her forearm and brought her ring finger up alongside his ring finger.

Col wished he could hide his hand, but it was too late. He knew what was coming next. Sephaltina compared the two gold bands and let out a squeal of surprise.

"They match! They're the same! My husband!"

Col released her, and she twisted around to stare into his face. As far as he could tell, she still didn't recognize him. But she didn't need to.

"I've found my husband," she said. "And my husband has found his long-lost bride. Why didn't you come looking for me?"

Col was taken aback by the sudden sharpness of tone. "I thought you'd left with your family."

"You should've *searched*. That's what a husband is for. It's not the kind of behavior I would have expected."

"Well, Sephaltina," said Gillabeth. "We're taking you to see the Revolutionary Council."

"No," said Col. "Let's take her back to the Norfolk Library first."

"I shall go where my husband wants me to go," said Sephaltina decisively. "Even if he hasn't been a very good husband."

38

Gillabeth tidied Sephaltina up and made her presentable. She removed the candies from Sephaltina's dress and, with the aid of a flask of water and a pillowcase turned inside out, wiped the smears of dirt from her face, arms, and legs. With the tangles raked out of her hair, Sephaltina looked more like her old self again. She submitted demurely, and protested only when Gillabeth insisted on removing her pearl choker and tiara.

"But they're my wedding things."

Col stepped in. "That was three months ago, Sephaltina. It looks odd to keep wearing them."

Sephaltina yielded with just a touch of sulkiness. "Oh, well, if my husband says so. I don't want to look odd for my husband."

When they set off for the library, she walked side by side with Col, but not particularly close. Gillabeth and Antrobus walked side by side behind.

The more Col thought about his situation, the less he liked it. Sephaltina was the saboteur, yet she was also his wife. He couldn't help feeling responsible for her. Even her madness was partly his fault, since he was the husband that she thought had abandoned her. He wasn't happy with the idea of just handing her over to the Council.

By the time they got back to the Norfolk Library, clean-up operations were well advanced. Already the bookcases had been returned to their original positions, and most of the mattresses. The library's residents looked up from their tasks when Col, Gillabeth, Antrobus, and Sephaltina appeared in the doorway.

"You didn't find them?" Orris asked, meaning Victoria and Albert.

"No," said Col. "We found someone else, though."

Everyone stared at Sephaltina, who was now quite recognizable, thanks to Gillabeth's ministrations.

"That's the Turbot girl."

"So she didn't leave with the rest of her family."

Quinnea was overjoyed. "Sephaltina Turbot! My daughter-in-law!"

She approached Sephaltina with outspread arms. However, her emotions were too much for her, and she sagged on her feet three paces away. Orris, coming up behind, caught and supported her. Col suspected that Sephaltina didn't recognize his mother or anyone else.

"Where has she been?" asked Mr. Gibber.

"She's been hiding out in her pink bridal suite," said Gillabeth. "Ever since the Liberation."

"Ah, I remember your wedding day." Quinnea managed to prop herself upright again. "And your wedding reception. We were all so happy then."

The mention of her wedding reception engaged with Sephaltina's muddled mind as nothing else had done. "Flowers and banners and dancing," she reminisced.

"Little glasses and little spoons. Cupcakes and trifle, rice pudding and blancmange."

"So many guests and so many servants." Quinnea thrilled to the same memories. "Ten kinds of cakes. Fifteen kinds of biscuits. And éclairs, macaroons, jelly, and fruit salad."

"I don't know about jelly." Sephaltina frowned. "I don't remember *that*."

Gillabeth cleared her throat. "There's something everyone should know before getting too carried away. Sephaltina is also the saboteur."

There were gasps as the final word sank in.

"*Her?*"

"A female saboteur?"

"She doesn't seem capable."

"She's already confessed," said Gillabeth.

"She didn't know what she was doing," Col put in quickly. "She's been a bit unbalanced. Not in her right mind." He appealed to Professor Twillip. "That makes a difference, doesn't it?"

"Not in her right mind." Professor Twillip nodded. "Yes, that's an old ethical principle. She's not morally responsible if she's non compos mentis."

"I like it when things go smash," said Sephaltina sweetly. "I like breaking things."

"You see?" Col turned to the others. "And she was worse when we found her."

Sephaltina nodded agreement. "Yes, I've been a bit unbalanced. I think I still am."

"No, no, don't say that," Quinnea moaned, and pressed her hands over her ears. "I can't have these emotional ups and downs. They're not good for me."

Sephaltina only smiled. "Of course, I won't do any more breaking, now that my husband has found me again. Even though he took so long about it. I want to be charming and lovable and wifely. I was always very lovable in the past. I'm sure it will all come back to me."

Gillabeth scoffed. "You should've thought about being lovable before you bashed Zeb's head in with a wrench."

"Wrench?" Sephaltina pouted. "I wouldn't dream of touching a wrench."

Col jumped in at once. "What, you deny it?"

"Such nasty, dirty, metal things. I don't even like to think about them."

"So you didn't try to sabotage a steam elevator on First Deck?"

"I've never been down as far as First Deck." Sephaltina shuddered. "Too close to Below."

"I believe her." Col nodded. "She's the saboteur but not the murderer. Look at her. She's too innocent to lie."

Gillabeth wasn't swayed. "Well, we'll let the Council decide that. We should hand her over now."

"They won't give her a fair hearing," Col objected. "Not with Lye and Shiv in charge."

"I expect they'll execute her," said Mr. Gibber.

"No-o-o-o!" Quinnea had uncovered her ears just long enough to hear Mr. Gibber's fateful words. She let out a long wail. "Not executed! Not my daughter-in-law!"

She stood before Sephaltina protectively, defensively. Although she looked barely able to withstand a puff of wind, no one wanted to push her aside. Instead they tried to argue with her—and Quinnea argued back.

It turned into a heated quarrel. Everyone except Quinnea and Col wanted to hand Sephaltina over and avoid further blame for the acts of sabotage. But Quinnea had hysteria on her side. She quivered from top to toe and shook her head until her hair flew out in a hundred wisps.

"Look what you're doing to me!" she screeched.

Col felt as if his head were stuck in a cage of parrots. Unlike Quinnea, he knew they couldn't just continue to keep Sephaltina in the Norfolk Library. There had to be some alternative—but he couldn't think for all the shouting and screeching.

Then a different voice cut through the clamor. "It may be relevant to point out that not all members of the Revolutionary Council are as unfair as Lye and Shiv."

The clamor fell away. One by one the library's residents turned to stare at Antrobus.

"Was that . . . ?"

"Did he . . . ?"

"Antrobus?"

"His first words!"

"Yes, he only speaks in sentences," said Gillabeth. "We heard him a while back."

The quarrel was forgotten. For the moment Col's

baby brother had become the center of attention.

"Say it again, Antrobus."

"Or something else."

"Say anything about anything."

But Antrobus was far too serious to speak merely for the sake of speaking. He remained silent in the face of all requests.

"He worked out the clues and led us to Sephaltina," said Gillabeth.

And perhaps he's helped me again, thought Col. Now that his head was no longer in a cage of parrots, he worked through the implications of what Antrobus had said. There was still one moderate with influence on the Council—Riff. Maybe he could make a deal with her? He could offer to expose the saboteur if Riff promised she wouldn't be executed.

"I'm going to talk to Riff about Sephaltina," he told anyone who would listen. "Don't do anything till I get back."

39

All the way to Riff's room Col tried to keep his mind on practicalities. He was going to see Riff because it was the only way to save Sephaltina. It wasn't because he had changed his mind about their relationship being over. He wasn't going to plead with her or appeal to her for his own sake. But still . . . he *was* going to see her!

"Come in," said a flat-sounding voice when he knocked.

She was sitting on her bed, with a pillow at her back, propped up against the wall. Half a dozen books lay beside her on the bed, but she didn't look as though she'd been reading.

She stared at him.

"Colbert Porpentine," she said slowly.

At least he wasn't just another Swank in her eyes. He had cleared the first obstacle: This time she really recognized him.

"I wanted to talk to you," he began.

"There's nothing you can say." She made a vague, weary gesture. "You can't bring them back. Nobody can."

She was still brooding over her parents. Col's first relief gave way to disquiet. She seemed sad and apathetic, a mood that wasn't natural to her. He could never have imagined her like this.

He repressed the urge to comfort her. Anything he said about her parents would surely backfire. Instead, he changed the subject. "It's not that. I came about the saboteur."

"Oh? What about him?"

"Her."

"*Her?*"

"Yes."

Riff sat up a little straighter on the bed. "So you know who it is?"

Col nodded. "I'll hand her over to you if we can make a deal."

"You think you're in a position to bargain? You must be mad."

"No. She is."

Without giving away Sephaltina's name, Col explained what she had and hadn't confessed. She was certainly guilty of repeated acts of sabotage, but she denied murdering Zeb and appeared to know nothing about the note pinned to the barracks door in Botany Bay. Riff listened and kept her thoughts to herself.

"And even with the acts of sabotage," Col concluded, "she hardly knew what she was doing. She's been half crazy ever since the Liberation."

Riff shot him a shrewd look. "You seem to know her very well?"

Col drew back at once. "Not necessarily."

"Is she one of your people in the Norfolk Library?"

"No. She's a loner."

"She must have been living with other Swanks somewhere."

Col held his tongue.

"Where is she now?" Riff jumped up and stood facing him. *"Tell me!"*

"Do we have a deal?"

Her eyes were flashing with anger. He wondered if she would slap him again. But no, it wasn't the same out-of-control violence as last time.

"What do you want from me?" she asked, subsiding.

"No execution."

"Hmm."

"And a fair trial. She can be guilty of the sabotage without being guilty of the other things."

"Lye and Shiv will want to execute her anyway."

"You have to win over Padder and Gansy, then."

"I don't have as much influence as you think."

"No influence at all, if you don't attend Council meetings."

Riff almost bit his head off. "How did you know that?"

"Will you promise to use all your influence?" He kept his voice carefully calm.

"Phah!" She swung away, then back again. "I can't guarantee anything."

"If you promise . . ."

"Why would you trust my promise?"

It was on the tip of Col's tongue to say, *Because I once used to trust you in everything.* But he restrained himself.

"Okay," she said. "I promise. Now tell me who it is."

"Sephaltina Turbot."

"Who?"

"My wife. You met her at the wedding reception. The one with the jelly."

"*Her!* How could *she* do anything?"

"She's been hiding away on her own. It's a long story."

"You can tell me on the way."

"The way where?"

"To see her. Where is she hiding?"

"She's in the Norfolk Library now. I thought you'd summon a meeting of Council, and I'd bring her to you there."

"I want to see her first. Your *wife*." She gestured toward the door. "Let's go."

Col hoped it would turn out all right. He was still wary of Riff, who seemed strange and unpredictable. But at least she had cast aside her apathy.

They went out into the corridor. Col was about to start telling Sephaltina's story when he sensed a sudden shift in Riff's attention.

Then he heard it too: a murmur of noise. The whole juggernaut was astir with excitement and alarm, with cries and calls and running feet.

Col and Riff halted in their tracks. A moment later a group of Filthies came hurtling along the corridor.

"It's the other juggernauts!" they shouted as they rushed past.

"Coming straight at us!"

"They've arrived!"

40

Riff took off running, and Col ran after her. He could barely keep her in sight. There was no time to wait for a steam elevator to arrive—she went up the staircases from level to level. She was heading for the bridge, of course.

He remembered what Septimus had said about the superior armaments of the other juggernauts. What would they do? How many were there?

He followed Riff up the final flight of stairs, through the door to the bridge. The place was seething like an ants' nest. Bells rang; levers clanged; whistles shrilled; orders were shouted. Everyone was far too busy to question or even notice him.

Riff seemed hardly aware that Col had followed her. A dozen Filthies were on the main floor, and she joined in with them, operating the control units.

Other Filthies stood on the raised level at the front, scanning through the windows and calling out everything they saw.

"That's the Russian flag!"

"Why have they stopped?"

"Changing to rollers."

"Not like our rollers."

"Not like us at all."

"What's it pulling?"

The Russian juggernaut? That was the *Romanov*, Col recalled. He *had* to see for himself.

He moved forward to the steps that led up to the raised level. But before he could mount up, a Filthy above him swung round to shout an order to the operators.

"Steer to the right! Why aren't we moving yet? *To the right!*"

It was Riff's brother, Padder. He glanced down, and his eye fell upon Col.

"Why the—?" His choleric face burned with anger. "What's he doing here? No Swanks on the bridge. Get him out. Now!"

Col didn't wait to be hustled. He spun on his heel and headed back the way he'd come. Seeing him leave, the other Filthies didn't bother to escort him.

He didn't deliberately choose to walk close by Riff. In fact he didn't know she was there until she jabbed him with her elbow as he went past.

"Up on the platform," she said out of the corner of her mouth.

He was four paces farther along before he understood. She was giving him an alternative suggestion: Instead of returning the way he had come, he could go up to the viewing platform above. He veered away from the door and meandered casually toward the metal staircase at the far side of the bridge.

No one was paying attention as he ascended the stairs. He entered the turret at the top, unbolted the door, and stepped out into the open.

The sun was low in the sky like a molten orange ball. The light was fading toward dusk, and the clouds had taken on a rich plum color. It might have been an ordinary twilight except for the twin columns of yellow-brown smoke staining one quarter of the sky.

Two juggernauts, then. One was too low to appear above the barrier that encircled the platform; the other showed as a forest of masts, with what looked like a dozen tangled birds' nests woven between them. And yes, there on one mast fluttered the gold flag of the imperial Russian family.

Col had just closed the turret door behind him when a mighty shudder shook the platform under his feet. The sound came a moment later: a deep, grinding rumble like thunder. Then the whole juggernaut started forward with a lurch and a sudden turn to the right.

He found himself thrown through the air. He crashed to the deck, slid across to the side, and put out his arms just in time to avoid smashing headfirst into the barrier.

He gripped the barrier and hauled himself to his feet. He was near the back of the platform looking out toward the buildings of Botany Bay.

The end of the coal loader had detached from the open flap on Bottom Deck. With a scream of metal it scraped along the flank of the juggernaut, catching at the rope ladders and cradles where the Filthies liked to lounge. Luckily, there was nobody outside now.

As Col watched, buckets of coal like tiny thimbles tumbled down from the end of the loader. The entire structure was starting to topple in slow, slow motion. He didn't wait to see it hit the ground. The view that mattered was on the other side.

With nothing for support, crossing the platform was a challenge in itself. He reeled and staggered as the juggernaut pitched and swayed. He took the last fifteen paces in a single rush.

The imperialist juggernauts had stopped between the headlands of Botany Bay. The *Romanov* was the larger of the two, almost as large as *Liberator*. Col understood now why the Filthies had asked, *What's it pulling?* The Russian juggernaut was in three articulated parts, a main segment towing two smaller segments. The segments were painted khaki and appeared to be all slab-sided hull. There was no superstructure except for the bristling masts and birds' nests on the main segment. The two towed segments were solid blocks, flat-topped and featureless.

The second juggernaut was lower and smaller, but more sinister. It had a single domed shell of armor like a crab, painted a dull black color that swallowed the light. Having no obvious front or back, it looked as though it might move off in any direction. Camouflage nets swathed its sides; higher up, its metal surface was dotted with blisters; higher again, four bulbous funnels stuck up in the shape of onions. Col read its name from white lettering on the black shell: GROSSE WIEN. It was the Austrian juggernaut.

Col also understood why the Filthies had cried, *Not like our rollers*. The *Romanov* had caterpillar tracks under its segments of hull, a great many sets of them. The

Grosse Wien had a smaller number of gigantic rubberized wheels, which protruded beyond the edges of its shell.

Even as Col watched, the wheels started to turn, and the caterpillar tracks started to roll forward. On the *Romanov* crackles of electricity flashed like lightning along the wires between the masts. Steam burst out from under the shell of the *Grosse Wien*. The two juggernauts had completed the changeover from sea propulsion to land propulsion. Now they were commencing their final advance upon *Liberator*.

41

Liberator continued to veer to the right, away from its enemies. It completed a lumbering half turn, then straightened and surged forward.

The imperialist juggernauts came after it. They split up as they advanced, obviously aiming to cut *Liberator* off on either side. The *Grosse Wien* blew a blast on its horn, an unearthly, wavering sound that went tunelessly up and down the scale. It made the hairs prickle on the back of Col's neck.

He remembered how his grandfather had described the speed of their own juggernaut as "faster than a galloping horse." But the imperialist juggernauts seemed to be moving at least as fast, especially the *Grosse Wien*. Churning across the bay on their wheels and tracks, they threw up a great spray of liquid mud. Soon they were both more brown than khaki or black.

The *Grosse Wien* had already taken a lead to the right. *Steer left,* Col willed, wishing he could communicate with the Filthies on the bridge.

Someone on the bridge must have reached the same conclusion, because in the next moment *Liberator* altered course to the left.

Suddenly, there was a loud *crump!* and a brightness in the air.

Looking down, Col saw that their prow had plowed over the steel tanks where he'd waited with the attack force nine days ago. The contents of the tanks had exploded, one setting off another all along the line. *Liberator* rolled on indifferently through the flames.

Veering to the left had brought them closer to the *Romanov*—and now the Russian juggernaut was starting to overtake them. A new sound boomed out even above the thunder of engines, the crunch and grind of rollers: a megaphone voice speaking in Russian.

"*Sdavaisya! Sdavaisya! Sdavaisya!*"

The words made no sense to Col, but the tone of menace was clear in any language.

Little by little the *Romanov* edged forward alongside. Its prow came up level with *Liberator*'s stern—then up to the back of *Liberator*'s superstructure—then level with the last of *Liberator*'s six funnels. In spite of every effort they couldn't pull clear.

Neither juggernaut swerved aside from the coal loaders that lay in their way. Girders buckled and burst apart as they smashed into the huge spidery structures: Compared to the juggernauts, the loaders were frail as matchsticks. There was a scream of metal, a convulsion of up-flung ribs and struts. Then the loaders went down, and the juggernauts rode on over the wreckage.

The impact slowed the *Romanov* more, perhaps because the mangled metal snagged on its caterpillar tracks.

Beyond the loaders were pyramids of coal, and again

both juggernauts rumbled on regardless. They didn't go over the top but simply bulldozed the pyramids aside. *Liberator* had the more difficult passage and a greater mass of coal to push through. By the time they emerged from the pyramids, the *Romanov* had made up for lost ground.

"*Sdavaisya! Sdavaisya! Sdavaisya!*"

The gold flag of the imperial Russian family flew out behind; electricity crackled between its masts. Now its prow was level with *Liberator*'s middle funnels—and it was gaining all the time. Col couldn't see the *Grosse Wien* on the other side, but he was sure it wouldn't have been left behind.

What was their plan? They seemed in no hurry to use the special weapons of which Septimus had talked. Rather, they were trying to box *Liberator* in and force it to a standstill. And they had almost succeeded.

Only one way of escape remained—and *Liberator* took it.

With a sudden lurch the great juggernaut slewed again to the right. Col clung to the barrier as the scenery swung around him. The *Romanov* was slower to change direction, moving farther away.

Now *Liberator* approached the chain of hills at the back of Botany Bay. They rose like a green sloping wave, as high as the bridge of the juggernaut itself. No gaps, no breaks, no valleys. The juggernaut couldn't bulldoze through so much solid rock; it would have to go up and over.

"Straighten course!" Col yelled a warning, though

there was no one to hear. "Straighten course!"

But the hills were too close and the juggernaut travel- eling too fast. They needed to go up the slope head on, but they were approaching at an angle. *Liberator* was still in the middle of its turn when the prow began to lift.

He felt the tilt under his feet. As *Liberator* reared up at the front, so it also canted over to the left.

For Col it was as though the whole world was coming unhinged. He had lived all his life on the juggernaut; it was his base and foundation, his measure of stability. It couldn't lose balance and capsize. It just *couldn't*.

Still the tilt increased. The platform dropped down on Col's side and up on the other. He felt as if he was about to be tossed out over the barrier.

The ground was far, far below. No spreading tiers or gray metal decks; as the juggernaut listed farther away from the vertical, he looked straight down at the dense green vegetation of the coast. He was hanging over a sheer, dizzying drop of a thousand feet.

He turned away, squatted on his heels, leaned with his back against the barrier—and immediately wished he hadn't. The other side of the platform towered over his head. He gazed up at the sky, and the clouds seemed to be falling on top of him. When he looked away, his eyes met the impossible sight of the juggernaut's fun- nels angled at forty-five degrees.

Still *Liberator* struggled to heave itself up over the hills. The turbines labored on with a thunderous roar . . . and there were other more ominous noises too. A thrumming whistle—could that be the sound of the rollers becoming airborne on the uphill side, spinning round and round without friction? And that low, grating vibration—surely the rollers on the downhill side skidding and digging deeper and deeper into the ground. So far as Col could tell, *Liberator* had lost all forward momentum.

Then came the very worst sound: a terrible creaking throughout the juggernaut's vast body, every metal beam and wall and joint straining under unnatural stress. *Liberator* hung suspended at the tipping point.

Col had the sense that he was going over backward. He closed his eyes—or they closed themselves. Any minute now the slow, inevitable fall would begin, and the whole weight of the juggernaut would come down like a mountain on top of him. At least it would be quick.

But it didn't happen. *Liberator* was moving forward again. He felt the change of angle as its prow came over the top of the hills and started to level out. With another mighty creaking of metal its weight shifted, and it tilted gradually back toward the vertical.

Col had slid unawares from a squatting position to a sitting position. He opened his eyes and gazed up at the bands of cloud passing across overhead.

In his mind he was still off balance . . . but finally the truth sank in. The juggernaut had returned to an even keel and was picking up speed. They had made it!

He hauled himself to his feet and looked out over the barrier. The tops of the hills were relatively flat, a high plateau covered with patches of forest. The small gullies and gorges were no obstacle at all to *Liberator*.

Col was more worried about what lay behind than what lay ahead. He looked back, and yes, there was the *Romanov*. Only the tips of its masts were visible above the hills, still crackling with flashes of electricity, brighter than ever against the darkening sky. It hadn't yet climbed the slope.

Did it intend to? Col watched for a few minutes and decided that the *Romanov* had come to a dead stop. The Russians dared not risk their juggernaut on so steep a gradient!

If only the Austrians had given up too . . . He rushed across to the other side of the platform.

No such luck. The *Grosse Wien* had already climbed up onto the plateau. It followed them a few juggernaut lengths to the rear, a few juggernaut breadths to the right. Col groaned. Something told him that the sinister dome-shaped shell wouldn't be so easy to shake off.

42

The sun set, and twilight dimmed to darkness. The sky was too cloudy for moon or stars. Still the pursuit went on. *Liberator* veered to the left and veered to the right, but the *Grosse Wien* shadowed every move. In the end there was nothing to do except travel on in a straight line.

The dull black shell of the Austrian juggernaut was invisible in the blackness of the night. What was visible were the gouts of fire that rose from its onion-shaped funnels. Every few minutes a glowing blob of bright red and yellow formed at the top of a funnel, then shot suddenly skyward.

The *Grosse Wien* also continued to blast its horn at irregular intervals. The wavering sound was even more unearthly by night, as mournful as the baying of some great beast.

Col stayed watching for what seemed like hours. The distance between the two juggernauts hardly varied. No doubt the *Grosse Wien* was sending wireless telegraph messages to all the other juggernauts. The imperialists were obviously determined to hunt down the one liberated juggernaut, no matter how long it took.

He'd hoped Riff would come up and talk to him on the platform, but either she was too busy, or she had forgotten, or she had never intended that in the first place.

He must have read too much into her suggestion.

His thoughts turned to his family and friends in the Norfolk Library. Would they understand what was happening? Perhaps Mr. Gibber would be able to gather news for them. . . .

He would have liked to return to the library, but when he crossed to the turret and peered down from the top of the staircase, there were still two dozen Filthies on the bridge. They were less frenetic now, going about their tasks with grim determination. Four of the Council members were engaged in discussion around Gansy's map desk at the back. Col had no chance of sneaking past unnoticed.

Instead he went back to watching the pursuit. Endless blobs of fire rose from the *Grosse Wien*'s funnels; again and again he heard the baying of its horn. It was nerve-racking and monotonous at the same time.

After a while he found himself a sheltered corner at the back of the platform, between the turret and the barrier. He curled up and fell into a fitful sleep, full of uneasy dreams.

In one he stood before Victoria, who seemed to be conducting his marriage ceremony. But it wasn't in the Imperial Chapel, and Victoria wore a sunflower in her hair, a chain of poppies round her neck. He turned to his bride—and instead of Sephaltina Turbot it was Riff.

"We're getting married," he said in wonder.

"Phuh! Who needs to get married?" Riff made a rude noise. "We're getting partnered."

He was roused by someone shaking his shoulder.
The world all around was lost and hidden, not only in
darkness but in a thick, enveloping mist. He felt damp
and cold and stiff. At first he could hardly see the face of
the person kneeling beside him. But he recognized her
when she bent closer to give him another shake.

"I've been searching all over the platform for you,"
said Riff.

She had come after all! Still under the influence of the
dream, his heart leaped, and he grinned with delight.

"What have you got to be so happy about?" she
demanded.

"You're here. I'm . . ."

Then he saw she was scowling, and he came back
to earth with a bump. Too much had happened; things
could never be simple between them again. *Don't let it
show*, he told himself.

He changed his tone. "You were looking for me?"

"Who else? What sort of dumb question is that?"

"We're in a mist, then."

"Yes, inside a cloud. It's our best chance to escape."

"The Austrians are still after us?"

"Same as ever. We think they're following us mainly
by sound. They can't see us in this mist, and they can't
see our track along the ground."

"You have a plan to escape?"

"We're going to surprise them with a sudden burst
of speed. Lye is ready for a supreme effort down Below.
We'll get as far ahead of them as we can, then swerve,

stop, and shut down our engines. If we're lucky, they'll keep on accelerating and shoot past us."

"Chasing a phantom?"

"Yes, they won't expect us to stop dead. When they can't hear our engines, they'll think we're too far ahead to hear."

"It might work."

"Thanks for the enthusiasm. It *has* to work."

"No, I mean, it's a good plan."

And it was—the best possible plan in the circumstances. Col couldn't focus on practicalities, though. He could tell from Riff's voice that she had recovered her old energy, but had she recovered her old feelings for him? He hardly dared hope it.

"Who thought up the plan?" he asked.

"Me and Lye. She proposed the burst of speed. I had the idea of stopping and shutting down the engines."

Me and Lye. So nothing had changed. Although Riff had come up to tell him about the plan, it was a plan she had worked out together with Lye. He couldn't help the bitterness that welled inside him.

"She caused all this in the first place," he said.

"What? Who?"

"Lye. She kept *Liberator* loading coal at Botany Bay when we should've left long ago."

"Hmm. That was Shiv and Lye together."

"Shiv just goes along with what Lye wants."

Another pause for thought. "Maybe. It was a bad decision."

"It was stupid and perverse and arrogant."

"No, just bad." Riff clicked her tongue. "What is it
with you and her?"

"With her. She hates me."

"Well . . . she says you keep leering at her."

"What? She says that to you?"

"She thinks you're always watching her and touching
her in your mind. She says you make her skin crawl."

"She's mad."

"It's not true?"

"No! How could you listen to her?"

"Okay, okay. Calm down."

"What about my side of the story? You never asked me."

"Let's change the subject."

"You brought it up."

"No, you did."

"How could you believe her? You'd have to be as mad
as her!"

"Enough!"

Riff jumped to her feet and stalked off into the mist.

Col sat there nonplussed. He stared at the blank
nothingness before his eyes, but she had vanished as
if into another world. He listened for the sound of the
turret door swinging open and slamming shut, yet no
sound came to his ears. She *must* be still on the platform
somewhere.

Was she punishing him? Was she angry with him on
behalf of Lye? Or some other reason? *Let her go*, he told
himself.

He maintained that resolution for about thirty seconds.

"Come back," he called out. "We can talk."

No reply. There was only the drawn-out note of the *Grosse Wien*'s horn, very faint and muffled. It had never sounded more mournful. A strange sense of loss swept over him. He stood up and flexed stiff muscles.

"Where are you? Riff?"

He walked back and forth with his arms spread wide. Why wouldn't she answer?

"Riff!" he cried. *"Riff!"*

He covered every part of the platform, and touched nothing more substantial than the mist. How could she have disappeared? He came back to the turret and found the door shut. When he tested the handle, it gave a loud, metallic creak—he couldn't have failed to hear that. His bewilderment was beginning to turn to panic.

Then his sweeping hands made contact with her. She was leaning out over the barrier at the back, only a few paces away from where he'd been sleeping. He had started his search too far away.

"There you are!"

He took her by the elbows and rotated her toward him. She didn't resist.

"Why didn't you answer?" he demanded.

"Sometimes I don't know who you are." She wasn't angry but quietly reproachful. "You act like a stranger."

"What? Why?"

"Of course I never believed Lye." She shook her head at him, and tiny drops of water flew out from her damp hair, sprinkling his face. "What do you think? I told her it was all in her imagination. I've been standing up for you. I never believed that nonsense for a moment."

"Oh. I didn't know."

"You *should've* known. You should've trusted me."

"Yes," he agreed.

"It's pathetic. We're in a life-or-death situation, the whole juggernaut, and all you can think about is your little private feud with Lye. It's so *petty*."

He was still holding her by the elbows, he realized. He wished he could see the look in her eyes, but the mist obscured the pale oval of her face.

"I've never changed from loving you," he said. "I can't stop."

Riff snorted. "You'd better not," she said.

He replayed her words over and over in his mind, and every time he liked them more.

"Do you . . . ," he began, faltered to a halt, started up again. "How do you feel about me?"

For a long moment she didn't speak. He waited in agony. Her answer might be far worse than any physical slap.

"Let go of my elbows," she told him.

As soon as her arms were free, she reached up and touched the side of his face.

"Is this really you again?" she asked.

He nodded. She ran her fingertip down his cheek and over his chin.

"The you that I know?"

Again he nodded. He couldn't have spoken to save his life.

"Then I'm the same. I can't stop either."

For Col it was a moment like no other. He wished it could go on forever. Instead it was broken by a deep rumbling sound from far below.

"Ah. That's the engine room." Riff transferred her attention, leaving the moment behind. "Lye's preparing for our burst of speed."

Even the mention of Lye's name no longer bothered Col. "Do you have to go?"

"I'm needed on the bridge. I should be there already."

She drew away without another word and vanished into the mist. This time he heard the creak of the turret door opening, then the clang as it slammed shut.

He leaned against the barrier and looked out, as Riff had been looking out before. He still felt the sensation of her fingertip on his face, like the lingering ghost of a touch.

How could he have gotten it so wrong? He had been on the brink of the greatest mistake in his life. Blind, blind, blind! He'd declared their relationship dead, he'd been trying to crush it in his own heart—and all the time Riff had never even questioned it!

Looking out over the barrier, he saw a dim, dull glow through the mist. It was a blob of fire from one of the *Grosse Wien*'s funnels, reduced to the merest hint of red and yellow. Impossible to tell how near or far, but he guessed the Austrians were following at the same distance as before.

Luckily, *Liberator*'s funnels emitted no telltale light.

Riff didn't even know how badly he'd failed her. Long, long ago she'd asked for his trust, and instead he'd given up on her. He'd lost faith and betrayed her in his mind, because he'd been afraid of getting hurt. He was a coward as well as a traitor. He could hardly forgive himself—and yet somehow, miraculously, he was already forgiven. *I can't stop either,* she'd said.

The rumble of the engine increased, until all at once the juggernaut surged forward. Col felt a tiny tap between his shoulder blades, then another on top of his scalp. Wetness?

He tilted his head and looked up. Though he could see nothing in the mist, he guessed that droplets were falling from the overhead wires, shaken down by the vibrations as *Liberator* accelerated. When another drop fell on his cheek, the wet spot was like a benediction.

The world that had seemed so tangled and fraught had become suddenly very simple. His doubts and despairs, his self-inflicted torments over Riff—all dissolved and gone away! None of it had ever happened!

Faster and faster the juggernaut accelerated. A drop of water fell into his open mouth and trickled back over his tongue. It was cool and delicious.

43

The gap between the two juggernauts widened. Minute after minute went by, and still the Austrians hadn't realized they were falling behind. Col stared out in the direction of the glow from the *Grosse Wien*'s funnels, which dimmed and faded until it was completely lost in the mist.

Liberator drove on at unsustainable speed. After a few minutes ominous hissings and wheezings rose from the depths below. Col couldn't imagine what conditions were like for those working among the boilers and turbines. The juggernaut was shaking itself apart. In the meanwhile, though, he could feel the wind of their speed in his hair and the damp strands of mist blowing across his face. They were outstripping the pursuit!

It couldn't last—and it didn't. Suddenly the *Grosse Wien* blew a new kind of blast on its horn: loud and long like a bellow of rage.

Now the Austrians had realized; now they would be taking action to catch up. *Time for the next part of the plan,* thought Col.

Even though he was expecting it, he was still thrown off balance by the sudden change of direction. He clung to the barrier as *Liberator* swung to the right. Thirty seconds more—then the gears disengaged and the engines cut out. The rollers rolled on under their own momentum, slower and slower, until the juggernaut came to a halt.

In the lull that followed, the only sound was the approaching thunder of the *Grosse Wien*. The glows of red and yellow loomed through the mist again. The Austrians were traveling along to the left, pursuing at tremendous speed.

Col held his breath. They were barely three hundred yards away. But so long as he couldn't see their hull, presumably they couldn't see *Liberator*, either.

Another angry blast of the horn rang out—and the *Grosse Wien* rumbled on past. They were chasing their idea of where *Liberator* had gone.

He let go of the barrier and brandished his fists in silent triumph. His knuckles were white from gripping so hard. He wondered if the Filthies were celebrating on the bridge, and wished he had someone to celebrate with.

Gradually the glow diminished and vanished. The next blast of the horn was muffled and far away, swallowed up in the heavy air.

If the Austrians were smart, they would stop and wait until they were able to see *Liberator*'s track again. He hoped they weren't smart, and that they would overshoot by a hundred miles.

After a while *Liberator* restarted its turbines. It was the quietest possible noise, a low thrum of minimal power. The rollers turned, and the juggernaut moved forward slowly and cautiously.

Col nodded to himself. They would need to keep swerving away from the place where they'd last been sighted. And then? Probably a wide loop that would bring them back to the coast far away from Botany Bay. Once on the ocean they could easily lose their pursuers.

The only problem was the lightening sky. Already the mist was gray rather than black, with a strange depthless pallor. It was like swimming in some murky liquid.

What would happen in the full light of morning? The mist would still hide them, but not as well as darkness and mist together. And then, how long before it dispersed?

For the next twenty minutes the juggernaut moved quietly onward. Little by little the mist changed from gray to white. It grew patchy, too, dense in some parts and thin in others. Col shivered as long streamers floated eerily around him. A breeze sprang up, sighing and whispering with a soft swishing sound.

The breeze was a threat if it blew away the cloud.

After twenty minutes the engines were suddenly cut again. What now? *Liberator* slowed and rolled to a halt. Col strained his ears and heard what some Filthy with very sharp hearing must have heard. The rumble of another juggernaut's engines!

His heart sank. The Austrians must have realized their mistake, turned, and come back on a different route. By chance their route had intersected with *Liberator*'s route.

He looked for a glow of fire from the funnels, but there was only the white mist. Perhaps the fire hardly showed in the daytime. No blasts of the horn, either.

Where was the rumble coming from, exactly? The mist multiplied and confused the sound. Col ran to the front of the platform and stared this way and that. Louder and louder—the *Grosse Wien*'s engines were roaring as never before. To the left? To the right?

Straight ahead!

The other juggernaut was rushing toward *Liberator* on a collision course!

The Filthies on the bridge were already aware of the danger. Hiding in the mist was no longer an option. *Liberator*'s engines surged into life again.

But acceleration was a slow process for a mechanical mountain weighing three million tons. *Liberator* lurched forward and made a half turn to the left.

The approaching noise seemed to surround Col and tower over him. A mind-numbing roar accompanied by clanking, grinding sounds—wait a minute! That wasn't right! A doubt entered Col's mind—

—and was confirmed one heartbeat later. The shape that loomed through the mist was the *wrong* shape, too high and blocklike to be the *Grosse Wien*. When he glimpsed color as well, he knew for certain. Khaki!

It was the Russian juggernaut, the *Romanov*. The Russians must have found an easier place to climb over the coastal hills.

He let go of the barrier and backed away—a mistake, because he had nothing to hang on to when the two juggernauts collided.

At the last moment the mist dissipated, driven away by the immense onrush of metal on metal. For a split second Col saw with perfect clarity every detail of the *Romanov*'s prow and masts and birds' nests.

Then the crash.

It jarred through him as though someone had taken a hammer and struck the end of every bone in his body.

It pealed out with a clang and a bang and a screech of tearing metal.

It rattled his teeth and sent him sprawling face-first. The reverberations in the deck shuddered through his hands, his chest, his cheekbones.

He rolled over and saw the *Romanov* swinging away under the force of the impact. Its prow had struck *Liberator*'s side amidships. Violent flashes of electricity fizzed and sputtered in the tangle of wires between its masts.

Col's ears were ringing, and his legs were like jelly. By the time he finally staggered to his feet, both juggernauts had slewed to a stop. He propped himself up against the barrier and surveyed the damage.

Two of *Liberator*'s funnels leaned to the left, and a third had collapsed and toppled down over the upper terraces of the superstructure. The *Romanov*'s main segment had separated from its trailing segments, and many of its masts had snapped, now held up only by the tangle of wires. The electricity that had fizzed in the wires seemed to have died away. The juggernauts were roughly side by side: three hundred yards apart at the front and twice that distance at the rear.

Then Russian officers appeared on the deck of the *Romanov*. They shouted and gesticulated one to another. Obviously, the collision had taken them completely by surprise.

Col didn't try to hide, and he was soon noticed. The officers shook their fists and hurled what sounded like Russian curses in his direction. Then they disappeared.

Three minutes later a force of fifty or more armed officers emerged on deck. Col ducked as they raised rifles to their shoulders and started shooting.

The *crack-crack-crack!* of rifle fire came faster and faster, and the *tang!* of bullets hitting metal plate, the whizz and zing of ricochets. They seemed to be wasting a great many bullets on just one person.

He scuttled along to a different part of the barrier. If he stuck up his head for only a moment, they wouldn't have time to draw a bead on him. At least he hoped not.

He took a deep breath and looked out. The Russians were still shooting, but he was no longer the main target. Filthies had taken up position in the sorting trays all along the flank of the *Liberator*. They were mostly hidden behind their cover, but he could see the flash of their rifle fire.

They seemed to be giving as good as they got. So long as the Russians didn't start using special weapons . . .

Col ducked down again and moved to a farther part of the barrier.

When he rose for another look, he saw that the Russians *had* started using special weapons. At the very moment he popped up his head, a glass sphere was fired from the *Romanov*'s deck. It arced through the air and crashed down on one of the sorting trays. Immediately an evil-looking cloud of yellow gas spilled out.

There was no more rifle fire from that particular tray. The cloud expanded and spread, wider and wider.

But Col had stayed watching too long. A bullet whistled past, so close that he felt the wind of it on his cheek. He dropped down in a hurry and moved on to a new vantage point. He counted to twenty before sticking his head up again.

The situation had changed—thanks to the breeze. The cloud of yellow gas had continued to spread, but not where the Russians would have wanted. Now it was drifting back toward the *Romanov*.

Col heard cries of panic, saw officers dropping their rifles and pulling out handkerchiefs to cover their mouths and noses. Then a megaphone voice boomed out—the same megaphone voice he had heard from the *Romanov* at Botany Bay. This time it didn't sound so much like a threat against *Liberator*, but more like an order to the Russian officers themselves.

He dropped down below the barrier again. When he next looked out, the officers had gone, and the *Romanov*'s deck was deserted.

The first round of fighting was over. It was a stalemate so far, but Col knew that wouldn't last. All the advantages were on the Russian side.

44

He stayed watching a long while. The cloud of yellow gas dispersed, but the officers didn't return. No doubt the Russian leaders were working on a more calculated strategy for their next move.

As the sun climbed higher, the mist also dispersed. Leaning over the barrier, Col had a clear view a thousand feet down to the ground. It was like looking into a canyon, with the juggernauts so close at the top and the ground so far below.

At the bottom he could see the skidding tracks that both machines had carved through the natural scenery. What remained was a multicolored patchwork of grassy mounds, bushy hollows, dry gullies, and clumps of trees. A lake of scummy gray sludge had formed round *Liberator*'s rollers at the back, presumably leaking from the juggernaut's own bilge.

Col groaned at the sight of the damage. Steam and smoke trickled out from a dozen places low down on *Liberator*'s hull, which had been completely staved in. By comparison the *Romanov*'s flat prow appeared relatively unharmed. The Russian juggernaut was immobilized only because its caterpillar tracks had broken away from the wheels over which they ran.

Looking down at the two hulls, Col thought of the

two engine rooms—and the two populations of Filthies. No doubt the *Romanov* had its own Below and its own workforce of long-suffering slaves. No doubt the Russian Filthies were still trapped among the boilers and turbines, as *Liberator*'s Filthies had once been.

He wondered if the Russian Filthies ever dreamed of revolution. . . .

According to Professor Twillip, every European nation had developed its own slave class to labor in munitions factories during the Fifty Years' War. And the same slaves had been put to a new form of slavery in the imperialist juggernauts constructed after the war. Wouldn't the Russian Filthies hate their oppressors every bit as much as *Liberator*'s Filthies had done?

But if they had no Riff to inspire them . . . They couldn't know that one group of Filthies had already triumphed over their oppressors. There they were, so close to the one liberated juggernaut ruled by people like themselves—yet, closed off behind impenetrable walls, they might as well have been on the other side of the world. And the cruelest twist of fate was that they wouldn't even know why they'd been made to work the engines so hard—in order to overtake and overpower people like themselves.

If only there were some way to get a message to them . . . Col racked his brains in vain. He was still pondering the problem when the *Grosse Wien* hove into sight half an hour later.

Obviously the Russians had been communicating

with the Austrians by wireless telegraph. Was this the signal for an all-out attack?

However, the *Grosse Wien* slowed as soon as it made visual contact. Keeping its distance, it circled to the right and came to a stop a quarter of a mile away.

Col watched and waited until he grew bored. Nothing was going to happen yet. He wondered what was happening in the Norfolk Library. *Don't do anything until I get back,* he'd told them—how long ago? Were Gillabeth and the others still looking after Sephaltina?

He walked across and entered the turret. Kneeling at the top of the metal staircase, he peered down into the room below. There was no sign of the Council around the map desk—or anywhere else. In fact only a few operators remained on the bridge. Now was his opportunity.

He descended the stairs nonchalantly, as if he had every right to be where he'd been. He was halfway to the exit at the back of the bridge when one Filthy stepped forward and blocked his escape.

"Been taking the air up there, have you?"

She had red hair that stuck out in spikes around a crinkled, puckish face. A scar in the center of her forehead lifted her eyebrows and gave her an oddly quizzical expression. In spite of her challenge she didn't seem particularly hostile.

"I've been keeping watch. The Austrian juggernaut is a quarter of a mile away."

"I know. Who asked you to keep watch?"

Col didn't intend to get Riff into trouble. "Nobody."

"Hmm. How long have you been up there?"

"Since Botany Bay."

Wry quirks and creases came and went on her face. "You must've had quite a ride. Was it you they started shooting at?"

"Yes."

"So you must be a hero." She didn't mean it, yet there was no malice in her irony. "You'd better take your bravery off home, then."

Col turned to go, then paused with a question. "Where is everyone?"

"Yes, it is very quiet here, isn't it?" Again the quizzical eyebrows. "They've been called away to an emergency general meeting."

"In the Grand Assembly Hall?"

"Of course. Big decisions to be taken. Shiv's security force has been going round to announce it." The twist of her features suggested that she didn't exactly approve of Shiv or his security force. "Unfortunately, some of us still have to run the bridge."

"What are they deciding?"

"Ah, now there you have me. I won't know till they decide it."

"I meant—"

"Why don't you go and find out?"

Col changed his plans on the spot. Not all Filthies were against him . . . and in a time of crisis like this . . .

"Right, I will," he said.

45

By the time Col reached the Grand Assembly Hall, the meeting was already under way. The crowd was small, but densely packed toward the front of the hall. Col stepped swiftly across the open space and mingled in at the back of the throng. It seemed that everyone around him was wearing a red armband, and many of them carried rifles. Luckily, all their attention was focused forward.

A furious discussion was going on at the front of the hall. There was a smell of stale sweat in the air, and a tension so thick it could have been cut by a knife. Everyone looked drawn and haggard. Unlike Col they'd had no chance to snatch some sleep during the night.

"We have to attack before they attack us!"

"We'll go down fighting!"

"If they use more gas bombs against us . . ."

"The scum! The evil, murdering scum!"

"How do we fight against gas?"

Lye, Shiv, Padder, Gansy, and Riff were all there, trying to make their voices heard above the noise. Riff dragged a chair into place and climbed up on it.

"Never surrender!" she shouted. "Never! But we have to use our heads. No suicidal charges. We've already seen their gas bombs. We have to find out what else they've got."

"How can we?" a voice shouted back. "Except we attack them!"

"We find out the same way the Council has always found things out. Right?" Riff appealed to the other Council members. "There are people on board who can research those other juggernauts. If we put them to work . . ."

"She means *Swanks*," another voice interrupted, in a tone of disgust.

Col was dying to speak out and tell them that Septimus and Professor Twillip had already done the research. But the crowd's angry mood made him think twice about attracting attention.

"We don't have time for grudges," said Riff. "We need all the help we can get."

"I wouldn't trust *their* help," snorted Padder. Even Riff's own brother wouldn't support her.

"We have a better plan," cried Lye, and rose up suddenly as high as Riff. She had found and mounted another chair ten feet away. She looked once at Riff, then turned to address the crowd. "Airborne assault. Shiv and I have discussed it. We shoot ropes across from our superstructure to their superstructure. Then our assault troops slide across on the ropes."

"Where do we get the ropes?" Gansy asked.

"Plenty of coils of rope on Fourth Deck. All we need are grappling hooks to go on the end."

"The manufacturing decks can manufacture them," put in Shiv. "Bits of metal welded together. It'll be easy to snag the hooks in all those masts and wires on top of the Russian juggernaut."

Riff had a thoughtful expression on her face. "They'll bring up a thousand defenders before we get a hundred attackers across."

"We'll take them by surprise," Lye answered. "It's better than a suicidal charge, isn't it?"

Riff nodded. Obviously, she wasn't opposed to the plan in principle. "How would we shoot the ropes across?"

"We'll work it out. Some sort of spring or bow."

"Why not bring in the Swanks to help? There may be previous examples. That's the sort of thing they can find out about."

Yes, thought Col, *that's exactly the sort of thing Septimus and the professor can do. And if they manage to locate the Maxim guns as well . . .*

"No," said Lye. "We don't need them. They're just waiting for their chance to go over to their fellow imperialists."

"This is a battle for survival," Riff insisted.

"Yes, and they make sure of their survival by helping the Russians. They know what'll happen to them if *we* win."

"What?"

Lye shook her jet-black hair, which gleamed and flashed under the lights of the chandelier. She turned to the crowd and raised her voice.

"We don't need traitors on our side. We don't need fence-sitters. We need strong, pure souls who can change the world. Who *will* change the world! A hundred strong, pure souls to lead the assault!"

She was filled with burning conviction and absolute belief. Her voice had the same thrilling intensity that Col had overheard in Riff's bedroom.

"The imperialists fight only out of self-interest. But we fight for something bigger than ourselves. We fight for justice. For a world made fair and equal. What we do now lights a beacon for the oppressed. We make a revolution here in our hearts that will last a thousand years. Win or lose, live or die, the whole world will hear about us!"

"It sounds like you *want* to die," Riff interjected, as Lye paused for breath.

"I'm not afraid to die. I'm not going to hide and cower as though I might be in the wrong. I'm prepared to die because I'm in the right. We're *all* in the right. This is our test, to prove ourselves. Our truth over their lies! Our justice over their tyranny! Our future over their past!"

She was magnificent. Col didn't want to admit it, but she was. Her beauty only added to the effect. He could see Gansy watching her with shining eyes, Padder following her every move with admiration.

When she raised her arm and shook her fist, people imitated the gesture all around the hall. There was a general murmur of approval and a forest of fists in the air.

Only Col kept his arm at his side. It was a serious mistake, marking him out as different. The red armbands nearby turned and stared, becoming aware of him for the first time.

"Swank here!" one called out.

"Traitor!"

"Spy!"

Col tried to shake off the hands that clamped down on his shoulders. Too late. He scanned the faces all around him, and none of them were friendly.

"Bring him forward!" came the order from the front.

Col found himself propelled roughly toward the front of the hall. Riff and Lye were still on their chairs, with the other Council members standing between them.

Shiv eyed Col with cold distaste. "He heard our plan of attack."

"So what?" Riff shrugged. "He won't betray us."

"You don't know that."

"You think he's going to make hand signals to the Russians?"

Padder weighed in on Shiv's side. "Someone betrayed our attack to the soldiers at Botany Bay. We never thought that was possible."

"Perhaps *he's* the saboteur!" cried someone in the crowd.

Shiv glanced up at Lye on her chair. "Now?" he asked.

Perhaps Lye gave a tiny shake of the head; at any rate she turned her attention to Riff.

"Why do you support him?" she demanded. "He doesn't deserve it."

"Yes, he does. He's a good person. I believe . . ."

"What?" Lye snapped out the word as Riff hesitated.

"I believe in him."

The conversation had become a private exchange between the two of them, conducted over the heads of the other Council members. Then Riff broke the connection. She stepped down from her chair, and went across to stand beside Col.

"I'd trust him with my life," she said.

Col could have bathed in the glow of her words. Padder tried to draw his sister away by the arm, but she refused to budge.

"Don't do this," he muttered.

Shiv had somehow moved across to stand right at the foot of Lye's chair. "Time to announce it now," he advised.

Lye's gaze bored into Riff's. "He's a danger to us," she said.

"Announce it," Shiv repeated.

Still, Lye's eyes were locked upon Riff's. "You *know* he's a danger to us." Her face looked so gaunt, it was almost haggard. "Shall I announce it?"

Riff frowned. "What are you talking about?"

Lye switched focus from Riff to the crowd. "The saboteur has been discovered!" she proclaimed in a loud voice. She indicated Col. "It's his wife!"

Col gasped—along with everyone else in the hall.

"How did *you* find out?" he exclaimed.

His question was lost in the general hubbub.

"Her name is Sephaltina!" Lye went on remorselessly. "She's been our secret enemy all along!"

Riff must have been as baffled as Col, but she took a

different approach. "Wait a minute. He didn't know what his wife was doing. He didn't even know she was still on board."

"No?" Lye expressed her disbelief in a sneer. "Doesn't seem very surprised, though, does he?"

Shiv pointed an accusing finger at Riff. "What about you? How long have *you* known?"

This time there were gasps of horror as well as amazement. To accuse Riff, the leader of the Liberation . . .

"What's this?" Padder rounded on his sister. "Why didn't you tell us? Why didn't you tell *me*?"

Riff recovered her breath. "I was going to tell you."

"The imperialist juggernauts turned up," said Col. "We were working on a deal."

It was the wrong thing to say. There was a long moment of silence.

"*Deal?*" roared Padder.

"Behind our backs!" cried someone in the crowd.

"Where's his wife now?" Gansy demanded.

Riff exchanged despairing glances with Col. "Er, in the Norfolk Library, I think."

"What? Still free? With the Swanks?"

"I want the saboteur arrested." Lye's voice lashed out like a whip. "And the whole Porpentine family. Starting with *him*."

Half a dozen red armbands jumped forward to secure Col, who decided not to make a fight of it. He could hardly win, and he would only create more trouble for Riff.

"Take him down to the dormitory decks," Lye snapped.

The hall was in an uproar. Shiv stepped up onto the chair vacated by Riff.

"This is an emergency situation," he told the crowd. "We're under attack from outside and in. We need emergency powers. I propose a war leadership to take charge of security and our assault on the Russian juggernaut. Since Lye and I planned the assault, we'll need to be in charge. The other Council members—"

"No, this is wrong!" Riff turned to appeal to Padder and Gansy. "Do something! Make a stand!"

"The other Council members will share in all duties," said Lye.

There was a stamping of feet, and several voices called out, "Lye and Shiv!" "Lye and Shiv!" "Yes! Yes! Yes!"

Padder and Gansy appeared at a loss. They were obviously reluctant to go against a crowd so strongly in favor of emergency war leadership.

"It's a grab for power!" Riff stormed. "It's a takeover! It's a new tyranny!"

But she had no influence on the mood of the crowd. The sound of stamping grew to a thunder; the shouts of approval became a continuous swelling roar.

Riff glowered up at Lye, eyeball to eyeball. "You won't get away with this!"

Lye's face was like a mask. "Arrest her, too," she said.

Col couldn't believe it. More red armbands leaped forward to seize hold of Riff. She was too surprised to react.

"Take her to the dormitory decks too," said Lye, and

just for a moment there was a quiver behind the mask. Still she stood erect and maintained her self-control.

Col expected the crowd to turn against the new leadership. Surely they couldn't allow *this*? Surely Lye had gone too far this time?

But there was no backlash. The crowd continued to roar and stamp their feet. Col scanned around and noticed for the first time just how many red armbands there were. In fact virtually everyone in the hall wore a red armband—including a large proportion of Botany Bay convicts who hadn't even been present at the time of the Liberation.

It was then that Col remembered what the woman on the bridge had told him—about Shiv's security force going around to announce the meeting. Obviously, they had announced it only to other red armbands.

Lye and Shiv had won again.

46

Col and Riff were hustled away under a guard of red armbands while the meeting continued. Lye and Shiv had further specific proposals about emergency powers that required endorsement.

Once outside the Grand Assembly Hall, the red armbands produced leg irons, which they locked around their prisoners' ankles. Although they had appeared to spring spontaneously from the crowd, they hardly seemed like random volunteers. Would random volunteers be equipped with leg irons? Col and Riff were forced to shuffle in small steps with chains dragging between their legs.

They traveled by steam elevator down to Twenty-first Deck. This was one of the dormitory decks, where Menials had once slept. Riff must have slept here too, Col recalled, in the period when she was playing the part of a Menial.

Their guard of red armbands marched them along main corridors and side corridors. Other red armbands stood on sentry duty at corners and intersections. Their dormitory was DORMITORY NO. 5, according to the label on the door.

Inside were rows and rows of bunks, bare metal frames supporting narrow racks of crisscross wire. The racks rose up one above another like shelves in a bookcase. There were no other occupants.

The red armbands had a well-practiced routine for every operation. While four held Col immobilized, a fifth fastened a chain from the frame of a bunk to the chain between his leg irons. They repeated the operation with Riff. Someone put a folded gray blanket on each of their bunks, and a bucket nearby. Then they went out, locking the door behind them.

Col and Riff faced each other across the alley between two rows of bunks. They sat leaning forward, hands on knees.

"How could they know?" Riff mused.

Col understood that she was talking about Lye and Shiv and the saboteur. "You didn't tell anyone?"

"Never mentioned it."

They talked over and over what had happened in the Grand Assembly Hall, but the mystery remained.

"Lye and Shiv have been working toward this all along," said Col.

Riff nodded miserably. "We've been thinking about the imperialists while they've been thinking how to take power."

Half an hour later a different gang of red armbands brought Sephaltina and the rest of the Porpentine family to the same dormitory. They were all shackled in leg irons—Orris, Quinnea, Gillabeth, and even little Antrobus. Col's baby brother carried Murgatrude in his arms.

When Sephaltina saw Col, she cried out and clapped her hands.

"My husband! Now I've found you!"

Her rosebud lips parted in a childlike smile. Instinctively Col sat up straighter and distanced himself a little from Riff. Riff looked at him in surprise, then frowned and shrugged.

When the red armbands fastened each of the new arrivals to the frame of a bunk, Sephaltina ended up on the opposite side of the room from Col.

"It's not right!" she objected, and pointed to Riff. "I ought to be where *she* is."

Col's family knew that *Liberator* had collided with the Russian juggernaut, but not much else. As soon as the red armbands were out of the room, Col gave them the full story of what had happened since. Orris, Gillabeth, and Antrobus looked worried, Quinnea looked shaken, and Sephaltina continued to smile as though she hadn't a care in the world.

A little later a further pair of red armbands brought Mr. Gibber down to the dormitory, also shackled in leg irons. He protested and resisted violently. When the red armbands chained him to the same row of bunks as Riff, he kicked out until he lost his balance and fell flat on his face.

"It's all a mistake! I've done nothing wrong!"

One of the red armbands paused in the doorway. "We follow our orders," he said.

Eventually Mr. Gibber quieted down, though he still refused to get up from his position on the floor. "Why pick on me?" he grumbled.

"Because you're associated with us," Col told him.

"You? You're Porpentines. I didn't ask to be associated with you. I'm just a humble ex-schoolteacher."

He addressed himself to Col and Riff, since Gillabeth, Orris, and Quinnea were absorbed in their own conversation.

"I've been disappeared," he said. "That's what it is. I've been abducted, and nobody knows where. Just like all those others."

"I suppose they're imprisoned in other dormitories," said Col.

Riff shook her head. "I suspect there's more to it than this."

Mr. Gibber sniveled loudly. "I'm going to meet the same fate as Dr. Blessamy!"

"And Victoria and Albert." Col chewed at his lip. "Surely they'd show a little compassion to Victoria."

"Why?"

"She's pregnant."

Riff clicked her tongue. "That's not good."

"But if she explains to them . . ."

"I mean, it's not good if they find out. An heir to the royal family. Can you imagine what Lye and Shiv would think about that?"

"Oh." Col fell silent, more depressed than ever. That was an angle he hadn't considered.

Mr. Gibber had fallen silent too. He yawned and curled himself into a sleeping position on the floor. After a while Riff spread a blanket over him.

She talked on and off with Col, but she was starting

to yawn herself. Gillabeth, Orris, Quinnea, and Antrobus had all settled down for sleep.

"You're tired, aren't you?" said Col.

"Very," Riff agreed. "I didn't get a wink last night."

She stretched out on her wire rack, rolled herself up in her blanket, and dropped off almost at once.

Col might have thought he was the only one to remain awake—until Sephaltina caught his eye across the room. She held up the third finger of her left hand and proudly displayed her wedding ring.

He groaned inwardly and looked away. Still, he sensed that she was waiting to catch his eye again. To avoid further displays, he pretended to go to sleep himself. He turned in on his wire rack, faced the other way, and snuggled under his blanket.

Soon enough the pretense became a reality. He drifted off and slept right through until morning.

A rough bellow aroused him. "Wake up, you lot!"

A dozen red armbands had entered the room.

"Say good-bye to your dormitory," yelled one. "We're taking you down."

47

They descended to Bottom Deck. There were armed guards around the stairwells, and newly painted signs on doors and bulkheads.

NO VISITORS
ENTRY FORBIDDEN
THIS AREA PATROLLED

Col hadn't visited Bottom Deck for a couple of months. As his eyes adjusted to the shadows and occasional pools of light, he saw that the coal mounds had slipped and fanned out, no doubt under the impact of the collision. Large areas were cordoned off by ropes, from which hung more warning signs.

NO LOITERING
KEEP OUTSIDE THE ROPES
SUPERVISED WORKERS ONLY
BE PREPARED TO SHOW IDENTIFICATION

The red armbands marched their prisoners forward between the iron piers. Huddled groups of Filthies sat around everywhere, seemingly aimless and dispirited. They were blackened with coal and grease, and looked as all Filthies had looked before the time of the Liberation. Col guessed that they were workers from Below, who tended the great boilers and turbines. Right now they weren't tending anything.

He wondered what had happened. The metal floor was colder than he remembered, and there was no rhythm of thrumming vibrations underfoot. It didn't bode well for the juggernaut's engines.

A hundred paces along they came to a different group of people, lined up in a queue. Their clothes were dirty, in some cases very dirty, but they were all instantly recognizable as Swanks. They stood with heads hanging, shackled by chains between their feet.

"Now we know what happened to the disappeared," Col muttered.

"Lye and Shiv," growled Gillabeth behind him. "I should've guessed."

There were forty or fifty Swanks in the queue. Many of the faces were familiar to Col—they looked up and nodded when he went past. Finally he saw Victoria and Albert: Albert with his arm round Victoria's waist, Victoria with her head against Albert's shoulder.

Col waved a hand, and Victoria gave him a sad smile. Albert called out, "They got you, too?"

Col had no time to answer as he was hustled forward. One of the red armbands thumped him in the back with the butt of a rifle.

Another ten paces brought them to the end of the queue. Beyond the last of the disappeared, a chain snaked over the floor and looped around the next pier. Col now understood the nature of the queue; the chain stretched from pier to pier, and everyone's leg irons were fastened onto it.

His understanding was confirmed when the red armbands proceeded to fasten *his* leg irons onto it.

He found himself between Riff and Gillabeth. On the other side of Gillabeth was the last of the disappeared—a strange figure swathed in bandages. Col assumed it was a male from his short-cut hair, but his face was entirely covered apart from a slit for the eyes. When Gillabeth was tethered next to him, he uttered indecipherable grunting sounds through his bandages.

"Oh, be quiet," Gillabeth snapped. "You're not helping."

The red armbands stood around waiting, rifles cradled comfortably in their arms.

After a few minutes a murmur rose up farther down the line. Col heard the names "Lye" and "Shiv," spoken in fearful tones. The red armbands sprang to attention.

Lye and Shiv walked the length of the queue and stopped before the new prisoners. Lye was perfectly composed, though her pale eyes avoided Riff.

Instead she focused on Sephaltina, looking her over from head to toe. "And this must be the saboteur. Our secret enemy, the wife of Colbert Porpentine."

Sephaltina simpered sweetly at being referred to as "the wife of Colbert Porpentine." Then a puzzled expression came over her face. She looked Lye over in her turn.

"I've seen you before," she said.

"Likely enough, if you've been sneaking around," said Lye. "But your days of sneaking around are over. Now you're in my domain. This is where I rule."

"And rule like a tyrant," Riff broke in.

Still Lye didn't look at Riff.

Instead it was Shiv who answered on Lye's behalf. "We expect a maximum effort from every worker. How else do you think we could make *Liberator* travel so fast? You asked for speed, and we delivered."

He spoke in terms of "we," Col noted, whereas Lye had spoken in terms of "I." It was painfully obvious that Shiv was trying to have himself included.

Then someone else claimed Lye's attention. There was a clank and rattle as Mr. Gibber stepped forward in his leg irons. He almost toppled forward as the chain tightened behind him. He bowed his head and cleared his throat.

"Ah, you have something to say, my little spy?" said Lye. "What have you found out for me now?"

48

Mr. Gibber smirked from ear to ear, but he didn't speak out immediately. First he reached into his inside jacket pocket, brought out a key, and held it up as if examining it. When he was sure that everyone was watching, he went down on one knee, swiveled the leg iron on his left ankle, inserted the key, and unlocked the cuff. Then he did the same for his right ankle. He pulled the cuffs open, kicked them aside, and came up to stand next to Lye.

He was making faces to himself, grins and grimaces of self-delight. Lye nodded and allowed him to whisper in her ear. He stood very close to her—closer than necessary. At least Shiv seemed to think so.

"What is it?" he demanded. "Tell us."

Mr. Gibber completed his tale-telling, then fell back with obvious reluctance.

"Wait here," Lye said to Shiv. She snapped her fingers at two of the red armbands, who accompanied her back along the queue.

After the initial shock Col's mind was working at top speed. If Mr. Gibber was spying for Lye, then a great many things fell into place. It was no longer a mystery that Lye and Shiv had known about the saboteur. Of course—Mr. Gibber had been there in the Norfolk Library when Col

and Gillabeth had presented Sephaltina and announced
the news.

A moment later Lye returned with the two red
armbands—and Victoria and Albert. Col's spirits sank.

"What's this?" asked Shiv.

"She's pregnant," Lye told him.

"Pregnant?"

"A royal child."

Victoria tried to intervene. "Not royal. An ordinary
child. A very, very ordinary child."

Lye ignored her. "We could make this work to our
advantage," she said.

"How do you mean?"

They turned aside and continued their discussion in
lowered voices. Col caught only a few words: "Commitment . . . everyone responsible . . . no going back . . ."

Mr. Gibber hovered on the edge of the discussion.
He wasn't listening to their plans for Victoria and Albert,
but he appeared very eager about something else. In his
hand was a small tin, much like the ones in which he had
once kept his blackboard chalk. He held it out hopefully
in Lye's direction.

Lye paid attention to him only when she had finished
her conversation with Shiv. "Ah, you want your reward?
Very soon, my little spy. Business first."

By "business" she meant arrangements for the new
prisoners.

"I need a selection of volunteers to go down Below

and inspect the engines," she told them. "Inspect to see if repairs are possible. I think the saboteur and her husband can be our first volunteers. And his parents and sister and little brother. What about you?"

The last words were addressed to Riff, who merely glared in response. Lye didn't quite meet her eye.

"So be it. You too."

There was a loud, muffled roar, and the bandaged prisoner next to Gillabeth began jerking violently this way and that. Gillabeth planted her feet apart and just managed to avoid getting dragged over by the chain.

Lye curled her lip. "Her as well," she said. "She can go with the rest of the troublemakers."

Col was still digesting that as the red armbands unfastened their leg irons from the chain. Including the bandaged prisoner, there were now eight so-called volunteers. Two red armbands stayed with Victoria and Albert; the others propelled the volunteers forward, while Lye and Shiv led the way. Mr. Gibber trailed along behind like a faithful dog.

They arrived soon enough at the nearest viewing bay. Shiv raised the hatch, and a cloud of white steam blew out in a gush. Curled up in Antrobus's arms, Murgatrude stuck out his head and answered the hiss of the steam with a hiss of his own.

As the prisoners halted in front of the hatch, Mr. Gibber came forward, bowing and grinning like a goblin.

"Now?" he suggested to Lye.

He twisted the lid off the top of his tin. Inside, Col

caught a glimpse of something black—jet-black.

"Hmm, how many this time?" Lye studied Mr. Gibber with contempt.

He licked his lips. "Three?"

"No, don't be greedy. Three is what you got when you brought Victoria and Albert to me. Information about them is only worth two."

She reached up and plucked out two strands of her jet-black hair. When she presented them to him, he handled them like purest gold. With infinite delicacy he placed them inside his tin, then snapped the lid shut on them.

Col turned away from the scene. Mr. Gibber's expression of gloating avarice made his skin crawl. He found himself standing beside the bandaged prisoner—who, in spite of her close-cut hair, wasn't a he but a she.

"Who are you?" he asked.

The answer was a muffled sound that might have been anything. But Col already had an idea.

"Nod your head if I'm right," he said. "I think—"

"Quiet!" barked one of the red armbands.

Lye must have been following the exchange with one ear, because she swung round suddenly to face Col.

"He wants to know who she is." The smile on her lips came nowhere near her eyes. "Why not?" She nodded to Shiv. "Cut away the bandages. Let's show him."

Shiv shrugged, reached into his undershirt, and drew out the same knife with which he'd threatened the Botany Bay officer. He sliced through the knots, and two red armbands came forward to unwind the bandages.

In a moment the prisoner was revealed—exactly as Col had suspected. It was Dunga, the missing Council member.

She was boiling with rage. She tried to hurl herself at Lye, but the leg irons around her ankles brought her crashing to the ground. Perhaps fortunately, since Shiv had his knife raised and ready to strike.

"She seems to have made an excellent recovery," he mocked.

Lye indicated the open hatch. "Push her in," she ordered.

The red armbands leaped to obey. Dunga tried to clutch onto their boots—in vain. She had no time to clutch onto the ladder. With a crash and clatter she dropped down into the wire cage of the viewing bay.

"Now the rest of you," Lye ordered. "Climb down or be thrown down."

They chose to climb: first Orris and Quinnea, then Sephaltina, then Antrobus carrying Murgatrude. As Col, Riff, and Gillabeth prepared to follow, Lye gestured to Mr. Gibber.

"You too, my little spy," she said. "You can keep an eye on them for me."

Mr. Gibber looked up, surprised and not at all happy. "But . . . but they'll . . ."

"They won't hurt you. You watch over them, and the security force will watch over you."

"But where are you . . . ?"

"We have to prepare for the trial of Victoria and Albert." Lye turned on her heel. "You can report back to me later."

49

The viewing bay hung down from the ceiling of Below, high above the immense engine room. In the past Col would have expected to see boilers and furnaces, turning wheels and rocking beams; he would have expected to hear a mighty din of pounding machinery. At present, however, the whole chamber was silent and shrouded in steam. Descending the ladder, he couldn't even see the wire floor of the cage until he stepped on it.

Mr. Gibber was last to come down, and he kept very close to the bottom of the ladder. The red armbands remained on guard above. They sat around the open hatch with their legs dangling, the barrels of their rifles angled down.

Col stepped across to where a wire door had been slid back at the side of the cage. Under the old regime it would have served for hooking Filthies up from Below, as he himself had once been hooked up. Now, apparently, it was left open all the time. He looked through the opening at a system of pulleys suspended from the ceiling, just outside. Two taut ropes dropped down vertically and vanished into the steam; two loose ropes were tied to the side of the cage.

Presumably, the pulleys and ropes had been installed since the Liberation as a means of going down or coming up from the engine room. It was a dangerous-looking system, but hardly a problem for the acrobatic Filthies. Not so easy for himself or Gillabeth or Sephaltina, though . . . and very, very difficult for his parents and baby brother . . .

"Come over here," Riff called out.

Col turned to see Riff and Dunga on the other side of the cage, sitting with their backs against the wire. He went over to join them.

"Listen to this," said Riff. "Tell him."

Dunga pointed to a scar just above her knee. "I recovered from the bullet long ago. Just a flesh wound. But Lye and Shiv wanted me to stay injured. They had me moved to one of the dormitories and wrapped up in bandages. Pretending to take care of me, saying my wound might open up again. Huh! They even tied me to a bed."

Col whistled. "They dared do that to *you*! A Council member."

"That's why they did it. They knew my vote would go against them on the Council, so they found a way to stop me attending."

"What about the others?" asked Riff. "All the Swanks in chains?"

"Revenge," said Dunga. "Punishment. They've been sending groups Below to work alongside the Filthy workers. They want the Swanks to live and die as the Filthies did before the Liberation."

"Mostly die, then," said Col.

"Yes, they don't usually last long among the machinery. Even some of the Filthies have been dying. Lye makes them work longer and longer shifts, and confines them to the dormitories when they're not on shift. The red armbands are always watching and driving them on. They made a free choice to work with the engines, but they've ended up almost like slaves again."

"What about you?" asked Riff.

"I was selected to work Below a couple of days ago. I survived—in spite of all the bandages."

Riff raised an eyebrow. "Before the collision?"

"Of course. Everyone's been brought up since then."

"So why us?" Col asked. "Why select *us* to inspect the engines?"

Dunga shrugged. "Don't know."

"I don't like it," said Riff.

Col wasn't sure what to think. But at least Riff and Dunga had the skills to help them all survive Below.

He surveyed the cage. Orris, Quinnea, and Sephaltina occupied one corner, Gillabeth and Antrobus with Murgatrude occupied another, while Mr. Gibber sat by himself at the foot of the ladder. Mr. Gibber had his tin open in front of his chest and was sneaking a peek in under the lid.

Col frowned. He had never understood his old schoolteacher, but this latest revelation was the most incomprehensible of all.

Mr. Gibber must have realized he was being looked at, because he snapped the lid shut on the tin and stared back at Col with an expression that was half defiant and half cringing.

"You don't have to look at me like that," he said. "I know you all hate me anyway."

Col made no response, just continued to look at him. Mr. Gibber grew more and more uneasy under the scrutiny.

"You don't understand about love," he burst out at last. "Love that knows no reasons. Love that knows no bounds."

"Love?" Col blinked. "What, you and Lye?"

Gillabeth leaned forward and joined the conversation. "You sad little man. You're nothing at all to her."

"Of course I'm not." Mr. Gibber wasn't crushed by the comment—on the contrary. "She's everything, and I'm nothing. Every strand of her hair is worth more than my whole body. Beautiful, beautiful hair! And her body! So tall and straight and elegant!"

Thanks to her corset, thought Col, but he kept the thought to himself.

"And what am I?" Mr. Gibber rolled his eyes in all directions as though seeking an answer—or at least everyone's attention. "With my stupid nose and my stupid face and my stupid short little legs! Don't think I don't know! I'm just a washed-up, discredited schoolteacher. No one has any use for *me* anymore. Everything I taught has been thrown in the garbage. But I don't need her to love me. My love expects no return."

"What started all of this?" asked Col.

"All of *this?* You mean my love?" Mr. Gibber put his

hand on his heart. "Ah, she came looking for me at the academy. She needed a sign writer, and I offered to help. She appeared before me as a vision of perfection."

It made sense to Col. The Filthies had mostly learned to read, but they couldn't yet write. If Lye wanted new signs, she would need a Swank to write them. And where better to look than a school?

"All the signs you see on Bottom Deck—all my handiwork," said Mr. Gibber. "First I became her writer, and then I became her devoted worshipper."

"And her spy," Riff put in.

"I was helpless. I had to do whatever she asked. My reason was drowned and overwhelmed by passion."

"You were cunning with it, though," said Gillabeth.

"Oh, yes. Cunning enough to fool all of you." A kind of conceit mingled with the other expressions on Mr. Gibber's face. "You never imagined that a humble ex-schoolteacher could do such things. You never thought I had it in me."

"You're the one who abducted Victoria and Albert," Col accused.

"Of course, of course. I tricked them into leaving the library. I told them a fairy story about Beddle and Morkins getting into a quarrel with some Filthies out in the corridor, so they had to come and help. You should've seen their faces when the red armbands pounced!"

"And Dr. Blessamy?"

"He was putty in my hands. I don't even remember

what I told him. I could make him believe anything."

"And now?"

"Now what?"

"Where is he? He wasn't with the other prisoners on Bottom Deck."

For the first time Mr. Gibber looked a little uncomfortable. "I haven't seen him lately."

"No, probably because he was sent to work down Below. Probably because he never came back up."

"I don't know about that." Mr. Gibber grimaced and flung out his arms. "I can't think of consequences. I'm weak, I'm weak, I'm utterly helpless. The victim of my emotions. You can't blame me. My new love makes me do crazy things."

"Oh, we blame you, all right," said Gillabeth.

"Blame me, then. Blame me as much as you want. See if I care."

Col pointed to Murgatrude on Antrobus's lap. "Your old love didn't make you do crazy things. I liked your old love better."

Murgatrude stirred, raised his head, and appeared to take an interest in events. Mr. Gibber looked at his pet, then looked quickly away again.

"He rejected me," he said, with a hint of petulance. "He stopped loving me first."

Antrobus rose with Murgatrude in his arms. He toddled across to stand in front of Mr. Gibber. He was holding Murgatrude in such a way as to direct the animal's amber gaze onto the ex-schoolteacher.

Then he took a deep breath. "Have you considered the possibility that your pet may have rejected you only because he observed and morally disapproved of your new attachment?"

While everyone worked out this latest sentence, Mr. Gibber appeared almost transfixed by Murgatrude's eyes.

"In spite of which," Antrobus went on, "being both a loyal and high-minded pet, he kept your secrets and may now be willing to allow you an opportunity to redeem yourself."

Two sentences one after the other had exhausted Antrobus's lungs completely. He leaned forward and deposited Murgatrude in Mr. Gibber's lap, then returned to his place next to Gillabeth.

No one said a word. Murgatrude made himself cozy on Mr. Gibber's lap but continued to stare at his old master with hypnotic intensity. After a while Mr. Gibber reached out, very cautiously, and scratched him gently behind the ears.

50

They stayed in the cage for more than an hour. Col didn't understand, and called up to the red armbands sitting above. "Why are we waiting?"

He received several simultaneous answers, of which one at least was informative.

"Shut up!"

"That's our orders!"

"Until she comes back!"

The rifles angling down through the hatch continued to follow their every move. Col, Riff, and Dunga discussed plans of escape, but they could do nothing as long as the red armbands remained alert. After a while there was nothing left to discuss except their own gloomy fears.

Col turned his attention to another conversation—or half conversation, since it only involved one voice. Mr. Gibber was communicating with his pet.

"Oh, Murgy," he murmured. "Please don't look at me like that."

"What did you expect?"

"Now you're making me feel bad."

Mr. Gibber might have been answering the thoughts in Murgatrude's head. To Col it sounded like the first prickings of conscience.

"I admit I'm not perfect, Murgy."

"She was so beautiful, like a goddess."

"I didn't know, did I?"

Mr. Gibber was now stroking Murgatrude with smooth, pacifying strokes all the way from ears to tail. There were long silences when the conversation lapsed— or perhaps Murgatrude had some very drawn-out thoughts to communicate.

"All right, all right, don't make my life a misery."

"You pushed me to the extreme, Murgy."

"We're both a couple of old has-beens, aren't we?"

Finally Lye reappeared. There was a stir and bustle around the hatch, and she climbed down the ladder into the viewing bay. Three red armbands descended after her, all unarmed. Half a dozen rifles continued to point down from above.

"Stay where you are," she told the prisoners. "This doesn't concern the rest of you. Only *her*."

She crossed the cage and stood before Riff, looking down. The red armbands came up on either side, forming a screen around the two of them. They kicked Col and Dunga out of the way, but Col crept back and peered in around their legs.

"I wanted to talk to you without Shiv," Lye said.

Riff raised an ironic eyebrow. "Behind his back, you mean?"

Lye ignored the question. "So, is this what you wanted?" she asked.

"Seems it's what *you* want."

"No. *No.*" There was a sudden fervor to Lye's tone. Col couldn't see her eyes, but he could tell she'd cast aside her mask of cool composure. "I *never* wanted this. You should have been so much more."

"According to your version of me."

"You've been my guiding light. You *know* you have. You made me believe in something bigger than myself. How can I ever forget? You were so absolute for justice."

Riff shrugged. "So why are you here, really?"

"To give you one last chance. The revolution needs you. I need you. The world needs you."

"What about Shiv?"

"Shiv doesn't matter, not compared to you. I *believe* in you. You can be what you were again. You still have the will and the power and the spirit. You can overcome the weakness."

"What weakness?"

"Emotional weakness."

Riff nodded toward Col, who had been gradually edging farther forward. "You mean him."

Lye looked at Col, and her eyes flashed with hatred. She made no move to strike him, however, nor did she order the red armbands to do it for her. Col drew back his head and continued to observe around their legs.

"Yes, *him.* Your liking for that—that boy—that Swank— has corrupted you. He's dragged you down."

"Because he's a boy? Or because he's a Swank?"

"It's just a dumb itch, that's all. You find him physi-

cally attractive—so what? Pathetic boy-and-girl feelings. You ought to be above all of that."

"Like you."

"A revolutionary leader must be strong and pure.
You're always being distracted by thoughts of him. You
don't see clearly anymore. You let your heart overrule
your head."

Riff affected a yawn. "You've said all of this before,
you know."

"Yes, but now you *have* to listen. Being attracted to
him is an irrelevance." Lye ground her fist into the palm
of her hand. "Crush it out of you."

"And if I don't?"

Lye glared at Riff and continued the crushing gesture.
There was a long silence.

When Riff finally spoke, she jumped to a different
topic. "What about Dunga?"

"What about her?"

"You say the revolution needs me. Doesn't it need
her, too?"

"She's not . . . ," Lye began, then changed her mind.
"Okay, we can arrange it somehow."

Col could see the look of triumph on Lye's face. She
thought she was winning. He thought so too.

"You'll be a leader again," she urged. "We'll lead this
assault on the Russian juggernaut side by side. Surprise
and defeat the Russian imperialists. Then the Austrian
imperialists. Then all imperialists everywhere."

"So long as we get rid of *him*?"

"Yes! Say you will. Say you haven't changed."

"I haven't changed," said Riff.

Lye laughed. "Now we can achieve anything! You and me together. We can make the impossible happen!"

"I haven't changed, because I was never the person you thought I was."

Lye's expression seemed to sag and slip. "What do you mean?"

"I mean you made that person up."

"You won't . . ."

"No."

"That's your choice?"

"You can't blackmail me."

Lye took a moment to recover. Her body was very stiff and very straight. On her mouth was the old drawn-down, pained expression.

When she finally spoke, her tone was cold as ice. "I'll have to be the person you should have been, then."

She turned away and addressed the three red arm-bands in the cage. "You can start lowering now. Her and him first." She redirected her attention to the other red armbands sitting around the hatch above. "Rifles at the ready. Keep them covered at all times."

One of the men in the cage spoke to her. "Do we take off their leg irons first?"

"No."

"But . . ."

"But what?"

"They won't be able to inspect much in their leg irons."

"There's nothing to inspect. The engines are unrepairable."

Mr. Gibber spoke up, or started to speak. "I thought—"

"They're going Below to stay Below," said Lye. "They can all rot down there."

Col gaped. It was a death sentence, then. He had no doubt that Lye would happily get rid of him and his family—but Riff? After all the friendship and devotion and hero worship . . . could it switch across to hatred as instantly as that?

Lye avoided looking at Riff. "You can come with me now," she told Mr. Gibber. "I have to get back to the Grand Assembly Hall."

The three red armbands went across to the lowering tackle and untied the ropes at the side of the cage. Lye mounted the ladder. Mr. Gibber still sat with Murgatrude in his lap.

"All right, all right," he muttered.

It might have been in answer to Lye, but it wasn't. Mr. Gibber was communicating with his pet. Murgatrude broke into a sudden loud purr.

"Hurry up, my little spy," Lye called back down through the hatch.

Mr. Gibber rose with Murgatrude in his arms and headed toward the ladder. His tin remained on the floor of the cage—the tin that contained his collection of Lye's precious strands of hair.

"You've left your . . . ," Col began automatically, then stopped short as he felt something fall in his lap.

Detouring on his way to the ladder, Mr. Gibber had dropped some small shiny object in Col's lap. It was the key he had used to unlock his leg irons!

51

Col stared. Just because the key worked for Mr. Gibber's leg irons didn't mean it would work for anyone else's. But if Mr. Gibber thought it might . . .

Before he could gather it up, Riff's hand flashed across and grabbed it.

"Let me try," she hissed.

She bent forward and inserted the key into the cuff on her right ankle—it went in. She rotated it—and there was the faintest click as the cuff came unlocked.

Meanwhile the red armbands were still readying the tackle. A ratchet made a clacking sound as they hauled on the pulley system. One vertical rope moved up and the other down, bringing into sight a series of dangling loops.

Riff unlocked her cuffs but didn't pull them open. She completed the operation just as the red armbands completed theirs. One of them swung round and came across to Col and Riff.

"Me first," said Riff.

She rose to her feet, half turning to Col.

"Bye," she said, and gave him a farewell handshake. Under her breath she added, "Wait till I give the word, then start fighting."

It wasn't only a handshake. Col felt the cold metal

of the key pressed into his palm, and closed his fingers around it.

The two red armbands gripped Riff by the shoulder and escorted her to the open door at the side of the viewing bay. She moved in tiny steps with her ankles close together, so the cuffs wouldn't fall off by accident. Her escort pushed her toward the vertical ropes.

"Feet in the loop."

"I know what to do."

Col waited until all three red armbands were focused on getting Riff's feet into the loop. Then he inserted the key into the keyhole of his left cuff. One twist and a click. He did as Riff had done, leaving the cuff unlocked but closed.

As the red armbands paid out rope through the pulley, Riff descended a foot at a time. *Clack-clack-clack-clack* went the ratchet.

Col unlocked the cuff on his right ankle.

Then the ratchet stopped. Riff had disappeared below the level of the viewing bay's wire floor. Another loop in the rope awaited, dangling just outside the open door.

One of the red armbands came across to him. "You next."

Col copied Riff's tiny steps. He would have passed the key to Dunga or Gillabeth if he'd had time—but his father was closest. He flipped the key to Orris out of the back of his hand.

There was no clatter, so the key must have landed in his father's lap. But would Orris work out what to do with it?

"Feet in the loop," said a voice.

Col stood on the sill of the open door. Looking down past the loop, he could see Riff on the rope six feet below. She was a mere vague shape in the obscuring steam.

"Feet in the loop!"

A thump on his shoulders propelled him out through the door so that he had no choice but to grab onto the rope with both hands. He swung his feet forward, ankles together, and slipped them into the loop.

When would Riff give the word? How much longer? What was the plan?

"Lower away!"

With the first clack of the ratchet Col dropped a foot, then jolted to a halt. Then another clack, another drop, another jolt.

Clack-clack-clack-clack!

The red armbands went past in front of his eyes: waist-level, knee-level, foot-level.

"Now!" shouted Riff.

He let go of the rope and leaned forward just in time to get his elbows in over the floor of the cage. He seized hold of the nearest ankle of the nearest red armband.

Instant uproar! The red armband whose ankle he'd seized tried to pull away, but Col hung on ferociously. All three of them were shouting, all trying to kick at his hands.

In one corner of his mind he registered that the rope below his feet had started to swing back and forth.

Someone changed from kicking at his hands to

kicking at his head. A blow to the cheek rocked him back and almost dislocated his neck. Then someone's heel ground down on his wrists. He lost his grip and started to slide.

He was almost out of the cage when he managed to catch onto the sill.

The swinging rope below twisted him this way and that, making it even harder to hang on. He threaded his fingers in through the wire. But now someone was kicking at the wire from the other side.

One moment his fingers were on fire with the pain; the next moment they were numb and dead. He could no longer feel to hang on. . . .

He lost his grip on the cage and missed catching hold of the rope—any rope. He fell backward in the void, cartwheeling through a hundred and eighty degrees.

Only the loop saved him. Upright, he had been standing on the soles of his feet, but as he fell backward, his feet slipped in through the loop. When he reached the bottom of his arc, the loop tightened around his ankles and jerked him to a stop, upside down.

It felt as though his joints were being wrenched apart. The blood rushed like an explosion to his head, and for a moment everything blanked out.

He came back to the world with his head hanging down in the steam. Riff should have been below him, but so far as he could see, she wasn't. Just the rope, swinging loosely from side to side.

The ratchet clacked, then clacked again. He

descended headfirst, a foot at a time. The sounds from the viewing bay seemed strangely far away: voices of the red armbands yelling orders.

He twisted his neck to look up, and gasped. He was now about ten feet below the floor of the viewing bay—and there was Riff, clinging with fingers and toes to the underside of the wire! Riff the acrobat! While he had been fighting and distracting the red armbands, she must have swung through the air and flung herself across from rope to cage.

She looked down and saw him looking up. She detached one hand from the wire and pointed to the open door at the side of the cage. Then, like a spider on a ceiling, she began making her way toward it. She was going to take the red armbands by surprise.

Col wished he could be part of the plan, instead of dropping farther away with every clack of the ratchet. The steam rose around him until he could no longer see Riff or the underside of the cage. He released his aching neck muscles and let his head dangle.

From above he heard a sudden outburst of shrilling and screeching. Surely that was his mother? What was happening?

The feeling had returned to his fingers, enough to take a grip on the rope. Hand over hand, he began hauling himself right way up. The leg irons had slipped from his ankles in the violence of the fighting.

"Aaagh!" Another scream from above—a male voice this time.

He sensed rather than saw the flailing body as it fell
and struck him a glancing blow on the way down. He lost
his grip and dropped headfirst, until his feet in the loop
jerked him to a halt once again. The body continued to
fall, vanishing into the steam with a despairing wail.

Was it one of the red armbands? Riff's doing? He had
no time to think about it, because suddenly the ratchet
went crazy.

Clacker-clacker-clacker-clacker-clacker-clacker-clacker-
clacker-clacker-clacker . . .

No one was holding on to the control rope! Col plummeted faster and faster, down, down, down.

He plunged through dank clouds of steam. The
counterweight flew up on the other vertical rope and
missed him by inches. He wrapped his arms over his
head, but at the speed he was dropping, it wouldn't
make much difference.

He glimpsed great shapes of machinery rushing up
all around. When he hit the bottom, when he smashed
headfirst into—

But he didn't. Instead he came to a sudden stop. For
the second time the deceleration almost wrenched his
joints apart.

He must have fallen a hundred feet or more. Upside
down on the rope, he hung suspended and slowly rotating. Nothing else happened.

His legs ached; his fingers throbbed; his whole body
was a mass of many pains. On one side he saw the vast
cylindrical shadow of what might have been a boiler; on

the other side, what looked like a series of ascending ladders. Unfortunately, the ladders were out of reach.

The machinery down here was motionless and silent, but a new sound had started up above. Col heard it faintly yet distinctly: the crack of rifle fire. There were half a dozen shots in rapid succession, followed by a lull, then more shots and another lull.

What did it mean? He could only hope and pray.

After a while the shooting stopped altogether. Col remained dangling and rotating for several minutes. Then he felt a tug on his legs. At last! A tug and a pause. A tug and a pause. Someone was pulling the rope back up!

52

The ascent seemed to take ages. By the time he approached the viewing bay, Col had managed to haul himself right way up, standing with his feet on rather than through the loop. Inside the cage three figures were working the ropes. Gillabeth was doing most of the pulling, with help from Quinnea and Sephaltina.

The only other people in the cage were stretched out on the floor—five red armbands. Three were bound hand and foot; the other two appeared to be either dead or unconscious.

Col clambered in over the sill of the open door.

"My husband!" cried Sephaltina, and sprang forward with outspread arms. She reached up on tiptoe and kissed him on the cheek.

Col was astonished—and perhaps Sephaltina was a little surprised at herself. "I thought you might be dead down there," she said. "I'm so glad you're alive."

She spoke shyly, but in a more natural tone than Col had ever heard before. For once her sweetness didn't set his teeth on edge. But there was no time to think about it now.

"Where are Riff and the rest?" he asked.

It was Gillabeth who replied. "Up on Bottom Deck, unshackling the other prisoners."

"We won?"

"You should've seen us!" Quinnea jumped in, a flush of excitement on her normally bloodless cheeks. "The red armbands tried to lower me after you, but I wouldn't go. I had a panic attack."

"That's a good thing?" Col didn't understand the pride in her voice.

"Yes, because I was flapping and fussing so much the red armbands couldn't catch hold of me. I made a distraction. And they couldn't work out how I'd escaped from my leg irons."

"Father used the key, then passed it to Mother," Gillabeth explained. "She passed it to Dunga, then Dunga to me."

Quinnea rattled on. "So I made a distraction, and that girl Filthy came in through the door and attacked the red armbands from behind."

"Riff," said Gillabeth.

"Yes, yes. Punching and kicking and dancing around so fast you could hardly see her. Then the other Filthy joined in too."

Again Gillabeth supplied the name. "Dunga."

Col had seen Riff in action and knew all about the Filthies' hand-to-hand fighting skills. "But what about the rifles? I heard shooting."

He indicated the hatch at the top of the ladder, and Gillabeth nodded.

"The other red armbands were still up there," she said. "They didn't realize what was happening at first. By the time they started shooting, it was so confused they couldn't tell who was who."

"I got shot," said Sephaltina, and lifted a corner of her wedding dress to display the bullet hole. "Right through my dress."

"They shot one of their own, too." Gillabeth pointed with her foot at one of the motionless bodies on the floor of the cage. "Then—"

"Let me tell it!" cried Quinnea. "I thought of it first! They were sitting round the hatch with their legs dangling down, so I reached up and got hold of a foot and pulled!"

She clapped her hands with delight. Col struggled to adjust to this new side of his mother's personality.

"Yes, she pulled the first one down, and his rifle with him." Even Gillabeth had a smile on her face. "We all copied her and did the same. We grabbed the rifles off them before they knew what was happening. Then Riff gave them a chance to surrender, and they did. Except for the ones who ran off on Bottom Deck."

"Is that where she is now?" Col took a step toward the ladder.

Gillabeth nodded. "Riff and Dunga and Father took the captured rifles and went up to Bottom Deck. Antrobus, too. There was no more shooting, though. We stayed behind to raise the rope."

"Let's go see," said Col.

He led the way up the ladder. At first glance Bottom Deck appeared exactly as it had appeared before: quiet and cavernous, with scattered pools of blue-white light.

But when he looked along to the prisoners, they no longer formed a queue. They were moving freely about, rub-
bing their ankles. He breathed a sigh of relief.

Other figures stood around too: Filthies in undershirts, talking with the prisoners. Obviously, Lye's labor
force must have changed sides and turned against the
red armbands. From what Dunga had said, they had no
reasons for loyalty.

Emerging from the hatch and striding forward, Col
saw Riff and Dunga unlocking the last of the leg irons
with Mr. Gibber's key. Farther along, his father with a
rifle stood guard over a couple of red armbands.

A tug on his sleeve brought him to a halt. It was his
baby brother, appearing suddenly out of the shadows.

"What is it, Antrobus?"

Antrobus pointed to a sign that hung from a cordon
between two nearby piers.

KEEP OUTSIDE THE ROPES

Gillabeth, Quinnea, and Sephaltina caught up and
gathered around.

"What's so important about a sign, Antrobus?" Gillabeth asked. "We've seen dozens like that. Mr. Gibber
wrote them."

Antrobus seemed to swell as he prepared for one of
his long, grammatically perfect sentences.

"Since Mr. Gibber served as Lye's writer, might she
not also have ordered him to produce the note that was

pinned to the door of the barracks in Botany Bay?"

Col frowned and looked at his sister. Gillabeth pursed her lips.

"'You die tomorrow. Attack at dawn.'" Col recited the words. "But who would've pinned it to the door? Not Mr. Gibber."

"Lye herself," said Gillabeth.

"You think she had time before the attack?"

Gillabeth nodded. "It wouldn't have taken long. She could have gone down in a scoop while everyone was getting prepared."

"I saw her," said Sephaltina suddenly.

"What?"

"I saw her go down in a scoop."

Col stared into Sephaltina's wide, guileless eyes. "You *said* you'd seen her before."

"Why were you there?" asked Gillabeth.

"I wanted something to smash. I looked at the cranes, but they were too difficult. Then I saw someone go to operate the crane controls."

"Who?"

Sephaltina shrugged.

"Not Lye, then," said Gillabeth.

"Perhaps Shiv," said Col.

"Then *she* climbed into the scoop," Sephaltina went on. "With her pale face and black, black hair."

Another voice broke in. "What's this?"

Riff came forward into the group, with Dunga behind her. They must have finished freeing the prisoners.

Col explained Antrobus's theory and Sephaltina's evidence. Riff wasn't immediately convinced.

"Why would Lye betray our attack? She hates the imperialists more than anyone."

"I can think of a motive," said Gillabeth.

She seemed very certain about it. Col had no idea what Lye's motive could have been.

"We need to find Mr. Gibber," he said. "If we can get *him* to admit he wrote the note . . ."

"He's probably still with Lye," said Dunga.

"And Lye will be at the trial," added Riff.

Col had forgotten all about the trial. "Right. They were taking Victoria and Albert away to be tried, weren't they?"

"What for?" asked Quinnea. "What will they do to them?"

Col didn't know, but a sudden sense of foreboding gripped his guts. "Didn't Lye say she had to get back to the Grand Assembly Hall?"

"Obvious place to hold a trial," said Gillabeth.

"They'll all be there," said Dunga.

"It's now or never," said Riff.

"Win or lose," said Gillabeth.

"Let's go," said Col.

53

They went up by steam elevator: Riff and Dunga, Orris and Gillabeth, Col and Sephaltina. Sephaltina insisted on accompanying her husband, which was fortunate, because they needed her to present her evidence in person. She was the only one not carrying a rifle. Antrobus and Quinnea had been left behind.

Gillabeth made a useful suggestion on the way up. "I know a special side entry into the Grand Assembly Hall, if we want to sneak in at the front."

Everyone agreed. They had no definite plan except to stage a confrontation and exploit their advantage of surprise. Still, it was better to sneak in at the front than get stuck at the back of the crowd.

Gillabeth led them by way of tunnel-like service corridors and dimly lit storerooms. Col could imagine how Menials had once shuffled along these passages, wheeling trolleys, carrying food and drink. One storeroom was filled with unwanted urns and statues from the time of the old regime; another was packed with flags and banners bearing the imperial initials, v & a.

Finally Gillabeth halted them at a closed door. On the other side they could hear a voice declaiming and the background murmur of a large crowd.

"The Grand Assembly Hall?" Col asked in a whisper.

Gillabeth nodded. "The trial's already begun."

"Sounds like Lye's voice," growled Dunga.

Gillabeth turned the handle and pushed the door a fraction ajar. Everyone craned forward to peer through the crack.

There was little to see, but enough for Col to get his bearings. This door was on the right side of the hall, and their view through the crack angled toward the wall behind the speakers. They could hear Lye, but they couldn't see her.

"All done in her name," she was saying. "All that we suffered, every death and disfigurement. None of it could have happened without Queen Victoria's stamp of approval. There was a chain of command, and she was at the top."

Gillabeth pushed the door a fraction wider. Now they could see a raised dais that had been set up at the front of the hall. To Col it looked very much like the one on which the band had played at his wedding reception. Shiv sat on the dais behind a table, and appeared to have taken on the role of presiding judge. Victoria and Albert stood in shackles alongside.

"And all of you others from Botany Bay." Now Lye was addressing the convicts. "To whom did your governor owe ultimate allegiance? Who founded the original colony? The system of tyranny began with the British Empire. And this woman *is* the British Empire."

Gillabeth kept opening the door until they could see as far as the front of the crowd. With all attention focused on Lye, nobody noticed the widening crack.

"Where's Mr. Gibber?" muttered Riff.

"Could be further back." Col indicated the stacks of folded tables that blocked their view.

"We have to be sure," whispered Gillabeth.

Lye was pacing about before the dais, swinging her arms as she spoke. Padder and Gansy stood a little farther along, looking very ill at ease.

"You've heard that this ex-queen is pregnant," Lye went on. "Does that incline you to mercy? But what mercy can *we* expect from the Russians? I say it's too late for mercy. Now is the time for justice. She must pay with her life, and her consort with her."

If anyone in the crowd put a higher value on mercy, they didn't say so.

Only Gansy raised an objection. "Why now? If now is the time for justice, why wasn't it time three months ago?"

"Because now we *must* have total commitment!" Lye raised her voice. "Before we launch our assault! When we execute these two, we reject the old ways forever! No reservations, no going back!"

Col eyed the stacks of folded tables. What blocked their view also hid them from view. If he could creep up behind the folded tables, he could scan for Mr. Gibber in the crowd.

Out in the hall Victoria cleared her throat. "Am I allowed to speak?" she asked Shiv.

"Are you allowed to speak?" Shiv exchanged glances

with Lye, who gave the tiniest shrug of indifference. "Yes, I'll allow that."

Victoria stood facing the crowd, all eyes upon her. Now was as good a moment as any for Col. He lowered his rifle and left it on the ground.

"I'm going to take a look," he whispered.

He crouched down low, gave the door an extra push, and slipped through. If anyone at the front of the crowd had glanced toward his side of the hall, they would easily have spotted him. But no one did. He scurried across the floor and into the shadow of the stacked tables.

"I never wanted to be queen," Victoria was saying. "And I know Albert didn't marry me to become prince consort. We were only ever figureheads, and we never enjoyed it. We like it much more being ordinary people."

Albert snorted agreement. "The Liberation was the best thing that ever happened to us."

"We want to be an ordinary mother and father." Victoria touched a hand to her visibly swelling belly. "And Henry—or Henrietta—will be our beloved child. We promise to live quietly and not be a trouble to anyone."

Narrow channels separated the stacks of folded tables. Col squeezed his way forward in one channel, and peeped out.

"Ordinariness isn't a possibility for you," Lye answered Victoria. "You are what you represent. What you represent is a line of tyrants."

The crowd was mostly made up of red armbands, about a third of them wearing the brown, numbered uniforms of Botany Bay convicts. Even among the Filthies few faces were familiar to Col. But there was Mr. Gibber—not standing with the crowd, but lurking behind one of the marble columns. He was at the side and near the front, not far from Col.

"Your unborn child represents the same." Lye went on with her harangue. "The continuation of the line. An ongoing tradition of injustice. It represents a potential future of suffering for us."

Col doubled back in the channel between the stacks, looked toward the door, and gave a thumbs-up. He couldn't see faces in the crack, only a space of darkness. Hopefully, they had observed his signal.

"That's not fair!" Albert spluttered with indignation. "You can't say that about an innocent child!"

Lye sneered. "What do *you* know about fairness? You don't have the right to talk about justice."

"Maybe not!" The door swung open, and Riff marched out. "But *I* do!"

54

Behind Riff marched Dunga, then Gillabeth, then Orris, then Sephaltina. They were all unarmed.

The crowd was shocked into silence—but not immobility. As Col sprang to his feet and stepped forward to stand with the others, the only sound was the raising of rifles, the clicking of safety catches. Dozens of barrels were trained upon them.

Lye was beyond words, blazing with fury. Riff confronted her, eyeball to eyeball.

"You like to talk about justice," she snapped, "but only for other people. You're the one who should be judged and punished for what you've done."

Shiv recovered the power of speech before Lye. "What are you doing here? You've been convicted, all of you. You were sent down as prisoners."

"Yes, and when we were down there, we found a whole lot of other prisoners." Riff swung to face the crowd. "People who'd never been convicted. Shiv and Lye's hidden prisoners."

"Only Swanks," said Shiv.

"No," said Dunga, stepping forward. "I was one of them."

There was a murmur of amazement as the crowd

focused on Dunga. "A Council member?" "What crime?" "I thought she was injured."

Then Padder spoke up. "I don't understand. What are you doing here, Dunga? Where have you been?"

"I've been tied to a bed and wrapped up in bandages. On their orders. Ask them why."

Gansy turned to Shiv and Lye. "Why?"

Again it was Shiv who answered. "She needed time to heal properly. We had to keep her still, or she'd have reopened her wounds."

"Do I look as if I needed time to heal?" Dunga demonstrated with a whirl of her arms and a kick of her legs. "They wanted to keep me from voting at Council meetings."

"You recovered eventually," said Shiv. "Thanks to our care. Then you volunteered to go Below and inspect the engines."

"Not true!" Dunga barked. "You planned for us all to die down there!"

"Enough!" Lye cut in suddenly. "No one believes you." She appealed to the crowd. "It's nonsense. Does anyone believe we would actually try to kill a Council member just to keep her from voting?"

There were scattered cries of "No!" and a general shaking of heads. The idea was too much for anyone to swallow.

"Shall we send the prisoners down again?" Lye asked.

More shaking of heads. The crowd didn't believe Dunga, yet they didn't totally disbelieve her either.

"Not including Dunga, of course," said Shiv.

Still the crowd wavered. Col exchanged glances with Riff. It was time to move on to the most telling accusation.

He stepped forward. "That's not all. Lye and Shiv have committed a crime against everyone on board this juggernaut."

"This is stupid," snarled Shiv. "We're not the ones on trial here. I won't allow it."

Col hurried on regardless. The red armbands at the front of the crowd had lowered their rifles and showed no inclination to use them.

"Remember the ambush at Botany Bay? When our attack was betrayed because someone wrote a warning note and pinned it on the door of their barracks? We know who wrote that note—and it wasn't the saboteur."

He was aware of the risk he was taking. He hadn't said "we suspect" but "we know." Lye and Shiv didn't appear worried; the expressions on their faces conveyed only scorn.

"Not Lye and Shiv?" said Padder. "You can't be accusing them?"

"Yes," said Riff firmly.

Lye laughed outright, and there were a few titters from the crowd. But everyone was still listening, still waiting for further developments.

"Why would Lye and Shiv betray our attack?" Gansy asked. "They hate the imperialists more than anyone."

Col and Riff looked to Gillabeth—and she didn't let them down.

"*Because* they hate the imperialists so much," she said. "By warning the enemy, they turned a secret raid into a full-scale battle. They needed people to die on our side so that everyone would hate the imperialists as much as they do."

"Right." Suddenly it all made perfect sense to Col. "It was supposed to be an attack without bloodshed. Take hostages and force the imperialists to supply us with coal. But Lye and Shiv wanted more than that."

"They probably never expected so many deaths," said Gillabeth. "But they were willing to sacrifice lives in order to drive everyone to extremes."

The expression of contempt had frozen on Lye's lips. Shiv glared.

"You've forgotten one thing," he said.

Riff took the lead again. "You think so? Are you going to say you couldn't have written the note, because Filthies can't write?"

Shiv's mouth opened and closed. Obviously, that was exactly what he had been going to say.

"We're not accusing *you* of writing the note," Riff went on. "We're not accusing *her* of writing it either. We're accusing her of ordering *him* to write it." She pointed. "Come forward, Mr. Gibber."

Mr. Gibber was most reluctant to come forward. He seemed to be trying to make himself invisible in the shadow of the column.

"Come forward, Lye's little helper."

With every eye upon him Mr. Gibber had no option.

He came out in front of the crowd and stood looking at his feet. Riff propelled him farther on toward the dais.

"Stand up there," she said. "We want everyone to see and hear you."

Mumbling to himself, Mr. Gibber stepped up next to Shiv's table, alongside Victoria and Albert.

"Speak out loud and clear, Mr. Gibber. You wrote those signs on Bottom Deck, didn't you?"

Mr. Gibber's eyes flicked toward Lye, then back to Riff. "Yes."

"You do all the writing for Lye?"

"Yes."

"And you'd do anything for her? Whatever she asked?"

"Yes."

"So you'd write a note if she asked you to?"

"Yes."

"'You die tomorrow. Attack at dawn.' What about that?"

"What about it?"

"You wrote those words under Lye's instructions?"

Mr. Gibber shuffled his feet, licked his lips, and grimaced as though he'd just swallowed a nasty taste. Everything about his demeanor showed that their deduction was correct.

Lye tossed her head and cried out in a loud voice, "Tell the truth, Mr. Gibber!"

Col understood what she was doing. She didn't want the truth, only *her* truth. She was trying to re-establish dominance over her devoted worshipper.

Mr. Gibber's lips moved, but nothing came out. Col wished that Murgatrude could have been there. Without the influence of his pet, Mr. Gibber was falling back under Lye's influence.

"Tell the truth, Mr. Gibber!" she called out again.

"I don't remember," he said at last.

"You wrote those words for Lye," Riff insisted.

"I don't remember."

It was so obvious, yet he wouldn't confess it. He looked like a trapped rat.

Gansy spoke to Riff, sounding almost apologetic. "We need more evidence than this. I still can't believe it."

"Nor me," agreed Padder.

"No?" Riff remained undaunted. "Okay. Stand down, Mr. Gibber."

Mr. Gibber didn't have to be told twice. He jumped down from the dais, smirking with relief.

"Come forward, Sephaltina," Riff called.

Sephaltina performed a tiny bobbing curtsy and came forward.

The crowd was baffled. "Who's this?"

"This is our next witness," said Riff.

"It's the saboteur!" cried Lye. "The wife of Colbert Porpentine! The saboteur!"

The crowd responded with angry hisses. White spots of rage had appeared on Lye's cheeks.

"Stand up on the dais, Sephaltina," said Riff.

Sephaltina mounted the dais and faced the crowd, oblivious to their hostility. She had her hands clasped before her and the most demure expression on her rose-bud lips. Col was reminded of their wedding ceremony—she seemed ready to say "I do" all over again.

"Now, Sephaltina." Riff's tone was stern and serious. "You have owned up to many acts of sabotage."

Sephaltina smiled prettily. "Yes."

"It was you who smashed the wireless telegraph offices?"

"Yes."

"And you wanted to do something to the cranes? You went to look at them?"

"Yes."

"When?"

"I don't remember times."

"Was it at night?"

"Yes."

"Was it when we were at the coaling station?"

"What's a coaling station?"

"Mountains of coal. Huge metal structures."

"I remember. Yes, that's where."

"Did you see someone going down in a scoop?"

"Yes."

"All by herself in the middle of the night?"

Sephaltina pointed at Lye. "Her."

There was absolute silence all around the hall.

"She's making it up," said Lye automatically.

"Oh, no," Sephaltina simpered. "I was brought up to always tell the truth. You went down in a scoop and came back up half an hour later."

Although her smile was too sweet and her voice too sugary, Sephaltina had a childish simplicity that was somehow hard to doubt.

"That's . . . it's . . ." Lye appealed to the crowd. "This girl is the saboteur. You can't believe anything she says. She should have been executed long ago."

The crowd broke into an excited clamor, all talking and arguing at once. It was impossible to tell whose side they were on.

Lye advanced toward the dais. Sephaltina took a backward step and bumped into Shiv's table. Lye sliced the air with the side of her hand.

"She should be executed!" she hissed. "I say, put her to death *right now!*"

At her words Shiv rose from his chair and reached in under his undershirt. His hand came out holding the long-bladed knife with the pearl handle. He stepped forward around the table and stabbed Sephaltina in the throat.

55

Sephaltina's mouth was an O of amazement as red blood ran down her neck and spread out over her chest. When Shiv drew out the knife, she staggered sideways, held on to the table for a moment, then sank with a soft swish to the dais.

Shiv looked down at her. Even he seemed shocked by what he had done. "I think she's dead," he muttered.

Voices spoke up here and there in the crowd.

"He killed her," someone said.

"Murdered her," said someone else.

Shiv dropped his knife on the table as if it were burning hot. "I executed her," he said.

"No, murdered her," the second voice said again.

Shiv flinched, and his eyes darted in every direction. "She was the saboteur. She deserved to die."

"He did it to shut her up," a third voice said.

"Because of what she was saying."

"They didn't want us to hear."

The crowd was turning against Shiv and Lye. One woman reached up, pulled the red armband from her arm, and flung it to the floor.

"That's what I think," she said.

Watching the crowd, Lye had swung away from Shiv.

"She should've been executed long ago." Shiv

repeated her phrase. "Someone had to do it."

More and more people in the crowd began tearing off their red armbands, throwing them to the floor. Shiv stared at Lye's back.

"You said it." A note of desperation had crept into his voice. He was almost pleading for Lye's endorsement.

When Lye turned to respond, her face was cold and expressionless. "I didn't say to do *that*."

Shiv stared at her in growing horror. "'Put her to death right now,'" he quoted.

Lye shook her head. "Not before a proper vote of the meeting. Not with a knife."

All movement in the hall had ceased, even the removal of armbands. Everyone looked from Shiv to Lye and back again.

"Don't do this," said Shiv.

"You went too far," said Lye.

"You *need* me. You and me together."

Lye shook her head. "You always went too far."

"Only by your instructions."

It had become a battle of wills. Lye was glaring at Shiv, trying to dominate him as she had dominated Mr. Gibber. But Shiv wouldn't be dominated, not this time.

"I won't be tossed aside," he said. "I *won't*."

"Be quiet."

"I'll toss you aside first."

"You wouldn't dare."

"Watch me."

Their eyes were locked on each other as though

nobody else in the hall existed. Then Shiv broke eye contact and turned to the crowd.

"This wasn't the first killing I did for her," he said.

"Be *quiet!*" hissed Lye.

Shiv's eyes glittered with a perverse kind of triumph. "I killed Zeb for her," he announced.

"I . . . it wasn't . . ."

"You and me together." Shiv couldn't stop himself now. "We talked about it. She was determined to be elected onto the Council, and there was only one sure way to create a vacancy."

"You did it. You swung the wrench. I wasn't even there at the time."

"No, but you planted the idea in my head and made it grow."

"That's not true. You wanted to change the balance of Council votes in your favor. You did it for your own sake."

"My sake? You think I care about *my* sake? You know I only care about us."

Padder broke in. "So you were investigating a murder you committed yourself?" He stared at Shiv, goggle-eyed.

"*We* committed." Shiv didn't so much as glance in Padder's direction. "She helped afterward, too. She had the idea of blaming the saboteur. She was the one who unscrewed the nuts and bolts on the elevator to make it look like an interrupted act of sabotage. I couldn't do it, I was shaking too much." Shiv held out his trembling arm. "Same as I'm shaking now."

Then something in Lye snapped.

"You *weakling!*" she spat at him. "You never cared about the revolution. You'd never sacrifice anything for the cause."

"I sacrificed everything for *us,*" said Shiv in a bare whisper.

"Then you're a fool as well as a weakling. There never was any *us.* Just feeble little dreams in your feeble male head."

The Filthies in the crowd had had enough—and the convicts too.

"They're both mad!"

"To kill someone just for a place on the Council!"

"Monsters!"

"Each as bad as the other."

Now they were stripping off red armbands as though the fabric were infected with disease.

"I won't be a part of this."

"Not what we joined up for."

Lye scanned the hall defiantly. She had never looked more beautiful: mouth drawn down, nostrils flaring, cheekbones like cut glass.

"You don't *deserve* this revolution!" she cried.

But she didn't go on. The crowd's hostility was as palpable as heat, beating against her.

"Cowards," she muttered

She sprang across to the nearest convict and wrested his rifle from him before he knew what was happening. She swung the barrel toward the crowd.

"No!" warned Riff. "You shoot and you're dead!"

Filthies and convicts were already raising their rifles. Lye's mouth tightened.

"I'm dead anyway," she said.

She redirected her aim—at Victoria. Victoria closed her eyes; Albert made a move to step in front of her.

But now Lye's rifle was swinging again. This time it picked out Shiv.

"You come with me," she commanded.

Amazingly, he obeyed. He stepped around Sephaltina's body and came down from the dais. Then Lye spotted Mr. Gibber lurking nearby.

"You too, my little spy." She gestured with her rifle. "We're leaving."

She herded her collaborators at rifle point toward the doors at the back of the hall. When one Filthy tried to block their way, she curled her lip and aimed her rifle at his head.

"You want more deaths?"

The events of the last few minutes had left everyone stunned. Nobody wanted more deaths. The crowd parted and let them through.

"They're dangerous!" Col shouted. "Don't let them—"

He was about to add "get away," when a new drama distracted him. Riff had jumped up on the dais and was kneeling beside Sephaltina's body. She held Sephaltina's wrist with one hand while bringing her ear very close to Sephaltina's mouth.

"Not dead!" She lifted her head and sang out. "She still has a pulse! She's still breathing!"

56

Col was the first to rush up, then Dunga and Gillabeth and a number of Filthies from the front of the hall. In no time at all the dais was packed with would-be helpers.

Riff rose to her feet and appealed to the crowd. "Someone with medical skills! Is Elber here? Or Hatta? Or Shayle?"

"Hatta is."

"I'm coming."

Hatta was a young woman with a raw, red complexion and a patch over one eye. She shouldered her way through the throng and mounted the dais.

"Give her air!" she ordered, and began whirling her arms like a windmill. "Stand back! Make room! Shoo! Go on! Further! Right off the dais!"

Col retreated with the rest. He had seen the dreadful gash in Sephaltina's throat, and the blood bubbling out. Had the blade severed an artery?

Hatta seemed to know exactly what she was doing. She demanded towels, clean strips of cloth, and some form of alcohol, and immediately Gillabeth hurried off to search. When it came to finding anything anywhere in the juggernaut, Gillabeth also knew exactly what she was doing.

Hatta wanted only one assistant, and that was Riff.

Col watched and waited, feeling useless. The hall buzzed with a hundred animated conversations, but he took no part in them.

When Gillabeth returned with towels, cloth, and alcohol, Hatta and Riff busied themselves over the prone body of the victim. At one stage Sephaltina gasped and whimpered; a little later she fell very quiet. After ten minutes Hatta sat back and wiped her hands on a towel.

"That's all we can do for now," she said.

Riff also wiped her hands, then rose to her feet. Col wanted to ask about Sephaltina's chances, but before he could attract Riff's attention, there was a disturbance at the back of the hall.

"Let me through! I need a member of the Council!"

Someone was pushing forward, shouting at the top of his voice. Riff looked out to the source of the disturbance.

"What is it, Gart?"

"Come quick! Tell us what to do!"

"Is it Lye?"

"Yes."

Riff jumped down from the dais and ran for the back of the hall, weaving a way through the crowd. Col took advantage of the channel she created, and ran after her.

The Filthy who had shouted was probably the only person in the hall still wearing a red armband. He hardly waited for Riff to arrive before he turned and sped off.

He headed for the nearest elevator. Riff followed him and Col followed her—diving onto the platform only just in time. Gart pulled the lever, and the platform rose up amid clouds of steam.

Gart had a shaved bullethead and grizzled chin. He paid no attention to Col at first, but addressed himself to Riff.

"She said it's time to start the assault."

"Lye?"

"Yes. With Shiv and some old Swank. It's crazy. There's only the three of them. Where's the proper assault force? We're nowhere near ready. Most of the teams are still building their catapults."

"Catapults?" asked Col. "What catapults?"

Gart stared at him suspiciously. "Who—?"

"He's okay." Riff spoke up for him. "What catapults?"

"You don't know?"

"I've been busy. Is this the airborne assault?"

"Yes. The catapults to shoot the grappling hooks across. Lye and Shiv wanted fifty built, but we've only finished five so far. You have to stop them. You have to stop *her*."

Riff chewed her lip and said nothing. The elevator continued to rise past deck after deck.

"How high are we going?" asked Col.

Gart seemed to have overcome his suspicion. "Fifty-third Deck," he answered. "The catapults are on the terrace under the funnels."

They came out at the top of the elevator and followed Gart through one corridor after another. This part of the juggernaut was new to Col; he had never explored it even after the Liberation. There were many blank gray doors of what looked like offices or wardrooms.

Then Gart stopped and opened a more solid-looking door. Col blinked in the sudden hazy sunlight. It was like stepping out onto the platform above the bridge, except that here they were at the side rather than the front of the superstructure.

There was no solid barrier, only a succession of descending terraces with railings at the front. Rows of white-painted, hornlike pipes stuck up on every terrace—ventilation ducts, presumably. Above their heads towered the black cylindrical shape of one of *Liberator*'s immense funnels. Aft of that was another funnel leaning ten degrees out of the vertical; aft again was the funnel that had collapsed in the collision. Crumpled sheets of curved metal splayed in all directions like a crushed black flower.

"They've started!" Gart cried, pointing.

Col followed the line of his arm and saw two parallel ropes that arced from *Liberator* to the Russian juggernaut. The grappling hook had already been fired across, and had snagged successfully in the *Romanov*'s masts and wires.

Gart set off running along the uppermost terrace, with Riff and Col at his heels. They passed a number of unfinished metal constructions hidden behind tarpaulins that had been thrown over the railings. Groups of Filthies crouched around the constructions; at present they had all stopped work to watch what was happening.

Three figures came into view, moving slowly along

the ropes. The ropes were about half a yard apart, and each figure balanced with a foot on either rope. Mr. Gibber was at the front, then Shiv, then Lye. Lye kept her rifle trained on the other two.

"Too late," groaned Gart, and eased his pace.

By the time they came up to the catapult, the trio was thirty paces away, suspended over the void. Five Filthies stood watching them go, one a muscular, sandy-haired woman with a red armband.

"Why didn't you wait?" Gart demanded. "I said to stall her till I got back."

The sandy-haired woman shrugged. "She wouldn't be stalled. You didn't expect us to shoot a Council member, did you?"

Mr. Gibber advanced in a monkeylike crouch, sliding one foot forward at a time, often wobbling but never quite falling. By contrast Lye and Shiv possessed the acrobatic skills that all Filthies had acquired for survival Below. Lye had no difficulty maintaining her balance while carrying the rifle. However, she seemed somehow different in her way of moving, though Col couldn't work out why.

"That's not how it was supposed to work." Gart shook his head. "Not walking on top of the ropes."

Col looked at him in silent interrogation.

"The proper assault force would have used slings," Gart explained. "Sitting under the ropes and sliding across."

"Except we don't have the slings yet," added the sandy-haired woman.

Col understood the idea. Because the catapults were

being built on the uppermost terrace, the ropes sloped down to the Russian juggernaut at a slight angle. The assault force could have slid down in slings.

He looked at the catapult directly in front of him. It was a clever piece of construction, a giant bow welded from lengths of flexible metal. On either side it was fixed and braced against two of the projecting hornlike pipes.

Then he spotted something else on the ground nearby: an odd-looking bundle of cream-colored fabric.

"What's that?" he asked.

It was the sandy-haired woman who replied. "Something she wore. She stripped it off. I don't know why."

Col picked up the garment. The stiff material was fastened with laces and reinforced with whalebone ribs.

"It's her corset," he said.

He spread it out and held it high. Riff's eyes widened in amazement.

"So *that's* the reason," she breathed. She too must have noticed the difference in Lye's way of moving. "She's walking without her corset."

Everyone turned to stare at the trio on the ropes, who were now a hundred paces away. There was a visible tension in Lye's body, a prodigious effort of will. At the same time her stance had never been more upright.

"She must be in unbelievable agony," muttered Riff.

There had been no reaction from the *Romanov* as yet. However, as they watched, one head appeared, then another and another. Col imagined that the Russian officers were as astonished as he was. A moment later half a dozen of them crossed to the side of the deck and stared out.

Lye redirected her rifle and fired off three rapid rounds. She was hardly aiming and had next to no chance of hitting them. The recoil transmitted itself to the ropes, which bucked and swayed. Mr. Gibber let out a piteous cry and barely kept his balance.

The officers turned tail and ran. They were armed and could easily have brought down the attackers, yet they fled as though from superhuman beings of incalculable power. Col understood their fear. Why else would a force of three advance so confidently against a force of thousands?

"Keep going!" Lye's shout of command drifted back across the distance. "Faster!"

The three figures were almost halfway across, and moving at twice their original speed. For one mad moment Col really wondered if Lye might achieve the impossible.

Then the Russians came back in greater numbers. A hundred officers and troops marched to the side of the *Romanov*, lined up in military formation, and raised their rifles to their shoulders.

Lye didn't bother to shoot this time, but just yelled at the top of her voice, "Long live the revolution!"

Mr. Gibber gave up even before being shot at. With a drawn-out wail he jumped. He was still in a monkeylike crouch as he plummeted down and disappeared from view between the two juggernauts.

In the next moment the gunfire began. Flashes leaped

from a hundred barrels; a hundred bullets cut a swathe through the air. Shiv, at the front, took the full force of it. Like a twitching puppet he was buffeted this way and that. Then he toppled from the ropes and followed Mr. Gibber's long fall to the ground.

Lye must have been hit too, but not in any vital organ. She teetered and dropped her rifle. One arm hung limply at her side, and something seemed to have happened to her hip.

Still she refused to fall. Slowly, painfully, she drew herself upright. She was twisted and lopsided, yet she began to move forward again on the ropes. Faster and faster she accelerated.

"Surrender to the revolution!" she screamed. "You're all doomed! You'll never win!"

She was still screaming as the second volley from the Russian rifles smashed into her and knocked her down.

57

The Russian troops peered over the barrier encircling the *Romanov*'s flat top. They pointed below and cheered until their officers called them away. For Col and Riff, the lower terraces of *Liberator*'s superstructure cut off their view of the ground between the two juggernauts. Many more Filthies and convicts had by now appeared on the lower terraces.

"She always wanted to die as a martyr," said Riff. "I don't think she cared much about life or death."

"Nor other people's lives or deaths," said Col.

"She was an extraordinary human being. Absolute like an arrow."

"There was something missing in her. Murdering Zeb just to gain a place on the Council."

"Having Zeb murdered," Riff corrected. "And she never wanted power for personal satisfaction. I don't believe that. She wanted power for the cause, so that she could do the things she thought had to be done."

"Like getting rid of the Swanks. And me and you and Dunga."

"She never understood ordinary people. She never accepted that other people couldn't be the same as her."

"You, for example."

"Yes. Me."

They remained silent for a while. Col wasn't satisfied; he wanted to hear Riff condemn the murderous treachery of her former friend. Riff's oddly respectful mood didn't make sense to him. But he could see it was no use arguing the point.

Below them there was a general surge of Filthies and convicts making their way to a particular terrace twenty levels further down. It was a wider terrace that stuck out far enough to give a view to the ground.

"Let's go look," Col suggested.

"Okay."

Before Riff could leave, Gart had a question for her. "What about the ropes?"

"What about them?"

"If we let them stay up, the Russians might cross over and launch an attack on *us*."

"Right. Of course. Cut them loose."

She didn't wait to watch the operation completed, but led the way down to the lower levels. There were now so many people on the wider terrace that it was difficult to find a space, but she managed to push forward to the railing. Col squeezed in beside her.

It was like peering over the edge of a cliff. Far below they could see the lighter green of grass, the darker green of trees, and the winding brown lines of dry gullies. Farther back was the unwholesome-looking gray of the liquid that had leaked from *Liberator*'s bilge.

Everyone was pointing to two tiny spots of red that showed against the green of the grass.

"Lye and Shiv," one convict exclaimed.

Col wondered which was which. The two shapes were huddled and broken; even Lye's jet-black hair was indistinguishable. He guessed that she was the one farthest away from *Liberator*, since she had covered the greatest distance along the ropes.

As for Mr. Gibber, he was nowhere to be seen. Col studied the ground closer in to their own hull, since the ex-schoolteacher had been the first to fall. There were several patches of darker green, so he'd probably crashed down into a clump of trees.

"Look!"

"What are *they* doing?"

There was a murmur of interest as a dozen Russian officers emerged from between the *Romanov*'s caterpillar tracks. They were clearly visible in their white-and-gold uniforms. They fanned out over the ground and soon located the objects of their search: the bodies of Lye and Shiv. Everyone craned forward to watch.

Half of the officers made a beeline for the nearest body, while the rest moved on to the second body. Both bodies lay in puddles of their own blood. The officers stood talking for a while, then unslung their rifles.

Crack-crack-crack! The sound of rifle fire echoed across the distance. Lye's body—as Col assumed—jumped and jerked under the impact of the bullets, then lay still.

Crack-crack-crack! The other group did the same for Shiv's body.

"What's that for?" someone cried.

"Anyone can see they're already dead."

"It's disrespectful!"

The officers moved forward again, presumably to search for Mr. Gibber's body. But the Filthies and convicts had had enough. Some of them raised their own rifles and started shooting.

The officers looked up, realized their peril, and fled. They ran like scurrying insects, zigzagging left and right. One stumbled as if hit, and needed the aid of two companions to hobble along, but all made it back to the shelter of the caterpillar tracks. Filthies and convicts jeered and shook their fists.

"Hold your fire!" shouted Riff, as shots continued to ring out. "Don't waste bullets."

The shooting ceased. Col was staring at the *Romanov*'s caterpillar tracks. "No, wait," he said as Riff turned to go.

"What?"

"They came out between the tracks."

"And now they've run back there."

"Which shows there's a way in at the bottom of the hull. Perhaps there's a hatch."

"So?"

"It's something I was thinking about before. The airborne assault is impossible now, right?"

"I suppose. We've lost the element of surprise. The Russians will be prepared and waiting for us."

"But they won't be prepared for an attack from *underneath*."

Riff furrowed her brows. "You mean . . . if Russian officers can get down through their engine room, then we could get up the same way?"

"Yes. Or even better—we could make contact with the Russian Filthies and stir them up to revolution. We could attack the Russian juggernaut from within."

"Like our Liberation!" Riff snapped her fingers. "Go on!"

"We wouldn't need a full-on attack, just a few people to sneak inside and talk to the Russian Filthies. Tell them what we did and how they could do it too."

"Right, right, right!" Riff's eyes were alight with excitement. "I bet they're treated as bad as we used to be."

"What do you think?"

"I think it's the best plan yet." She flung her arms round him in a celebratory hug, then disengaged herself with a laugh. "I'll talk to Dunga first, then call a Council meeting. They *have* to agree. I'll *make* them."

58

When Col returned to the Grand Assembly Hall, he was told that Sephaltina had been moved to a more suitable room nearby. It turned out to be a small reception room with paintings on the walls, gilded chairs, cabinets of polished walnut, and a magnificent long divan. A bed had been made up for Sephaltina on the divan, with pillows, sheets, and a quilt. Her neck was swathed in bandages that went up to her chin and down to her collarbones.

Hatta sat on a chair beside her. She had a bowl of water on her lap and a pad of cloth in her hand. When Col entered, she looked up with a grumpy expression.

"Before you ask, she's doing well enough. No reason why she shouldn't get better."

"How can I help?" Col asked.

"You can take over this job, for a start."

She passed the bowl and pad to Col, and sat him down on the chair.

"You'll come back to check on her, though?"

"When I have time. I do have other patients, you know."

Hatta's healing skills didn't include a caring bedside manner. She marched off and left Col to take over the role of nurse. He dampened the cloth and, every few minutes, pressed it against Sephaltina's forehead. She was running a high temperature.

One hour passed, then another. Sephaltina's eyes remained closed. Occasional wheezing sounds came from her throat, and, once, a horrible gurgle that made him think she was choking. He was about to run outside and call for Hatta, but the gurgle stopped as suddenly as it had started.

Liberator's corridor lights had dimmed for the night when someone knocked at the door. Col turned as Riff entered.

"So there you are! I've been looking all over."

Col put a finger to his lips and pointed to the prostrate figure on the divan.

"Ah, right. Your wife." Riff didn't seem particularly interested, but she did lower her voice to a whisper. "We've had the Council meeting, and they've agreed to your plan. A small team going in underneath."

"When?"

"Tomorrow night. We need the cover of darkness, and we won't have time to complete preparations tonight. You'll be on the team, of course."

"I'll try."

"You can help me pick the others and . . . what do you mean, *try*?"

"I have to look after Sephaltina."

"Why?"

"I don't trust Hatta."

"Nothing wrong with Hatta." Riff frowned. "Why you?"

"She's my wife."

"I thought it was just an arranged marriage. That's what you always told me. You didn't choose Sephaltina. It was an alliance between families."

"Yes, but I still feel responsible for her."

"Because of that silly bit of gold around your finger?"

Col looked at his wedding ring. Not for the first time he wished he could annihilate it by sheer force of will.

"I went through the ceremony and said 'I do.' I can't help it. I *am* married to her."

"Too married to help me, then. I come second."

"No, you come first."

"But not right now."

"She'll probably be better by tomorrow night."

"Phuh! I think you need to find a way to get unmarried. *If* you want to have anything to do with me."

"Unmarried?"

"You have a ceremony for getting married, so you ought to have one for getting unmarried. Say 'I don't' or something."

"I never heard of anyone getting unmarried. What happens when Filthies get partnered?"

"That's different. It's not an alliance between families."

"There is a ceremony, though?"

"Not like your Upper Decks ceremonies."

"Tell me."

"No." Riff sniffed. "We'll probably all be dead soon anyway. Slaughtered by the imperialists. This plan of yours is our last chance."

"I want to be part of it."

"Then you'd better decide."

"Can you come back for me later?"

Sephaltina broke out suddenly in a violent fit of wheezing. Spasms racked her body, and her eyes flickered open and closed.

Col bathed her forehead with one hand and tried to hold her still with the other. By the time the spasms passed, there was a tiny red spot on the bandages round her throat.

He turned to continue the conversation with Riff, but she had already left the room.

59

Sephaltina's condition remained stable overnight. When Hatta looked in the next morning, she examined the patient and said, "She'll heal in her own time. It's up to her now."

Col wasn't happy with that, but Hatta hurried off without waiting to hear his complaints. Sephaltina didn't do any more gurgling, and her fits of wheezing were milder than yesterday. He could only continue to bathe her forehead.

He had one group of visitors early in the morning: Orris, Quinnea, and Antrobus. Antrobus carried a bunch of flowers and a box wrapped up in pink paper.

"How is my poor daughter-in-law?" Quinnea asked.

Col repeated what Hatta had said. Quinnea fluttered all around the patient, murmuring, "We can't lose her now. We just can't. I couldn't bear it."

Col changed the subject. "What's happening with the juggernaut?"

"Your sister has become the main organizer," said Orris with a touch of pride. "She's in charge of all kinds of things."

"So active." Quinnea raised a hand to her brow. "She makes me tired just looking at her."

"The Filthies don't object to her being in charge?" Col asked.

"Not at all," said Orris. "There's a different attitude since the radicals were overthrown. Nobody wears a red armband any more."

"What about the imperialist juggernauts?"

"They haven't attacked *yet*." Orris stroked his long jaw. "But it could happen at any moment. The Austrian juggernaut moved in closer overnight."

"We're praying they'll wait another twenty-four hours." Quinnea turned to her husband. "Tell him, dear."

"I've been selected to take part in a mission." Orris actually smiled. "We're going to break into the *Romanov* from underneath."

Col was amazed—and envious. "Why you?"

"Because I learned a little Russian once." Orris composed himself for speech. "*Dobre den.* That means 'hello.'"

"Ah, right." Col had never even considered the language problem. Of course the team would need to communicate with the *Romanov*'s Filthies in Russian.

He turned to his mother. "You don't mind him going?"

Quinnea didn't miss a beat. "Everyone has to take a risk sometimes. I know he'll discover resources in himself that he never expected."

Col almost dropped the damp cloth and the bowl of water. His mother *was* a changed person! Her success in pulling a red armband down by the legs seemed to have given her a new perspective on life.

"You'll be surprised at what you can do when you have to," she told her husband, encouragingly.

"It's a pity you can't come, Colbert," Orris said. "I suppose you have to look after your wife."

If there was a hint of hesitation in Orris's voice, there was none in Quinnea's. "Of course he must. Oh, and I nearly forgot. We brought her some lovely flowers and sweets."

Antrobus stepped forward and held out the bunch of flowers and the pink-wrapped box.

"She likes sweets, doesn't she?" Quinnea asked Col.

"Dotes on them."

"We cut the flowers from a pot in the Westmoreland Gallery."

Accepting the gifts on Sephaltina's behalf, Col placed them on a nearby cabinet. He couldn't help wondering what deep thoughts were circulating behind Antrobus's solemn eyes. Did his baby brother understand that Col's only feelings for Sephaltina were responsibility and a kind of guilt because he didn't and couldn't love her? Antrobus uttered not a word, for which Col was thankful.

When they left soon after, Col went out and found a vase for the flowers. The rest of the morning passed by in a monotonous trance. At least there was no sound of any attack by the *Romanov* or the *Grosse Wien*.

Later in the day Victoria and Albert paid a visit. Col gritted his teeth as they asked questions about his wife and sympathized with him over his misfortune.

"She'll recover, no doubt of it." Albert clapped him on the shoulder. "No doubt at all."

The fact that their sympathy was so very genuine

made it somehow harder to bear. Why couldn't they remember that his marriage had only ever been an alliance between families?

He had questions of his own to ask, but somehow he didn't like to ask them in Sephaltina's presence, even though she was sleeping. Instead he waited until the end of the visit, then accompanied Victoria and Albert out into the corridor.

"When you abdicated as queen," he asked Victoria, "did you also abdicate as head of the Imperial Church?"

"I don't know." Victoria seemed bemused. "I just abdicated. Why?"

"Well, marrying people would've been something you did as head of the church, wouldn't it?"

Victoria nodded slowly. "Yes, that sounds right."

"So if you're still head of the church, you could still marry people?"

"Oh!" Victoria's face lit up with a smile. "You know someone who wants to get married?"

Col skirted the question. "Or unmarry them?"

The smile disappeared. "*Unmarry* them?"

"I know someone who wants to get unmarried."

Col tried to sound as casual as possible. He was relying on the fact that Victoria and Albert were known for having the best of feelings rather than the best of brains. He hoped they wouldn't make the obvious connection.

"Oh, dear," said Victoria. "What a shame. Do we know this person?"

"I can't tell you who it is. Is there a way to do it? There *ought* to be a way."

A look of distress had appeared in Victoria's large, liquid eyes. "I'd hate to have married anyone who didn't want to get married."

"Perhaps if they *both* wanted to get unmarried?" Albert put in. "Do they?"

Col had a sinking sensation in the pit of his stomach. "I'm not sure. I'll need to find out."

"Have to be both of them," said Albert. "Wouldn't be fair otherwise."

"No, I suppose not," said Col.

He walked on with them another twenty paces, as far as one of the steam elevators.

"I'd better be getting back to Sephaltina, then," he said.

He turned back with a bitter taste in his mouth. Riff had said that reversing a wedding ceremony ought to be as simple as saying "I don't," but he'd always known it couldn't be so easy. Now he knew just how difficult. He felt as if he were raveled up in a thousand strings—and they were tightening around him all the time.

60

Col would hardly have dared ask Sephaltina her views on getting unmarried, but he found out anyway. Later that afternoon she began to babble random phrases.

"Yes, Mama."

"I will be good."

"I'll wear the pink ribbons."

"I have to be pretty."

Col wished Hatta would put in an appearance. Sephaltina's voice had an odd, breathy quality. Was babbling a good sign, or was it bad for her throat?

"Shush . . . shush . . . ," he said.

Instead of shushing, Sephaltina suddenly opened her eyes very wide and looked straight at Col.

"My husband," she breathed. "Back again."

He managed a smile. "Do you remember what happened?"

"I don't need to remember. My husband is taking care of me. Everything is just as it should be."

"You're recovering well. The nurse says—"

"Of course I am. I have to get better for my husband."

Her eyelids flickered and closed, and she seemed to be falling back asleep. *I'm glad she's getting better,* Col told himself.

A few minutes later her eyelids flew open, and she

looked straight at him again. She remained silent while
he bathed her forehead with cool water.

"You're happy being married, then?" he said after a
while.

"Silly," she murmured.

"Even though it was an arranged marriage?"

Sephaltina's lips puckered in a smile. "I arranged it."

"You . . . ?" Col didn't understand.

"When we received your proposal. The Turbots from
the Porpentines. Daddy didn't want to give his consent,
but I made him."

Col had a distant recollection of Chief Helmsman
Turbot saying that his daughter had been very insistent.
"How?"

"I held my breath until I fainted. I threatened to keep
on doing it and doing it. I said I'd keep on doing it until
I died. I'm very strong-willed, you know. I always get
whatever I want in the end."

Col stared at her. With her heart-shaped face, rose-
bud mouth, and cheeks so prone to blushing, she was
sweetness and prettiness personified. But perhaps sweetness and prettiness didn't rule out a very strong will.

Soon she dropped back into a deeper sleep, and Col
was left alone with his unhappy thoughts.

He'd never really expected Sephaltina to give up on
being married, but he'd forgotten that she'd pushed
her father to agree to it. And even before then, what
about all the little presents that she'd left in his desk at
school? Packets of fudge, bars of nougat, and boxes of

chocolates—always with a note bearing the enigmatic initials ST. Every memory was like a twist of the knife. She must have loved him long before he was ever aware of her existence. Even if it was a slightly strange kind of love . . .

He felt ashamed of himself for probing her on her commitment to marriage. He should never have asked Victoria about getting unmarried. The strings that wound around him felt tighter than ever.

Ten minutes later Septimus Trant stuck his head in at the door.

"Hi! Sorry I couldn't look in sooner. I've been so busy on the project." He came up to view Sephaltina on the divan. "How is she?"

Col hadn't seen Septimus since Botany Bay. Since Septimus was aware of Col's feelings for Riff, he was one person who could share and understand Col's dilemma. Right now, though, Col didn't want any sharing or understanding.

"She's getting better."

"That's good," Septimus said neutrally. "She helped us, did you know?"

"No."

"If Sephaltina hadn't smashed up the wireless tele-graph offices, we'd never have known where to find mag-nets. They were inside the equipment, in the casings."

"Magnets?"

"For the project. It was a lucky accident for us."

When Septimus had mentioned "the project" before,

Col had assumed he was talking about the mission. But why magnets?

"You've been stuck in here a long time, haven't you?" Septimus asked, as if the thought had just struck him.

"I only hear what visitors tell me."

"You heard about the other juggernauts turning up?"

"*What?* No."

"The French *Marseillaise* and the Turkish *Battle of Mohacs.*"

"When?"

"Half an hour ago." Septimus half swiveled toward the door. "Come and look."

Sephaltina lay sleeping peacefully under the quilt. Col considered the time it would take to reach a place to look out, then return. If they moved fast . . .

"Okay," he said.

The lookout they chose was one of the sorting trays on Thirty-first Deck. They descended by elevator, hurried along corridors, and finally came out into the open.

There was no hint of a breeze, and the air was hot and heavy. It was already close to sunset, and the sky was streaked with orange and yellow bands. Hundreds of birds wheeled in circles, climbing higher and higher.

Col and Septimus came around the scoop that rested on the tray, and stood close to the edge at the front.

"The *Battle of Mohacs.*" Septimus pointed. "And the *Marseillaise.*"

While the vast bulk of the *Romanov* loomed before them, the other juggernauts were visible at a distance, left and right. They appeared in silhouette against the lurid sky, like crouching beasts encircling their prey.

The *Battle of Mohacs* was on the left, along with the *Grosse Wien*. It was even smaller than the Austrian juggernaut, with a curiously old-fashioned silhouette rising in steps to a great square poop at the back. At the front the tops of two enormous spoked wheels showed above the level of the deck. Both deck and poop were crowned with battlements like a castle.

On the right, the *Marseillaise* was a monster at least as big as *Liberator*. Two conical towers dominated its silhouette fore and aft, with a dozen strange cigar-shaped objects floating above them. Massive tethered balloons, Col guessed. The prow dropped away to a low snout or proboscis that stretched forward over the ground, half as long as the juggernaut itself.

"Now we know why the Russians and Austrians were waiting," said Col.

"For reinforcements."

"They won't wait much longer now."

"No." Septimus frowned suddenly and snapped his fingers. "Time I got back to help the professor."

He hurried off without another word. Col stayed on a few minutes longer, but there was less and less to see in the dwindling light.

Then he too turned, and headed back to Sephaltina in her sickroom. On the way he realized with annoyance that he'd forgotten to ask Septimus about this project involving magnets.

61

Would Riff come for him? Col went over and over their last exchange. Although he'd asked her to come back, she hadn't actually said yes. Now the sun had set, and it was time to launch the mission. . . . Perhaps the team had already left without him?

He could have whooped when the door swung open and Riff appeared. Unfortunately, his jump of excitement woke Sephaltina from her slumber. A tiny frown formed on her forehead, as though someone had done something offensive in her presence.

"Okay," said Riff. "Last chance. We're about to go."

Sephaltina answered first. "My husband is taking care of me," she said haughtily.

Riff ignored her and addressed Col. "It was your plan. Are you going to be a part of it or not?"

"I . . ."

"You can't take him away," said Sephaltina. "He's *mine.*"

Col turned to her. "I won't be gone long. You're improving all the time."

"Am not. I'm getting worse. I'll get much, much worse if you leave me." It sounded like a threat.

Riff stood by the door, ready to leave. "Well?"

"Go away!" Sephaltina shouted suddenly. "You don't understand about marriage. You're only a Filthy. A marriage is forever and ever. Through thick and thin. In sickness or in health."

Riff eyed her coldly. "You're crazy."

"In craziness or in sanity. Nothing matters more to him than me. It's not *allowed*."

Col tried to explain. "I can help save *Liberator* and everyone on it."

"Don't fib!" Sephaltina's shout became a shriek. "You're not doing it to save people. You're doing it for *her*. You want her instead of me!"

Sephaltina might be crazy, but she wasn't stupid. Col looked around, completely at a loss what to say.

Meanwhile Hatta had entered the room. She stood with folded arms a couple of paces in from the door.

Sephaltina drew breath and returned to the attack. "If you go on this mission with her, you'll be sorry. I'll die, and you'll be responsible."

"No."

"You want me to die, don't you? Admit it! So you can be with her!"

"No."

"Yes. You want me to die, so I'll die. Then you'll be sorry for what you've done to me."

Hatta chose that moment to stride forward. She took hold of Sephaltina's shoulder and pushed her back down on the divan.

"Well," she said, "you *are* getting better, aren't you? Much stronger, to be making all that noise. Even trying to sit up."

"I need lots and lots of looking after." Sephaltina pouted. "From my husband."

"Lots and lots of sleep, that's what you need. Haven't you tired yourself out with all your shouting?"

Indeed Sephaltina did seem tired. She sank back into her pillow, closed her eyes, and opened her mouth.

"I want a sweetie," she said. "I want my husband to give me a sweetie."

"There are no sweeties," said Hatta.

"Actually, there are." Col pointed to the box wrapped in pink paper on top of the cabinet. "My mother left some this morning."

"Yes!" It was as though Sephaltina had already sensed their presence. Her eyes flew open and her gaze homed in instantly on the box. "Sweetie, please."

"Stabbed in the throat, and she wants sweeties!" Hatta rolled her eyes. "Sweets are the one thing you must *not* have. Big, sticky lumps getting stuck in your throat? You can sip water, and nothing more. Absolutely out of the question."

Sephaltina's tongue played daintily over her lips. "Sweetie, please."

Hatta's answer was to scoop up the box from the top of the cabinet. The cabinet had a glass front and a key; she opened it up, deposited the box inside, then closed and locked it.

"There!" She removed and pocketed the key. "You can have your sweeties when you've fully recovered, and not before. Do you understand?"

"Please can I have a sweetie?"

"No."

"Please."

"No."

"I *want* a sweetie."

"Oh, be quiet, you silly girl."

Sephaltina screwed up her mouth in a very tight expression. "Not very nice to me," she huffed, and turned away on her side.

Hatta beckoned to Col with one finger. He followed her in the direction of the door, where she spoke to him and Riff together.

"She really is much improved," she said in a low voice. "There's no problem about leaving her."

"It's all right for me to go on this mission?" Col asked.

"Yes."

"She won't die?"

Hatta pulled a face. "As if."

Col swung to Riff with a broad grin. "I'm in. Let's go!"

62

The members of the team were Riff, Dunga, and Padder from the Council; Orris and Col; and three other Filthies: Jarvie, Cham, and Cree. Cree was the woman with red spiky hair who'd quizzed Col on the bridge and made a face at the mention of Shiv's security force. Col liked her already.

Orris had been converted into a passable imitation of a Filthy, with tousled hair, loose-fitting clothes, and greasy smudges on his cheeks. In an odd way the change suited him. "The Russian Filthies won't talk to me if they think I'm a Swank," he explained.

Col had to undergo a similar transformation. Cree surveyed him critically and grinned. "Nah. Your father's ten times the Filthy you are."

The preparations had gone far beyond Col's planning in another respect too. Along with their rifles everyone carried a canvas bag containing fancy foods and luxury items. The idea was to present small gifts to the Russian Filthies.

"To win them over?" Col asked.

"Yes, and show them how we live," said Riff. "How lucky we are."

"Which they could be too, if they liberate themselves," added Cree.

Twenty minutes later the team descended in a scoop lowered by one of *Liberator*'s cranes. The oppressive air weighed down like a fist and held the whole world trapped and still. Dry thunder grumbled in the distance, a continuous deep roll; sheet lightning lit up the horizon like a light switched on and off. No storm, no rain, no climax—just the menace without the fulfillment.

Some kind of activity was taking place up on the *Romanov*'s flat deck, but the high, fortresslike sides of the juggernaut made it impossible to see what it was. The other juggernauts were mere black masses visible only in flashes of lightning. Col could swear they'd moved in closer yet again.

He smelled the ground even before the scoop touched down. A hundred scents rose to his nostrils, full of mystery and promise. Sharp scents and sweet scents, woody scents and herbal scents . . . He had never been close to so much natural vegetation in his life.

The ground itself turned out to be far more broken and irregular than it had appeared from the terraces. It was a landscape of hummocks and hollows—and a great many obstacles. The team fell in behind Riff and marched in single file.

They walked over patches of short, bristling grass and waded through patches of tall, silky grass. Insects clicked and ticked; undergrowth rustled; small flying things whirred past in the dark. It was all far more alive than Col would ever have imagined.

At the crest of one higher hummock Riff called a halt. "What's that?"

The *Romanov*'s hull was a dark, blank wall across the night—but now, viewing it from ground level, they could see a glimmering strip of light at the very bottom. It shone out between the caterpillar tracks, from underneath the hull.

"I see shadows moving."

"Russians."

"What are they doing down there?"

"Don't know."

The march resumed. They crossed a gully and skirted a clump of trees. They were trudging over a marshy area when Riff suddenly froze. Following the line of her gaze, Col saw a shape like a lump of mud sticking up. Very, very slowly it moved.

"What the . . ." Dunga whistled under her breath.

"Leave it alone," Padder advised.

Riff had other ideas. "I want to take a look."

"Why?"

"Just because. Wait here if you want."

In the end everyone chose to follow Riff across the boggy ground. The thing moved again, then again. A furrow in the mud marked its progress.

Did Riff know what it was? A wild notion began to form in Col's mind as they approached. The thing looked more and more human . . . more and more like one particular human.

"Lye's little spy," said Dunga.

It was impossible yet true. Mr. Gibber appeared to have lost the use of an arm and a leg, never once raising his head as he dragged himself along. From top to toe he was exactly the same color as the mud on which he crawled.

"What's he saying?" asked Cree.

They gathered round. Mr. Gibber continued to plow slowly forward as though they weren't there. He was muttering a single word over and over to himself.

"Crawling . . . crawling . . . crawling . . . crawling . . ."

"He's out of his mind," said Jarvie.

"He shouldn't be alive at all," said Padder.

Col traced Mr. Gibber's telltale furrow back in the direction of the trees they'd just passed. "The branches must have broken his fall. I *thought* he'd come down in a clump of trees."

Riff nodded. "The Russian officers made very sure Lye and Shiv were dead. But they never got around to shooting Mr. Gibber."

Col bent down and spoke very close to Mr. Gibber's ear. "Hello, Mr. Gibber! We never expected to see you still alive."

Mr. Gibber stopped saying "crawling" and said something that sounded like "no."

"We're from *Liberator*. I'm Col Porpentine."

"Can't hear, can't see, can't think," Mr. Gibber muttered into the mud. "Not alive."

"Of course you're alive."

"I fell and died. Corpse of Mr. Gibber. Turning back to earth. Eaten by worms. Ugh."

"What did I say?" Jarvie shrugged. "Out of his mind."

"Not surprising after what he's been through," said Orris.

"How long has be been without food and water?" asked Cree.

"A day and a half," answered Riff. She pointed to Mr. Gibber's muddy mouth, which was almost touching the ground. "Though he probably found water."

Col had to keep changing position as Mr. Gibber continued to drag himself along. "Where are you going, Mr. Gibber?"

"Eternal rest. Nothingness. Earth to earth. Worms and maggots."

Then his head butted up against Padder's shins. Still he continued to press mindlessly forward, while Padder continued to block his way.

"Crawling . . . crawling . . . crawling," he muttered.

Finally his head slid off to the side, and, as if following its lead, he labored along in a new direction.

Col rose to his feet. "He won't stop. I think he believes he's a worm."

"We'll have to leave him," said Cham. "The mission comes first."

"At least let's point him in a better direction," said Col.

With help from Dunga he took hold of Mr. Gibber

under the chest, lifted, and turned him around. Though they tried to be gentle, he moaned and groaned pitifully.

"More broken bones there," said Dunga.

However, Mr. Gibber was now crawling in the direction of their own juggernaut.

"Can we spare him something to eat?" Cree suggested. "The Russian Filthies won't miss what they don't know about."

Riff nodded, and opened up the canvas bag she was carrying. She drew out a pack of biscuits and passed it across to Cree, who crouched down beside Mr. Gibber and slipped it into his jacket pocket.

"He'll find it there if he recovers his mind."

"*If*," said Riff, and turned to go. "Okay, we've wasted enough time."

They soon left the bog behind and came to an area of prickly bushes, where they had to zigzag constantly. One time, a bird shot up out of a bush with a great flapping of wings—and everyone jumped.

Riff peered ahead to the glimmering light at the bottom of the *Romanov*. "I know what they're doing," she said. "They're repairing the tracks."

It made sense to Col. Of course the Russians would be in a hurry to have their juggernaut moving again.

Peering ahead himself, he now realized that the light shone out from many separate bulbs rigged up beneath the *Romanov*'s underbelly. Thirty or forty dark figures moved about among the caterpillar tracks. They were all stooping because the underbelly came down so low to the ground.

Riff led the team around in the shadows to the left of the light. Closer and closer they came, moving more and more cautiously. The ground was churned up in some places, compacted and hard in others. Smells of crushed vegetation mingled with smells of oil and metal.

At twenty yards' distance they could see that the *Romanov*'s hull was composed of great metal plates bolted together. Each projecting bolt head was the size of a double fist. Below the hull the caterpillar tracks were mounted in parallel pairs and ran over countless tiny wheels. There were many, many sets of tracks all along the side of the juggernaut—and all the way underneath as well.

The team covered the last twenty yards in a sprint and slipped in under the hull. They continued on until they were well behind the outermost line of tracks.

"Where now?" asked Padder in a whisper.

"Don't say 'toward the light,'" Cree murmured in mock prayer.

"Toward the light," said Riff. "That's where the access will be."

They turned and advanced toward the light. It was like a low cavern under the hull. They flitted in silence from the cover of one set of tracks to another. Once, they had to scramble over a broken track that lay trailing on the ground, awaiting repair.

As the light grew brighter, the underbelly became a silvery roof, scraped and polished by all the rock over which the juggernaut had rubbed itself. A harsh spitting sound crackled through the air, along with shouts and commands in incomprehensible Russian.

They stopped on the edge of the repair zone and looked out from the last set of tracks.

The spitting sound came from welding equipment that sprayed out white, cascading sparks. There were two separate repair gangs, each made up of officers and workers. The officers carried rifles and wore white uniforms dripping with gold braid. The workers had the hunched stance of Menials and wore what looked like leather harnesses. Naturally, the officers gave all the orders and did none of the work.

But where was the access?

Then they saw it, on the opposite side of the repair zone. There was an opening in the underbelly where a metal plate had been slid back; emerging from it, twin pipes descended to the ground, ran horizontally for a few yards, then terminated in twin gaping mouths. The pipes were about six feet in diameter and made of some gray, corrugated, semitransparent membrane.

Dunga pointed to the armed officer on guard beside the twin mouths. "Not good."

"Bet he'll be there all night," said Padder,

"We'll never get up the pipes while he's there," said Orris.

"Think straight!" Riff hissed. "We don't want to get

up the pipes. You think eight of us can take on all their troops and officers?"

"The pipes would only take us straight to the Upper Decks," Col explained. "We need to get to the Russian Filthies in the engine room first."

"And I think I know the way," said Riff.

"You do?"

"Listen up."

63

Following Riff's plan, they divided into two groups. Padder and Cham had the task of creating a diversion; everyone else circled around in the shadows and approached the twin pipes from the other side of the repair zone.

"There." Riff pointed upward and nodded with satisfaction.

It was as she had predicted. Because the pipes were round, they didn't fit tightly together, but left a small triangular gap where they descended through the access hatch. On this side the gap was shielded from the sight of the repair gangs.

Riff, Col, Orris, Cree, Jarvie, and Dunga formed a line and waited. They held their canvas bags and rifles in front of their chests.

"*Yagh! Hai! Yarragh!*"

Padder and Cham began yelling and banging metal on metal. The guard beside the pipes swiveled and took a dozen steps in the direction of the sound.

There was no need for any signal. Riff sprinted forward, and the others followed. She pushed her bag and rifle up through the gap, grabbed the edge of the hatch, and vaulted upward.

Cree boosted her up from behind. In the next moment she reached back down to help Cree in her turn.

After Cree came Jarvie, then Orris. The diversion continued, but the yelling and banging sounded more distant now.

Only Col and Dunga remained. Col hoisted his bag and rifle up into the gap, where a pair of hands lifted them out of the way. He hooked his fingers over the edge of the hatch and hauled himself upward. He was more solidly built than the Filthies, and for him it was a tight squeeze.

He was halfway there when he realized there were no helping hands to pull him up from above. Nor anyone to give him a boost from below—Dunga had vanished. He understood why when he felt vibrations against his back.

The vibrations were footsteps descending rung by rung. Someone was coming down in one of the pipes.

He could only freeze and hang on. He molded himself against the edge of the opening. Was the semitransparent membrane enough to hide him?

It was like someone climbing down right over his back. The corrugated pipe was reinforced with rings of metal that dug deep into his flesh. Surely he must be making a dent; surely the dent was noticeable?

But no. The vibrations passed over him and continued step by step to the ground. In another moment the officer had left the pipe without noticing a thing.

Col stayed frozen until Dunga reappeared and gave him a forceful push from below. He almost flew up into the darkness above the hatch.

"Steady." Hands caught him by the arms. "Keep to the ridge."

The air at the bottom of the Russian juggernaut was like concentrated sewage. He blinked and staggered as the stench hit him.

He turned to help Dunga, but someone was already kneeling over the gap. Someone else thrust his canvas bag and rifle into his arms.

He was on a raised ridge between two troughs. Similar troughs spread out in all directions, shallow and rectangular. Whatever liquid was in them gave off the foul sewage stench.

He stepped away and took in the rest of his surroundings. The dim light seemed to come from everywhere and nowhere. He had an impression of a vast open chamber, but drive shafts bigger than tree trunks passed across overhead and blocked his view. Motionless at present, the shafts were a silvery color, gleaming with oil. The two corrugated pipes went up at a steep angle, then also vanished behind the shafts.

"Go," said Dunga behind him.

The team had begun to advance in single file. Col slung his bag over one shoulder, his rifle over the other, and clapped a hand to his nose as he walked. The ridge was like a causeway in an intersecting system of causeways.

Looking down at the troughs on either side, he almost jumped when he saw things move in the liquid. Was that hard shell or scaly skin? Better not to look too closely. The creatures made soft plopping sounds as they rolled and rotated.

Riff led them in a straight line until the troughs came

to an end. Now they faced a towering metal bulwark
pierced by apertures at various levels. On the lowest
level, which was their level, one aperture glowed with an
eerie, greenish light from within.

"Maybe we'll find them in here," said Riff.

She marched straight in under the arch of the aperture. Orris was behind her, then Cree, then Col. It was
like a tunnel, mantled over with knobbly cauliflower
growths. The growths appeared to be metallic; at least,
they were stained with rust and hard as iron to the touch.
Drops of water gathered overhead and dripped on their
heads and shoulders: warm water.

Thirty paces in they almost jumped out of their skins.
A face appeared upside down, as if hanging from the
ceiling.

"Aii-eee!"

The mouth opened to let out a shrill cry, display-
ing two rows of filed, sharply pointed teeth. The face
belonged to a young girl with a metal band around her
neck and blond hair trailing down in two long pigtails.

They barely had time to register that this was one of
the Russian Filthies. It was impossible to interpret her
upside-down expression. She was gone before anyone
could produce a friendly smile—or before Orris thought
to try out his Russian.

When they arrived at the place where the face had
appeared, they discovered an opening in the ceiling. The
tunnel had brought them to the bottom of a circular well
with a ladder going up. The source of the greenish light

was a lamp behind wire mesh, recessed into the wall.

They climbed the ladder. There was no sign of the girl or any other Russian Filthy. At the top they stepped off into a second horizontal passage similar to the first. At least they were leaving the sewage smell behind.

Eventually this passage opened out into another vast chamber. Here, instead of drive shafts, were great cogs and wheels suspended overhead. Cogs engaged with cogs in a bewildering intricacy of different sizes and mountings. Some of the wheels were connected by chains, others by belts on drums.

Nothing they could see was moving, yet there was a constant sound of machinery.

Whish-gaah! Whish-gaah! Whish-gaah! Whish-gaah!

It was like the slow wheeze and pant of some immense sleeping beast. Perhaps it came from the whole length and breadth of the *Romanov*'s engine room.

They moved forward again, under the cogs and wheels. All directions looked the same, all dim and shadowy.

"Maybe we should call out," Orris suggested.

"Maybe you're right," said Riff. "Okay, on the count of three."

"How do we call in Russian?" asked Jarvie.

"Just shout anything," said Riff. "One. Two."

They filled their lungs, but they never got to shout. Suddenly they realized that a host of figures had materialized out of the shadows. They were surrounded on all sides.

The figures stepped forward to form a ring around them.

64

The Russian Filthies were shorter and stockier than their counterparts from *Liberator*. They were half clothed in rags, as *Liberator*'s Filthies had once been, with signs and markings painted on their grimy skin. They wore ornaments as well: old bits of wire or metal strips bent into shape as bracelets, anklets, and collars. The women and girls all had pigtails, while the males had beards or the beginnings of beards. Both sexes had teeth filed to needle-sharp points, like those of the girl who had startled them in the tunnel.

She was there too, standing with a swagger, bold as brass. She looked to be about twelve or thirteen years old. Her face was broad, and her ears stuck out even farther. She seemed very pleased with herself.

The expressions of the other Russian Filthies were more menacing and malevolent.

Col gave his father a nudge. "Speak to them."

Orris took a step forward, assumed his most serious expression, and said, *"Dobre den."*

Instant pandemonium broke out. The Russian Filthies yelled, screeched, and shook their fists.

"No rifles!" cried Riff, as Dunga and Jarvie instinctively reached for their weapons. "Look harmless. Look friendly." She turned to Orris. "You must've said it wrong."

Orris shook his head, flapping his jowls. "I'm sure those are the words for 'hello.'"

"Try again."

Orris forced a smile and put his hand on his heart. The effort to appear both friendly and sincere made his eyes bulge alarmingly. *"Dobre den,"* he said in a slow, clear voice.

The words produced a different reaction this time. Now the Russian Filthies shrieked with laughter, beating their hands on their thighs in helpless hilarity.

"Better," said Riff.

"They still don't understand," said Orris sadly.

"It must be the accent," Col told his father. "You learned to speak like the Upper Decks Russians."

"Right. Same as I had to change *my* accent." Riff swung back to Orris. "Try saying it a different way."

"What way?"

"Different."

Orris tried saying it through his nose, then pinching his lips, then from the back of his throat. *"Dobre den. Dobre den. Dobre den."*

The Russian Filthies turned to one another and began gabbling a mile a minute. They seemed to be arguing, everyone talking over the top of everyone else.

"At least they've got the right idea," said Col.

"What idea is that?" asked Riff.

"That he's using language to communicate."

Riff let out a snort of frustration. "Say something else to them," she told Orris.

Orris reflected for a moment, then brought out a whole sentence. *"Biem chelom Vashim Imperatorskim Velich-estvam Tsar Aleksandr Shestoi i Tsarina Katerina."*

The Russian Filthies didn't like that sentence at all. They growled and showed their teeth.

"I think they understood." Orris nodded with satisfaction.

"What did you say?" asked Riff.

"'Humble greetings to Your Imperial Highnesses Tsar Alexander the Sixth and Tsarina Katerina.'"

"Wonderful." Riff groaned. "The only thing we didn't want them to understand. Let's try the gifts."

They emptied out their canvas bags and displayed the contents on the ground. As well as foodstuffs and delicacies, there were scissors, spoons, cups, combs, mirrors, rings, and necklaces.

"For you," said Riff, and made gestures of passing the gifts across.

The Russian Filthies understood. They came forward with caution—all except the young girl, who gave a whoop and rushed in to snatch up a spoon. With both hands she bent it round in a circle, then slipped it over her wrist as a kind of bracelet.

Her example encouraged the others. One by one they darted forward to pluck up a tidbit or trinket.

Riff pointed to herself, then to the Russian Filthies.

"Us. Same as you," she said.

The young girl tapped her own chest. "Unya," she said.

"That must be her name," said Col. "She thought you were naming yourself."

"Riff." Riff pointed once more to herself.

The girl pointed at Riff, and grinned. "Riff-ff. Riff-ff."

Riff waved an arm to include the whole team. "Filthies."

"Filth-ees," Unya repeated. She spread both arms to encompass all the Russian Filthies. "*Svolochi.*"

"*Svolochi?*"

Unya nodded violently up and down. "*Svolochi.*"

"*Dobre den,*" said Orris.

The girl screwed up her face quizzically, then suddenly clapped her hands. She turned to the others and repeated the words with a different pronunciation. "*Dobre den! Dobre den!*"

The ice was broken; now everyone understood. Again Riff indicated the team.

"Us," she said. "No tsar. No tsarina."

She shook her head to communicate the negative. Orris found a word for it.

"*Nema tsaria,*" he said. "*Nema tsarina.*"

The *svolochi* started to giggle, and seemed to think it was a joke.

"Wait a minute," said Orris. "I can do it. *Mi prishli . . . mi prishli vladet.*"

The giggling died away, replaced by expressions of gawking disbelief.

"I told them we rule," Orris explained. "We're the rulers."

"I'll show them." Riff unslung her rifle and directed it

upward, toward the Upper Decks of the *Romanov*.

"*Mi prishli vladet.*" She produced a perfect imitation of what Orris had said. "Bang! Bang! Bang!"

The *svolochi* watched with growing curiosity and a glint of eagerness.

"They know about rifles," said Col. "But only in the hands of their oppressors."

He raised his own rifle and squinted along the sights as if taking aim at a Russian officer high above. "Bang!" He squeezed the trigger with the safety catch on.

The whole team joined in the pantomime, aiming and pretending to fire, cheering and beating their chests in token of triumph. After a while the *svolochi* got swept up in the mood and began cheering and chest-beating too.

"*Mi prishli vladet!*" they shouted. "*Mi prishli vladet!*"

They reached out for rifles to try for themselves.

"Yes, let them," said Riff. "With the safety catches on."

For several minutes it was a wild scene of pretend shooting and cheering and dancing around. The *svolochi* aimed their barrels upward at imaginary targets and squeezed furiously on the triggers. The fact that the rifles remained silent didn't seem to bother them.

Col grinned at Riff. "I think they like the idea."

But someone must have jogged a safety catch from on to off. Suddenly a shot rang out.

Crack! Zwang! Zwang!

The bullet ricocheted off the metal overhead, then ricocheted again. There was a howl of pain, and two of the *svolochi* tumbled to the floor.

One was the woman who had accidentally fired the gun. Knocked backward by the recoil, she was more surprised than hurt. The other was a male with a bushy black beard who had been hit by the bullet itself. He lay howling and thrashing and clutching his shoulder.

Everyone gathered around. Col went to examine the wound, but Dunga held him back. "No, let them do it."

In fact the wound hardly deserved so much howling and thrashing. When Blackbeard at last allowed them to look at his shoulder, they could see that the bullet had barely pierced the skin. The double ricochet had taken all the speed off it.

It was Unya, with her small, nimble fingers, who performed the surgery. She nipped the end of the bullet between her fingertips and pulled it out with a swift jerk.

"Yarrraghh!" Blackbeard's howl surpassed all his previous howls.

He sat up with an aggrieved look on his face and glared at the offending rifle, which now lay on the ground where the woman had dropped it. He lurched to his feet, went across, and kicked it. Then he stamped on it. He seemed to regard it as a personal enemy.

Then he began lashing out at other rifles in other hands. There were no protests from the *svolochi*. Perhaps Blackbeard was a person of special importance, or perhaps the rifles' dangerous power had unnerved them all. One by one the weapons clattered to the ground.

Of the team members only Dunga still had possession of her own rifle. When Blackbeard came up to her, Riff called out a warning: "Don't fight."

Dunga dropped her rifle even before Blackbeard could knock it from her hands.

"And we were doing so well," Orris lamented.

"Not anymore," said Cree.

Indeed the mood had changed again. Blackbeard shouted something in Russian, and the *svolochi* closed in aggressively. Another shout, and the team was hustled across the chamber.

"Looks like we're prisoners," said Col.

65

They were moved to a nearby room, where the girl Unya took sole charge of them. They could have easily overpowered her, so they weren't exactly prisoners. But what was the point in trying to escape, when the aim of their mission was to win the Russian Filthies over?

The room was a bewildering maze of pipes. Copper pipes circled the walls low down; lead pipes ran round higher up and across the ceiling. The lead pipes were crusted with white sediment and tiny stalactites, dripping constantly. Some interior heat warmed the copper pipes.

Unya divided up the team and arranged them on different sides of the room. The places she chose were the few places where there were no drips of water. Col shared a dry spot with Riff between an array of copper pipes and a drainage grille.

"*Liazhesh,*" Unya ordered. "*Liazhesh!*"

Riff looked to Orris, but he shook his head. Unya leaned over as if preparing to lie down, then folded her hands against her cheek as if preparing for sleep.

"Ask her what's going to happen to us," Riff said to Orris.

Unya shook her head and put her finger to her lips. "*Babya,*" she said. "*Zavtra.*"

"I think *zavtra* means 'tomorrow,'" said Orris. "I don't know what *babya* means."

Unya imitated the sound of a snore.

"Might as well catch some sleep while we can," Riff said.

She lay down facing the pipes, and Col lay on his back beside the drainage grille.

"What do you think will happen tomorrow?" he whispered.

"Don't know. We're not finished yet."

"My plan hasn't worked."

"Don't blame yourself." Riff found his hand and gave it a squeeze.

"Shhh!" Unya came bounding across from the other side of the room and shushed them furiously. As soon as she saw the contact between their hands, a broad smirk appeared on her face.

She said something in Russian, and when Col and Riff didn't understand, she laughed at it herself. She had a very loud laugh, as loud as her boisterous body language.

Then she set about arranging their arms and legs according to her own ideas. Her first idea involved rolling Col onto his side and making him cuddle up against Riff's back as closely as possible.

"She thinks we're partnered," said Riff.

Unya next idea was to drape Col's arm over Riff's waist. They were like two dolls for her.

Col resisted. "No," he said. "Not partnered."

Unya sniffed and moved away. She went over and shushed Orris, then went and did the same for Jarvie. When Col looked over his shoulder a little later, she was half sitting, half lying in the doorway.

The room was now silent except for the dripping of water and the *whish-gaah!* of distant machinery. Riff had settled herself into a more comfortable position. *Easy for her,* Col thought. To survive Below, every Filthy would have had to learn to nap under any conditions.

Col was sure he would never go to sleep himself—he was too worried about what was happening to *Liberator.* When would the imperialist juggernauts attack? By day or by night? He hated to be stuck here, wasting time. He also felt a little guilty that Sephaltina would be left alone far longer than he'd intended.

At first he hardly noticed when his arm moved and slid comfortably across Riff's waist. Only when his hand cupped her hip did he realize he wasn't doing it himself.

He blinked, and stared at the arm that was guiding his arm . . . and the bracelet around the wrist, made from a bent spoon. When he twisted over to look behind his back, his eyes met Unya's.

She let go of his hand and sat up straight with a cackle of laughter. Then she pointed to Riff, smacked her lips, and made gross *slurp-slurp*ing sounds. Her version of a kiss. She was trying to encourage him.

Riff mumbled a drowsy question in her sleep. "What is it?"

Unya laughed so much she couldn't *slurp-slurp* anymore. She retreated back to her place in the doorway.

Riff continued to murmur to herself, without ever waking up. Her murmur sounded like a contented purr in Col's ears. He realized with surprise that his hand still rested on her hip. . . . It seemed glued there, and he couldn't make himself want to unglue it.

He broke the spell in the end, though. He removed his hand and went back to his own thoughts. Now he was thinking about Riff and himself. . . . Would it ever come good between them? *How* could it ever come good? It seemed like the ultimate cruelty that finally he knew he loved her, finally he knew she loved him, and *still* they couldn't come together.

Why, why had he ever gone through the marriage ceremony with Sephaltina? It was his own fault; he'd known it was wrong at the time, only it hadn't seemed to matter much then. Was he doomed to pay for the rest of his life?

His thoughts went round and round in circles, so hopeless and depressing that, in spite of himself, he fell at last into a shallow sleep. When he came back awake, it seemed as if he'd barely closed his eyes.

His arm was wrapped over Riff's waist, his hand cupping her hip, exactly as before. Unya up to her tricks again?

But when he looked over his shoulder, Unya was nowhere near. She was lying across the doorway, stretched out like a dog. So he must have done it himself. . . .

Just a little longer, he thought, letting his arm rest.

Then Riff snuggled back against him. "Don't move," she said. "That's nice."

"You're awake?"

"Sort of."

"How long have . . ."

"Don't move. Nobody can see. Nobody needs to know."

He didn't pull away, but he couldn't help the tension in his fingers. She covered his hand with hers.

"Relax. It's meant to be."

Col was desperate to believe that it was meant to be. Only he couldn't quite forget the obstacle in the way. "I feel like I'm cheating."

"Cheating?"

"On Sephaltina."

"Oh, your little wife toy. She doesn't count. She's not a real person."

"That's not fair. She has feelings like anyone else."

"Like anyone else who's a spoiled child."

"She loves me. She really does. I'd forgotten how much, but it's true. I can't hurt her."

Riff let out a scornful breath. "I saw her performance. 'I'll die, I'll die!' That's not feelings, that's manipulation. Can't you tell the difference?"

She rolled over where she lay, so that they were face to face. Her mouth was very close to his; her eyes were huge and overpowering.

"You're so moral," she said. "You're still the respectable Upper Decks boy at heart."

Col was drowning. It was like the time when she'd been teaching him fighting skills, and they'd both fallen to the floor. . . . No! He struggled in vain to summon up an image of Sephaltina on her sickbed.

"You believe in abstract things instead of real things," she whispered. "Principles instead of feelings."

That was partly true, he knew; he would never escape the influence of his old ethics lessons under Professor Twillip. But still . . .

"Sephaltina's not a principle. And being married is very real for her."

The wave was receding. Riff drew back a fraction too.

"Did you find out about getting unmarried?" she asked.

"Yes." Col seized on the diversion. "It won't be easy."

"You want to wait?"

"Yes."

"But it *will* be possible?"

He couldn't tell an outright lie. "No," he said miserably.

"Never?"

"Never."

"Phh! Well, I know where I stand now."

A sudden distance had sprung up between them. Riff sucked in her lower lip, and rolled back to face the pipes again.

Col was in a state of utter confusion. The blood pounded in his brain until everything became a blur. For one moment the thought passed through his mind: If only Shiv had stabbed a bit more effectively, if only he had struck for the heart . . .

In the next moment he was attacked by remorse. That was a terrible thought. He shook his head and turned over to face the doorway.

I want Sephaltina to recover, he told himself. *I'm glad she's better.*

He heard no further sound from Riff, so he guessed she must have dropped off again.

When he dropped off himself, a long while later, his sleep was filled with jumbled, vivid dreams. One scene kept repeating: He was in the Imperial Chapel, and Queen Victoria asked, *Do you, Colbert Porpentine, take this woman to be your lawful wedded wife?* And, in the dream, he concentrated hard and said the words that he really meant: *I don't.*

Always the same: *I don't.*

The last time he dreamed those words, a voice started to sing. It was the most beautiful singing he'd ever heard, but it didn't sound like the kind of song to sing in the Imperial Chapel.

Then he understood what was wrong—it was in a foreign language. All at once he was no longer asleep but wide awake and listening to a real song in a real room with pipes and dripping water.

He could hardly believe that it was Unya singing. Such a pure, rich voice hardly seemed to fit with her personality. But there she was, sitting cross-legged in the doorway, singing to herself.

Col wasn't the only one awake and listening. After a while Unya realized she had an audience and broke off in mid-song.

"No, go on," said Dunga, propping herself up on one elbow. She raised a hand to her mouth, to illustrate sound coming out. Then to her ear, to illustrate listening.

Unya seemed the last person in the world to be bashful, but she grimaced and giggled and shook her head. Eventually, though, she took up her song again.

Col had never imagined that anything could be so deep and moving. His main experience of music before the Liberation had been of Gillabeth's agonizingly correct piano recitals. This was music that made the hairs stand up on the back of his neck.

Unya never did get to finish her song, however. This time one of the *svolochi* came up and interrupted with an important message. She rose and stood in the doorway, nodding as she listened.

Then she turned back to those in the room. "*Babya zhdet,*" she explained.

There was that word *babya* again. Who or what was *babya*? Unya beckoned to show they had to get up and follow.

66

Unya and the messenger escorted the team along tunnels and up ladders. It was like a warren of passages burrowed into a mass of solid iron. Finally they emerged into a larger space, where a crowd of *svolochi* had assembled. On one side a sheet of water came sluicing down in a perpetual waterfall. Underfoot the floor was slimy and slippery.

All eyes were upon the team as they came forward through the crowd. Unya pointed ahead and breathed the one word, *"Babya."* Her tone suggested awe and reverence.

Babya was a woman, though at first sight she appeared more metal than flesh. Little of her skin was visible because of the ornaments that encased her like gleaming armor. Bracelets covered the entire length of her arms, multiple rings encircled her neck, and bands of brass lapped around her waist and legs. She had copper coils braided in her hair, screws and bolts dangling from her ears, and silver wires woven through her eyebrows. It was a miracle she could stand upright under the weight.

She inspected the team one by one, clanking as she moved along the line. She was obviously the leader of all the *svolochi*. Perhaps she thought Col was a leader too; at any rate he was the one she chose to question.

"Romanov," she said, and spread her arms to take in

everything around them. *"Romanov."* Then she prodded Col in the chest and raised an eyebrow.

Col understood that she wanted to know where the outsiders came from. *"Liberator,"* he said, and pointed with both arms, trying to convey the idea of a place beyond the walls of the Russian juggernaut. He added a pantomime of shielding his eyes and pretending to stare into the remote distance.

Babya turned to the *svolochi* behind her. For the first time Col noticed that some of them carried the rifles that had been taken from the team. They held them at arm's length, very gingerly. Babya pointed first to the rifles, then to Col.

He could only guess. "Yes, they belong to us." He stuck out his chest, miming pride and power.

Babya nodded, and said something to her followers. At once the whole assembly moved off, with Babya and the team in the middle.

They made their way past alternating niches and buttresses. The buttresses were stamped with a double-headed eagle and the date 1857: the symbol of the tsars and the date of *Romanov*'s construction. Many of the symbols had been defaced with scratch marks.

Three turns brought them into another open space, and an even larger crowd of *svolochi*. Here the light was orangey-red, radiating from open trays of glowing coals. Great cast-iron blocks towered up like black cliffs all around.

The *whish-gaah!* sounds were louder here, and seemed to come from somewhere deep within the blocks. Intricate pipes zigzagged like veins over the front of the metal. So far as the eye could see, the cliffs had no summits and the space no roof; it might have been a dark night sky overhead.

Col was still trying to make out a roof when somebody caught him by the shoulders and swiveled him round to look where everyone else was looking. Two large pipes sloped up at an angle of forty-five degrees in front of a featureless black wall. He recognized at once that these were the same corrugated pipes that came out beneath the *Romanov*'s underbelly—and presumably ascended all the way to the *Romanov*'s Upper Decks.

Babya took a rifle from one of the *svolochi*, beckoned Col forward, and walked out in front of the crowd. When Riff tagged along uninvited, nobody tried to prevent her. They halted twenty paces away from the pipes.

There were human figures going up inside one pipe, coming down inside the other. They appeared as mere gray shadows through the semitransparent membrane.

Babya handed the rifle to Col. *"Pokazhi,"* she said.

She made gestures that at first he didn't understand. Something to do with the rifle and the gray shadows?

"I think she wants you to shoot one of the officers in the pipe," said Riff.

"What?"

"To demonstrate the use of the rifle."

"What if they're Menials?"

"More likely officers."

Col focused on three shadows coming down in the

left-hand pipe. He could see them clearly enough to put a bullet through their heads.

He clicked off the safety catch, raised the rifle to his shoulder, and took aim at the first of the three. The officer—if it was an officer—had no suspicion, no sense of danger. He was an easy target through the membrane.

Col had his finger on the trigger, yet his finger refused to move.

It's an officer, he told himself. *An officer, not a Menial.*

But there was more to it than that. He pictured the bullet arriving out of nowhere, splattering the man's brains. Even a Russian officer didn't deserve to die without warning.

"Hurry up," Riff urged.

Already the first shadow was disappearing out of sight, where the pipe angled down through the floor. Col switched his aim to the second shadow. Still he couldn't bring himself to squeeze the trigger.

"I can't shoot an innocent man," he muttered.

Riff snorted. "Think what they do to their Filthies. Think what they do to make Menials."

"I mean that particular man. I don't know what *he's* done wrong."

The second shadow followed the first below floor level. Babya grunted with impatience.

"It's our only chance," Riff hissed. "The mission's finished if you don't demonstrate the rifle."

Col redirected his aim to the third shadow. But Riff's words made it even more difficult. To kill someone just as a demonstration seemed like the worst kind of murder.

He tilted the rifle barrel and fired harmlessly above the pipe. The bullet hit the wall with a loud *tang!* and went singing off through the air.

The shadow in the pipe stopped and turned. The second shadow came back into view, then the head and shoulders of the first.

"That won't do it!" Riff exploded. "Give it here!"

She reached out to take the rifle, but Col wouldn't let go. Babya, losing interest, turned to walk away.

Meanwhile the Russian officers were doing something inside the pipe. Naturally, they recognized the sound of a rifle shot. Three tiny vertical slots opened up in the membrane, and three sets of eyes looked out.

The men exchanged shouts of outrage and amazement. Col couldn't understand their words, but he understood their reaction. What they saw were two Filthies with a rifle who had just taken a shot at them.

In the next moment the tips of three rifles poked out through the slots.

"Down!" he yelled.

He gave Riff a violent push that knocked her to the ground, and dived to the ground himself.

In the same split second the officers fired. Their shots passed over the top of Col and Riff, and struck Babya instead.

Tang! Tang! Two of the bullets ricocheted from her metal ornaments. The third smacked into the back of her skull. She toppled forward, spasmed, and lay still.

67

A great gasp rose from the *svolochi*. The thought flashed across Col's mind—who would they blame most? The officers who had fired the fatal shot, or the outsiders who had brought trouble upon them?

"Come *on*!"

He heard Riff's scream and jumped to his feet before the officers could draw a new bead on him. Three paces only he ran, then flung himself down behind Babya's lifeless body.

Another volley of shots rang out. Babya's body jerked this way and that. Col felt the wind of one bullet brush across his hair.

He threw a glance toward the *svolochi*. Riff was already among them, shouting, "Like this! Safety catch off! Like this!"

He realized that he still had a rifle himself. No question of cold-blooded murder now. He looked out over the top of Babya, took aim at the middle shadow, and fired.

The officer crumpled and fell. In his fall he collected the officer beneath him in the pipe, and both tumbled down below the level of the floor.

The officer above took a wild shot, and there was a roar of pain from someone in the crowd. A moment later the *svolochi* started to shoot back. First one *crack!*

then another, then a whole barrage of gunfire.

The *svolochi* might not have learned to shoot straight, but they compensated by sheer volume of firepower. The last officer fell a short distance, then stuck. Bullet after bullet ripped into the pipe all around him. At least a few must have hit their target.

"Enough!" Riff yelled, and waved her arms. "Stop now!"

They didn't understand the words, but they grasped the message. The gunfire died away. In the silence, the *whish-gaah!* of the machinery sounded loud and strangely echoing.

Then the whole crowd surged forward around their fallen leader. A young boy no older than Unya was one of the first to reach her, to kneel and look into the dead, staring eyes. Others looked at the back of her skull, half blown away.

Col got to his feet and stepped back as the crowd pressed forward. The boy extended two fingers and gently lowered Babya's eyelids over her eyes. Tears rolled down his face, and many more faces besides.

They didn't speak their grief, however—they sang it. One voice began, and another joined in, then more and more, each taking a part as in a choir. It was haunting and beautiful and heartbreakingly sad.

Louder and louder rose the lament. Col had the impression that faraway voices were responding from every chamber of the engine room. He had hardly known Babya, but the song crept into his bones and filled his heart to bursting.

Then a different sound cut across the song like a knife.

Wooo-waaaa-wooo-waaaa-wooo-waaaa-wooo-waaaa!

It was the blare of sirens. Jarring, harsh, hateful, incongruous . . .

The *svolochi* looked up at the towering cast-iron cliffs all around. Col followed the line of their gaze but couldn't see the sirens. What he saw was a movement of wires and levers alongside the veinlike pipes that zigzagged over the metal. Then lids popped open and vents appeared. The *svolochi* held their breath, and so did Col.

Something was emerging from the vents . . . a yellow, spreading gas, as sinister as the hiss that accompanied it.

Col remembered that gas. The Russians had lobbed it over in glass spheres after the collision of juggernauts. Obviously, they used it as a means of controlling their own Filthies, as well as against external enemies.

When the breeze had carried the gas toward the *Romanov*, the Russian officers and troops had fled. But the *svolochi* didn't flee—didn't try to protect themselves in any way. Instead they stood staring up at the vents and raised their voices in a new kind of song. No lament this time, but a song of defiance, thrilling and terrible.

It was magnificent, swelling the heart and stirring the blood. But how could they defy a gas?

Voice by voice it multiplied. Col saw Unya nearby, puffing out her chest and putting her soul into every note. The song rose until it drowned out even the blaring sirens.

A hand plucked suddenly at his elbow. "We have to show them what to do!" cried Riff.

Col had no idea what to do, but he ran after her in the direction of the corrugated pipes. She seemed to have it all worked out. Dunga, Cree, Orris, and Jarvie ran too.

She stopped at the place where the last officer had fallen and the membrane of the pipe had been shredded by bullets.

"Where it's weakened!" She pointed to the bullet holes. "Tear it open!"

She inserted her fingers into one hole and pulled. It was harder than it looked, even where there were several holes close together. The fabric of the membrane was much tougher than any ordinary cloth.

The others used their fingers like Riff, but Col used his rifle. He pushed the barrel in through a hole, all the way up to the trigger guard. Then he worked it back and forth like a saw, extending the rip.

"Good!" cried Riff, observing his success.

"Look at this!" cried Orris. "Even better!"

He was referring to Unya, who had come up to join them. She wasn't using her fingers or a rifle, but her filed and pointed teeth. She knelt by a cluster of holes, between Col and Orris, and enlarged them by gnawing with her teeth.

Col redirected his own rip downward, to meet up with Unya's.

Riff swung to face the *svolochi*. "Here!" She waved her arms frantically. "Over here! Escape route!"

The *svolochi* saw what was happening and started to move. Their singing rose to a thunderous volume as they marched across. The yellow gas continued to spread through the air, thicker and thicker, but still above the level of their heads.

In another minute Col's sawing and Unya's gnawing met in the middle. Riff pulled the flaps apart, and the hole was just big enough to squeeze through. She entered the pipe, and Unya slipped in behind her.

Col was next, then Orris and the rest of the team. Behind them the whole crowd of *svolochi* pushed eagerly forward.

We've done it! thought Col in jubilation. His plan had worked after all. This wasn't just an escape route, but a route to the Upper Decks. They had started a revolution!

68

Going up in the pipe was an extraordinary experience. The rungs inside were like the steps of a staircase. As the *svolochi* behind the team surged upward, they propelled those ahead of them faster and faster. Col's feet hardly seemed to touch the rungs. It was less like climbing a staircase, more like being carried up in a steam elevator.

How long it lasted he could never have guessed. It seemed to take only a minute, yet there were many hundreds of rungs. The light coming in through the semitransparent membrane was a dim gray blur.

When the light changed to layers of brightness and darkness, they were almost at the top. In another moment the pipe came to an end, and they emerged all at once into a kind of lobby.

Col staggered and jumped out of the way as the human tide streamed out behind him. They had arrived at the lowest level of the *Romanov*'s Upper Decks.

Three Russian officers stood gaping in disbelief. All had fine, curling mustaches, white uniforms with epaulettes, and peaked caps with gold-braid trimming. They backed away toward a set of glass doors, fumbling to draw their pistols from their holsters.

Riff launched into instant action. She chopped one

officer to the side of the neck, tripped another, and punched the third in the solar plexus.

As they lay gasping or unconscious on the ground, she knelt and stripped them of their pistols. She kept one for herself and passed the others to the two nearest *svolochi*.

Unya whistled in admiration and flourished her arms in imitation of Riff's moves.

Col looked around. More and more *svolochi* were arriving all the time, still singing their song of defiance. They flooded out across the lobby, momentarily without direction.

"That could be a Russian steam elevator," said Orris.

He was pointing at the glass doors toward which the officers had tried to retreat. The glass was etched with fancy designs; on the other side Col could see a grille of intersecting metal struts. It was quite unlike the curtains and swing doors of *Liberator*'s elevators. But Orris's idea was a good one: For purposes of rapid transportation, the top of the pipes would surely need to be near the bottom of an elevator.

"Let's take a look," cried Cree.

She swung open the doors and tugged at the grille in vain. Jarvie, coming up behind, worked out the trick of it. He slid the struts sideways to reveal a large platform between vertical rails, with chains and cables hanging down. It was unmistakably a steam elevator, far larger than any on *Liberator*.

The crowd pushed forward with a cheer. Cree and

Jarvie were carried in by the surge, but the rest of the team was left standing. There was no more room on the platform.

"It's okay!" Riff called out to Cree and Jarvie. "You take the first lot up!"

"We'll send it back down when we get off at the top!" Cree called back.

Jarvie, meanwhile, had located the lever that controlled the elevator. He raised it to the up position, and the platform jolted and started to ascend. The *svolochi* in the lobby continued to whoop and cheer long after the *svolochi* on the platform had disappeared behind clouds of billowing vapor.

Col, Riff, Dunga, and Orris gathered together—along with Unya, who seemed to have attached herself as a new member of the team.

"We need to find another way up," said Col. It was obvious that one elevator could never cope with the numbers still emerging from the pipe.

"There has to be a staircase nearby," said Riff, and led the way out from the lobby.

They found themselves in a corridor with burgundy-colored carpet and wood-paneled walls. Unya must have caught on to the plan; she shouted back in Russian to the crowd in the lobby, and a horde of followers streamed after them.

They discovered a staircase round the very first corner. Similar to yet different from *Liberator*'s staircases, this one went up in a spiral, with brightly painted woodwork on either side. Archways led out onto each level of deck, while the staircase kept spiraling upward.

Around and around they went, past deck after deck. The *svolochi* pushed up behind them. There was no one on the stairs and no one on the floors when they looked out. The *Romanov*'s Upper Decks seemed surprisingly deserted.

After five floors Orris was wheezing and panting.

"I'm . . . not as young as . . ."

His mouth was wide, his complexion an unhealthy shade of puce.

"I'll stop and wait with you," said Col at once.

In the end the whole team stopped, and Unya, too. They left the staircase by the next archway, while the *svolochi* continued their upward rush.

"Dozens of decks above this," said Dunga.

"We could look for another elevator," Col suggested.

Everyone liked the idea. There were many elevators on *Liberator*, so no doubt the *Romanov* was similarly equipped.

"Look for glass doors," ordered Riff.

They set off as soon as Orris recovered his breath. Riff with her pistol and Col with his rifle marched at the front.

The deck they were on was even more lavish than the one lower down. The wood paneling here was more highly polished, and the carpet was like velvet under their feet. There were ornate mirrors on the walls, and the symbol of the double-headed eagle on every door.

In one corridor the team passed a group of Russian

Menials, instantly recognizable by their hunched posture. They wore elaborate harnesses of leather straps that buckled around their waists and over their chests and shoulders.

"Mi na vashei storone!" Unya called out to them.

They gazed at her with blank expressions, then went back to their cleaning and polishing. Each was tethered to a separate doorknob.

The team strode on in a straight line, avoiding side passages and branching corridors. However, their route came to an end at a grand arched gateway. It reminded Col of the entrance to Dr. Blessamy's Academy, but gilded and far more elaborately carved.

"The doors are open," said Dunga.

"Let's keep going," said Riff.

They walked through into a high-domed gallery and continued along a mosaic path through lush green vegetation. Somewhere ahead there were people talking and laughing. Splashing sounds too.

Col raised his rifle and Riff raised her pistol. They came up to a further archway and looked through into a very strange hall.

A huge pool of water occupied the center of the place, fifty paces long by fifty paces wide. Around the sides ran a walkway of tiles and an elegant colonnade of white pillars. Cubicle doors filled in the spaces between the pillars.

The water must have been warm, because wisps of steam rose from the surface. Six officers with mustaches and side-whiskers stood or swam in it, and an equal number of ladies in bathing caps. The officers wore tight-fitting, red-striped bathing suits buttoned up to the neck, while the ladies' suits were looser and puffed out like balloons above the water.

Then one of the ladies caught sight of the intruders and screamed at the top of her voice.

69

The officers rushed for the steps on one side of the pool. They were mostly middle-aged and paunchy, ungainly as walruses in their tight-fitting bathing suits. They flapped across the tiles and vanished into the cubicles.

The team skirted the pool on the opposite side. There was another archway at the far end of the hall. They ran past deck chairs, towels, the remnants of a picnic, and half a dozen dresses that stood up all by themselves, like human figures without arms or heads. Presumably, they belonged to the ladies in the pool, and only their hoops and stiffeners kept them upright.

The ladies, meanwhile, dipped down below the water until only their eyes and bathing caps were showing.

The team was halfway around when a voice barked out an order in Russian. Unya skidded to a stop and pointed. The barrels of six pistols stuck out over the tops of six cubicle doors. The whole team halted.

"We can match that," snarled Riff, and aimed her pistol at the head of one of the ladies in the pool.

Col did the same, squinting along his sights as if ready to shoot, while praying he wouldn't have to.

It was a stalemate. The Russian officers shouted to one another from behind their cubicle doors.

Then one door swung open, and one officer stepped

out. On his head was a brass helmet, which looked very odd in combination with his bathing suit. He had strapped on a sword belt and left his pistol behind.

He stalked around the pool with his nose in the air and a supercilious expression on his face. He marched up to Col, drew his sword, and struck the ground at Col's feet with the tip.

When he spoke, his tone dripped with contempt. "Kapitan Kodalski."

"That must be his name," Riff guessed, as Unya pointed to the officer's chest.

Then Unya swung and lunged with her arms, this way and that.

"Ah, swordplay," Riff interpreted. "I think Kapitan Kodalski is challenging you to a duel."

"I could just shoot him," said Col.

"And they could just shoot us."

"Why me, anyway? You're the expert in single combat."

Riff grinned sarcastically. "I don't think his code of honor would let him fight with a *girl*."

Col saw that the officer was still glaring at him, rigid as a statue. He shrugged and passed his rifle across to Dunga.

Kapitan Kodalski bowed to the ladies in the pool, then shouted *"En garde!"* and sprang forward. The fact that Col was unarmed didn't seem to trouble his code of honor.

Col jumped back, knocking against a deck chair. The sword swept past and barely missed his ear. Kodalski advanced to deliver another blow. Col flung the deck chair in his way, and the sword sheared through canvas and wood instead of flesh and bone.

"Use this!"

As Col sought desperately for a weapon, Riff tossed him a towel. A *towel*! And already Kodalski was preparing to lunge again.

Col did the only thing he could do with a towel: He darted forward and flicked it at his opponent's face. The corner of the towel caught the officer across the cheek. He howled with pain and lost control of his stroke, which scythed through empty air.

Unya hooted with laughter. Kodalski's howl turned into a splutter of mortification, then a roar of rage.

Col watched the man's eyes. Riff had trained him long ago to spot the movement in the eyes that comes a split second before the movement of the muscles. He saw where the next blow was aimed, and dodged easily. The thrust to his chest sailed past his left elbow.

Then he worked out another use for the towel. When Kodalski thrust forward again, Col sidestepped to the right and raised his arm so that the sword passed beneath—then whisked the towel under his arm to muffle the blade's sharp edges. He clamped down with his elbow and trapped the sword against the side of his body.

The officer's face was a picture of goggling outrage. Col swiveled from the hips and forced him round on the other end of the sword. When he took a step forward, Kodalski had to step backward. Two more steps—then

Col swiveled again and propelled him right off the edge of the tiles.

Too late the officer let go of his sword. For a moment his feet hung over empty air; then he landed in the pool with a mighty splash. When the spray cleared, he was standing up to his chest in water.

Col drew the sword out from the towel and waved it in front of Kodalski's nose. The officer was very red in the face and refused to look Col in the eyes. He raised his arms as a sign of surrender.

"You've humiliated him!" Riff laughed. "Beaten in a duel and tossed in the water."

In the next moment the cubicle doors opened, and the other officers trooped out with their arms also raised. The ladies in the pool seemed to have disappeared underwater completely.

Unya came up to the side of the pool and spoke in Russian to Kapitan Kodalski. He muttered in reply, and she raised her voice.

"What are they saying?" Dunga asked.

Orris's brow was creased in frowns as he struggled to translate. "Something about 'going up.'"

The exchange went on for half a minute. Unya's tone grew sharper and sharper; Kodalski's head hung lower and lower. Finally he made his way to the steps and climbed out of the pool.

Not once did he look in the direction of his fellow officers. He removed the brass helmet from his head and held it under his arm.

"*Davai, dvigaisya!*" Unya ordered.

"That means 'move!'" said Orris.

Kodalski marched stiffly toward the exit at the far end of the hall. Unya followed, and gestured for the others to follow her.

Riff grinned. "I think he has to do whatever we say. Very useful, this code of honor."

Beyond the exit there were more wood-paneled corridors. Col carried his newly acquired sword and let Dunga keep the rifle. Kodalski left wet footprints on the carpet and shivered as he marched. They passed another two groups of Russian Menials, laboring in domestic duties, but Unya didn't call out again.

It was no surprise when Kodalski turned down an intersecting corridor and halted in front of a set of glass doors. Unya made him face the wall and put his hands on his head.

"Steam elevator!" Orris exclaimed. "We're going up!"

70

They rode the elevator up forty-two floors, and stepped out at the top onto a deck more opulent than any they had yet seen. The walls were decorated with tapestries, the ceilings with gold and painted stars. Niches displayed artificial flowers or wax fruit arrangements under domes of glass.

"Listen," said Riff.

The fighting wasn't far away: a vast and confused hubbub of shouts and cries, with frequent cracks of rifle fire. The sound of the *svolochi* singing was a backdrop to all other sounds.

"Must be around the top of the first elevator," said Orris.

"And the top of the staircase," added Dunga.

"Probably hundreds of them up by now," said Col.

"Let's go," cried Riff.

They set off running toward the hubbub. The corridor became a broad highway, fifteen yards from side to side. Someone was coming toward them from the other direction.

"Hey! That's Cree!"

"And Jarvie!"

The two separated members of the team recognized them in the same moment. They slowed and waited.

"You made it," said Cree, as the two groups came together.

"What's happening?" Riff asked. "Who's winning?"

"We are—just," said Cree. "We're on the highest floor here. The imperial guards have retreated to the open deck above."

"There's not that many ordinary soldiers," Jarvie added. "And most of their officers are old."

Cree took over again. "But they've blockaded the stairs to the open deck. The Russian Filthies are trying to fight their way through. We're trying to find another way up."

"Good idea," Col agreed. "There must be other stairs."

"You'd think so." Jarvie grimaced. "We haven't found any yet."

"We'll all search," said Riff. "We'll fan out and—what's *she* doing?"

Unya had wandered off by herself. A short way back up the corridor was an imposing door flanked by marble statues. Unya had opened the door and was peering inside.

Then she turned and shouted, beckoned, and waved.

"Maybe she's found something useful," said Orris.

"Like she found the steam elevator for us," said Col.

The team members exchanged glances and came to an instant decision. As Unya vanished through the door, they hurried after her.

Col took a good look at the statues on the way in: one male and one female, carved in proud and formal poses, wearing robes and elaborate headgear. The nature of the entrance suggested there was something very special about these rooms.

Inside, the air smelled of tobacco and cigars. Col took in green-baize tables, stucco moldings over the ceiling, glowing lamps, and painted lampshades. On one side of the room was a black animal chained to a hoop in the wall. Larger than a cat yet smaller than a tiger, it showed its teeth and glared at them with bright, yellow eyes.

Unya was as if intoxicated. She caressed the lampshades and stroked the baize tops of the tables. It seemed she had to touch everything before she could believe it was real.

They went on through into the next room, which was even more luxurious. Col gasped at all the satin and velvet, amber and tortoiseshell, lacework and crystalware. Crimson drapes hung around a massive four-poster bed, and the walls were lined with mottled brown fur. Scent perfumed the air, exotic, sweet, and musky.

There was no one presently in the room, but many signs of hasty departure: clothes scattered over the floor, pillows tossed aside, an open book upside down on the quilt. From the room beyond came unmistakable sounds of movement.

Col, Riff, and Dunga advanced with their weapons raised. Col eased the door open with his foot, to reveal another scene of sumptuous magnificence—and the source of the sounds. Half a dozen Menial servants shuffled around in their leather harnesses.

They wore all-white uniforms emblazoned with the

letters A & K on their chests. Unya pointed to the insignia with great excitement. Riff pointed in another direction entirely.

"Here's how we go up," she said.

Just inside the door was an arch to the left and an ascending staircase. Riff went through the arch and started up the stairs. Col followed at her heels.

The stairs were narrow and dimly lit. The team climbed to a small landing, reversed direction, and continued up again. This was obviously a private and exclusive route for the occupants of the rooms below.

At the top they stood in a bare circular space. No luxury here. The air was cooler and fresher, and the light seeping in around the edges of the door had a different quality. Col thought at once of the turret above *Liberator's* bridge.

"We've come to the open deck," he said.

The bolts on the door were like the turret too, though already unbolted. He worked the door handle. Metal creaked and grated on metal.

"Carefully," Riff warned.

The rest of the team had gathered behind them. Col gave the door a tiny push, and it almost flew wide open, caught by a gust of wind. He snatched it back and held it just a few inches ajar.

Outside, the deck of the *Romanov* was an endless flat metal surface. Surprisingly, it was wet with puddles of rainwater. Col remembered the rumbling thunder when they'd crossed the ground between the two juggernauts. The storm must have broken overnight, while they were down in the *Romanov*'s engine room. Now, in the morning, the sky had cleared and the sun was shining.

The nearest people were fifty paces away. They had congregated by the side of the deck: a score of very grand ladies and gentlemen. The gentlemen wore short cloaks, sashes, and rows of medals on their chests, while the ladies were all in white, with veils, gloves, and high-piled coiffures. They might have been attending a ball in all their formal finery.

Unya pointed her finger and gabbled away in Russian. She was on her hands and knees, peering out at the bottom of the door. She was pointing to one couple in particular.

"*Ya ikh uznal! Eto tsar i tsarina!*"

Col registered the two words that made sense to him. "Did she say . . . ?"

"Tsar and tsarina!" Orris jumped in. "That's who they are. Tsar Alexander the Sixth and Tsarina Katerina. Of course. Initials *A* and *K*."

Col stared at the couple and noticed how much they resembled the statues flanking the doorway in the corridor. "We were in their rooms," he said slowly. "We came up by their private staircase."

Riff shushed them both. "Keep your voices down."

Tsar Alexander wore a simple black bearskin hat rather than any more elaborate form of headgear. As they watched, he removed the bearskin and passed it across to one of his subordinates. Then he took a short ceremonial sword from a scabbard at his waist, and passed that across to a second subordinate. His gestures were very deliberate, very regal; his subordinates bowed and received the items with great reverence.

Unya was pushing against the door, and Col allowed it to open a few inches wider. No one seemed likely to look in their direction.

The breeze blowing in ruffled their hair and clothes. Outside, it stirred the puddles and made the water glitter in the sharp sunlight. On the other side of the imperial family was a tangle of masts and wires like a forest of fallen trees.

"What *is* this ceremony?" Orris muttered.

The tsarina had now presented her gloves to one of her female attendants. Tsar Alexander stood erect with outthrust chest as a courtier in fur cloak and knee-high boots unpinned his medals and ribbons, one by one, and made a pile of them on a cushion held out by another subordinate.

Two further attendants were busy at the side of the juggernaut, where a ramp led up to the encircling barrier. They unfurled a tasseled white cloth and spread it over the ramp as if laying a tablecloth for dinner.

"Hear that!" said Dunga.

Col had grown used to the general background clamor of fighting and singing, but now the sound had changed. The song of the *svolochi* was no longer a song of defiance but a song of victory. It grew louder and clearer even as they listened.

"They've won!" cried Cree.

Jarvie whooped. "They're coming up on deck!"

It was all taking place on the other side of the turret, where they couldn't see. There was a redoubled uproar of shouting and rifle fire, as though the imperial guards were making a last stand.

What they could see were the reactions of the imperial family. The tsar and tsarina glanced in the direction of the fighting, and a new urgency came into their actions. The tsar began shaking hands with his subordinates, addressing a few words to each one.

"I could shoot him from here," said Dunga, sighting along her rifle.

"No, wait," said Riff. "I want to see what happens."

The tsar finished shaking hands, then turned to his tsarina and bowed. She responded with a tiny bob of a curtsy. Then they walked side by side to the ramp, ascended the incline . . . and stepped off at the end.

Col gasped. Everyone gasped.

He had to replay the sequence in his mind to be sure it had really happened.

"Why did they do that?"

The courtiers and attendants followed their master and mistress, two by two. They marched up the ramp and stepped off into the void on the other side of the barrier. The ones who had received the bearskin, sword, gloves, and medals went over with the rest, bearing the ceremonial items as they dropped.

"Perhaps I can explain," said Orris. "I learned something about the Russian nobility. They've always been known for their aristocratic code of honor. The tsar could never live with the disgrace of being overthrown by his own Filthies."

"So we've won?" Dunga looked puzzled.

"Easy as that?" Col could hardly believe it.

Riff believed it. She was exultant. "Our second revolution! First the British, now the Russians! No one can stop us now!"

She kicked the door wide, and they stumbled out into the open air. The breeze carried a sharp smell of gunpowder to Col's nostrils. He stepped away from the turret and looked to see what was happening on the other side.

The Russian imperial guards had formed a defensive line all across the deck of the juggernaut. Some were standing and some kneeling; some flourished swords and some fired rifles. Many lay bleeding on the ground.

The *svolochi* were on the other side of the defensive line. Col could hear them more than he could see them— their tremendous victory song like a booming peal of thunder.

"The guards don't know the tsar's given up the fight," said Riff.

"How do we tell them?" asked Col.

They reached the same answer in the same moment. "Unya can."

But Unya wasn't with them. They looked around and realized that she'd trotted off on her own. She was standing against the barrier, craning over the top. No doubt she wanted to see where the tyrants had fallen to their deaths.

"Unya! Unya! *Unya!*"

She spun around. They expected to see an expression of elation on her face, but instead they saw shock and dismay.

She let out a sound like a strangled squawk.

71

An incredible scene dawned before their eyes as they looked out over the barrier. Thousands of imperialist troops were drawn up in columns and squares on the ground below. It was a vast battlefield, closed off between *Liberator* on one side and the *Romanov* on the other, between the *Marseillaise* at one end and the Austrian and Turkish juggernauts at the other. Troops from the different juggernauts wore uniforms in different colors: red, gray, green, and blue. The battle was already underway.

"And we thought we were winning," Riff muttered.

"So much for conquering the *Romanov*," said Col.

"No wonder there were so few Russians."

"Just the old ones left behind."

Liberator was like a castle under siege. Filthies and convicts fired rifles from scoops that had been lowered halfway to the ground to serve as gun posts. Others fired from portholes in the juggernaut's side. Answering fire came from snipers stationed above in the tethered balloons of the *Marseillaise*.

The rest of the team joined Col, Riff, and Unya at the barrier. Jarvie and Cree gasped, Orris groaned, and Dunga cursed under her breath.

"So many of them."

"We don't stand a chance."

Riff grunted. "Not only troops. War machines, too."

She pointed to a part of the battlefield where hundreds of wheeled vehicles were lined up in rows. From this height they looked like black beetles with silvery wing cases.

And there was more. Col saw mighty brass tubes elevated at forty-five-degree angles, aimed at *Liberator*. He saw a huge red hose that stretched all across the battlefield from the *Romanov*'s second segment. And in the very center of the imperialist forces—

"What's that?" Dunga asked the question before he could ask it himself.

It was a kind of tower, an octagonal structure roofed over and closed in at the top. Flagpoles and flags rose from its eight corners; banners swathed its metal legs.

"Must be something important," said Riff.

A system of raised walkways converged toward the tower like ribbons, laid out between the troop formations. Four ribbons combined into two, then two into one.

Ferr-whooshh!

A ball of light drew everyone's attention—a ball of light shooting up from one of the brass tubes. It looped high in the air, seemed to hover for a moment, then arced down upon *Liberator*. Missing the scoops, it smashed against the side of the hull. A white flare of intense brightness radiated from the point of impact.

Ferr-whooshh! Ferr-whooshh! Ferr-whooshh! Ferr-whooshh!

Col had black dots before his eyes. From all parts of the battlefield, tubes fired off their balls of light. Some landed and flared in no-man's-land next to the hull, some passed clean over the top, and two splashed light over the superstructure. The gunners were still getting their range.

"We have to do something," said Col.

"What?" asked Cree.

"Cut off that hose for a start," said Riff. "See where it's coming from?"

Col already knew where it came from: the detached second segment of the Russian juggernaut. But now he understood the implications. "I bet it's for pumping yellow gas."

Orris grimaced. "The Russians' favorite weapon."

"They'll poison everyone on *Liberator*."

"But how do we get down?" asked Jarvie.

Col chewed at his lip. It would take ages to go back down by way of steam elevator, pipe, and engine room. . . .

"I know!" cried Dunga. "Look!"

They followed the line of her pointing arm.

Riff whistled in amazement. "Lye's ropes!"

A hundred yards along the side of the *Romanov's* hull were two ropes dangling down. Although Riff had ordered the ropes cut loose at the *Liberator* end, they were still attached by grappling hook to the *Romanov* end.

The Filthies were elated, but Orris pulled at his chin.

"I don't think I can climb down there," he said.

Col wasn't too sure about it himself. Though half his father's age, he was still heavier and less agile than the Filthies.

"You don't need to," Riff told Orris. "You stay here with Unya and complete the revolution."

"How?"

"Can you say, 'The tsar is dead'?"

Orris thought for a moment. *"Tsar mertv."*

"Unya?"

Unya looked round, and Orris repeated the phrase. *"Tsar mertv."*

Unya clapped her hands. *"Tsar mertv! Tsarina mertva!"*

"Yes, tsarina too." Riff turned to Orris. "Your job is to shout that to the imperial guards until they give up fighting." She turned to Col. "How about you? Can you do it?"

She meant the climb down the ropes. Col pulled a face. "What have I got to lose?"

Riff grinned. "Right. We can't survive anyway."

"Not against the whole imperialist army."

"We're finished." Riff's grin broadened. "Nothing matters anymore."

"Nothing at all."

He was watching her eyes. Suddenly it was as if no one else were there. This wasn't a combat, yet he was waiting for the movement in her eyes that foretold a movement of the muscles. He had the strangest sense of freedom. . . . The strings that had been tying him down were all at once dissolved. If they were going to die anyway . . .

He sprang forward as she sprang forward. He seized her in a hug—the tightest, hardest, fiercest hug. She squeezed back just as hard. Then she kissed him, not softly or tenderly, but as though to imprint herself onto him. He returned her kiss with a kind of consuming desperation. They clung to each other until they could hardly breathe.

"*Tsar mertv!*" yelled Orris at the top of his voice.

"*Tsarina mertva!*" yelled Unya.

They were advancing across the deck, telling the imperial guards that their rulers were dead.

Col and Riff pulled reluctantly apart. They were still looking into each other's eyes.

"I guess luck was against us," Riff murmured.

Col shook his head. "I feel lucky," he said. "I feel like the luckiest person in the world."

"Come on, you two! We're going!"

Dunga, Cree, and Jarvie were already running toward the ropes. Col and Riff turned and ran after them.

72

Col and Riff started down the ropes side by side, but Riff, being nimbler, soon moved ahead. Col had slid his sword through his belt so that the blade hung down safely out of the way. He let the rope pass around his shoulder and lowered himself hand over hand, walking down backward with his feet braced against the hull.

He had never felt so intensely alive in his life. He had the breeze on his skin, the sun on his back, and fresh air in his lungs. Nothing mattered, nothing at all—and he went down the rope as if on wings.

The last stretch was the hardest, when the rope stopped short fifty feet above the ground. Looking down, Col saw Riff moving like a crab, clinging to bolt heads with fingers and toes, pressing herself flat against the metal.

He copied her technique. It was even more difficult with the sword swinging against his side, but he was infallible. He clambered to within ten feet of the ground, then jumped the rest of the way. The point of the sword stabbed down into the soft earth beside him.

Riff, Dunga, Jarvie, and Cree were discussing the next move as they waited for him. There were no soldiers or officers nearby; the troop formations had all moved up toward the besieged *Liberator*. A number of soldiers stood around the hose where it emerged from the *Romanov's* detached second segment—but not many of them. No doubt that was why Riff had made it their first target.

Col saw no reason to delay. There was a hose to cut, and he had the sharp-edged blade with which to cut it. He plucked the sword from the ground and flourished it over his head.

"Let's go!"

He set off running, and the others sped after him.

The grass was wet from the recent rain, and it sparkled in the sunshine. Col kicked up spray as he ran, sploshing through puddles as if they weren't there. Not once did he glance back to check that the others were following. He was utterly carefree and utterly reckless.

Looking ahead, he saw how the hose passed at intervals through lumpish bits of machinery. Pumping engines, perhaps? The Russian troops were gazing toward *Liberator* and hadn't yet noticed his approach. Naturally, they had no idea of the revolution that had just taken place in the main front segment of their own juggernaut.

Col kept as far away from the troops as possible and ran right up to the hose. It was two feet in diameter, red and rubbery. He lifted his sword and swung. The blade sliced down—deep enough to reach the hollow core, though not deep enough to cut all the way through.

A hiss of yellow gas escaped. It had an evil reek, sweet and bitter at the same time.

A voice cried out in Russian, a shout of alarm.

Col had a vague sense that the rest of the team had come up around him. He raised his sword for a second blow, but Cree dragged at his elbow and yelled, "Run! Run! Run!"

It wasn't the Russian soldiers they needed to flee, but the gas itself, pouring out of the gash in the hose.

Col ran with the rest—but still had the sense of a job unfinished. Was it so difficult to patch a hose? He skidded to a halt and looked back.

"Wait up," he cried.

"What?"

"Give me cover."

He ran in again, heading for a different part of the hose. This time he was close to one of the bits of machinery: a strange contraption mounted on wheels, with a great central bellows puffing in and out. Even better! There would be no way to repair a wrecked pumping engine.

He veered toward it. Shots were fired, but he didn't know if they came from the Russian soldiers or from Riff's pistol and Dunga's rifle. He was still in his crazy mood of exhilaration.

He swooped on the pumping engine, which was chugging quietly away, and thrust his sword into the heart of its moving mechanical parts. There was a screech of metal, and the chugging ceased. Again and again he thrust—and, for a coup de grâce, plunged the blade into the bellows.

With a wheezing gasp the bellows let out a great

cloud of yellow gas. Col jumped back a moment too late, and the poisonous stuff blew into his face. His eyes streamed, his nostrils stung, and the back of his throat was on fire.

"Don't breathe it in!" shouted Riff.

The rest of the team had come up around him again. They half pulled and half carried him away to fresh air. Someone thumped him on the back, and he coughed and spat and spluttered.

"Can you run?" Riff asked.

He took a shallow breath and discovered that the gas hadn't invaded his lungs. He nodded.

A hand that felt like Riff's caught hold of his hand. Still blinded by tears, he stumbled along where he was led. Plants whipped at his legs; mud sucked at the soles of his feet. He heard gunshots that might have come from Russian soldiers, but the sounds grew less and less frequent.

"This'll do," said Riff.

The hand pulled him down, and he found himself lying among twigs and leaves. He rubbed the tears from his eyes and looked out blearily. The team had taken shelter in the middle of a dense patch of bushes.

He scanned around and saw no signs of pursuit. Behind them the cloud of gas had expanded enormously, drifting toward the *Romanov*. Ahead of them the nearest troop formations wore green uniforms. To their left a branch of the raised walkway ran along on a kind of low scaffolding.

"We did it," said Cree.

Dunga shook her head at Col. "You were mad," she growled.

They watched as balls of light continued to lob against *Liberator*, staining the sky with slanting columns of smoke. The troop formations were still marching, and the battlefield was still humming with activity. Their success in disabling the Russians' favorite weapon seemed to have had little effect on the overall siege. No doubt the other imperialist forces had favorite weapons of their own.

Suddenly an amplified megaphone voice boomed out far and wide. The words were in a foreign language, but the tone was clearly a tone of command. After half a minute a second voice took over, speaking a different foreign language.

"It's coming from the tower," said Jarvie.

"Orders to the troops," Riff deduced. "So the tower must be their central command post."

Cree nodded. "That's why the walkways lead up to it."

"All their generals gathered there," said Dunga.

"Their supreme commanders," added Col.

"Do you know what I'm thinking?" Riff asked.

A long silence. Everyone had had the same thought—and wished they hadn't.

"There's only one way to make a real difference," Riff continued.

"Attack the tower," said Dunga grimly. "Take out their commanders."

"Right. We're the only ones that can do it. We can creep up under the walkways. Well?"

Cree shrugged. "Yeah. What else have we got to do?"

"Might as well go out trying," Dunga agreed.

73

Patches of bushes gave them cover as far as the walkway. They kept their heads down and crawled along on their elbows and knees.

Once in under the walkway, they rose to a crouching stance. The deck was solid wooden planking, four feet above the ground. The struts and braces of the scaffolding hid them from view at the sides.

Now they could move much faster—except when they heard footsteps tramping on the planks overhead. Four times they had to stop and hold their breath until the footsteps passed on.

After a while they came up level with the rear lines of the main imperialist forces. They were all on one side of the walkway and wore not only green uniforms, but green helmets with plumes of green feathers. Col guessed they were Austrians from the *Grosse Wien*, since they had the letters GW painted in white on their helmets.

"What do you make of those?" Riff hissed.

She pointed to the strange devices that the soldiers nursed in their arms. They had copper-colored bodies, projecting nozzles, and a great many steel spikes. Some sort of special weapon, presumably. Septimus might know what they were, but Col didn't have a clue.

Farther on again, imperialist forces of a different kind

appeared on the other side of the walkway. Col peered out through the scaffolding at the same silver-and-black vehicles he had observed from the deck of the *Romanov*.

Their silvery parts were their open-spoked wheels and torpedo-shaped snouts; their black parts were their frames and riders. No part of any vehicle or rider rose more than two feet above the ground. The riders, who wore masks and goggles, were almost horizontal on their backs. They steered with rods on either side and propelled their vehicles by pedaling with their feet.

The vehicles were all in motion now, hundreds upon hundreds of them, like a glittering sea. The waves of the sea were the riders' knees rizing and falling in perfect unison. Like a swarm of beetles, they advanced in close-packed formation, with a murmurous sound of thrumming and drumming.

The team continued to advance underneath the walkway. The planking over their heads came down lower, until they were forced to scuttle along bent almost double. It was particularly difficult for Col, who was taller than any of the Filthies. After a while their walkway joined up with another walkway.

Keeping a watchful eye on the planking, Col failed to notice a sudden hump in the ground ahead. Riff went around it, but he caught his foot and fell flat on his face.

"Ow!" said the hump in a muffled voice.

Two eyes and a mouth appeared in the muddy shape of it. Col disentangled his legs and sat up. It looked like a pile of earth, but it was actually Mr. Gibber.

"I know you." The voice was a little less muffled now. "You're Colbert Porpentine."

"Right." Col scrambled to his feet. "Glad you're not dead anymore."

"Wait." Mr. Gibber reached out a muddy arm and gripped Col by the ankle. "Don't you want to talk to me? Don't you want to hear about my experiences?"

"Not now."

"I had a vision in the night, you know." Mr. Gibber maintained his grip. "I died and came back to life."

Riff had already moved on. Dunga, Cree, and Jarvie detoured around Mr. Gibber and followed her. No one wanted to waste time on Lye's little spy.

"Let me show you!" Mr. Gibber let go of Col's ankle and dug into his clothing at the side. "The evidence! A miracle!" He held up the now-empty pack of biscuits that Cree had slipped into his jacket pocket. "It came out of nowhere. Redemption in the night! I believe an angel did it."

Col was five paces away, but he couldn't help grinning. "You ate them all, then?"

Mr. Gibber didn't understand the grin. "This is no joke, Porpentine. I've been given a new life. I want to be a better person."

"Sorry, I can't wait," said Col. "We have to stop these imperialist troops before they storm *Liberator*."

"Let me help." Mr. Gibber propped himself up on one arm and one leg. "I hate them too. They kicked and stomped on me. That's why I hid under here."

He blew muddy bubbles out of his nostrils and began to crawl after Col. He was moving much faster than the last time Col had seen him.

"Let me prove I'm a better person. I can help you."

By now the rest of the team was thirty yards away. Mr. Gibber sounded genuine, but he was still a liability.

"Another time," said Col, and hurried to catch up with the others.

He caught up sooner than he expected. The rest of the team slowed to a halt as the deck of the walkway sloped down suddenly over their heads. Three feet, two feet . . . lower and lower.

By the time Col came up, they were all on their hands and knees.

"Can't we crawl?" he asked.

"Not even that." Dunga pointed ahead. "It gets worse."

"No way through," said Jarvie with a groan.

"What, then? Out in the open?"

Riff snorted. "And fight a whole army face to face?"

They crossed to the side of the scaffolding and looked out. They had passed beyond the silver-and-black vehicles now; the soldiers here wore gray uniforms and stood massed in squares a thousand strong. Their rifles were curiously ornate, with carved wood and inlaid silver, but looked every bit as deadly as the rifle Dunga bore.

"We have to find a way," muttered Cree.

The others looked to Col and Riff as the ones most likely to come up with a plan. But not this time. Col's mind stayed empty, and Riff shook her head in frustration.

Time passed. Outside, the megaphone voices boomed more orders, then fell silent again. The orders were obviously not addressed to the soldiers in gray, who remained standing at attention, rifles sloped against their shoulders.

Then a different voice called out in a language they could understand. "I'm coming to help!"

It was Mr. Gibber, still crawling along after them. He had covered the distance at remarkable speed considering his broken arm and leg.

They shushed him to silence. Luckily, the nearest square of soldiers was forty yards away. Mr. Gibber continued to approach without another word.

They were all watching him except Dunga. Peering out through the scaffolding, she gave a sudden low whistle. "What's that?"

Even Mr. Gibber turned to look. Something was approaching outside the walkway—a type of vehicle they hadn't seen before. At the front was a steam-powered traction engine, with the driver riding behind on a small platform.

"It's going our way," said Col.

"Heading toward the tower," Cree agreed.

"I wonder . . . ," said Riff.

It was moving very slowly, parallel to the walkway at a

distance of twenty yards. Now they could see what is was hauling: a long, low trolley on wheels, laden with straw inside a perimeter of wire netting. The rounded tops of two huge glass flasks stuck out high above the straw, glowing with eerie brightness.

"If we could sneak on board . . . ," said Riff.

"Hide in the straw," muttered Cree.

"Catch a lift," said Jarvie.

Col clicked his tongue. "We need it to come closer."

"I can help," said Mr. Gibber.

Before anyone realized what was happening, he had crawled out through the scaffolding and was heading straight into the path of the traction engine. He looked like some creature from the muddy depths as he flopped along on his one good arm and one good leg. With every movement he let out a groan or a howl of pain.

The driver slowed down and shouted at him. Mr. Gibber bellowed back and kept moving. He only stopped when he was right in front of the engine's wheels.

At the last minute the driver swerved—closer to the walkway, right next to the scaffolding.

"*Yes!*" Col said breathlessly. "He's done it!"

"Get ready," ordered Riff, as the traction engine went past.

The side of the trolley was now just a couple of yards from the side of the walkway. They scrambled through the scaffolding and jumped up onto the wire netting above the slowly turning wheels.

For one split second they might have been visible as they went over the top of the netting. But no one was nearby; no one was watching. They plunged down and burrowed into the straw. By the time the traction engine swerved back to its original path, they were completely hidden from view.

"Thank you, Mr. Gibber," murmured Col.

74

Col rolled over. He had someone's leg weighing on his shoulder and someone's head against his knee. The straw was surprisingly cold, and the chill seemed to come from the two huge flasks.

He slid a hand through the straw and touched the surface of the nearest flask. No doubt about it: The glass felt like ice.

He pushed aside the straw to take a look. The brightness behind the glass was overwhelming—and now he could see exactly what it was. The flask was full of balls of light, packed side by side as if floating in some transparent liquid.

"I know," whispered Riff. "It's what they fire from those tubes."

She was the head against his knee, observing the same view through the glass.

The trolley trundled on for a hundred yards. But their hopes of reaching the tower were dashed when they began a slow, gentle curve to the right.

"We're moving away," muttered Riff.

"Where are we going?" Col wondered.

"What do we do when we stop?" asked Jarvie. It was his leg weighing on Col's shoulder.

For the present they could do nothing but wait. Col

shifted Jarvie's leg to the side, but he was happy with Riff's head against his knee.

After another hundred yards there were hisses of steam from the traction engine, and the trolley began to slow down. Col risked raising his head and saw at once where they were going. One of the great brass tubes reared up against the sky ahead. Of course—the balls of light in the flasks! They were delivering supplies of ammunition.

He ducked his head back down when he realized there were soldiers all around. He passed on the news to Riff and Jarvie, who repeated it to Dunga and Cree. Dunga and Cree had burrowed all the way across to the other side of the trolley.

"We're closer to the tower," Jarvie whispered.

"But not close enough," said Riff.

The trolley shuddered to a halt. Col heard the clink of weapons and the creak of boots . . . then someone shouting orders. The soldiers seemed to have come up right beside them. Did they suspect something? Col gripped the hilt of his sword.

Bad move! He hadn't realized that the tip of the blade stuck out from the straw. It must have flashed in the sunlight, because there was a sudden shout of surprise.

"*Qu'est-ce que c'est?*"

The barrel of a rifle came through the wire netting, probing into the straw. Col felt Riff stiffen. She must be trying not to cry out as cold metal dug into her flesh.

In the next moment he struggled to repress a gasp

himself. A second rifle had pushed forward and made contact with his calf.

Cry or no cry, the soldiers were sure there was something in the straw. The rifle drew back from Col's calf, then pushed forward again. This time it prodded his thigh.

It was the end for their plan of reaching the tower. Now they could only sell their lives as dearly as possible. Col waited for Riff's command to spring out and start fighting.

Instead he heard a faraway noise of singing. Somewhere, on another part of the battlefield, a multitude of voices rose up like a choir.

The battle song of the *svolochi*!

Col could have laughed out loud. A whole new army had joined the fight against the imperialists!

The soldiers had heard it too. They grunted with surprise and called out questions. The rifles withdrew from the straw.

Then the megaphone boomed from the tower again: fresh orders from the generals. The orders were repeated in French, German, Russian, and Turkish.

There was instant commotion. Nearby officers barked their own orders; soldiers clicked heels, wheeled around, and marched off.

Had they forgotten there was something in the straw? Even if they hadn't forgotten, they seemed to have lost interest—or their officers had. Unit after unit marched off in the direction of the singing.

"We helped them, and now they're helping us," Riff breathed.

"I bet Unya made it happen," said Col.

Still they hardly dared to believe the danger was gone. They waited as troops marched past in a never-ending tide.

They raised their heads above the straw only when the sounds of marching faded into the distance. Many troop formations still remained, still standing at attention, but none so close as before. Col looked out toward the tower; Riff looked up at the brass tube soaring above them.

"Let's put that out of action first," she said.

It turned out to be easier than expected. On Cree and Dunga's side the trolley had pulled up next to a canvas shelter erected round the base of the tube. Cree and Dunga slipped unobserved over the top of the netting and in through the flap of the shelter. Col, Riff, and Jarvie wriggled their way across between the glass flasks and followed behind.

There were imperialists inside the shelter, but Cree and Dunga had already dealt with them by the time the others arrived. Three men lay doubled up on the ground, no match for the Filthies' fighting skills. They wore padded jackets, balaclavas, and gloves so thick and heavy that their hands looked like paws.

Col looked around at stores of flasks, canisters, and rubber-sealed jars. The place was unnaturally cold, and their breath made clouds of mist in the air.

Dunga dusted her hands as over a job well done. "What next?"

"Tie them up." Riff turned to point to an array of taps,

pipes, and other apparatus at the base of the tube. "Then wreck this stuff."

"It'll be a pleasure," said Cree.

"Then what?" asked Jarvie. "Are we still trying for the tower?"

"Don't know." Riff sucked in her cheeks. "First I'm going to look out and see what the Russian Filthies are doing."

Col followed the direction of her gaze and saw a line of rungs that ran up along the top of the tube's sloping barrel.

"Me too," he said.

75

Riff scampered up rung by rung like a monkey; Col climbed after her, a little less acrobatically. They came out above the canvas of the shelter and continued on past knobs, pipes, and attachments of every kind. The brass tube was like a tree trunk covered in metallic growths and vines. Col hoped that he and Riff would pass for just another couple of attachments if anyone happened to see them from a distance. The diameter of the barrel hid them from anyone closer in.

Riff went up to the very top, and Col halted on the rungs below her. He looked out to where the *svolochi* advanced in an arrowhead formation across the middle of the battlefield. They must have streamed back down through the *Romanov*'s engine room, because they were emerging from underneath the hull.

"See!" cried Riff. "They'll split the enemy troops in two!"

Col nodded. Whether or not it was a deliberate strategy, the *svolochi* were driving a wedge between the main imperialist forces. The amplified voices of the generals in their tower boomed out orders to avert the threat. Troops in blue, gray, green, and red uniforms wheeled and maneuvered and got in one another's way. The fighting had swung in favor of the revolutionaries.

Col extended his survey across the whole field. On one side was the cloud of yellow gas he'd released himself; the imperialist troops had abandoned that area completely. On the other side was *Liberator*, looking much the worse for wear. The balls of light appeared to have melted metal where they hit, so that parts of the superstructure sagged down like coagulated liquid. Everywhere the hull was pitted with scars and blackened with residue. However, the scoops had mostly survived; only two hung down broken on the ends of their cables.

Riff's gasp of indrawn breath called his attention back to the *svolochi*. The generals had brought a new force onto the battlefield, surging forward from the direction of the Turkish juggernaut. It was the start of a counterattack.

"What are *they*?"

"Don't know. Cavalry."

"Those aren't horses."

"No, dogs. Monstrous dogs."

"Where are their riders?"

The dogs came forward at fearsome speed: square-headed wolfhounds covering the ground in huge, springy bounds. Wide bands of fabric encircled their backs like saddles, but no one sat in the saddles.

Then Col realized that the riders rode not above but below. They were strapped in under their mounts' bellies, their helmeted heads just visible in the space between the great pistoning forelegs. Each rider lay alongside some kind of long-shafted weapon.

Soon the nature of the weapon was revealed. As the hounds leaped toward the *svolochi*, rockets shot forth from under their chests. The *svolochi* had no answer. First the rockets smashed into them; then the dogs did. The dogs began snapping this way and that, white froth flying from their slavering jaws.

The *svolochi* wavered but fought back. They must have taken rifles from the Russian soldiers and officers, because most of them were armed. They stopped singing and drew their lines closer.

"Yes! Go on! Keep moving!" Riff urged them forward.

But the advance had come to a halt, and the *svolochi* were now on the defensive. Little by little they had to give ground. The wolfhounds they managed to shoot served as their only means of protection; they crouched behind the shaggy-coated bodies and aimed their rifles over the top.

Now the megaphone voices blared into life once more. New activity stirred, and new deployments started up in other quarters of the battlefield. With the surprise attack from the rear blocked off, the generals were going back to their own plans. Once more the siege was underway.

This time it was the turn of the silver-and-black vehicles. Since Col had last seen them, they had moved up to the front line facing *Liberator*, along with the green-uniformed soldiers who carried the spiky copper devices. Two hundred vehicles were in the first wave of the new offensive.

Col couldn't see the drivers, but he imagined them pedaling madly as they lay with their backs flat to the ground. The swarm glided forward like two hundred beetles in crescent formation.

Shooting from the scoops and portholes, the defenders hit and halted maybe a dozen. But twelve out of two hundred was nothing. The swarm parted to pass around the immobilized vehicles, then recombined and flowed on the same as ever.

We're just outnumbered, thought Col.

The swarm advanced right up to *Liberator*'s rollers and vanished briefly out of sight. When they reappeared, they were smaller, shorter than before. They had left their torpedo-shaped snouts behind!

They sped frantically away, no longer in close formation but dispersing, escaping. The defenders continued to shoot from the scoops and portholes, but they could do nothing about the snouts.

Kerrr-umph!-umph!-umph!-umph!

A series of muffled explosions shook the bottom of the juggernaut, shook the ground, even shook the brass tube and its rungs. There was little flash or fire, just a dull shock that spread out in ripples. For a moment the air went blurry, and everything seemed to dissolve.

When the scene steadied and became solid again, *Liberator* had settled lower to the ground like an old, tired dog bedding down. The bottom part of its hull had folded up in huge corrugations; its rollers had ceased to exist. It tilted at an angle of several degrees, and another two funnels had collapsed.

Col felt it as a blow to his own body. *But we're still upright,* he told himself.

Meanwhile the offensive was entering its next phase. As the wheeled vehicles merged back in among the imperialist troops, the green uniforms stepped forward with their spiky devices. Once again rifle barrels stuck out from portholes and over the edges of the scoops. The juggernaut might have reached its end, but its defenders were still fighting.

The green uniforms advanced only part of the way across no-man's-land. They knelt down, placed their devices on the ground, and did something that involved a sudden jerk of the arm, as if pulling a cord. Then they stepped back—and the devices began to move forward under their own power.

"What *are* they?" Col heard Riff mutter.

"More bombs?" he suggested.

"I don't think so."

As the devices moved forward, they jetted streams of gray smoke into the air. Soon the streams of smoke joined together in a dense, impenetrable mass. Already, large parts of *Liberator* were hidden from view—which meant that the imperialist forces were also hidden from *Liberator*'s view.

"Must be a smoke screen," said Riff.

Megaphone orders rang out; officers barked supplementary orders. The entire body of imperialist troops marched forward across the battlefield.

It was the final assault. The advancing front line remained a constant hundred paces behind the smoke-producing devices. Farther back other troops carried sections of ladder—many sections to combine into many ladders.

"Ow!" Col protested as Riff stepped on his hand.

"Down!" Her tone was urgent. "Move!"

"What are we—?"

"Hurry! I have a plan."

Hand over hand he went down as fast as he could.

"Back to the fighting?" he asked.

Riff didn't reply, and didn't need to. Everything else had failed. There was nothing to do but return to their original goal.

Attack the command tower, he thought. *Oh, well, I never expected to survive anyway.*

76

Riff explained her plan. "We'll ride on *that* to the tower." She jerked a thumb toward the trolley outside the shelter. "Drive right through their troops."

No one understood. "How? Who does the driving?"

"We'll make their driver take us."

"So . . ." Dunga knitted her brows. "We go out in the open now?"

"No point trying to stay secret."

"The tower will be heavily guarded," said Jarvie doubtfully.

Riff grinned. "Yes, but we don't need to fight our way into it. We can blow it up."

They looked at her in blank astonishment. Col was the first to grasp the idea.

"The ammunition," he said. "The balls of light."

"Right. We saw what happened when they hit *Liberator*. We've got two big flasks full of them. If we crash the trolley into the bottom of the tower . . ."

"They'll explode on impact?"

"Why else are the flasks bedded in straw? I reckon they'll go up with a boom."

"And of course we'll have plenty of time to jump off first," said Cree.

The others gaped at her, then realized she was being

ironic. Their chances of making it through alive were infinitesimal. They weren't even likely to reach the tower before being shot down.

"So why are we waiting?" Dunga asked, and spun on her heel.

They hurried to act before fear could unnerve them. Leaving the three men tied up on the ground, they slipped out through the flap of the shelter. Dunga went first, with Col right behind her.

The driver was still on the platform at the back of the traction engine. A pock-faced, middle-aged man not wearing a military uniform, he perched on a small, high seat, half dozing, awaiting orders.

His orders came from a source he didn't expect. Dunga prodded him under the ear with the tip of her rifle, and Col held his sword against the man's throat.

"Drive!" gritted Dunga.

The driver gurgled and went pop-eyed. He didn't speak Dunga's language, but he understood her meaning, especially when Col mimed a show of turning the steering wheel.

While Riff, Cree, and Jarvie piled into the trolley behind, the driver twisted a handle, lowered a lever, and pressed down on a pedal. The engine started forward with a hiss of steam and a smooth back-and-forth motion of sliding rods and shafts. Imperialist troops marched past on the other side, preoccupied with their own role in the final assault.

There was room for only one person to ride with the

driver on the platform, and Col's sword was handier at close quarters than Dunga's rifle. Dunga dropped back and jumped up to join the rest of the team in the trolley. She kept her rifle trained on the back of the driver's skull, while Col continued to menace him with the sword.

They were exposed on both sides when they passed beyond the tube and shelter. The command tower looked bigger than ever, less than two hundred yards away. But two hundred yards was an eternity given the odds against them.

Col pointed to the tower, but the driver shook his head. Perhaps he had guessed the nature of their plan; at any rate he refused to cooperate further. Not bothering to argue, Col seized the steering wheel and worked it with one hand himself. It was a huge circle of iron three feet in diameter. With the sword still at his throat, the driver cursed but didn't fight for control of it.

The engine veered to the left, and the trolley followed. Col aimed at the tower as if aiming a gun. There were units of troops in the way, but he didn't try to navigate around them.

They scattered with shouts and cries. They had seen him now—and also the rest of the team. Dunga, Riff, Jarvie, and Cree stood facing out from the flasks, fully visible.

Soldiers raised rifles, and officers shouted orders. Col tried to duck lower as the first shots rang out. One bullet ricocheted from the steering wheel; another struck Col's sword and almost wrenched it from his hand. Miraculously, Col himself wasn't hit.

With a sound like a cough the driver jerked back, then toppled forward onto the wheel. Col tried to pull him off but couldn't make him move. His head weighed down on the upper part of the wheel, his chest on the hub, while his left arm had become somehow trapped in the spokes.

Dead, Col realized. He couldn't see the wound, but he could see blood dripping onto the platform. The man must have died instantly, shot from the other side.

It made no difference to the progress of the traction engine. The driver's foot still weighed down on the pedal, while his slumped body locked the steering wheel in position.

More shots, more shouting. The Filthies on the trolley behind were screaming at him.

"Col! Up here! With us!"

Suddenly hands gripped him under the armpits, and he found himself hoisted up and over the wire netting.

It didn't make sense to Col. "Why?"

They hauled him back over the straw until he was leaning against one of the flasks. The cold of the glass pierced through to his bones.

"They can't shoot you here," Riff told him.

"Of course they . . . ," Col began, then trailed off.

The shooting had stopped. He looked out and saw hundreds of raised rifles, yet not one soldier pulled his trigger.

"They were only aiming at you," said Riff. "They can't aim at us here because they might hit the flasks."

Col nodded slowly as understanding dawned. "And set off an explosion."

Riff grinned. "Neat, ain't it?"

Her eyes were alive with wild energy, desperate and jubilant at the same time. It was an unexpected stroke of luck . . . along with their luck over the dead driver, who was keeping them right on course for the tower.

How long would it last? When would the officers have second thoughts? At present they were arguing furiously among themselves. Col felt like making faces and sticking out his tongue at them. Instead he turned to see what was happening to *Liberator*.

The smoke screen was starting to thin, enough to reveal thousands of troops marching across no-man's-land. Red, blue, gray and green uniforms were all taking part in the final assault. The front lines had probably reached the juggernaut already. . . .

A flurry of shouted orders brought him back to their own situation. The trolley had covered half the distance to the tower, but the officers had finally worked out a way to act. On their orders a mass of soldiers dropped their rifles and ran forward.

Riff fired her pistol and Dunga her rifle. They stopped a few, but the rest flowed around the trolley in a great wave. They didn't try to attack the team, but they grabbed hold of any projecting part of the chassis—and leaned back.

The wheels of the traction engine started to skid. Dunga and Riff kept shooting, while Col swung his sword. The soldiers soon learned to jump away from the flashing blade. But he could only threaten a few at a time, and there were far too many of them. The weight of a hundred soldiers pulling backward brought engine and trolley to a dead stop.

"I'm out of bullets!" Dunga yelled suddenly.

"Me too!" cried Riff. "Do what you can!"

Dunga and Riff used the butts of their weapons; Cree and Jarvie used their bare hands. Col stooped over the netting and slashed with his sword. He was in a kind of trance, dancing from place to place, keeping his mind open everywhere at once, as Riff had taught him.

Another flurry of orders rang out, and a new wave of soldiers ran up. These retained their rifles, but they didn't risk shooting with them. Instead they wielded them like clubs as Dunga was doing. While the soldiers of the first wave crouched lower over the chassis, the newcomers swung out above their heads. Now Col and the Filthies had to deal with rifle butts before they could even approach the hands that held back the trolley.

There was a sudden cry as Jarvie took a terrible blow. He collapsed into the straw with blood spurting from the side of his head.

For one moment Col's attention was diverted, and he came out of his fighting trance. In that same moment he failed to dodge the swing of a rifle butt that crashed down on his sword hand.

The sword fell from his numbed fingers, bounced on

the wire netting, and fell to the ground outside the trolley.

Disarmed! He stepped back in shock, temporarily helpless. In that moment his eyes swept over the whole battlefield, near and far.

Liberator was doomed. Eight ladders rose out above the thinning smoke screen, reaching up to the lower tiers of the juggernaut's superstructure. Climbing troops were already almost at the top, tiny as insects in the distance. They carried protective shields of some kind, and the defenders appeared powerless to stop them.

It was all coming to an end. Megaphone voices continued to blare out a steady stream of orders to the assault forces. The trolley was immobilized eighty yards away from the tower, and several soldiers had leaped up onto the wire netting. Only a miracle could save the revolution now.

Zwackk!

Something came whistling through the air and arrowed into the ground twenty paces away. It quivered where it stuck, bright and shiny with many prongs.

Col gaped. The ropes attached to it went all the way back up to the uppermost terrace below *Liberator*'s funnels. It was one of the grappling hooks.

77

More and more grappling hooks came shooting down. A dozen, two dozen, three dozen, all within a hundred-yard radius.

The soldiers on the wire netting dropped off, and the soldiers all around stopped fighting. One man had been impaled by a hook and pinned to the ground, but his comrades were too stunned to notice his screams of agony. The generals must have seen what was happening, because the megaphone voices fell suddenly silent.

Riff, Cree, and Dunga whooped and cheered, but Col couldn't adjust. The hooks had been intended for an assault on the *Romanov*. What was happening now?

"Look! Look!" Riff pointed. "It's the project! They've done it!"

She was pointing toward the uppermost terrace. On each pair of ropes was a sling, and someone sitting in the sling. Even as he watched, the figures kicked off and started the long ride down.

The project . . . He remembered Septimus talking about a project, something to do with magnets. It had all happened while he was looking after Sephaltina.

The slings passed into the murk of the smoke screen

and emerged again on the other side. The figures in the slings grew larger and larger, accelerating under their own momentum. Now Col could see that the weapons they cradled in their arms were much bulkier and heavier than ordinary rifles.

He understood the nature of the weapons when one of the rope riders began firing at the troops below.

Rat-tat-tat-tat-tat-tat-tat-tat-tat! Rat-tat-tat-tat-tat-tat-tat-tat-tat!

Flash after flash burst from the barrel. Only a Maxim gun could fire a nonstop stream of bullets like that.

"That's the project!" he exclaimed. "Maxim guns!"

"Maxim guns," Riff agreed. "But that's not the project. Look closer!"

Dozens of figures came swooping down like great birds out of the sky. The troops nearby didn't wait for their arrival, but broke and fled. By the time the first rope-rider hit the ground, a wide clearing had opened up all around.

There was a blur of speed and a tremendous thump. Col didn't see the rope rider bend at the knees to absorb the impact; he only saw as she straightened up, stepped out of the sling, and swung her gun menacingly in all directions.

She was a solidly built Filthy, with hair tied back in a bun and a face that Col didn't recognize. The most remarkable thing about her was her clothing—a loose gray Menial uniform.

Col turned to Riff. "Why is she wearing Menial clothes?"

Riff laughed out loud. "Because she's a Menial, of course!"

"But . . ."

"*That* was the project."

"What?"

"To turn Menials back into Filthies."

Col stared and stared again. The woman with the Maxim gun didn't shuffle like a Menial or hunch her shoulders like a Menial. Her eyes were bright and clear, her movements swift and light. But the hair tied back in a bun . . . that was as much in the style of a Menial as the pajama uniform.

He could hardly believe it—yet he had to believe it. Septimus and the professor had found books explaining how to turn Filthies into Menials, he remembered. They must have worked out how to perform the operation the other way around. Though where *magnets* came into it . . .

Meanwhile, more and more rope riders continued to land, all wearing pajama uniforms, all armed with Maxim guns. They fired a few short bursts of gunfire.

Rat-tat-tat-tat-tat-tat-tat-tat-tat! Rat-tat-tat-tat-tat-tat-tat-tat-tat!

The imperialist troops scurried off as fast as their legs could carry them. They understood the lethal effects of a nonstop stream of bullets.

Cree bent down to examine the injured Jarvie. Dunga turned to Riff with a puzzled frown.

"Why are they landing here?"

"Same plan as us, maybe."

"What, take out the command tower?"

"Let's go find out."

They jumped down from the trolley and hurried across to the first rope rider.

Col looked up toward *Liberator*'s superstructure and saw new slings being attached, new rope riders preparing to slide down the same pairs of ropes. Lower down he saw defenders leaning out from portholes, lassoing the ladders, and trying to pull them off balance. The tide had turned, and the siege was faltering everywhere!

The first rope rider accompanied Riff and Dunga back to the traction engine. The driver's body lay now half on and half off the platform; the soldiers must have dislodged him from the steering wheel, and presumably from the foot pedal too.

Riff called up to Col. "Can you drive this thing?"

"What, back to our plan? We blow up the tower?"

"Yes, but now we have help. Can you drive it?"

Col rehearsed in his mind the steps he'd seen the driver employ: Turn the handle, lower the lever, and press down on the pedal. It wasn't complicated. "I think so."

The rope rider gestured with her Maxim gun. "Let's do it."

She sounded so much like any other Filthy it was hard to believe she'd only recently regained her power of speech. Col hardly knew how to address her.

"Right," he said, and put off thinking about it till

another time. He turned to Cree. "What about Jarvie? Can we move him?"

Cree looked up from the injured Filthy. "Yes. He's conscious. The blood looks worse than it is."

So Col and Cree lifted Jarvie over the wire netting, while Riff and Dunga stood below to receive him. He gave a lopsided grin as they lowered him to the ground.

"Are we winning?" he asked.

"Good as won," Riff told him.

The dead driver also lay on the ground, dragged clear of the engine by the rope rider. Col mounted the platform and took his place on the driver's seat.

He located the handle and gave it a turn. The engine let out a great *swoosh* of steam.

When he lowered the lever, the platform rocked under his feet.

He pressed down on the pedal—just a little at first, then more and more. Suddenly the rods and shafts came to life, and the whole engine trundled forward.

Riff came running alongside. "I'll keep you company," she said, and sprang up next to him.

Col applied all his weight to the pedal, but the engine had already reached its sluggish top speed.

"Do we jump off before the crash?" he asked. "It'll be an almighty explosion."

"No crash," said Riff. "Change of plan. Now we can use the Maxim guns." She gestured toward the rope riders, who had formed a loose half circle and were advancing behind them. "They'll set off the explosion by shooting the flasks. I've arranged it all with Vassa."

Vassa must be the first rope rider, Col realized. And she had her own name—not a slave name but a proper Filthy name! The world really was changing!

The tower straddled the end of the walkway, rising to a height of fifty feet. Its lower part was an open frame of eight metal legs, draped with the banners of France, Russia, Austria, and Turkey. Its upper part was a solid octagonal box with shuttered windows on every side. Glinting brass telescopes stuck out through the shutters, but it was impossible to see the faces behind them. Higher up, huge silver cones were mounted on the roof like the mouths of trumpets.

Col and Riff were thirty yards away when the telescopes swiveled toward them. Twenty yards away, and the trumpets spoke in megaphone voices. The generals had realized their danger.

Col swung the steering wheel to guide the trolley alongside the frame of metal legs. He could see steps spiraling up to the octagonal box above. He took his foot from the pedal and brought the traction engine to a halt.

The megaphone voices were going frantic—no longer deep and authoritative, but shrill and frightened. It sounded as though the generals were squabbling for control of the microphone. Though the words were incomprehensible, they were doubtless commanding their troops to remove the trolley at all costs.

Riff jumped down, and Col was right behind her.

Now the megaphone voices were pleading for help. But the rope riders had the area covered, and there were no soldiers or officers nearby. No one was foolish enough to invite a hail of bullets from the Maxim guns.

Col and Riff raced for safety. Fifty yards away the rope riders stood with their guns raised, aiming at the two glass flasks. Col and Riff dived flat to the ground as the guns spat fire.

Rat-tat-tat-tat-tat-tat-tat-tat-tat-tat!

There was a sharp sound like breaking glass, followed by a first explosion.

Whumpff!!

The second explosion was a hundred times louder.

WHUMPFF!!

A tidal wave of light and heat picked Col up and flung him through the air. It pummeled his head like a giant fist and knocked him into oblivion.

78

When he came back to consciousness, his eyes were still dazzled from the light. Even the grass in front of his face was etched in black and white. He turned his head to look at the tower—but there was no tower anymore. All that remained was a mass of tangled, blackened wreckage at the end of the walkway. The octagonal box had disintegrated; the metal legs had melted and collapsed. Two guttering fires still burned where the flasks had been.

He rolled over and discovered Riff lying on her back beside him. Her eyes were closed, and he wasn't sure if she was breathing.

"Are you okay?" He jogged her arm. "Can you hear me?"

She blinked and looked at him. "It's a miracle I can hear anything after that blast." She raised her head and studied the wreckage. "We did it," she said. "We really did it."

Col sat up. As his vision returned to normal, he could see how the imperialist troops were reacting to the fate of their command tower. All across the battlefield the will to fight had gone out of them, and they were starting to head back to their respective juggernauts. Some of the ex-Menials fired in the direction of the troops, but there was little need. The momentum of the retreat was already unstoppable.

Col laughed with sheer relief. "I thought we were gone back there."

Riff laughed with him. "Until the grappling hooks came down."

She sat up too, and something seemed to catch in her throat. Suddenly she was no longer laughing. Col looked at her with concern, and saw that her eyes were wide and staring. For a moment he wondered if she had a concussion. Was this an aftereffect of the explosion?

Then he saw where she was staring—at a particular ex-Menial standing with other ex-Menials fifty paces away. Although the woman had her back to them, her hair was instantly recognizable: black in some places and blond in others.

"Your mother," he exclaimed. "That's your mother."

Riff only nodded.

"Don't you want to go over to her?"

Riff made no move to get to her feet. "My da too. On her left."

She was breathing in and out in shallow, nervous breaths. Col was baffled. Surely she should have been overjoyed?

"Well?" he asked.

"They might not recognize me. They haven't recognized me yet."

"You haven't given them a chance."

"Maybe they can't remember back that far."

"Wait till they see you close up."

"They *ought* to remember me. I remember everything about them. Everything."

She was afraid, Col realized. He thought back to the time when Lye and Shiv had brought her face to face with her parents. *Nod your heads if you remember me,* she'd said, and they'd nodded their heads. Then, *Nod your heads if you don't remember me,* and they'd done that, too. He recalled her sick-looking face and the way she'd seemed to crumple inside.

So even Riff could be afraid. She must have been hurt beyond hurt. At the time he'd been more aware of his own hurt, but now he felt what she must have felt. She was simply terrified of experiencing the same pain again.

He understood—and also understood what he had to do.

"It'll be all right," he said. "You'll see."

"I can't . . . I couldn't . . ."

"Just give them time. You've grown a lot since they last saw you. I bet they'll be so proud of you."

He slipped a hand in under her elbow, encouraged her to rise, and walked her forward. She didn't resist, yet he could tell she'd stop dead the moment he let go.

He kept talking to her the whole way, saying the same calming things over and over. The last twenty paces were agony. His confidence was all on the outside, for her sake. He really didn't know whether her mam and da *would* recognize her—and if they didn't, he felt as if his own heart would break too.

Five paces away Riff's legs appeared to lock. She couldn't take another step, and she certainly couldn't speak. Col looked in her face and saw the hope behind the fear. So much hope—she was brimming with it like a glass full of water.

He walked the last few paces by himself, cleared his throat, and said, "I've brought someone to see you."

Riff's mam swung sharply around, and Col found himself staring into the barrel of her Maxim gun. She cradled it against her hip, while a strap over her shoulder took the weight. She was wary and alert and very much in combat mode.

This is good, Col told himself. She had the quick reactions of a Filthy, not the dullness of a Menial.

"What is it, Masha?" asked the man to whom she'd been talking.

Col recognized the other Menial that Lye and Shiv had brought to Riff's cabin. Yet although the face was similar, the impression was transformed. Both the man and woman were strikingly attractive in a way Col hadn't realized before. The woman had Riff's cheekbones and overall facial structure; the man had exactly the same eyes.

"Someone to see you," Col repeated.

He had intended to prepare the ground and lead their thoughts gradually back to the past, but their staggering similarity to Riff swept his plans away. They were so obviously her parents. They *had* to recognize their own flesh and blood!

"It's Riff," he muttered. "Your daughter."

Riff had been almost hiding behind him. When he stepped aside, she stood with lowered head like a guilty child.

Her mam and da looked at her, looked at each other, looked back at her again. Col couldn't interpret their response: surprise or puzzlement or something else?

Please, please, please remember her, he prayed inwardly.

And then it happened. The two of them sprang forward—perhaps Riff sprang forward too. In the next moment they were all caught up in a three-way family hug. Crying and laughing, they began to rotate to the left, to the right. It was like a mad, glorious dance.

Everything was going to be all right! Col felt a huge surge of relief. He felt even better when Riff's eyes met his over her mam's shoulder—eyes swimming in tears— and she mouthed the words "thank you."

79

Soon the imperialist juggernauts started to move off. The *Marseillaise* backed away from one end of the battlefield; the *Grosse Wien* and the *Battle of Mohacs* backed away from the other. They seemed in a great hurry to leave the scene of their humiliation.

The Russian troops, meanwhile, could no longer return to their home juggernaut; they fled cross-country with the *svolochi* in pursuit. All that remained were the bodies of the slain and injured, and the shells of wrecked or abandoned machines. A smell of burning and explosives still hung in the air.

Riff introduced Col to her parents, and he even shared in a four-way hug. He didn't go with them, though, when they went off to sit on the walkway. They had too many personal memories to talk over, he reckoned, and they needed time to catch up on their own.

It wasn't long before *Liberator* began lowering its scoops, carrying Filthies, Swanks, and convicts to the ground. They were all in a mood of wild celebration and jeered and brandished their fists at the departing juggernauts. Like Col they had believed themselves doomed—and their impossible triumph was all the sweeter. The scale of the imperialist defeat would have satisfied even Lye.

Col grimaced at *that* thought. It hadn't happened in the way Lye had intended, yet they *had* lit a beacon for the oppressed. He seemed to hear her voice crying out with that strange intensity: *Our truth over their lies! Our justice over their tyranny! Our future over their past!* Yes, it was all coming true—the future was beginning, and the Age of Imperialism was drawing to an end. Their own Liberation was no longer a unique case, now that the Russian Filthies were liberated too.

He walked over in the direction of the descending scoops. Gillabeth was in the first scoop to touch down and, being Gillabeth, immediately took charge of tidying up the battlefield. Everyone else wandered around, laughing and talking in a kind of euphoric daze.

"Colbert!"

He turned at the sound of his name. It was Septimus and Professor Twillip running across from another scoop. The professor's eyes were shining behind his glasses, while Septimus was grinning from ear to ear.

For a moment it was impossible to talk. They hugged and thumped one another's backs, until the professor started to wheeze and had to adjust his glasses.

"What a battle!" Septimus cried. "All their special weapons! We beat them all!"

Professor Twillip pointed to one of the spiky, smoke-producing devices that had rolled to a stop nearby. "That's a pufferbug, did you know?" He pointed to one of the great brass tubes fifty yards away. "And that's a mortar firing loblights."

"Loblights!" Col laughed. "We used them to blow up the command tower. We turned their own special weapon against them."

"You did that?" Professor Twillip beamed. "Well done! We wondered how that happened."

"We only succeeded because you used *your* special weapon first." Col gestured toward the ex-Menials with their Maxim guns.

"It was Gillabeth who found the guns," said Septimus. "They were in a hidden armory on Twenty-second Deck."

"We never thought of ex-Menials as a special weapon," said the professor, suddenly serious. "We changed them back to Filthies because it was the ethical thing to do. Righting a terrible wrong."

"It was their choice to fight." Septimus nodded. "More than a choice—they insisted. They were determined to create a special revenge force. The different plans only came together after they were changed back."

"I suppose they had more to revenge than most," said Professor Twillip.

"How did you do it?" Col turned to Septimus. "*Magnets*, you said."

"Yes. We discovered the limiters were made of stainless steel. We could never have done it by surgery. We used magnets to dislodge the metal from where it was implanted in their brains."

"It was his idea." The professor spoke proudly of his protégé. "Credit where credit is due."

Septimus flushed. "Well, yes, but you . . ."

Another voice hailed from a distance. "Colbert!"

This time it was Col's father hurrying toward them. He was actually smiling, and his face seemed to have discovered new upturned creases it had never known before.

"We won!" he exclaimed. "We survived! Can you believe it?"

He shook Col's hand, then the hands of Septimus and the professor. Then he shook Col's hand again, even more vigorously.

"Well," he said. "Well, well, well, well, well."

At last he released Col's hand. He seemed momentarily uncertain what to do.

"It's a whole new world," Professor Twillip said, beaming.

"Yes, indeed." Orris nodded. "I even invented a joke on the way down through the pipe. Just made it up without thinking. Do you want to hear? Or what about this? Watch!"

He raised his arm and snapped his fingers. Loud, sharp, clear—snap!

"I can do it every time." He demonstrated again. "I can't wait to show Quinnea." He turned to Septimus and the professor. "She's all right, isn't she?"

"She's fine," said Professor Twillip.

"And Antrobus and Gillabeth?"

"Fine too. They're all fine."

"Er . . . no," said Septimus.

The professor's face fell. "Oh. I was forgetting." He

turned to Col, though he spoke to Septimus. "Will you tell him, or shall I?"

"You."

"Tell me," said Col.

"Yes, tell us," said Orris.

Professor Twillip adjusted his glasses, ran his fingers through his fleecy white hair, and finally managed to bring out the words, "It's your wife, Colbert."

"Sephaltina? What? What's wrong?"

"I'm so sorry. I'm afraid she passed away."

Col stared at him. "How? In the fighting?"

"No, before the battle started. We only heard about it secondhand. I don't know the details. Hatta could tell you. . . ."

"She's over there now," said Septimus.

More and more people had come down in the scoops, and Hatta was one of them. Col followed the line of Septimus's pointing finger.

"I'd better go and ask her, then," he said numbly.

"Yes," Orris agreed. "That would be best."

80

The others offered to come with him, but Col waved them away. He felt like a criminal. Sephaltina had begged him to stay and look after her, yet he'd abandoned her to go on the mission with Riff. And even that wasn't the worst of it.

The scene came back to him with damning clarity. Sephaltina on the divan, head propped on her pillow, shouting and screaming: *You want her instead of me. . . . If you go on this mission with her, you'll be sorry. . . . You want me to die, so I'll die. . . .*

What had she done to herself? She hadn't been killed in the battle, and the wound to her throat hadn't killed her—so what else was there? Had she done it because she loved him and couldn't live without him? He felt sick to his stomach with guilt.

Hatta was on her knees examining an injured soldier, a basket of bandages and ointments on the ground beside her. The man wore the green Austrian uniform, and his arm stuck out at an unnatural angle. Perhaps he had fallen from one of the siege ladders. . . .

"Hatta."

She glanced around with a scowl. "I'm a healer, not

a warrior. I can't leave him suffering just because he's an enemy."

"I never said you should."

"Good, then."

She bent over the man again, took a grip on his arm and shoulder, and gave a sudden wrench. The man screamed and fainted.

"There." Hatta smiled with grim satisfaction. "That's the bone back in its socket. He'll be grateful when he wakes up."

She swiveled to face Col. "Right. Now you. I suppose you want to hear about your wife?"

Col hated that scowl on her face. Was *she* blaming him? But she was the one who had told him to leave Sephaltina and go on the mission.

"It makes me mad." Hatta snorted. "The most stupid, unnecessary death I've ever witnessed."

"What did she do?"

"Fool of a girl! How can I heal people who don't want to be healed?"

"I never thought she'd go through with it. I thought it was just a form of blackmail."

"What was?"

"She killed herself, didn't she?"

Hatta let out a harsh laugh. "Oh, yes, she killed herself."

"Don't laugh. How do you think I feel?"

"You've got nothing to do with it."

"What?"

"She didn't do it because of you. She killed herself by being greedy."

"Greedy?" The wheels spun round in Col's mind. "You mean the sweets?"

"Yes, her beloved sweeties. You heard me tell her she couldn't have any till she was fully recovered. You saw me lock them away in the cabinet."

Col remembered something that Sephaltina had once told him. "She always gets what she wants in the end."

"Hmph! She got what she wanted this time, all right. She must have attacked the cabinet in the middle of the night. She smashed a chair leg right through the glass front of it."

Col remembered how Sephaltina also loved smashing things, but he didn't mention that.

"One sweet would have been dangerous," Hatta went on, "but it might not have killed her. But one sweet wasn't enough for Miss Greedy-Guts. She stuffed a whole handful into her mouth and tried to swallow them all at once."

"That killed her?"

"I found her in the morning on the floor by the cabinet. She'd bled out through her bandage, but she probably choked to death first. There was a whole mass of sweets stuck in her mouth and throat."

"That's horrible."

"No, it's stupid. It's the most stupid thing I ever heard." She stared and pointed at his face. "What's that?"

"What's what?"

"You're not *crying* for her?"

Col brushed a hand over his cheek and felt the wetness.

"Well, now we have two fools," said Hatta angrily. "Enough of this. Let me look after people who *want* to be healed."

She rose, collected her basket, and stomped off to take care of other injured soldiers. Col watched her go.

It wasn't fair to be angry with Sephaltina. Hatta didn't understand how Upper Decks girls had been brought up under the old regime. Perhaps Sephaltina *had* been spoiled and self-centered and irresponsible, but she'd never had the chance to be otherwise. Only Gillabeth was an exception.

The victory celebrations were still going on all around, but a sad, mournful feeling overshadowed Col's elation. Although he no longer felt guilty, he couldn't stop thinking about Sephaltina's horrible death. He wiped the wetness away from his other cheek.

81

Two days later a great gathering took place in the Grand Assembly Hall. Filthies, Swanks, convicts, and ex-Menials all attended. Riff, Col, Gillabeth, Orris, and the remaining Council members stood at the front of the hall, along with six representatives of the Russian Filthies. Unya was one of the six; another was the new *svolochi* leader, who wore the massive metal ornaments that had once belonged to Babya.

The hall itself was dimmer than before, with many blank gaps in the lights of the chandelier. The damage caused by exploding torpedo snouts had added to the damage caused by the original collision. Even the floor had a slight tilt underfoot.

Gillabeth stood forward to address the meeting.

"The Council has asked me to speak on their behalf," she announced. "With the help of my father I've been conducting negotiations with the new rulers of the *Romanov*."

She gestured toward the *svolochi*, and their leader inclined her head solemnly.

"They want to express their gratitude for what we did. They owe their liberation to us, they say."

A burst of enthusiastic cheering ran round the hall. Everyone was in high spirits, still bathing in the afterglow of victory.

Gillabeth stayed calm and crisp and competent. She was in her element, as though she'd been born to this role. Long ago she'd said she would have made a better supreme commander than Col ever would, and now she was vindicated. He was proud of her.

She went on to give a summary of *Liberator*'s condition and prospects. In short, there were no prospects. The juggernaut's turbines were irreparable, and its generators were dying. As if to prove her point, the lights flickered even as she spoke.

Her words dampened the mood in the hall, but only a little. Everyone had known this was coming. They waited to hear the news about the negotiations.

"However," said Gillabeth, "the Russian juggernaut *can* be repaired. With a little more work on its tracks, it'll travel as fast as ever." She paused. "The Russian Filthies have plenty of room since they let the officers' families leave. They're willing to share their juggernaut with us."

The hall erupted in wild applause. On and on it continued, with whistles and whoops of delight. Mr. Gibber appeared suddenly in front of the assembly and took it upon himself to act as cheerleader.

"Rah! Rah! Rah!" he yelled. "More! More! More!"

He had one leg in a splint and one arm in a plaster cast. Murgatrude sat on top of the cast, half hidden inside the supporting sling. Mr. Gibber waved his other arm like a conductor and incited the crowd to greater and greater heights of enthusiasm.

"Thank you, Mr. Gibber," said Gillabeth, and quelled him with a meaningful look.

She spoke again as the crowd quieted. "They've offered us a combined leadership. They'll be setting up a new council, and we can have three places on it. Three places out of eight."

Padder nodded. "Very fair."

"I think so," said Gillabeth.

She went on to talk about arrangements for the move. She calculated it would take another three weeks to complete repairs on the caterpillar tracks. In the meanwhile there were rooms to sort out, personal possessions to choose and carry across, food provisions and other stores to transfer.

Col listened until someone distracted him by taking hold of his arm. It was Unya, popping up suddenly behind him. He stood side by side with Riff, but not close enough to satisfy Unya. She took his right arm in one hand and Riff's left arm in the other, and tried to twine the two of them together.

Col and Riff laughed. They didn't exactly resist, but they didn't help her either. She clucked her tongue with annoyance as the arms kept falling apart. After a while she began trying to arrange their arms around each other's waists.

When Gillabeth stepped back and Gansy stepped forward, Col paid closer attention. This was about long-term planning, he knew, and he was eager to hear the details.

"We've been talking about where to go in the *Romanov*," Gansy said. "The new combined council will decide, but we've been working on a proposal."

She carried a scroll of paper under her arm, which she now unfurled and held up. The crowd craned forward to see, though only those closest could distinguish the colored shapes of oceans and continents. Apart from Gansy and the Swanks, hardly anybody understood how to read a map anyway.

"This"—Gansy tapped a particular area of green—"is North America. It's a whole continent with almost no coaling stations. The only red dots marked are right at the top or the bottom. There's only one dot in the middle, and it's black. See here?" She tapped again. "We don't know if the middle is uninhabited or what. But we think it's a good sign."

"That's where we think we should go," said Gillabeth.

The leader of the *svolochi* was watching Gansy's tapping fingers. She clanked her ornaments for attention and spoke out in Russian.

"Vot novaia zemlia gde mi budem zhit v mire."

It meant nothing to Col, but his father had clearly been working on his Russian language skills.

"The, er, new place," Orris translated, pausing over every word. "Life . . . peace . . . to live in peace."

The crowd was all in favor of living in peace, and roared its approval. Once more Mr. Gibber began to act as cheerleader, waving his one good arm. He must have ruffled Murgatrude's composure, or perhaps Antrobus communicated something in silence; at any rate Murgatrude let out a deep-throated growl, and Mr. Gibber desisted.

Gillabeth took charge again. "Any further business?"

There was no further business—until Unya's voice rang out. *"Eti dva dolzhny byt partnerami!"*

Orris struggled to translate. "These two. Something to do with partners."

It was Gillabeth who shook her head. "No, Unya. Be patient." Just for a moment she sounded less like a supreme organizer and more like a sister. "Let them decide in their own time."

Patience, however, was not one of Unya's virtues. She reached up to Col and Riff, and brought their heads together—so suddenly that the top of Riff's skull banged into Col's jaw. It wasn't a kiss but a clash of bone on bone.

Col rubbed his jaw ruefully, as the entire assembly burst out laughing. The *svoiochi* and their leader laughed loudest of all.

82

It was their last night on board *Liberator*. The ceremony was over, and the witnesses had left, closing the door behind them. For a while Riff's cabin had been packed with people: Col's family, Victoria and Albert, Septimus and the professor, Riff's parents, and—inevitably—Unya. Now only Col and Riff were left.

Through the porthole they could see the silver disc of a full moon and a few tranquil banners of cloud. There was no glass in the porthole; during the battle a loblight had smashed out the glass and left a huge, bulging dent in the wall. Cool air as well as moonlight came in through the hole.

Even apart from the dent, the room looked different inside. Riff had finished transferring her personal possessions to the Russian juggernaut—including her books, which were her most valued possession of all. The empty bookcase, wardrobe, bed, and washstand were the only furnishings that remained.

The two of them stood side by side, casting sharp silhouettes in the circle of light on the floor.

"Our last night," said Riff. "It'll be strange to leave."

"But *our* first night," said Col. "You and me."

"True."

"We'll be the same on the *Romanov*. Better. Because now we're partnered."

"No."

"Uh?"

"We're not partnered."

Col didn't understand.

"There's more," Riff told him.

"But I thought . . . We've just done the ceremony before witnesses."

"The public ceremony. There's a private ceremony too."

"You never told me that."

"Always a private ceremony too," she said.

Col had butterflies in the pit of his stomach. "What is it?"

"Exactly the same."

"Are you making this up?"

No hint of a grin appeared on Riff's face. Col had never seen her so serious.

"We've made promises in front of other people," she said. "Now we have to promise each other."

"Just the two of us?"

"Yes. *Really* promise. In your heart."

She turned to stand facing him. "You remember the first thing we promised in public?"

"Yes."

"No need to say it out loud. Just think it and feel it."

Col nodded as she held up her right hand, fingers outspread. Matching his hand to hers, he slid his fingers between her fingers. They had done the same thing fifteen minutes ago.

"I promise to . . . ," he said automatically, then stopped.

In your heart, Riff's eyes reminded him, speaking without words.

He interwove his fingers even tighter with hers, and continued the promise in silence.

I promise to put you first in my life in every way. What we make together, no one else can come between.

They raised their hands, gripping hard to form a single fist. Then they unlaced fingers, dropped arms, and stood facing each other again.

Riff nodded and put her hands on her hips. She leaned forward and blew very gently on his face. He felt the warmth of her breath on his skin, playing over his cheeks and nose and chin.

I promise you love in four kinds, he thought. *Love of the heart, sympathy of the mind, heat of the body, tenderness of the spirit.*

He blew gently back at her. Her hair stirred, and her eyelashes quivered. She was looking at him, looking into him. *Do you really mean it?* she wanted to know. *Do you really and completely mean it?*

And he did, he realized. This wasn't a mere ceremony; this was the actual thing. Not willed or spoken, but the feeling and intention inside himself.

Riff nodded again, reached out, and held him by the elbows. He held her in the same way. Now came the third and last promise.

He looked into her eyes and saw that the feeling was there in her, too.

I promise to keep no secrets from you. They leaned forward and touched foreheads. *Whatever happens to me, I shall tell you. Whatever happens to you, I shall listen and share.*

They touched foreheads. It was a symbol of telling and sharing, but very close to a kiss. Col couldn't help the tension in his arms, which transmitted itself to her. He struggled to keep control . . . touching face to face without kissing . . .

Then she drew back and dropped her hold. His eyes had been closed, but he opened them now. She read and answered his silent question.

"Yes," she said, meaning that they were finally, truly partnered. Her solemn expression disappeared, and a broad grin spread over her face. "That's the serious part done. You only just lasted it out, didn't you?"

The moonlight caught on her cheekbones, and she was beautiful. He could hardly believe the way she looked. What had he ever done to deserve someone like her?

He reached out to take her hand, and as he did so, the gold wedding ring flashed on his finger.

He frowned at it. "I wish I could take this off."

"It's not important."

"It says I was married before."

"You're not married now. You're partnered. Like Filthy to Filthy. It's different."

And it was, he discovered. Very, very different.